# HALF BROKEN THINGS

*by*

Morag Joss

**Magna Large Print Books**
Long Preston, North Yorkshire,
BD23 4ND, England.

**British Library Cataloguing in Publication Data.**

Joss, Morag
   Half broken things.

   A catalogue record of this book is
   available from the British Library

   ISBN   0-7505-2098-1

   ⟍⟍⟍

First published in Great Britain in 2003 by Hodder & Stoughton
A division of Hodder Headline

Published in Large Print 2003 by arrangement with
Hodder & Stoughton Ltd.

Magna Large Print is an imprint of Library Magna Books Ltd.

Printed and bound in Great Britain by
T.J. (International) Ltd., Cornwall, PL28 8RW

For Iain Burnside

*'But this is what ... people are so often and so disastrously wrong in doing: they (who by their very nature are impatient) fling themselves at each other when love takes hold of them, they scatter themselves, just as they are, in all their messiness, disorder, bewilderment...'*

*'And what can happen then? What can life do with this heap of half broken things that they would like to call their happiness, and their future?*

*'And so each of them loses himself for the sake of the other person, and loses the other. And loses the vast possibilities ... in exchange for an unfruitful confusion, out which nothing more can come; nothing but a bit of disgust, disappointment and poverty.'*

# *January*

This is not what it might look like. We're quiet people. As a general rule extraordinary things do not happen to us, and we are not the type to go looking for them. But so much has happened since January, and I started it. Things began to happen, things I must have brought about somehow without quite foreseeing where they would lead. So I feel I must explain, late in the day though it is. I'm going to set out, as clearly as I can, in the order in which they occurred, the things that have happened here. And I shall find it difficult because I was brought up not to draw attention to myself and I've never been considered a forthcoming person, never being one to splurge out on anything, least of all great long explanations. Indeed, Mother always described me as secretive. But that was because, with her, I came to expect my reasons for things to be not so much misunderstood as overlooked or mislaid, and so early on I stopped giving them.

Father was usually quiet, too. When I think

13

back to the sounds of the house in Oakfield Avenue where I grew up, I do not remember voices. I think we sighed or cleared our throats more often than we spoke words. I remember mainly the tick of Father's longcase clock in the dining room we never ate in, and then after the clock had gone, a particular silence throughout the house that I thought of as a shade of grey. And much later when I was an adult, still there looking after Mother, the most regular sound was the microwave. It pinged a dozen times a day. In fact, until recently, whenever I heard a certain tone of ping, in a shop or somewhere like that, I would immediately smell boiling milk. But when I was a child there was just the clock, with silences in between.

Mother had few words herself. She often went about the house as if she were harbouring unsaid things at great personal cost, with a locked look on her mouth. That being so, I suppose Father and I felt unable to open our own very much. What happens to all the things you might say or want to say, but don't? Well, they don't lie about in your head indefinitely, waiting to be let out. For a time they may stay there quite patiently, but then they shuffle off and fade until you can't locate them any more, and you realise they're not coming back. By then you're past caring.

So I grew to think of myself as someone not in particular need of words. I did not acquire the habit of calling them up; not many at a time at least, not even to myself in my own head. Things in my head had been very quiet for a long time, before all this.

But I have been wrong about this aspect of myself, as about others. I find that there are words there after all. Now that I need them, my words have come crowding back, perhaps because I have a limited time in which to get them all down (today is the 20th, so only eleven more days). I am pleased that my hands remember the old touch-typing moves without seeming to involve me at all. The letters are hitting the paper in this old typewriter almost as if they were being shot out of my finger-ends. Which is just as well, because I'm busy enough dealing with all the clamouring words that are flinging themselves around in my head, fighting over which gets fired out first. I'm in a hurry to let them loose. I want to explain, because it is suddenly extremely urgent and important that, in the end, we are not misunderstood.

And I shall try to put down not just what, but *why* things have happened and why none of it could have turned out any differently. Until now I really haven't thought about the why. Time's the thing. I haven't had time, not time of the right kind, to ask myself why things have gone the way they have. I've been too busy being happy; even now I'm happy, although the time left is of the other kind. But I'm quite content to spend it trying to puzzle it all out and write it down. It's a pleasant way to pass time, sitting over the typewriter at the study window and looking out now and then to wave at them (that's Michael, Steph and Charlie) down there in the garden. They're not doing much. Steph is singing to Charlie and rocking him on her lap: *Row, row, row the boat* – that's one of Charlie's favourites – and the more she rocks the more he likes it. They're waving back now. I've told them I've got to write a report for the agency and in a way, that's almost true, so they're making pretend-sad faces up at me because I can't spend the afternoon with them. And now Steph's got hold of Charlie's wrist and she's making him wave too. Behind them, I can see three different kinds of Michaelmas daisy in the border, three nice shades of purple. But the roses are on their second flowering now and look as if the air's gone out of them, as if they've stayed too long at the party.

Anyway, I'm going off the point. I was saying that I'm going to explain everything. And while I cannot imagine any explanation for anything that does not also contain an element of justification, I am not trying to offer excuses for what we have done. But

16

nor am I apologising, quite, except for the mess and inconvenience, which are bound to be considerable.

So how did it start? With the letter from the agency? Or with the advertisement I placed? Perhaps much earlier, years and years ago, with Jenny. Jenny is the niece I invented for myself. Yes, perhaps that reveals a tendency. She started as just a little, harmless, face-saving white lie which of course led to others, and in no time at all the fact that she did not exist was neither here nor there. My niece became quite real to me, or as real as somebody living in Australia ever could be, in my mind. I haven't travelled abroad.

No, now that I reflect, it started with this place, with the house itself. Because the house made me feel things from the very first which perhaps I should find strange, it being my fifty-eighth. Memories are a little blurred after fifty-seven in eighteen years, but I do know I'd never felt things before. This is the fifty-eighth house, although I've sat some houses more than once because people used to ask for me again. I specialise, or I did, in long stays. 'We have the perfect lady, flexible, no ties, usually available' was how I was recommended. I spell this out just so that it is clear that I have been well thought of. Inexperience has nothing to do it. Nor was it anything to do with malice or jealousy.

17

The house when I came was full of old things; fuller than it is now, for reasons I will come to. Many of them were not in mint condition, and I liked them like that. I liked the way they sat about the house in little settlements, as if they had sought one another out and were sticking together, little colonies of things on small island table tops. There were the boxes: workboxes with velvet linings and silver spools and scissors and dear little buttonhooks, boxes with tiny glass bottles with stoppers missing, writing boxes still cedar scented and ink-stained on the inside, yellowed, carved ivory boxes, and painted and enamel ones – I suppose for snuff, those ones – but I wasn't concerned about their original purpose. Then there were the small silver things in the drawing room, the heavy paper knife with a swan's head, the magnifying glass, a round box with a dent, the filigree basket with the twisted handle, a vase for a single rose. The blue and white porcelain in the dining room, some of it chipped, and the fans in the case in the library, of beaded lace, faded painted parchment and tired-looking feathers. Even some of the books: nearly everything else was modern, but on three shelves there were sets of very old books with cracked spines and faint titles. They all had that look of being dusted in cinnamon and gave off a leafy smell that reminded me of church. Inside, many of the pages were loose, and so thin that the print on the other side grinned right through the words when I tried to read, as if they were not unreadable enough already.

But all these things seemed content in their imperfections; they were not shouting out to be mended the way new things are. New things so often break before there has been time for them to fade and crumble. Here, it was as if the things had simply been around long enough to be dropped or bent or knocked, and every one of these minute, accidental events had been patiently absorbed, as if the things knew themselves to be acceptable and thought beautiful just as they were. If objects could give contented sighs, that's what these would have done. I wanted to be like that. I wondered if I, also fading and crumbling as everything does in the end, could be like that. Yes, I remember wondering that right from the start, in those first few days of January.

The third day, like the first two, slipped away and got lost somewhere in the folds of the afternoon. As before, Jean had made the dusting of the objects in the house last for most of the morning. She had vacuumed the floors again and cleaned her bathroom, unnecessarily. After her lunch of milky instant coffee and biscuits she tidied round the kitchen. When she could fool herself no longer that there was anything left to do she mounted the carved wooden stairs and walked the upper floors, again feeling mildly inquisitive, as if the house and the rest of the day might be conspiring to withhold something from her. Again, pointlessly, she tried the three doors she knew to be locked. Then she wandered with less purpose, pausing here and there, her vague eyes watching how light displaced time in the many other rooms of the house. Light entered by the mullioned windows, stretched over floors and panelled walls and lay down across empty beds. It lay as cold and silent as a held breath over furniture and objects and over Jean lingering in each doorway; it claimed space usually taken by hours and minutes which, outside, continued to pass. Through windows to the west Jean saw how the wind was moving the bare trees that bordered the fields; through the south windows she watched grass shivering in the paddock, watched as clouds pasted on to the sky bulged and heaved a little. Inside, the afternoon aged; its folds sank and deepened, closed over the last of the daylight and sucked it in. When it was quite dark Jean walked again from room to room, touching things gently and drawing curtains. So the third day passed, with Jean watching as it seemed not to do so, unaware that she was waiting.

She was keeping the letter from the agency in the pocket of her thick new cardigan, the Christmas present she had bought and wrapped for herself so that she would have something to open 'from my niece Jenny in Australia' in front of the other residents on Christmas morning. For this year, finding herself again between house-sitting jobs over the holiday, she had been obliged to spend Christmas at the Ardenleigh Guest House. It was Jean's fifth Christmas there in eighteen years, and Jenny had sprung into being the very first time when, one day at breakfast, a depressed old lady had invited Jean to agree with her that Christmas was quite dreadful when you were getting on and nobody wanted you. It had sounded like an accusation; Jean had then been in her late forties but suspected she looked older. She ignored the assumption about her age and concentrated on the 'unwanted' allegation. She heard herself saying, *Oh, but I didn't have to come here! In fact my … my niece begged me to come to her! But I told her oh no, I shan't come this year, thank you, dear. Thank you, Jenny dear, I said, but no, I'll make other arrangements.* And then of course the old lady had asked her why. *Oh, well. Well, she's having a baby soon, her third. So I thought, it wouldn't be fair to add to the workload this year.* Then she added, in a voice loaded with dread, *You see, she's not having an easy pregnancy.*

Several of the residents were permanent, and the next time Jean had to spend Christmas there one of them asked, too eagerly, how the niece was getting on. She could not bear to disappoint – it was as if during the intervening two years the residents had been on the edge of their seats waiting for news – so she found herself telling them about the baby (*quite a toddler now, into everything!*) adding that this year they were away, spending Christmas with Jenny's husband's family. And it was the same the next time, at which point Jean lost her nerve and packed them all off to live in Australia. But she discovered that the Ardenleigh residents had formed a high opinion of Jenny, and it did not seem right to Jean to sully her niece's reputation by allowing her, just because she had emigrated, to forget her old aunt in England. It did not seem the kind of thing Jenny would do. So for Ardenleigh Christmases she now produced Jenny's thoughtful present, relieved not to have to produce also another reason, beyond the unbearably long flight (at her age), for not spending Christmas 'Down Under'.

But this year it seemed that Jenny had slipped up, because the cardigan was not a success. Jean had chosen it thinking its colour 'amethyst' and realised, now that it had been hers for over a week, that it was just a muddy purple. But it did not occur to her not to wear it even though it now disappointed; she wrapped herself snugly into her mistake just as she kept the letter close as a reminder to be at all times braced against the temptation to forget it. It lay in her cardigan pocket. In the mornings, bending to dust the feet of a table or to unplug the vacuum cleaner, Jean would sometimes feel it crackle next to her, as if a small, sharp part of herself had broken off and was hanging loose against her side. It puzzled her, almost, to find that she was not actually in pain. Sometimes she would take the envelope from her pocket and look at it, but she did not read the letter again.

Yet, somewhere in the course of the afternoons, Jean would arrive at an amnesty with the presence of the letter. As daylight took its leave, it seemed to wrap up and bear away the threat that seeped from her cardigan pocket. She could feel that the letter itself was still there, but she would begin to regard it with a sort of detached astonishment, which grew into simple disbelief, that marks on a piece of paper should hold any power over her. Walking from room to room, switching on lamps, it seemed amazing to her that only this morning she had thought the letter had any meaning at all. Here, in this soft lamplight, how could it? And as the day darkened further, the picture of herself accepting some pointless words in an envelope hidden inside her cardigan grew more and more improbable. By night time, when she had settled at the drawing-room fire and the peace of the house was at its deepest, the very notion of eight months hence was simply incredible. Here, if she wanted it, the future could be as dim and distant as she preferred the past to be.

On the fourth day Shelley from the agency telephoned.

'Hello?'

'Is that Walden Manor?'

'Yes? Hello?'

'Who is this? Jean, is that you? Jean? It's Shelley, from Town and Country Sitters. Did you get our letter?'

'Oh. Oh yes. Yes, I got the letter.'

Jean disliked Shelley. She had met her in person only once, when a householder had insisted that his keys should not be sent through the post to the sitter and Jean had had to travel to the office in Stockport to collect them. She knew she ought to try to feel sorry for her. Shelley was burdened both by asthma and by a disproportionately large chest, which together gave the impression that her breasts were actually two hardworking outside lungs, round and wide, inelastic and over-inflated. Jean now pictured them rising and falling and pulled her purple cardigan round her own neat shoulders, swaying in a wave of panic that suddenly washed through her. She waited with the receiver held some distance away, trying to calm herself, while Shelley caught her breath at the other end. She guessed that Shelley would be at her desk, winding the telephone flex around the ringed index finger of her free hand, her unbuttoned jacket of the navy businesswoman sort skimming the sides of her blouse-clad bosom with the whish and crackle of acetate meeting acetate. Possibly this was adding to the gusts of noise that Jean could hear over the phone, now, as if some battle that she could not see were being fought somewhere in the distance.

'Right, well, Jean,' Shelley managed at last, 'so you've had our confirmation. Basically I just wanted to check if you've got any queries. You're okay as regards the contents of the letter, are you? Unfortunately we won't be in a position to offer you any further employment after the expiry of this current contract. I mean, we had said, hadn't we. I did say.'

Jean said nothing, knowing that her silence would be considered a difficult one.

Shelley told her, 'We don't like terminating people but it's company policy. Town and

Country's not in a position to keep people on past retirement age, we're not allowed. It's the insurance.' Breathing of a struggling, bovine kind followed this long speech. 'I mean, you've done sterling work. But you've already had four years past sixty. Right. So.'

Still Jean said nothing, so Shelley changed tack. 'So, you're doing okay, are you, Jean, as regards the location of the property? Okay popping out and getting your bits and pieces? Because they did say it'd be better for a car owner as you've got over a mile to the village and it might be lonely. They said really it'd suit a slightly younger person with a car and maybe a part time job in the area, though I did tell them you were very professional and okay with a mile. You are okay, Jean, are you?'

'There's been a breakage,' Jean announced. 'Today, while I was dusting. A teapot on the sideboard. Blue and white, Chinese, with silver mountings. Not very large.'

There was another wait while Shelley prepared the tone of her reply and Jean heard the breathing grow unmistakably irritated. 'Well you've just proved my point. We have to fork out the excess on that now. You'll need to find it on the inventory and notify us and we'll have to tell the owners. You have got the inventory, haven't you? It was in with the rest of the paperwork, with our letter and the owners' list, you know, all

26

their do's and don'ts?'

'Yes, I've got the paperwork. And the list, all the do's and don'ts. Plenty of *them*.'

'Yes, well, that's their prerogative. People can go a bit over the top, especially when they can't meet the sitter themselves. The Standish-Caves had to fly out the day before you arrived, that was all explained, wasn't it?'

The list of instructions and grudging permissions for the house sitter that had come from the owners, via the agency, filled several typed pages. They were wide-ranging: no open fires, no candles, do not use the dining room or drawing room, use TV in small sitting room, use only kitchen crockery, do not use the cappuccino machine or the ice cream maker, always wear gloves to dust the books, beeswax polish only – no silicone sprays, you are welcome to finish any *opened* jars, unplug the television at night. Jean hugged her cardigan closer.

'You'd think I'd never house-sat before. You'd think I don't know the first thing.'

'Well you can't blame them, can you, especially not now something's broken. It is their house.'

'I could have a go at mending it. I've still got the bits.'

'Don't touch it! They'll want it properly mended, if it's even worth doing. These clients are very particular, that's why they're using us. That's why you're there. Oh, *Jean*.'

There was more laborious breathing from Stockport until Jean finally cleared her throat and said, 'Sorry.'

Shelley said, rather quickly, 'Well I'm sure you are but I mean this is the point, isn't it? This is just the point. You are sixty-four. Suppose it happens again? Suppose you had a fall or something – well, our clients are paying for peace of mind, which they'd not be getting, would they, not in that particular scenario. No way they'd be getting peace of mind if Town and Country let their sitters go on too long.'

'It's only small. They probably wouldn't even miss it, there are hundreds of things here.'

'Jean, you're in a *people* business. The client's needs come first. That's key. Isn't it? You're in the client's home.'

Jean sniffed. 'You don't have to tell me that. I have been doing this eighteen years.'

'Yes, and maybe that's why it's time to call it a day, isn't it? After all, we've all got to retire sometime, haven't we? I should think you could do with a rest! Where is it you're retiring to, again?'

There was another wait while Jean said nothing because she did not know, and Shelley shored up her elective forgetfulness against the disturbing little truth that for

28

eighteen years the agency had corresponded with Jean, on the very rare occasions when there was a gap between house-sitting assignments, care of a Mrs Pearl Costello (proprietrix) at the Ardenleigh Private Guest House in East Sussex somewhere. St Leonard's, was it? This year Jean had asked as usual for an assignment that would span Christmas, and they had nothing for her until this one at Walden Manor, beginning on January 3rd. Shelley sighed with an audible crackle as her jacket shifted on her shoulders. All right, so Jean had no family. But today was Shelley's first Monday back from 'doing' Christmas for fourteen people of four generations in a three-bedroomed house, and she told herself stoutly that family life could be overrated. Jean probably had a ball at the Ardenleigh.

'Going to retire to the seaside, are you, Jean?'

'I'm looking at a number of options. I haven't decided.'

'Good for you. Right, well, I'll let you get on. Send us on a notification of the breakage. Oh, and can you remember in future when you answer a client's phone, you should say, "Walden Manor, the Standish-Cave residence, may I help you?" It's a nice touch. You don't just say hello, all right? Company policy. And careful with that duster, at least till you're enjoying a long and happy retirement!'

Jean put down the telephone in the certain knowledge that Shelley in Stockport was doing the same with a shake of the head, a crackle of her clothing and a despairing little remark to the office in general about it being high time, getting Jean Wade off the books.

That evening Jean lit a fire in the drawing room. When it was well alight, she drew the agency's letter from her pocket and laid it carefully over the flames. Its pages curled, blackened and blazed up as the logs underneath settled with a hiss and a weak snap of exploding resin that sounded to Jean, smiling in her deep armchair, more like an approving sigh followed by faint and affectionate tutting. Only as the flames died, and to her surprise, did she become aware of a dissatisfaction with the emptiness of the room. Jean did not acknowledge loneliness. She had long recognised that two states, solitariness and a kind of sadness, were constants in her life, merely two ordinary facts of her existence. The two things might have been related, but as far as she could she left that possibility unexamined. Because even if they were, what could she do about it? Like many people who cannot abide self-pity, Jean sometimes felt very sorry indeed for a buried part of herself whose very existence irked her. And of course she was alone now, sitting in the glow of the fire and of warm-shaded lamps, in the low, beamed drawing room with its deep rose carpet and the heavy drapes pulled against the dark outside. She occupied a solid wing armchair, one of several chairs in the room which, along with two sofas, were covered in materials that were all different but belonged to the same respectable family of chalky old shades of green, pink and grey. She had never been more comfortable in her life, and she was, of course, alone. And so what dissatisfied her suddenly, she thought, could not be simple loneliness, not some unmet desire for a companion, but more a regret that she was the only person in the world who had seen the short but satisfying burning of the letter. For it had been a ceremony of a kind, watching the maroon, swirling print of the letterhead 'Town & Country Sitters *for total peace of mind*' go up in flames; and ceremonies should be witnessed even if they are not quite understood, Jean thought. She could not say exactly what the significance of hers had been, whether it marked an end or a beginning, a remembrance, an allegiance, a pledge – but it had been in a way purifying, and there should have been somebody else here to watch it with her. Somebody who might afterwards stay a while, and to whom she might talk in her underused voice, all about the letter, and Mother, and houses and growing old, and who, occupying the other chair by the fire, would nod and understand. And who, later perhaps, almost carelessly admiring her cleverness and good taste, would assure her that one smashed teapot among so many half broken things did not matter, that all would be well, even that her ill-chosen cardigan was, in fact, a beautiful shade of amethyst.

I felt that way about the objects even before the teapot. And also before the teapot, there was another thing. I felt, walking through the house, that time itself had stopped passing or rather, since that is impossible, that its passing had begun to seem irrelevant in the way that a war fought in another country becomes, eventually. For it seemed to me that in this house the only purpose of time, before it grew dark, was to let something beautiful happen to the light that was coming in through the windows. The hours of those first afternoons just moved over and made space for me to be quietly entertained by the light entering, fading and then leaving us, the things and me. I thought it was the kindest present I had ever been given.

I tested this second feeling for the first few days and reached an accommodation with it. I realised that in a house like this time passes so gently it seems not to be doing so at all unless you pay attention to the way light changes. Time had stopped pulling me along the way it had begun to, with that letter. It was as if time would let me linger for as long I wanted, would even linger along with me, but so quietly that I would not notice it at my side.

All this is the wisdom of hindsight, of course. I couldn't have put it into words at the time. All I could have said for certain back in January was that I was happy in a beautiful house. Also that I saw, for certain, that people are mistaken when they say that joys are fleeting. It's the opposite. I had arrived thinking, worrying, really, that it wasn't long until September. But in the first week here I learned that a part of joy is the apparent infinity of it. When you are happy, happiness stretches out ahead of you, its end forever receding even as you suspect that something this good can't last. But it does. It goes on, and you're confounded, you ought to be expecting it to finish, and it doesn't. Then something quite giddy gets into you, and then you start to think you *need* it to go on. And it does, it does. It's one of the things about it. Suddenly, because I was happy, the time until September was so, so far away. Happiness surrounded me like trees so I couldn't see September, waiting.

She had not told Shelley the half of it about the teapot. When it fell and shattered on the dining room floor after what seemed the merest push from the feather duster, it had spilt keys. Several, perhaps forty of them, had skittered and skidded across the flagstones like enamelled seeds from a spent case. Jean was at first offended by the accident, feeling that she had been almost forced into it. The owners' list had commanded, 'Use the feather duster. Do not lift objects to dust them' and Jean had so far been obedient. So really, the breakage could be said to be their own fault, for if she had been using a cloth, or if she had been holding the teapot instead of pushing the stupid feather thing at it as it sat on the sideboard, it would not have slid off and smashed.

But the broken teapot ceased to matter when she picked up the keys from across the floor and considered them, for this was a house with a great many locked doors. Householders varied, Jean had found. Some encouraged a house sitter to move in and treat the place as their own, proffering so much access that it was embarrassing. In her time Jean had been invited to use computers, drinks cupboards, dubious videos, occasionally a sauna and once, the client's electric hair rollers. Others were less profligate but still welcoming, sometimes dust-sheeting and closing unneeded rooms as much for the house sitter's convenience as their own. But few locked rooms the way these people had, without explanation, but still leaving open four empty bedrooms upstairs and all the downstairs rooms that Jean was supposed to clean and maintain but not use. They had also locked what they called, in their instructions, the pool pavilion, the garages, the potting sheds and implement store. Desk drawers and small cabinets throughout the house also had been locked and the keys taken away. And had been placed in the blue and white teapot at the back of the sideboard, Jean now supposed, lifting and dropping handfuls of keys, letting them clank softly in her palm. Or to be more accurate, placed in the teapot so that they would be hidden from her. Her vague offence over the owners' behaviour was warming into resentment. They were practically saying they did not trust her. Did they assume that a humble house sitter would be unable to resist the temptation to sully their beautiful and valuable possessions?

The keys that were obviously for cars were of no interest to Jean, who had never learned to drive. Nor did she think she would ever need or want to operate garden machinery using the keys with paper tags marked *mower*, *old saw* and *new saw*. But the largest mortice keys would surely open the locked doors upstairs. They would show her the rooms that were thought too good for her, which would offer up their spaces, grateful that she had come to claim them. The smaller keys, she guessed, would be for cupboards. They would reveal even finer things that would console her for the destroyed teapot, treasures yet more precious, even now waiting to be brought into the light. And the smallest keys would surely turn the locks of some of the carved boxes, of hidden drawers in exquisite cabinets; they would yield with scarcely a click and she would pull out tiny handles and lift lids on secrets that these people, in their insulting way, had thought to keep from her. Next to these pewter-coloured keys, whose dullness merely disguised the scale and richness of what they protected, the bright blue and white, silver-mounted teapot was already losing its glamour. Jean retrieved the porcelain shards, now as discarded and irrelevant as shed skin, and put them in a bag.

You might think it's a perfect recipe for bitterness, living all alone in the house of somebody much richer than you are, but I don't think I have ever fallen into that particular trap. Besides, this house isn't the biggest place I've done or the most luxurious, nor did I mind not having neighbours. It's a solitary job anyway, you accept that, and a mile from the village isn't really that far. Thinking about it I've been much more solitary in towns, behind electronic gates in huge opulent houses full of expensive trash, usually in places that are both popular and disgusting, like Bournemouth. Or Wilmslow. I could never be anything other than solitary in places like that. Those houses have carpets so thick you think you're walking on squashed animals, and big upholstered chairs with huge cushions, like corpulent women in tight dresses in too young a colour. Most often it's peach. In places like that you are lonely, comfortable and revolted all at the same time.

So, this house, the fifty-eighth, is not the biggest, nor the loneliest nor the richest. It is the most gracious. Put simply, it is beautiful. From the first, I knew it was the first truly beautiful house I'd ever seen, because I could imagine really living in it, as distinct from just staying a while. It's beautiful in the old way, quietly. I don't think I'm a snob but there's such a thing as good taste – though there's more to it than that. I never really associated this house with its owners. It seems strange even to call them that. I thought about them, a little, in the first week or so, but gradually less, and hardly ever after Michael came.

When I arrived, three of the rooms upstairs were locked. So was the door to the cellar, various other cupboards around the place, and the garages and outbuildings. I was a bit cross about that, clients shouldn't do that. First of all, one of my jobs is to keep rooms aired and how can I if they're locked? Second is the fire risk. What if there's an electrical fault, and a fire starts that you can't get to? You're wondering all the time what could happen behind the door and all you can do is rattle the handle and pray that everything's unplugged. People just don't think about that, not until they've experienced a house fire for themselves. The irony was that on that very long list of things they wanted me to do or not do, they'd put 'avoid any fire risks'! So, no candles, no open fires, unplug the television. I could have taken that personally, but I kept reminding myself they knew nothing about me and fires and houses. They couldn't, because Town and Country Sitters didn't; if they had I should never have been taken on at all. No, the 'owners' were just being cautious in case I was as stupid as they were afraid I'd be, being only a house sitter.

Other things on the list that annoyed me: after 'no open fires' it said that the radiators were turned off in the library, drawing room, dining room and upstairs, but not in 'my' bedroom or the smallest bathroom, or in the small sitting room where the television was. That was an assumption, wasn't it? That I'd just watch telly and go to bed. Well, I may have been in the habit of doing so, but I didn't care for the assumption. Straight away it reminded me of the Ardenleigh where it's a choice between the bedroom (heating off, discouraged in the daytime) or what they call the lounge, where the television is on all day with nobody watching it but not really doing anything else either, except looking offended. And oh yes, the Aga kept the kitchen warm, the list said. If that wasn't a hint about where I belonged I don't know what was.

So almost from the very beginning I lit a fire in the drawing room every evening, right up till the beginning of June. There are enough logs stacked outside in the open shed in the courtyard to last for years and plenty of trees round about anyway. Michael has been lighting a fire again since last week. August evenings can be chilly.

Anyway, I'm supposed to be trying to explain. I admit I wasn't in the best frame of mind about Mr and Mrs Standish-Cave, but it wasn't malice. It was more a case of things just coming round in a particular way, starting with me coming here after another Christmas at the Ardenleigh. The Ardenleigh is dreadful at Christmas. It's half holiday guesthouse and half old people's home. She (Mrs Costello) takes anybody who pays as long as they're not geriatric, and I daresay it suits her to have people there all winter. But at Christmas it's neither one thing nor the other. A plastic snowman on every storage heater, wisps of tinsel (turquoise to match the carpet) sellotaped on to the pictures, the barometer and the cuckoo clock, even on the stainless steel cruet on every table. This year there was an artificial Christmas tree with flashing lights that played *Santa Claus is Coming to Town*, until one of the residents had a nightmare about it and wet her bed. It was the talk of the place, would she be allowed to stay? The pictures on the walls are like the tablemats and the tablemats are like the pictures, and I've never known grapefruit segments in syrup (first course on Christmas Day) improved for being eaten off a coaching scene from Olde Englande. It's not uncomfortable exactly; you get used to the sound of the traffic outside and the television, and at least the heating goes on in the bedrooms at six. But the irony was that even though I loathed the Ardenleigh it was better than where I would probably end up, because I wouldn't be able to afford even the Ardenleigh's terms for permanent residents after September.

Later, it was the three of us together,

Michael, Steph and me, and then the baby, and its seeming suddenly so clear what was important. This is hard. I've just read that last bit back to myself and it doesn't really tell you much, does it? Suppose I put it like this: it wasn't just the thought of the Ardenleigh or worse, or this house, or the things in it, or just me, or just Michael, or Steph, or the baby. Not any one single thing, not one thing more than any of the others. It was all of us, and all of it: the way this place allowed each of us to stop struggling in our various ways, how it seemed to give us strength, how it seemed right to care for it so much, and for one another. All of it added up to more than just us.

We came to it late, you see, we came late to the idea of belonging in a place and belonging to other people. I mean we'd all had goes at it in the past, it's hard to avoid, but it was us being here, the family we made, that was the point. If you think that sounds like an attempt to justify what's happened, you'd be quite right.

Six tapestry kneelers at maybe eight pounds each would hardly make it worth the trip. Michael's whole trip had been planned round the pair of 16th century alabaster effigies in the display case and now, just because the vicar wasn't here and thanks to this stupid woman, he wasn't going to get his hands anywhere near them. The consolation prize of six tapestry kneelers made it worse, somehow. Michael was thinking this in his head while smiling and listening to the woman – she must be some church volunteer – who had interrupted him between the sixth and seventh kneeler and was now following him round the church.

He had called at the vicarage to ask if he could handle the alabaster figures, to be told by a preoccupied woman at a computer screen that the vicar was away and she knew nothing about the procedures for unlocking the case holding the figures, but he was of course welcome to look round the church. He had been glad to find it empty, and not too disheartened. He had half-expected to find the figures inaccessible, but he might still find out useful things such as the strength of the lock on the case, perhaps even where the key was kept (pathetically often with church people, simply in a drawer in the vestry). It would not be the first time he would have to make a return trip, and in the meantime a decent number of kneelers would make this one worthwhile. So when this other woman had appeared eight minutes later he had been sitting in one of the pews with his backpack beside him, half prepared for the interruption.

Long ago he had learned that the quiet of

country churches was deceptive and that people came and went all day, self-importantly engaged in parish drudgery of one sort or another. So he always made sure that he was ready to assume, at the split second's notice usually given by the clack of an iron latch, an attitude of prayerful contemplation. Until such time as he might be interrupted – today, a mere eight minutes – he would be quietly busy. This time he had been stuffing the boring but quite saleable hand-stitched kneelers into his backpack. It could have held twenty. Twenty might have fetched well over a hundred quid; still only a fifth of what the alabaster figures would make, so it would have gone down as a poor day. But still respectable, at least worth his while.

But he would have to revise those calculations, because he had only managed to get six of them. And the woman was now into her twentieth minute of telling him that the vicar wasn't here because his wife had died three weeks before Christmas and the poor man had had to go on a retreat.

'Just yesterday, how unlucky! Poor man. I said to him, you just never know how it's going to take you, we're all different. We are, aren't we? But he said he would see things through to Epiphany, that was yesterday of course, and then he would take a break. He's finding it much more difficult than he expected, if you ask me.'

Michael smiled and said he quite understood. 'But if perhaps *you* could open the case? As I explained, I've been looking at artefacts from this period for several years and it's only by–'

'I said to the parish clerk on Sunday, I said if you ask me that man is heading for a breakdown, he said oh I know, but at least he's off for a week, off to Columba's Lodge on the seventh and I said well I'm glad to hear it–'

'You see, handling the figures is the only way–'

'What? Oh, no, I am sorry, I wouldn't be comfortable. I am churchwarden as I said, but I'm not sure I've got the authority. I've never been asked, you see, and the vicar keeps the key at the vicarage, so– I mean if the other churchwarden was here as well, but no, he's away, I know for a fact it's this week. He's in the Canaries, they always go in January. Lucky for some!'

Michael pulled his mouth into another understanding smile but doubted if he could say 'it doesn't matter' without hissing, so said nothing. He wandered off down the nave, raising his eyes to the roof as if it held some interest, blinking several times to disguise the faint flickering of muscle that tugged at one side of his face whenever he got upset. Then like a familiar ache came

44

the realisation that she was not going to finish talking and push off to leave him alone again in the church. He would have to leave first.

'You see, it's Jeff, you said, isn't it, you see, Jeff, I think the vicar would say it's not the value so much as the fragility. Do you know, nobody's even meant to touch them without gloves? I couldn't take it upon myself, you see. But the vicar might let you handle them, if you came back when he's here.'

Michael pressed his eyebrows into an angle of scholarly disappointment. 'Yes, yes, that would be marvellous, except I'm due back in Norfolk by the weekend, you see. And one does so need to examine them. The main idea for my little book revolves round certain dating uncertainties, as I said, and only close examination gets one any further forward...'

'Oh, but we're quite confident they're genuine sixteenth century, because–' Michael was too taken up with noticing how hamstery she looked to hear the details. Her hair might have been red once, and was still abundant. Twisted wires of it were held under a knitted hat and a gingery down surrounded her small mouth, which worked too quickly. Michael took a deep breath for one last effort and interrupted her to explain that his hypothesis, based on his understanding (imperfect, of course, just a little interest of his, though a publisher *may* be getting keen) of the religious iconography of Northern Europe, the details of which he would spare her, was that the figures might be much older.

'They might, in fact, even be 12th century. Though one must get them in one's hands, you see, as the weight and density of the material is key. And a little scrape test on the base would confirm, and so on. But if I'm right, they'd be so rare you could say they were priceless. *Immensely* valuable.'

This had worked before. It was extraordinary how the unwillingness of some people to put their important and valuable objects into his hands could suddenly evaporate at the suggestion that a closer examination might reveal even more importance and value. But infuriatingly, inexplicably, it was not working now with Hamster Woman. Was she simple?

'Oh my goodness! That would be something for the PCC, wouldn't it! But oh, you *should* have telephoned the vicarage first, it's too bad you've missed the vicar! Though to be honest I'm not sure if he'd have been up to it, he's *exhausted*. It's only four and half weeks since she finally went and such terrible timing, just in the run-up to Christmas and you can imagine Christmas nearly finished him but no, he wouldn't bow out of a single service, he's like that, throws himself into everything, *too* hard if you ask me. And oh, he did need the break, we could all see that. She was only fifty-nine and towards the end, you see, with the nursing, well. The bishop's quite good about things like that. The new bishop I mean, the last one wasn't quite so *aware*, not at the grass roots. Though as a parish, we all try to be terribly–'

'No, well! Sadly, I didn't know. Ah well, very sad. Another time. Well, I won't…'

Michael was not finding the right words in the way he had once been able to, and his face was definitely ticking now. Why was it calling for greater effort each time? This part of it, the part of the whole business that should be fun, that might even in a strange way have been the point of it once, was now becoming more and more difficult. His attention tended to wander, and that was dangerous. Or perhaps, Michael considered, pulling a hand across his face, he was allowing his attention to wander *because* it was dangerous, because the fire he was playing with had been cooling over the course of the last few trips and a little more danger might generate a little more heat from it. Or was he just tired, tired beyond words, like the vicar, *exhausted?*

Michael bestowed his curatey smile on the woman once more and concentrated hard. He was not Michael, he was Jeffrey 'everyone calls me Jeff' Stevenson. He adjusted his voice to reveal his gratitude, his smile to show his regret, his eyes to leave her in no doubt about his sincerity. He ran it over again in his mind. He, Jeff, was a Church of England curate taking a few days' holiday, researching his special interest in devotional objects. He was a curate; disappointed and philosophical, but (because they all were) demonstrably, quintessentially *nice*.

Nicely, he said, 'It's my own fault, I should have planned better, but sometimes it's good to wander whither one wilt, so to speak, and just drop in. Ah well, back to Norfolk, disappointed! Unless we can prevail upon someone else...'

'Oh, Norfolk! I'm very fond of Norfolk! So where is your church, exactly?'

Michael swallowed and tried not to stare at her with the naked hatred he was beginning to feel.

'St Margaret's, Burnham Norton,' he told her, also reminding himself that today he was Jeff Stevenson of St Margaret's, Burnham Norton and that there was no need to panic. He could, if required, reel off the biographical details of Jeff Stevenson that he had memorised from Crockford's Directory of the Clergy. Part of Michael's brain now pictured the real Jeff Stevenson going about his pathetic business in Norfolk, unaware that he was being impersonated (and rather well) on the other side of the country. Michael knew that whatever the day might hold in the line of duty for Jeff Stevenson, it would include a little light comforting of the old, the lonely, the sick: jollying up, calming down, smoothing over the truth that most people's lives stank whether there was a God or not. Michael believed that comforting was just another form of lying, which made Jeff Stevenson no better than he was.

'Oh, yes, but just where *is* that?' asked the woman, her voice squeaking with what sounded, unbelievably, like genuine interest. How was it possible, Michael wondered. Really, how was it done? And most of all, *why*, why this curiosity, this caring about details in the lives of strangers? Then the thrill that had been missing from the day stole over him. Beyond its being in Norfolk, Michael had not a clue where Burnham Norton was. And it would be such an exquisite disaster if, by one of those coincidences that were so common, he was about to be found out. He waited, perhaps half wanting it, to hear the 'because my sister lives there, you *must* know her!' or the 'but the curate of St Margaret's is my goddaughter's nephew. You're not the curate of St Margaret's!' One day it was bound to happen. Was it to be today? The more little trips he made the more he risked it, and with every time he got away with it, the closer came the day when he would not.

'Is it on the coast?'

The question seemed to ring off the walls of the church and eddy round the display case where the pair of effigies stood smug behind the glass. Michael moved casually towards the door.

'Well, if you know where Norwich is it's not so far from there, I suppose. Look, I think I'd better–'

'But in what direction? How many miles? Is it anywhere near oh, what's it called... I can picture the place, I went there as a girl – twice in fact–'

'Oh, is this your leaflet?' Michael blurted. 'May I take one?'

'Oh, do! Here, take a few and you can hand some on,' she said, pushing a wad of pale green leaflets at him. 'There's quite a bit there about our effigies, we are rather proud of them! And we do like our visitors!'

'Oh, *may* I? Thank you.'

'Take plenty, do. Well, remember where we are, won't you? The vicar'll be back by the end of this week. Have you signed our visitors' book? There *should* be a pen but they do walk!'

'Oh, not to worry! It's been lovely just to see the church. Yes, I've signed the book,' Michael gushed back. 'As soon as I arrived, before you came in. Thanks so much!'

'And do, *do* come back at the end of the week when the vicar's here!'

'If I possibly can, I will! Thank you!'

'Give my regards to Norfolk!'

'I will!' And if you say one more word, he thought, beaming at the woman before he turned to go, I shall club you to death.

Michael parked in a lay-by on the edge of Sherston, swiped up the pile of pale green leaflets from the dashboard, wound down the window and pushed them out. He stared at them as they settled and shifted on the ground. The twitch in his face had travelled down to his throat, and he began to cry. The van needed work, the electric bill was overdue and even supposing he could shift the six kneelers straight away, once he counted in his petrol he would be no better off. He sank his head on to the steering wheel and gulped. He was due back in court tomorrow for falling behind with his fines again, and he had nothing for the arrears. But even that was not the worst of it. The unbearable part was that, despite the practical clothes and the shiny clean hair for today's little performance, he was not Jeff Stevenson. Once again, inescapably, he was only himself.

On Tuesday, the day after the teapot and Shelley's telephone call, Jean filled her cardigan pockets with keys and set off round the house. The largest key opened the locked room at the front, which turned out to be a study, not of the proper working kind but with a battered, easy-going air, as if any studying ever done in it had been allowed to evolve in its own fashion. The furniture was comfortably mis-matched, apparently brought in piece by piece and then allowed to stay, however useless it became. One solid mahogany desk had been joined by an oak one, smaller and less attractive, on which stood an ancient IBM golfball typewriter. A four drawer filing cabinet stood next to one of another colour, half its size. There was a computer and printer, and a disconnected fax and answering machine. Next to the computer squatted an old adding machine, and behind the cordless telephone sat a white plastic one with a round dial.

Jean was not especially curious about what business might have been conducted here, but it seemed to her, peering at the shelves of Cricketers' Almanac, the stacked software boxes with titles such as Mensa Ultimate Challenge and British Plant Guide, that it was less than all-absorbing, and perhaps indistinguishable from recreation. Quite possibly no business at all, in the commercial sense, but only household matters were run from here. She looked round blandly. All offices and businesses were, in the end, the same to her. She had worked in several, the last in 1984, when she had left just in time to avoid having to grapple with word processing. Work in offices bored her and always had: all it ever came to was the talking, typing, sending, filing of what were in the end just words and numbers. The people around her had seemed unaware of the futility of what they did all day, so she had learned to keep her mouth shut, do what was expected of her and look as if she gave a damn. But it amazed her. The wonder of offices, she felt, was that so many people could waste so much of their lives in them and think their time well spent.

Two of the newest and smallest keys opened the filing cabinets. Jean flicked through the folders in the top drawer, marked with names such as *Current Account 1*, *2* and *3*, *Telephone*, *Insurance (Buildings)*, *Insurance (Contents)*, *Appliances*, *Oil*, *Electricity*, *Pool*, *Suppliers: Various*. In the lower drawers the first few files were labelled *Bonds*, *Deeds* and *Inland Revenue*. Jean could not be bothered to look further. It was all financial or legal stuff, statements and accountants' letters about trusts, investments and so on, and a lot of correspondence with some firm called Sadler Byng & Waterman who called themselves Independent Financial Advisers. Jean closed the drawer. It was sure to be disappointingly mundane in the detail, even if she were ready to make the effort to understand it. If she found herself at a very loose end some wet afternoon she might come up here and take a proper look. Before she left the room she checked that the computer and fax were indeed unplugged, but noted reproachfully that the old electric typewriter on the oak desk by the window was not. She left it as it was.

She tried another of the large keys in the carved door at the end of the main landing. It turned. The door opened with a sigh of its hinges, and showed to Jean – as if a curtain had been raised on a scene from a glamorous play – a room so light, pristine and pale that she felt immediately dirty and unworthy. She hesitated, finding it necessary to gaze from the doorway as if to check that the room was indeed empty; for something inside, something surely alive though not human, was beckoning to her. She stepped out of her shoes and walked in, where the perfection of the room expanded and grew inclusive. As she moved, she stirred the trapped smells of dry grass, clean cotton and lemon oil, which now began to animate and scent the air she breathed. With every step across the white carpet she summoned magic; she was rousing spells long asleep in the stillness. Moving from window to window she looked out at the dank gardens and then back, trying to accustom herself to the changed picture that she must make, framed by the room. Slowly she grew used to the thought that now she was in the room she was also *of* it, transformed from the sneaking outsider on the threshold into the perfect room's perfect occupant. She looked round at the pattern of faded flowers on the thick curtains, the soft carpet and green rugs, the bleached stone fireplace and the silver candlesticks on the mantelpiece. They seemed to be congratulating her on her safe arrival; they breathed their acceptance and conferred their brightness upon her. Jean sat down on the edge of the large bed, then slid into the centre of it and stretched out. The room was cold, and at once the goose-down quilt beneath her grew warm and nest-like. She lay and allowed something that felt very like happiness to lap through her, wondering if this feeling might be the live thing that she had sensed in the room as she had stood on the threshold. But then, had she not herself brought the feeling with her into the room? She lay smiling, pleasantly unsure whether she were the giver or recipient.

Later, she wandered into the dressing room where she found that the wardrobes, which lined three walls, still had keys in their doors. Opening one, Jean was dismayed that the full-length mirror on the inside should so nearly spoil things. It showed her that she did not, after all, quite perfectly belong; in her heavy skirt and cardigan she was the only dark thing in the room and was not merely dark, but a muddy, lilac dark. But that she should now be shown this was a kindness, really, in the manner of the room's many kindnesses, because the door's swinging open like that and offering Jean her own reflection was revealing also the most obvious and natural solution. The wardrobe was full of women's clothes, most of them hanging from silk padded hangers. Jean counted eight cashmere twin sets and perhaps ten skirts, several blouses of white and cream silk and linen, at least a dozen striped and plain cotton shirts. The drawers alongside held trousers, heavy sweaters, belts, scarves, underwear. Behind the next door hung suits and dresses. For many years Jean had bought clothes of the better sort second-hand, from discreet little places invariably called 'dress agencies'. She had almost developed the necessary blindness to evidence of previous ownership that was betrayed by a slightly bagging skirt, an armpit crease, a curl in a lapel. But nearly all of the clothes in these wardrobes had been so little worn that it was like staring at shop rails. They had the pleasantly impersonal, un-owned look of clothes in the classic English style – yet they might be, Jean

56

thought, biting her lip, just slightly too young and daringly coloured for her. Or perhaps, she thought, with a nip of elation that the prospect of new clothes had not induced in her for three decades, perhaps only too young and daringly coloured for her current view of herself, which now seemed, suddenly, unduly and unnecessarily depressed. The dark figure she had seen reflected in the long mirror was already an embarrassment, a mystifying guest who had turned up uninvited and looking all wrong. As she sifted along the rails she began to see that really, the clothes were actually already hers and always had been; it was only she who had strayed from herself. These clothes would restore her to her proper self – the version of herself that she and other people had mislaid so long ago that everyone had ceased to notice that the dark, muddy Jean who had been going about in her place was the wrong one. The real, elegant, cared-for Jean had been found, and now she was burning to get out of the wrong clothes and prepare herself for the right ones. Turning carefully away from the reflection she undressed and slipped on a long dressing gown of cream alpaca.

In the large bathroom next to the dressing room she ran a deep bath, poured in two or three scented oils, and stepped in through the steam that had formed in the cool air.

She lay back and waited. She would not wash away her old self. The violence of rubbing at her own skin would be almost crude and impatient, and she felt only the magnanimity of a person who is content to wait for her true status to be recognised. She lay in the lapping heat until, as she knew she would, the old Jean simply detached herself, rose up and disappeared into the steam, like a person dissolving into fog. Jean lifted a hand and stirred the water almost in a gesture of farewell, and sighed, looking down the length of her own body. She found she quite liked it, and was finding also that she had all at once become a person who knew that little sensory pleasures were not proscribed; that taking a slow bath in the afternoon was not merely permitted, but smiled upon. What else but approval could be meant by the sight of her own limbs and stomach, the reward of the slippery hot water, such sweet-smelling steam and soap, the thick towels?

After her bath she dried and scented herself, and spent the next hour in a thrill of experiment, trying on her new clothes. The underwear was no good, made for some-body whose bosom and backside were larger than hers. The shoes were a little too wide, but not bad if she could find some insoles. Most of the clothes were com-fortable and also rather too big, so that they bestowed upon Jean the extra little compliment of making her feel dainty. The sight of herself in them was so gratifying it was as if the mirror were a new and encouraging friend. Wearing a deep raspberry-coloured cashmere skirt and sweater, Jean rearranged the wardrobe, pushing the few things that did not suit or fit her to one end. She then brought her own few bits of underwear from the tiny back bedroom and moved them in. She binned the toothbrushes in the bathroom and placed her own by the basin. In the bedroom she unlocked the dressing table and set out on its polished top the hairbrushes, scent and jewellery she found in the drawers. Before gathering up her key collection and leaving the room, she turned on the radiators, closed the curtains, switched on the bedside lights and turned back the bedclothes.

Bringing her new warm scent with her back on to the long landing, Jean opened the third locked room which, when she entered it, seemed to have been longer uninhabited than the other two. Silence and stillness were more deeply in possession; the baby's cot and shelves of toys seemed never to have moved or had a moving thing come near them. The rocking chair stood balanced and fixed in its immobility. A touch of Jean's hand sent a wooden mobile of woolly sheep, hanging frozen over the

Moses basket, into a reluctant spin. At least three dozen pairs of eyes watched her from the shelves; peering through acrylic fur fringes, a menagerie of toy bears, ducks, cats, tigers, elephants and pelicans stared out, glassy and despairing.

In the chest of drawers Jean found volumes of unworn baby clothes, many still in their wrappings, and unopened bottles of every imaginable unguent for the washing, scenting and soothing of baby skin. A baby alarm, still in its box, stood on a small antique nursing chair along with a breast pump, also new and unpacked. Jean saw at once how it all fitted together. Mrs Standish-Cave must be pregnant, which accounted for the quantity of temporarily redundant, non-maternity clothes in the wardrobe, and she and her husband must have gone abroad for the obvious reason. She was going to spend her pregnancy abroad and have the baby there. Perhaps she was even foreign herself and had gone to be with her mother, or perhaps she just had views about the standards of English hospitals. She could, in either of these cases, afford options. No doubt they planned to return with the baby when it was a few months old, where the perfect nursery would be waiting. Jean picked a white bear with maroon velvet paws off the shelf and stroked it, allowing her jealousy of the woman's wealth and, a more familiar envy, her motherhood, to wash through and leave her. It was perhaps a little more understandable now, the peremptory, selfish list, if only marginally less exasperating. Even the locking of the rooms might be thought almost forgivable. Didn't women get fussy and obsessional about their homes when a baby was due? Nest building, fixing, sorting and controlling and having everything just so? Jean fingered the sleeve of her raspberry cashmere jersey and smiled. She could imagine it, the sweet anticipation of preparing for a baby – she had imagined it often enough, though long ago now. But for a reason she did not examine she could imagine it now quite painlessly, rather than with a vague though sapping sense of regret.

Was it loneliness? A matter of not having enough to do? The beds in all the other bedrooms (I mean not counting the two they'd locked) except the one I was meant to have (which, I did note, was the smallest) were stripped bare when I arrived. It doesn't do much for a bedroom, a bare mattress. It looks as if someone has died or at least left forever, whereas a bed newly made up tells you that someone is expected. The bare mattresses were sad, but it was on the same afternoon that I discovered my new bedroom that I began to mind about them very much indeed.

It was the baby's room, perhaps. All that expectation. Such a cheerful thing, a room waiting for a new person. Or maybe it was my new clothes and my new room that were already making me feel so different, so that the idea of a child of my own seemed just another thing that I'd almost managed to forget about wanting very badly, but could now have.

Please don't think I lost my marbles or anything like that, because certain realities never quite left me. Not even I thought for a moment that I could produce a child at sixty-four. But that evening I took my supper into the drawing room and ate in front of the fire. ('Do not take food out of the kitchen'. Of course the list had said that, but I didn't even think of the list that evening and it would have made no difference if I had.) Afterwards I sat thinking.

I have always liked the sound owls make and that evening the owls were the only thing I could hear apart from the fire. I think they nest in the barn or the eaves of the pool pavilion. As I listened, the thought came to me that this house has stood for over four hundred years; even the teapot made it through a couple of centuries before I turned up. All the bits and pieces I'd seen that afternoon – the candlesticks, the clothes, the white bear with velvet paws, even the typewriter – they had all been chosen by somebody at some time, acquired somehow and put here, for reasons which must have been valid enough and perhaps even compelling at the time. But now those reasons didn't matter any more, nor whose reasons they were. Less still did it matter *when* those reasons mattered, whether last month, last year or 1600, because they were in the past.

I saw then that everything that is ever thought or done by people disappears. All human reasoning and actions die, because the minute they're done with, they belong to a time past and they don't come back. Oh, but you might say, what about memory, or the consequences of what people do? They last, don't they? Well, they may survive for a while, but they are on borrowed time. I mean that quite literally. Though it may be longer in coming, the death even of memory comes around, and the effects of actions grow weaker until they are unfelt and cease, and then it is as if they have never been. What is history, then, I suppose you might ask next, if not the past lasting into the present. And I would reply that history is only what we keep hold of in order to explain the present in a way we like. If history is a sort of looking through a window into the past, we choose not just the shape of the window but the view we get from it too. I have read enough historical biography to see that. History is not the remembering of events that were significant in their own time, it is only the resurrecting and preserving of things dead and past upon which we hang our reasons for the way things are now, in the hope that those reasons may seem less paltry. Nothing in the history of anything, not one thought or deed of a single soul, can ever outlive its use-fulness in providing acceptable reasons for the present. So not even history lasts.

But things, things last. They last beyond the time when their significance, or that which originally made them significant, has been forgotten. Whatever the things in this house had meant to someone once, whatever fond stories were attached to them no longer mattered, because time had passed and now the things simply belonged here, neutrally. I could disregard the old stories and tell new ones, and who's to say mine would be less true? That teapot – I looked it up on the inventory – was made in Canton around 1650, silver gilt mounts added later at Augsburg. Insured for hundreds of pounds (I forget the exact figure, it isn't important). Isn't that ridiculous? Now suppose I were to add that it had been bought by, let's say John Walden, an ancestor on my father's side. I could put that it was mentioned in a Deed of Probate (since lost) at Walden Manor in the mid 19th century. Suppose I were to go on to say that it was used by my beloved great-aunt as a button box? Who's to argue? I will admit that these thoughts, as I sat that evening with the owls calling in the dark outside, quite excited me.

I had already begun to picture this kind great-aunt of mine sewing a button from the teapot on my favourite dress, talking softly as she did so to her little niece Jean, and it suddenly seemed perfectly right to continue with the story (this teapot was letting me tell any story I wanted) and say that at some point later on in all this huge, wasteful expenditure of time, Jean conceived a child out of wedlock, gave birth to a son and had him adopted. Forty-seven years ago, say, that would make it 1955, when I was seventeen, the year after Father died. A man of forty-seven might well have children of his own by now, perhaps even grand-children! How happy I would be to find him again. This would be a fine house for a large family, with its gardens, the pool, the paddocks, so many fine rooms.

I swear that this notion that I could once have had a baby and that nobody could insist that I hadn't, it actually made me happy, because it seemed not at all an invention but more like a forgotten thing remembered. So later that evening before I retired to my new bedroom for the first time, I made up all the other beds, too. There was any amount of bed linen. I chose the best, pure linen with lilac piping for Michael and Steph's room, the one with pale dove-grey walls and darker grey velvet curtains (although of course I didn't know then, precisely, that this room would be *theirs*).

Oh, and that was the evening I burned the inventory, too. Over the course of that day it had become an even greater irrelevance than Shelley's letter, and so it went the same way. I remember that it was still less than halfway through January, and perhaps there was something of a Resolution for the New Year in what I did.

The next day Jean left the house in a beautiful olive tweed coat. In the hall she caught sight of her reflection in the long mirror and noted almost with complacency that she looked elegant. How could one fail to, in such a coat? There was a kind of clarity in the silhouette she made. And the same clarity was beginning to enter her mind, pushing aside anxieties and opening it up to small pleasures, such as the way she could spin almost like a dancer as she twisted to see the swing of the coat from the back. The coat she had arrived in, already in her mind just *that old navy thing*, was still lying slung across the oak chest. Turning from the mirror, she picked it up gingerly, as if it were a heap of used bandages. It already felt much less hers than the olive tweed, so the feel of the inferior cloth disturbed her only for a moment, off-handedly; but the smell of it, sacky and with a tang of railway station about it, pulled her dangerously close to acknowledging the old Jean who had worn it last. She bundled it into the cloakroom and as she closed the door on it she lifted one olive tweed sleeve and took a deep breath. The new scents, floral, English, reassuringly her own, glided up to her. She still had on the raspberry cashmere things underneath the coat and had taken from the wardrobe some black shoes, gloves and a leather bag, all of which, she hoped, would make sure that the old Jean did not waylay and follow her when she left the house.

The walk down the drive took twenty minutes. She had never seen it in daylight except in the distance from the upper windows, because she had arrived by taxi long after dark on her first evening. Since then she had been outside the house only to walk round the gardens, bring in logs and to try the doors of the outbuildings. Now, walking between the fields of Walden that bordered the drive on both sides, she felt there was little to see beyond their mild contours except for lines of drystone walls and stands of trees. The landscape itself, empty of livestock, people or buildings was pleasant; it harboured no threat and so held little interest. Jean felt mildly grateful, for that was all she required of it for now. In fact the kind of people (Mother was one) who noticed things in the countryside – interestingly shaped roots or poisonous fungi or how many berries there were – had always rather irritated her.

Jean did not hurry in the new shoes; she liked to look down at them as she walked along and feel the slight slipping contact of her feet with the leather lining. The rain and winds of the previous few days had blown a thin layer of mud on the tarmac drive into tiny patterns, like sand on a beach after the ebb tide. Trickles of water, dammed by clumps of saturated dead leaves and flung twigs, had found their channels. Jean did not avoid the wet particularly but she was already looking forward to her return, remembering that in the wardrobe there were some warm-looking slippers that she had not yet worn. She would light the fire in the drawing room and spend a quiet afternoon there; she might even stretch out on the sofa and nap after lunch, because her morning in Bath was bound to be rather exciting and tiring. Today the housework would be skipped, of course, but since that did not matter to her, it could hardly concern anyone else. This afternoon she would rest in the drawing room wearing the soft felt slippers while her wet shoes, stuffed with newspaper, dried by the Aga. It was a privilege to own such good shoes and so it was a pleasure, as well as a responsibility, to look after them properly.

It was a further quarter of a mile along the road to the bus shelter where Jean stood and waited. As the rain began again, she thought a little sadly of the keys, quite definitely car keys, that had been among the others in the teapot. There were at least three cars behind the high doors of the stone garages behind the courtyard, but she could not drive. But almost certainly her son would, and as she climbed on to the bus and paid her fare to the driver she felt a slight, secret superiority over the other people on board. They looked resigned to travelling this way, but this would be the last time she would ever have to wait in the rain for a bus that was running late.

In Bath, she bought stamps, writing paper and a copy of *The Lady* at WH Smiths and asked for directions to the post office. Across the road from it stood one of those new coffee places with sofas, the sort of place she had never been in before, where they sold fourteen things with Italian names and where, she found, she had to ask carefully to get just a cup of coffee. The smell of the place was better than the coffee actually tasted, but Jean was already tired and grateful for the rest, and she needed somewhere quiet to do the next part. The places around her were filling up, so she shrugged her arms out of the olive coat and let it fall around her like a peel, lining side out. Then she spread her pink cashmere sleeves, as if she were resting heavy wings, across the low table. She set out her paper, envelopes and chequebook, establishing more territory, turned to the back of *The Lady* and began to read. When she had learned what she had to do, she printed on a sheet of paper:

WERE YOU BORN 1955 AND ADOPTED? Lady in country house seeks contact with her brown-eyed baby boy given (out of necessity but reluctantly) to adoptive parents, south of England, aged 3 weeks. All papers since lost. Mother longs to trace. Replies to Box No. only, treated in strictest confidence.

By the time she had printed out another copy to keep, filled in the form, calculated the cost, written out her cheque, and sealed everything in the envelope and addressed it, she was shaking slightly, and her coffee was cold. She wondered about ordering more but she had already spent half of her week's money on the advertisement and the stationery, and she was worried that if she delayed even to drink a cup of coffee she might be overtaken by objections (although from where she was not sure) to what she was doing. Her courage was fluttering and growing restive, like something trapped and uncomfortable. Her heart started to bang inside her chest, and in her throat. People were looking at her. Oh God, could they hear it? Did it show on her face, how terrified she was? She had to get home. She tried again to stop shaking, and could not.

'Excuse me, are you all right?'

So it did show. She had to get home. Now she was certain that all the people here, drinking from foaming cups and talking about their shopping, indeed every one of the thousands of people walking in Bath this morning, would stop her if they could. They would form a mob, a huge furious mob, and stop her. Already this woman at the next table was ignoring what her friend was saying and looking at Jean with what she wanted her to think was concern, but was really suspicion.

'I'm fine. I just need to get home. It's rather warm in here. Thank you.' Jean shrugged herself back into her coat, recovered enough now to see the woman noticing how good and expensive it was. With the woman's eyes still upon her, she crossed the road to the post office and posted the envelope. She stood by the post box until she felt calm again.

Briskly she crossed back and walked into Waitrose, because it had struck her suddenly that a house needed flowers, especially in January. She spent very nearly all of the rest of her money on lilies, roses and freesias, and also picked up a leaflet about Waitrose's home delivery service, hoping that she could place an order by telephone without having to use a credit card. She had never held with credit cards nor, it had to be admitted, had she ever been invited to own one. She had assumed before she arrived that while on this assignment she would go out and do her food shopping once a week or so, as she normally did. But the strain of being away from Walden had proved too great, she realised, walking as fast as she could back to the bus station with her armfuls of flowers. She would not risk it again.

Across town, at the moment when Jean was boarding her bus home, Michael was standing before the magistrates. The Bench – one kind-looking lady, one hard-faced one with dandruff and a man with sloping shoulders – had just re-appeared after having retired to discuss his case, and the hard lady was telling him again how disappointed they were to see him. Michael nodded in sad apology and submitted to another telling-off with the hangdog expression that the magistrates liked. He was lucky to be avoiding a period in custody, he heard, and he caught on the face of the kind lady a look of triumphant magnanimity which told him that he had her to thank for that. He answered in a hoarse voice their intrusive but by now expected questions about his earnings and outgoings. It was noted that he still was not working. Did he not have some experience of bar work? Michael gulped and tried to explain about the depression. So had he consulted his GP? They recommended that he see his GP again, leaving unasked the question of whether or not, after a string of missed appointments, his GP would see him. The mess that Michael was making of his life was expanding and filling the room, pressing down on the shoulders of the magistrates who all now seemed to be sagging, and leaving Michael short of enough breath for explanations. But it was not the exposure of his squalid life that suddenly touched him and made his chin wobble as if he were still a snotty kid; it was the novelty of being questioned. He should be used to the way the magistrates went on by now, but every time it took him unawares. When they asked him about himself, sounding as if it really mattered, he found himself wanting to cry. For a moment he nearly allowed himself to believe that these motherly, judging women cared about him. But he glanced up at the flaky shoulders of the hard-faced one, and remembered that it was not his poverty, nor his upbringing in care, nor his bare little flat, nor the absence of friends and prospects that concerned them. All they cared about was getting money off him, first for driving the van without insurance or tax, and then an extra load for falling behind twice with the payments. Tears of self-pity filled his eyes, and when the hard lady went on to tell him that they were not imposing a community service order on him in view of his health, but increasing his fine and generously re-scheduling the payments, he lowered his head further and his tears spilled down the lapels of the jacket that he had worn to encourage the magistrates' leniency. If he kept up to date with the payments from now on, he would clear his debt in four years. Michael opened his mouth and closed it again. There was no point in saying anything. It wouldn't work. Any institutional sympathy for a child brought up in care was exhausted long before that child had become a struggling adult of forty, so he would not mention it. Now they were asking if he would be able to keep up with the payments this time. He gave the expected yes. And as he was being told that they hoped never to see him again, the kind lady started writing something and did not look up when he left the court.

When Michael got back to the flat it was still freezing, but he was worried about the electricity bill so it was going to have to stay that way. He thought about going across to Ken's where it was always hot, but this would mean listening to Ken and he was not up to it in his present mood. A thread of guilt tightened inside him. Ken didn't see many people; he ought to go. But not now. He might look in later and see if Ken wanted anything doing. And if he did, if he asked Michael to get him a paper or cigs from the shop at the top of the road or something, or fill him a hot water bottle, it would make Michael feel a bit better about asking if he could have a bath. Ken's bathroom, with the hoist, the handrails and all the surgical what-have-yous on the window sill that Michael couldn't bear to study too closely, gave him the creeps, but the water was always hot.

Michael heated up a tin of soup and took a mug of it to bed. The backpack, empty and gaping open, sat on the bedroom floor next to the row of books against the skirting board. Mr David at Sulis Curios and Objets d'Art had taken the kneelers yesterday for

75

twenty-five quid for the six, which he had counted out and handed over with a dirty look. Bloody act of charity, he had said. Don't try this kind of thing on me again, all right? But they had both known that Michael would. The trouble, Michael decided, spooning up his soup, was his lack of a fallback position. He could not afford to walk away from even the meagre money Mr David put up, because there was always something that made his need for cash immediate and desperate: a bill, the rent, his fines, buying food, something. Every single time he did business with Mr David he came to the transaction with impending disaster at his back, unable to imagine how his life could go on if Mr David was not (as he sometimes pretended) in the mood to buy. Michael no longer thought it anything other than natural that when he went to Mr David he brought along with him a huge, palpable need to sell, like some outsized, embarrassing relative who had been foisted on him for the day.

If anything it was all getting worse. Michael was now further than ever from being able to build up enough stock to run his stall again at Walcot Market, further away now even than he had been on the day last year when everything had been nicked from the back of the van. True, the van doors had been held together only with twine and a twisted coat hanger, but Michael had thought that he had tied enough elaborate knots to put anyone off having a go. Since then he had not made enough on any deal to buy stuff get the stall going again. He was managing, badly, from one deal to the next. That meant he had to take whatever Mr David offered him, and it was clear from how very little he did offer that Mr David was well aware of this.

Michael had more or less promised him the alabaster figures, and Mr David had more or less promised to give him five hundred for them. That would have been enough for Michael to clear a few debts and start getting some stock together again, so that by Easter he might have the stall back and be well placed for the summer. But he had not got the alabaster figures. And meanwhile, the last mouthful of soup was stone cold, and even if he did get them another day, supposing he dared put himself through all that again, Mr David would sell them on for at least two, possibly three thousand. He tried not to think too hard about that. Mr David had contacts, and you needed the contacts. Contacts of the right sort were just another of the many things that Michael did not have. With this thought he dropped his empty soup mug on the floor, settled under the bedclothes and pulled them around himself.

When he woke it was already after six o'clock, and pitch dark. At least he was now warm enough. If he was lucky he would soon fall asleep again and not wake up until tomorrow.

In the Kiddies' Korner at the back of the beer garden next to the car park of The Masons Arms, Jace was about to hit Steph. There were no kiddies around to see him, it being half past six on a Wednesday night in January; there was nobody to see him at all, a fact that Jace knew perfectly well, and that was worrying Steph. She had miscalculated again. It would have been smarter to head straight for the car and wait while the sight of it calmed Jace down; he loved his stupid Renault 5 Turbo with the stupid alloy wheels and the stupid paint job, and once he was driving along with the sound system thumping he wouldn't hit her. But instead she had run off across the car park and ended up here. The trouble was that when she was pregnant her mind didn't work that way, thinking things out in advance – she just did things, or just came out with them. It was no good trying to tell Jace that, though. He wouldn't know a hormone if it jumped up and bit him on the leg. He was so mad with her for 'showing him up' he had started shouting even before they got outside. He was still shouting at her. Now it appeared he was angry with her not just for 'showing him up', but also for getting him angry. He was definitely working up to something, and since it was she who had made him angry, it would be her fault if he did give her a slap. Steph calculated that it would probably be just the one. But it would be a further miscalculation, she remembered in time, to try to stop him by saying he shouldn't hit a pregnant woman, because reminding him about the baby was never a good idea. It was the baby that had made Jace inclined to hit her in the first place. It was the baby's first kick that ten minutes ago had caused Steph to clutch her belly and squeal out in the public bar *Oh! Oh bloody hell Jace I just felt it! It just kicked me!* And if it hadn't been for the barmaid getting sentimental about the time she had *her* first, and three complete strangers laughing and going on about it, asking when it was due, Steph thought Jace might have let it pass with a grunt. But he had blushed with fury and embarrassment, picked up his car keys and told her to get outside.

She was standing next to a plump, lavishly graffitied, moulded resin elephant whose hollow insides were filled with cans and empty crisp packets that someone at some time had tried to start a fire with. She looked away, and with her head lowered she scraped with one fingernail at some peeling grey paint on one of the elephant's ears, finding that she was managing to turn the growing bare patch into a very good likeness of Marge Simpson. She could draw a pretty good Marge Simpson, and an excellent Homer. She had thought at one time of being a cartoonist, until her art teacher had told her cartoonists have to create original characters and not just copy things. She had actually come up with one or two quite good characters of her own, but then found that they refused to cooperate. They just looked at her from the paper. She had not been able to make them say or do anything.

*Are you listening to me, you two-ton cow?* As she looked up, Jace's hand cracked off the side of her head, which hit the grey elephant wall like a sounding gong. It was such a weird noise, so unexpectedly deep and grand that Steph, leaning against the vibrating elephant's side as the sound died and the singing in her ears became an echo, wondered about laughing. Instead she lowered her head once more and made her way over to the car, where she waited at the passenger side while Jace unlocked the doors with a single, bad-tempered click of his keys in mid-air. Steph understood that he intended only to unlock the driver's door for himself. She understood that it was nothing to him if the click happened to unlock the other doors at the same time because (and it made no difference to him) she could get in or stay out; she could spend the whole night inside the kiddies' elephant with the fag ends and crisp packets for all he cared. She got in.

It took me a day or two to get over the trip. Not for a moment did I feel sorry I'd done it, of course not. What took it out of me was having to be out there again, I mean on the outside, where nobody knew who I was. It made me feel angry that nobody was able to see that inside I had become so much more myself.

I was angry in the way I was when Father died. Father and his clock that became my clock, and the anger I felt apparently towards him but really, even before I found out he wasn't to blame, towards myself. I haven't gone over the clock business in my mind for such a long time. When I do think of it, I tend to remember the way Father would sometimes give me one of his kind looks when Mother was not in the room, and nod towards the dining room and the direction of the ticking and say never you mind, that clock's yours when I go and I would look upset and then he'd say you're not to mind selling it. It's to see you through college, you sort yourself out and you be a teacher, now. Like your Dad. He had been an English teacher, I think not a very good one. It was another of the things Mother kept ready in her mouth, seldom said but ready to sting him with, how hopeless he was not to have made it even to head of department, let alone headmaster. I thought I would like to teach history.

So he always meant me to sell the clock, to see me through university. I think that's why he never really explained to me how beautiful it was, how wonderfully it was made. He never showed me its workings or pointed out what made it so rare, so fine and valuable, for fear that he would not be able to hide from me how much it meant to him. If only he had! If only he had given me eyes to see his clock for what it was, and the words to understand it. I wouldn't have been so deceived over it later if he had just let me see it as he did. I wouldn't have spent so long cursing his memory and thinking he was as big a cheat as Mother.

After I went on the bus to Bath that day to do all that was necessary to place the advertisement, I resolved not to go out again. How it rained in the week that followed! But on the next fine day I found some paraffin and made a bonfire at the side of the orchard. I burned my old navy coat, and then all my other old clothes. Standing out there watching the clothes go up in flames I went on thinking about Father and the clock, and I remembered another of the things he would sometimes say if Mother was not in the room. I suppose it was the nearest he came to letting me see the clock as he did. I can't remember the exact words he used, but it was something about time passing painfully – so this must have been in his last year, then, though by some trick of memory it seems to me that he said it at times all through my life even if time had to pass painfully, even if your minutes and hours offered up nothing but indiscriminate and bigger doses of pain, it was still consoling in a way to have time measured so beautifully, on a clock like his.

And as I watched the old clothes burn I thought how solitary I must look, a woman standing by a bonfire in an orchard in winter. Yet I was not lonely, for I knew that the house and all that it contained would be company enough until such time as my son should come to me.

## *February*

A few weeks later a stale sense of familiarity with what he was doing surfaced in Michael's mind. He had had times like this before, times when dark and light became the same, when a part of him seemed to absent itself from the world that his body lived in and inhabit some ditch all of its own. Such times could come upon him without warning, but usually they followed something difficult such as his court appearance. And they were worse in the winter because around the end of the second week, when he might be feeling that he could wash or get out of bed, he would then have to overcome the cold and this extra battle could, as it had this time, delay him by several more days.

He was even thinner, because eating, like washing, was another thing that required unimaginable effort. When he absolutely had to, he would manage to trudge up to the shop and buy a half dozen or so cans of soup and a packet of bread. Over the next few days, as and when he became aware of a need to put something in his stomach, he would eat soup straight from the tin, cold.

Neither the sweetish, half-rotten vegetal smell that came from it, the sticky feel of the soft lumps in his mouth nor the message his stomach would afterwards send, of being sickened rather than satisfied, seemed to have much to do with him. Nor did the accruing pile of opened and unfinished tins by the side of his bed, whose metallic stink soured the room.

As if bitterly half-in and half-out of an affair with death, he lay for days waiting to see if it would come to him, in the belief that he would let it. Uninvolved, he would put up no resistance, but nor would he seek it out. So he thought about being dead without planning suicide, which would have required of him a degree of inventiveness and purpose of which he was incapable. To engage with the problem of his body for long enough to bring about an end to its improbable beating, breathing, filling and emptying seemed overwhelmingly effortful; even the smallest deviation from habit required what felt like impossibly original thinking. And it was that, rather than pride or even a vestigial notion of decency, that made him get up when he needed to pee. Dimly he realised that a wet mattress might eventually force him to get out of bed and stay out, but his torpor was so deep that he would put off the moment until he could barely stand up straight and then, with a nearly bursting bladder, he would stumble to the bathroom.

This time he ate his soup perhaps once a day, and slept off and on. At intervals, over the top of his bedclothes, he stared at the television with the sound off. Because he did not have a television licence and guessed (for he had no idea how these things worked) that a detector van must pick up the noise somehow, he was in the habit of watching in silence. And as he was anyway unable to connect with anything he saw, the silence was also a protection against the incomprehensibility of what was happening on the screen. He watched faces: listening, talking, laughing, shouting, weeping; seeing not just strangers but beings whose functioning he observed but could neither understand nor imagine sharing. He watched and half-wondered why it was that he was so different, for it was obvious that he lacked some fundamental understanding that bound all of them together, and excluded him. Where they had opinions, hopes, ideas, peculiarities, quirks and eccentricities, he detected in himself neither feature, form nor preference. He was unbearably flat and weightless. When he slept he sometimes had dreams in which he was not a person at all, although what he might have been instead was never clear. In other people it seemed that a river flowed, some animating liquid seemed to bubble and burst along their veins whatever they were doing. His were dry, still, and silent. If he was filled with anything, it was dust. Michael sensed in himself an empty space that in other people was occupied by any number of reasons for living.

Early one morning before it was light, on the way back from the bathroom, he picked up his copy of *Heidi* from the floor and took it back to bed. It lay there next to him unopened for several more hours, but he touched the cover from time to time, and thought about the story. It was one of his favourites, along with *David Copperfield*, *Oliver Twist* and *A Little Princess*; books that he had been given years and years ago, in special editions for children, by Beth. She had been no reader herself so she had given them to him just to encourage his apparent interest in reading. In order to dislodge the thought of Beth, Michael sat up and opened the book. It pained him to recall how she had always tried to encourage him, without managing to understand him at all; she made such efforts with the books, with his acting. She even tried to explain away how he made up stories when everybody else said he told lies. He switched on the light by his bed, not to read but to look at the pictures. As long as he could stop Beth taking hold in his mind, he thought he might soon be all right. He knew it for certain when, having begun almost by accident to read the words, his favourite part of the story (where the gruff old Grandfather made Heidi a soft little bed all of her own in the hay loft) made him cry as it always did.

Later he got up, gathered together a change of clothes and knocked on Ken's door across the walkway. Ken seemed grateful to see him. Michael had a bath and afterwards returned to Ken's sitting room. The community nurse had been so Ken was doped up and not saying much, parked in his day chair in his usual combination of clothes and pyjamas with a thing on a cord round his neck that he could press if he fell, which rang an alarm somewhere. On the plastic hospital tray table next to him the nurse had left his sandwich lunch on a plate covered with cling film, the remote control for the television, yesterday's *Express* and a jug of orange squash. A plastic cup with several tablets in it sat on a piece of paper with 12 O'CLOCK AFTER DINNER NOT BEFORE written on it. He seemed more bloated. His walking frame was within reach, though Michael noted that the commode chair was now positioned just behind Ken's day chair and not in the bathroom, and the telephone had been pulled across the floor from its little table by the door so that he could reach it without getting up. Not that it ever rang. Michael was not feeling completely better, so while Ken dozed he dried his hair by the fierce gas fire still unable to locate the space in himself that held any real pity. He did not ask if Ken had missed him. He would not have known what to do with the information, with the burden of having let him down, if Ken were to say he had. How he managed during Michael's bad spells, when his popping in to chat or fetch his little bits of shopping came to an abrupt stop, was something they never discussed.

'Got a big deal on today, Ken,' he said. 'In the Cotswolds. There's some nice stuff going in the Cotswolds. Nurse coming back, is she?'

The nurse always came back at four thirty to wash Ken and get him ready for bed and Michael knew it, but his checking up struck a note of concern that seemed to please Ken. He nodded and croaked that he was a lucky chap, and that Michael was to mind how he went, and when he had dismissed him with a valiant lift of a hand, Michael took his leave.

The van got to Sherston under protest, but Michael was feeling so much better now that this seemed merely an added challenge. After all, a groan under the bonnet was not a thing that would trouble Jeff Stevenson, curate of St Mary's, Burnham Norton. Michael had telephoned this time and spoken to the woman at the vicarage so the vicar was expecting Jeff Stevenson, and Michael, as he drove along, began to enjoy the transition from himself into Jeff.

It would be the usual doddle. Michael had always been able to act; he had shown a real ability in drama, his teacher had said so. In fact, he might have become an actor. If he had spent those years anywhere other than in Beth's house on that estate on the edge of Swindon he might have made it, but it was impossible to get started from a place like that. Beth had had no idea. But he had definitely had some sort of knack for acting, for forgetting altogether that he was Michael. Probably he had been born with it, because it was the one thing he could do that felt effortless and natural. He just shucked Michael off, left him somewhere and sailed away in his mind and his body, becoming somebody else. It was like taking a holiday from yourself, and always brought with it a whoosh of joy that would make him gasp.

People were wrong if they thought it was a game, though. It was a way of life. He owned clothes that he had picked up from stalls on Walcot Market, knowing they were not really for him but for one or other of the not-Michaels. He had shooting clothes, double-breasted suits, bomber jackets, flamboyant waistcoats – even a silk cummerbund – that he would never wear as Michael. Today, the unfashionably bright blue jeans, checked thick shirt and Timberland boots were helping him to be Jeff Stevenson, and as he drove along he rehearsed Jeff Stevenson phrases about the troublesome van for the benefit of the vicar, whose name was Gordon Brookes.

Gordon Brookes was waiting in the vicarage, which sat in the shadow of the church. From the window of the parish office at the front he could see down the churchyard to the lychgate, which needed re-thatching and where used needles and condoms had been found again two days ago. Sighing, he was trying to rearrange his restless dissatisfaction about the absence of his wife, coupled with the problem of his son, and re-mould them into the shape of the lychgate problem. The lychgate seemed to him, as he looked at it, more and more of an affectation. It wasn't as if it was ever used, he thought petulantly. Coffins came in by the south door, even Wendy's had, on one of those wheelie things, because all the hearses went straight round to the far side where the car park was. The lychgate had probably not been used properly since the last time a horsedrawn cart carrying a coffin stopped in the lane.

Jeff Stevenson was now three minutes late and the problem of his son Simon floated to the top of Gordon's mind. The problem troubled him because although it was as yet still vague, it was not vague enough. Certainly Simon's deciding that he needed to 'make a contribution to global equality' had seemed as flimsy as most of his previous notions about what he should do with his life. But his intention, announced a fortnight ago, that he and his wife and the new baby should embark on 'a new life based on service to others', was solidifying in a way that Gordon did not like. Simon was leaving in four weeks' time, and his wife was refusing to go with him. This morning his daughter-in-law had been on the phone in tears, asking him to change Simon's mind; Gordon had felt distressed for her but at the same time irritated. It was the sort of call that Wendy would have dealt with. And the ringing of the telephone had interrupted him in a mood of guilty introspection about Wendy, so that instead of agreeing with his daughter-in-law that Simon was simply running away from his responsibilities, he had heard himself suggest that perhaps, if a person feels a calling to higher responsibilities than the ordinary domestic ones, a wife might find her own happiness in supporting him in that calling. Wendy had been happy in *her* supporting role for thirty-eight years, he told her in a cracking voice, hoping very much that he was right. He had been met with silence. Then he had said that not for a moment did he underestimate the effort and difficulty, even sacrifice, that would be involved. 'Oh no?' his daughter-in-law had asked tearfully, and rung off.

Gordon sucked on his bottom lip, feeling misunderstood and a little peeved. Women were better at these things, that was all. It had been Wendy who made sure that Simon's many lurchings in and out of physical and psychological health, education, employment and relationships remained, to Gordon, vague; with Wendy gone Gordon now felt in danger of having too much expected of him. This raised in him a mixture of fear and indignation because, having forgiven himself within a year of Simon's birth for a detached paternal style which some might have called inadequacy, he no longer worried that inadequacy was what it was. Since Simon had been born he had devoted himself almost entirely to parish matters that, he had persuaded both Wendy and himself, were more deserving of his attention. He had wanted, he said, to set Simon an example of life and work that would be worth following.

So the lychgate, Gordon now considered, might be a problem whose time had come.

The lychgate could be his next project. And for as long as it would demand his energy (Gordon was known by his parishioners to be terribly focused) he could not be expected to lavish the kind of attention that Wendy had had time for on the grandchild with an absent father. In fact, he thought, with Wendy gone, he *needed* a project. Gordon liked to be committed. Over the years, 'commitment' was what he had come to call the habitual and sustained expenditure of his energy on a range of projects of his own devising. 'Commitment' was the personal quality of which he was proudest in himself. He no longer noticed much about the church or his parishioners except the things he disliked, one of which was a lack of commitment. He was just thinking he might bring it into the sermon on Sunday and also get in something about the needles and condoms (obliquely, of course) when he saw a man, presumably Jeff Stevenson, standing under the lychgate, his head raised in apparent admiration of the timbering of the roof. What was the attraction? It was not nearly as interesting as the church – you could say it detracted from it – and it was only nineteenth century, Gordon thought, simultaneously deploring Jeff Stevenson's taste and framing the first arguments he would have to meet and demolish on his way to reinstating the

95

lychgate in the parish's affections. Not wishing Jeff Stevenson to see him waiting at the window, Gordon turned, selected his deerstalker from several hats hanging in the hall, pulled on his jacket and set off from the front door of the vicarage to meet him.

'Hello there! Gordon, how *are* you?' Michael demanded, meeting him on the churchyard path and advancing with a handshake. Gordon submitted his hand, Michael seized it and grabbed Gordon's wrist with his left hand. As he beamed at him and yanked his arm up and down, Michael was trying to see beyond the smeared glasses, which reminded him of the chip shop window at the top of his road on Snow Hill. He searched through the lenses for eye contact and fixed him with a look of concern. The hat was perching so ridiculously on Gordon Brookes's head that he had to concentrate on not staring at it.

'How are you doing, Gordon? I'm Jeff. Jeff Stevenson.'

'Yes, yes, hello. You're expected. Gordon Brookes.' Gordon lifted the hat and replaced it. He always wore a hat of one sort or another; he thought of his hats as his little trademark. Oh, the vicar and his hats, he imagined people saying, affectionately casting their eyes upwards. He found it useful that a hat created an illusion of approachability and friendliness, and at the same time kept people away. Most people were wary of eccentricity, he had found. They seldom stopped him in the village to chat, for instance, unwilling to risk being thought, by association, as barmy as the man in the barmy hat. But clearly Jeff Stevenson was not most people. For one thing, he had a most persistent handshake.

'Great hat! How do you do?' Michael said, thinking that Gordon Brookes's lower lip looked too red and wet.

Gordon said, 'I didn't realise you knew my name. We haven't met before, have we?'

Michael swallowed. Although Gordon Brookes's tone of interrogation was mild, he was still asking a question. Michael had never before been asked how he knew a vicar's name. Vicars in general seemed to assume that everybody knew who they were. Thinking fast, he worked out that he could afford to be honest about the source of that small piece of information, and that it would be easier than coming up with a lie on the spot.

'Actually, I looked you up.'

'Oh?'

'In Crockford's. I looked you up in Crockford's; I like to do my homework, seems only right since I'm imposing on your time and goodwill,' Michael said in his carefully unplaceable accent, and tried to rest in the fact that this was quite true. Of

97

the books that Michael owned, many were volumes that he had acquired only because he had failed to sell them on the stall. Among them were *Crockford's Directory of the Clergy 1997*, and Simon Jenkins' *England's Thousand Best Churches*. It was the combination of these two that had inspired his curate impersonation technique for robbing churches in the first place, but Gordon Brookes would not, of course, be told that. Crockford's supplied him with his characters: the names, dates, backgrounds and present positions of the earnest churchmen, invariably curates, whom he impersonated. It supplied him with the same details of the incumbents of the churches he selected for his forays, for the rare occasions on which he might meet up with the vicar rather than a 'parish worker'. The Jenkins book gave him details of church treasures, both fixed and architectural (which were of course irrelevant to the purpose, though Michael had at times been grateful to be able to make an admiring reference to, say, the Norman reredos or the double hammerbeam roof), but also – and more to the point for Michael – Jenkins described the treasures small, easily liftable and saleable: the minor effigies and busts, silver, pictures, chairs, lecterns, embroideries. Over and above these Michael often found a pleasing range of more humble but attractive objects waiting to be opportun-istically pilfered, and the beauty of it was he wasn't taking things that belonged to *people*. He was not depriving anyone of anything personal, and if he did cause upset then at least church people had one another to turn to for comfort. And if God himself were offended, he hadn't so far got round to showing it. In the meantime, Michael had done well out of candlesticks, church candles, tooled leather Bibles, altar cloths, small and ancient rugs, even sheet music, all of which were the kind of thing that any number of Bath people would pay money for in order to reinforce their belief that they were complex and creative souls whose originality and flair were revealed in the arrangement of their homes. He now noticed that Gordon Brookes was looking at him with some curiosity.

'Sorry, where did you say you got my name?'

Michael swallowed again, and felt a tiny twitch of his face, the kind that might look to anyone watching like a deliberately tight blink of the eyes. The question, never before asked, was now being asked again. Perhaps it was the loss of the wife that was making this one so cagey, though he seemed to Michael more exasperated than bereaved.

'Crockford's. Fount of all knowledge! I say, it is all right for me to see the figures, isn't it? I've looked at them behind the glass, of course, but it'll be just tremendously exciting to get really close to them.' He beamed again and tried to look eager. Steady, Michael, he told himself.

In the church Gordon Brookes pulled on a pair of cotton gloves from a drawer at the base of the display cabinet, unlocked the glass door and lifted out one of the two figures. 'Here's our St John. Vestry's the best place, there's a proper table there,' he said, making his way to a door at the far end of the church. He could not carry both figures at once, but he seemed prepared to make two trips rather than hand one to Michael to bring. Michael, obedient to some etiquette that suggested it would be unseemly to do so, did not offer to help, but waited patiently by the open case. Gordon came back, took the second figure in his arms, saying only, 'St Catharine, slightly heavier,' and Michael followed respectfully.

The vestry smelled of paraffin and chrysanthemums. Two walls were lined with cupboards, and chairs were stacked in one corner. The only other door must lead outside, back towards the vicarage, Michael thought. From a large cardboard box on the floor with 'Waste paper for Afghanistan' written on its side in black marker, Gordon Brookes drew a couple of magazines. He spread them over the centre of the table.

Without smiling he placed the figures on top of them. Gordon Brookes then tipped his head on one side and gazed at them sentimentally, and it seemed sensible to Michael to do the same. The St Catharine sat on her magazine, partly obliterating the cover photograph of a middle-aged man standing on a rock on the edge of a lake looking through binoculars. The white, sweet-faced Saint Catharine, her eyes cast graciously downwards, was apparently reading the headline 'Whale watching in Manitoba'. Michael smiled, and Gordon Brookes smiled too.

'Lovely, aren't they?' he said, quite kindly. Michael got his notebook and magnifying glass out of his backpack and put on a pair of spectacles. But he did not sit down, feeling that the most delicate of transactions was being conducted and that even one off-balance move, one over-zealous gesture on his part would cause the whole fragile bargain to collapse. Gordon Brookes took a step back. Michael smiled at the figures again and then looked at Gordon.

'Carry on,' Gordon said, pulling off the gloves and handing them to Michael. 'I'm no expert so I'll leave you to get on with it. I'm assuming you know how to handle them.'

Michael almost burst into song. 'Right! That's terribly good of you. I do appreciate it. It's a marvellous opportunity.' He sat down at the table and squinted purposefully at the figures, wrinkling his nose. Gordon Brookes did not leave. Michael looked at him with the gentlest smile of dismissal he could manage.

'I'll be fine, now. Thanks so much,' he said.

'Right. Well, I'll let you get on, while I just potter.' So that was what he meant by leaving him to get on with it. Get on with it, but I'll be right here behind you. In the same room. I am not going to leave. Michael's face twitched behind his glasses. How was he going to manage the amount of bluffing that would now be required? He could drop out of the whole thing, just look at the figures and go. But how could he even think of leaving without them, after this much effort? His heart had been thumping in his throat since he arrived. He coughed. He dared not touch the figures in front of Gordon Brookes. He could not trust his hands not to shake.

'Don't let me, er ... I'm quite happy here on my own, if you've got things to do.'

'I gather it's a study of yours. Have you published?'

'Oh no! Oh, you know, the usual problem. Time! Takes so much time, getting anything knocked into proper shape for a publisher. That's life. But I chip away, live in hope. You know.' He turned and looked at the alabaster figures in what he hoped was an informed sort of way.

Gordon turned and started to busy himself with a precarious stack of books and sheets of paper. 'Choir. They will leave things higgledy-piggledy,' he murmured. Michael, pretending to consult his notebook, was getting desperate. He had to get Gordon Brookes to leave.

'Honestly, don't let me stop you getting on,' he said. 'I'm quite happy on my own for ... well, I should think twenty minutes should do it. But naturally I'd prefer you to come back to put them back in their case.'

'You were ordained when, Jeff?' Gordon asked mildly.

'Oh, only in 1996,' Michael replied. 'Latecomer.' He would volunteer nothing more lest it provoke more conversation. He needed the man to go.

'Yes. Yes, because you see, if you don't mind, Jeff, it's odd you're not aware. Trivial thing, of course, but if nobody's pointed it out to you ... we never say Crockford's, do you see. It's Crockford, not Crockford's. You just don't say Crockford'zzzz, except when you're saying the whole name, as in *"Crockford's Directory of the Clergy"*. Hope you don't mind my mentioning it.'

Michael fixed a look of polite amusement on his face and turned.

'Oh? Well! Well, my goodness. I, er...'

'It's odd you've not picked that up so far.'

It was too late for Michael to pretend he was hard of hearing, had to lipread and sometimes made mistakes. His mouth was dry. Gordon Brookes was about to say that he knew perfectly well that Michael was a fraud. But Michael knew, just as perfectly, that he needed the alabaster figures to get himself afloat again; he needed them so badly that he felt a rush of fury at the thought that Gordon Brookes might stop him. Just as he was thinking that the only course open to him now was physical assault, he wondered. Dare he try it again? He had done it once before with a punter who'd come back to the stall complaining that Michael had sold him some dud Cornish ware the week before. *'1930s you said and when I get it home I turn it upside down an' it says fucking dishwasherproof on the bottom.'* The punter had not been in the right frame of mind to be convinced that dishwashers had been around for a lot longer than people realised. Michael had had to think fast. It had worked then, and it had to work now.

He pretended to turn his attention back to the figures, but stirred, then coughed, started rigidly in his chair and sucked up a noisy breath. He swung back in his chair and pulled in another breath with a sound like air being blown into a balloon. He struggled to say, 'Asthma. Be all right ... in minute.' And then he took another, even more shallow, pained and laborious breath to show that he would not be all right at all.

'Oh good heavens – have you got something to take for it? An inhaler or something? Don't you carry an inhaler?'

Michael shook his head and lurched in his chair, sucking and heaving. 'Glass of water. Pills. Need water. Glass of water.' He now brought fear into his eyes, which swivelled wildly round the room in search of the sink and tap, which he had already established were not there.

'Oh! Oh right, I see, *right*. Hang on. I'll just have to ... er, look, will you be all right for a minute? I'll get one from the vicarage. I'll be back in a second, can you, are you sure you, er...'

Michael nodded. 'Please! Please, water.'

When the vestry outside door had closed behind Gordon, Michael waited for a moment, got up, wrapped each figure quickly in the magazine on which it stood and placed them both in his backpack. Then he dashed back into the church, crossed it swiftly, let himself out and raced down through the churchyard, keeping off the path, which he knew could be seen from the vicarage. By the time the van started on the third attempt Michael was half-dead with terror, but with the pulse of fear came also a quickening surge of relief because he was, after all, alive.

My mood changed. Something happened to remove any last trace of uncertainty. Two people turned up on bicycles – imagine, in February! They were Dutch, and I believe they did say that they had hired the bicycles for the day as it was fine and they wanted to see something of the countryside outside Bath. They had all that strange clothing that people wear on bicycles. I've never had the slightest idea where such clothing is even to be bought or what it is called, let alone what particular purpose it might serve, and it took me a moment to get over their appearance at the door, like giant tadpoles in some sort of brightly coloured race. And they had maps, of course, and showed me the special cycle route they were doing on which certain 'points of interest' had been marked, including Walden Manor. They had left the marked route and come all the way down the drive, even though there is a sign saying 'Private' at the top, next to the road. This is Walden Manor, yes? they asked me. I couldn't very well dispute it. So I said yes, and then I stood at the door waiting for them to go.

'We know that the house is not open to the visitors,' the man said. He smiled even more than the girl, which is unusual. At least the girl had the grace to look embarrassed.

'We are so sorry to bother you, we are the students of architecture,' she explained. The man hadn't stopped nodding and smiling. Lovely teeth, but I distrusted such a conscious effort to charm.

'It is so beautiful!' he said, 'we have nothing like this in Holland. So – we don't know, but if you might very kindly let us take a look round...'

'–a little look, only on the outside, perhaps,' the girl said. 'If you can bother with us so near your house.'

Rash of me. They could have been anybody, burglars, rapists. Quite apart from it being the last thing a house sitter should do, give strangers the run of a place. They could have had coshes, knives, rope, handcuffs, anything, in those saddlebags. Supposing they'd even left me alive, I would never have recognised them again, not out of those ridiculous clingy suits and helmets. So why did I let them in? It was the 'your house' that did it, I suppose. I suddenly felt so proud, and I swear that all of a sudden the thought came to me, if it's my house I can do what I like. So I heard myself saying I'd be pleased to show them round my house. They didn't stay long. I went a bit vague about dates after 'fifteenth century origins' (I just made that up, it sounded about right) which gave them the chance to show off and argue between themselves over when different bits might have been built. He said they were intrigued by the building materials and methods more than the design because, evidently, he said, the house was 'provincial' and not by a distinguished, or even a known architect. I said there was more to good design than fancy London names, and they were a bit taken aback, I think, and I was too, because I hadn't realised I thought that. They asked how long my family had lived here, and I simply told them, oh always. And would the house stay in the family? It was the man, of course, who asked that, and his girlfriend gave him a look that said of course it will and that was an impertinent question. So I said of course it will in a voice that justified her look (and as I spoke I did feel mildly though genuinely offended). I inherited the house from my parents, I told them, another thing I hadn't realised I thought. My Mother died eighteen years ago, when she was in her eighties. I nursed her for many years, I said, and now the house is mine and my son will have it after me. I have just one son, I told them, smiling. If they wondered about where my husband might be they didn't say. Though the girl would have sneaked a look at my ringless hands and concluded I was divorced, I suppose. Women notice things like that.

When they left I saw them off at the front door and closed it after them, and I had the sense that we both, me and the house, breathed a sigh, glad to be alone together again. I thought I would just walk through the rooms once more, and it was as I was turning to go upstairs that I caught sight of myself in the hall mirror, which by then I was describing to myself as a looking-glass. I had been smiling at those two young people. I thought perhaps I had smiled because of their youth and friendliness, smiled while putting them in their place and perhaps also at their deference and respect for me, 'the English lady', and for their admiration of my house. Whatever the reason, my face was much improved for it. It had not smiled like that for a long time and I liked the brightness in my eyes and the lift round my mouth. My skin looked warmer and my face rounder, as if I'd been plumped up with optimism, and I had a receptive look, as if the sound of human voices, including my own, had made me newly alert.

I was still half-smiling, long after they had gone. The reason for my continuing smile lay in the remembered pleasure of the words I had spoken, talking about my son to complete strangers.

Steph was carrying this one high. There had been a growth spurt and now it lodged right under her boobs like a strapped-on sandbag and her stretchy cotton skirt rose up at the front, well above her knees. It had been some time since her cardigan closed over the swell, and now the T-shirt she wore underneath was also too small and an acreage of skin like uncooked pastry was revealed where the T-shirt failed to meet the skirt top. She had taken the ring out of her navel, which now protruded, its vulnerable flesh like private, inside skin turned indecently outwards. She pulled the T-shirt over it a hundred times a day but always her belly shifted, the T-shirt rode up again and her navel reappeared like the inquisitive pink snout of a puppy sniffing at cold air. She had no money for new clothes.

'Cover that up, will you.' Jace's eyes returned to the road in front. Steph pulled the T-shirt down and shivered. The seat belt was uncomfortably tight, although she had let it out all she could. She thought that Jace probably could adjust it more but he would need to fiddle about with the bit clamped to the wall of the car. She had asked him to, once. She had no very clear idea how advanced her pregnancy was but it was not more than six months; she was going to get bigger still, and if Jace wouldn't adjust the seat belt for her then she was going to have to go without it. But she did not think it would be worth asking again. It was the least of her worries. Jace kept saying he had no money either, but he had more than her, that was for certain. They were on their way now to look at somebody's car stereo, for God's sake, that Jace had seen advertised in the paper. He fancied a better one, that was all, and he was ready to spend hundreds on it, so how come she had nothing to wear, and nothing for the baby, when it came? As they drove on in silence, she considered asking him again for some money. But if she did, the conversation would go like this:

*I can't help it showing. I need some new stuff to wear, don't I? This is too small.*

*Better get something then, hadn't you?*

*I can't. Aw, Jace, going to buy us something? I haven't got any money, have I?*

*Get your Nan to get it. She's the one supposed to be looking after you.*

Steph sighed at the wholly expected turn that the imagined conversation would take. It was true that she was still living, though Nan called it staying, at her grandmother's house. She had told Jace several times what the score was, that it was only temporary and Nan would rather she were not there at all, but the trouble with Jace was it didn't matter how many times you told him something, if he didn't like it he would just keep going on about it and in exactly the same way, whatever you said. So Steph could say now, yet again: *She's not looking after me. She says I should be in my own place. She says she's not having a baby in the house and when all's said and done she's got her own life to lead.* But it would make no difference. Actually, as far as Steph could see her Nan did lead her own life anyway whether Steph was there or not, but Nan often made the point and Steph supposed that, as it was Nan's house, she was entitled to make it.

She looked at Jace. He was doing three things: driving, smoking and poking his head forwards and backwards in time to the music. He would not add conversation to these, being quite absorbed already. The music was so loud you would think the drummer plus drum kit were riding along in the back of the car. Jace, if he had anything to say to her, would have to shout to be heard and what he would say would be:

*Well, then. You should do something about it, shouldn't you? Get your benefit sorted for a start. Don't think I'm forking out just 'cause you won't get your money sorted.*

*I can't go to the benefit office like this.*

*Shouldn't have fallen pregnant, then, should you?*

*It wasn't just up to me, Jace. You are its father.*

*So you say. I'm not forking out for a bloody kid that's maybe not even mine. You want to get yourself sorted.*

Steph stared straight ahead. The conversation always ended there, so she was right not even to have started it. It wouldn't have been worth the breath. Every conversation started with Jace going on about something to do with the way she looked, then went on to her lack of money, at which point she would tell him again why she could not go to claim any. Early on in her pregnancy she might also have pointed out something about having to give up college for the baby, reminding him that getting to college had been important to her, and Jace would have said something dismissive about doing A-level art in the first place. *Fucking useless. Where's that leading, fucking nowhere*, was how he put it. Then he would shift the attack on to different ground, saying just to torment her that he couldn't be sure that the baby was his and so why should his money support 'it'. And anything that she might say in reply to that would make no difference. So Steph squirmed quietly as they drove along, pulled at her T-shirt and knew she was right, again, not to have opened her mouth.

It was less exhausting to run the conversation in her head, which was the closest Steph could bear to go in confronting the mess she was in. Her Nan did not want her any more than Jace did, and she had no money for clothes or anything else.

And she could not go and register for benefit because she was going to keep this baby, and if they knew she was having it they would interfere. No more could she go to a doctor, or even have it in hospital, because they would take it off her the minute it was born. Not that Jace had ever suggested she should see a doctor, he didn't think about things like that. She should be all right, though. It was just nature, after all. She tried to swallow her fear. She would be all right, she had done it once before with no problems, and it got easier with each one, didn't it? That was what everyone said.

She looked across at Jace again and thought without emotion that he looked bloody stupid with his head going in and out like that. He was a thin person with a very small chin, and Steph suddenly realised that he looked just like the school tortoise, speeded up. If you held out a leaf of parsley to the tortoise – she remembered it had 4F, the class number, painted on its shell but she had forgotten its name – its head would pop out like that and pop back in, just like Jace's. Anyway, the tortoise was dead now and here she was, sitting here, knowing there was no point in saying *I can't go to the benefit office in this state, can I? They'll get the social workers at me and then they'll take it away when it comes and I'm not having that, right? I'm keeping this one, right?* She tugged her T-shirt protectively over her belly and felt like crying.

*You're mad, you're fucking mad, you are. And you got a bloody kid already. Jesus, look at the state of you.*

*I was too young. I told you that, I was only fifteen with Stacey. I wanted to keep her, it's not my fault they wouldn't let me.*

*And so what's different now? You've not even got a place to bring it up, have you?*

She remembered, it was called Tommy. Tommy the tortoise. Steph began to cry noisily. He had got run over by a teacher's car in the playground. That was the kind of thing that upset her now, silly things. Important things, like Stacey, upset her even more. Stacey would be nearly seven now. Seven, and somebody else's. Steph's sobs grew louder and more desperate. She had been too young and scared not to go along with what everybody told her to do.

*That's not my fault, is it? You said you'd get us a flat! And we're not too young, I'm twenty-three and you're twenty-one, there's loads of people our age with kids! Loads! You were meant to be moving out of your mum's and getting us a place. You said.*

Jace was looking at her crumpled weeping face with scorn, but there was no let-up in the poke-poke of his head nor in the volume of sound. He shouted, 'You do my head in, you do! Shut up, can't you!'

And Steph did, because Jace's voice was at a dangerous pitch and a whack might follow, even though he was driving. Jace stubbed out his cigarette. He had won that round easily and planned to win the next by changing the subject. 'I'm out of fucking fags.'

Steph sniffed and blew her nose. 'You shouldn't smoke in front of me, it's bad for the baby. And I'm not giving this one up, we're keeping it. You said we'd keep it. You said.'

Jace turned off the music. The sudden silence rang round the car. He said, 'Yeah, well, that was a bloody while ago.'

Steph pulled down her T-shirt again and squirmed as the baby trapped under the too-tight seatbelt wriggled and kicked.

He should not have done it. Michael was perching on the edge of the driver's seat as lightly as he dared to while driving, as if in some way this would make him less of a load for the afflicted van. He leaned forward, trying to squeeze a little more speed out of it, but actually speed was out of the question. Keeping going, even at twenty miles an hour, was as much as he hoped for now. He should not have done it.

Maybe it was because of the latest bad time he had just gone through, maybe he had not been thinking straight, but he just had not been ready. In fact; it had been mad to go and do a job like this, the first time he had been out of the flat in weeks, and without thinking about the state of the van, without its even crossing his mind that the vicar would see it and might remember it. In fact he might even have got the number if he had been quick. Michael was not sure. He had been too petrified getting the van started to dare look up the churchyard path to see if the vicar was coming after him. If he had been, Michael thought he would have died of fright, or worse, got out of the van and done something silly to him. Without defining to himself quite what might have lain on the other side, he knew that doing something silly to the vicar would have constituted the irreversible crossing of some line. It was not that he had decided not to cross it, it was just that he had not dared look up the churchyard path. And then the van had started.

He should not have done it. As he chugged hopelessly along, Michael's mind raced and churned with self-reproach. That bloody sprint down the path with the stuff bumping up and down in the backpack, that too had been mad. Not classy, like he took a pride in being. The smart, the *classy* bit was the impersonation, the getting-to-know-you thing, then lifting the stuff carefully, perhaps coming back later for it, not grabbing it then and there like some cheap little shoplifter. *Later*, when nobody was likely be around, when it wouldn't have mattered even if anybody was because he would be just that visiting curate, popping back again. *That* was classy, if not easy, so why had he been so stupid? Grabbing and running off with the alabaster effigies had been bad enough, but with the van in this state! There was another terminal-sounding cough from under the bonnet and Michael held his breath. He was so tense that his head pounded, and although he was staring through the windscreen he was not giving enough attention to the road. A white car swung angrily past him and cut in front with a blast of its horn. It must have been sitting on his tail for miles. The bloody van! On the way here he had been so busy feeling like Jeff Stevenson coping with a dodgy alternator or gearbox or whatever that he had not stopped to think about the van's next journey; it fell a little short of Criminal Mastermind standard for the getaway vehicle to be on its last legs. He was sweating now, and still barely seven miles from the bloody church. If that vicar had decided to get in his car and come looking for him, Michael could be in trouble. He tried to weigh up calmly the chances of the vicar taking such direct action against the more conventional ringing for the police and waiting at the church for their arrival. But all his practical calculations were fading in importance. The more comforting thought of going to bed and staying there (should he ever reach home) was tugging at him, a wanton and persistent desire for oblivion that Michael dreaded, but which his mind was now embracing like an old, disgraceful, but already forgiven friend.

He fought the desire, and two thoughts surfaced. The first was that the van would never make it back to Bath, and the second was that it would be safer to get it off the road than to have it break down, in full view of any passing vicars, at the side of the road. Michael roused himself, and a couple of miles farther on steered the van into the forecourt of a petrol station and garage. He drove in under the canopied petrol pumps, past ranks of second-hand cars for sale and parked at the far end next to some sheds, where a couple of lads in boiler suits were working on cars. Just in time, Michael remembered who he was for the purposes of getting the van fixed, and bounced out of the driver's seat with an attempt at Jeff Stevenson's smile on his face.

He was not sure that the young man in overalls with the strange curtain haircut really understood what a curate was, not even after he had explained it to him, and pleaded that he had to get the van back on the road at once because he had 'things to deliver to some elderly people'. (It was not much of a story but there was no time to embellish.) What the curtain-haired mechanic did know, and was telling Michael, was that no way could they sort it today.

'No way, booked solid with MOTs and Terry's behind anyway,' he said, motioning with his head towards a pair of legs poking out from under a car. 'Booked up solid. We don't do emergencies. You'd be better getting it home and sorting it there, mate,' he added.

Michael smiled at the bad news, as he imagined a curate would, and could not help feeling mildly scandalised at such a lack of respect for the clergy. He wished he were wearing a dog collar. Over the youth's shoulder he watched a pregnant woman get out of a car that had just parked on the forecourt. She stood by the open passenger door and followed with her eyes as her husband, or boyfriend more like, slammed the driver's door and stalked off to the garage shop. She looked uncomfortable, unhappy in her clothes and slightly ashamed, and Michael, only half listening to the mechanic, understood with a stab of recognition that she felt these things whether she was pregnant or not. He must have been staring, for she seemed to have caught his eye and now, to his horror, she was waddling over to him. He turned his attention back to the mechanic.

'Number's in the shop if you wanna call them,' the mechanic said, turning to go. He added over his shoulder, grinning, 'They'll sort it for you, but they'll charge.' He called underneath the car where the feet were squirming. 'Terry! They still charging eighty-five for call-out, Corsham Break-down? You know, whatsisname, that Steve at Corsham Breakdown. Still charges eighty-five, does he?'

The legs shifted again and a muffled voice replied, 'Oh yeah, think so. Eighty-five, mileage on top. Cash.'

'Yeah, well, there you go,' said curtain-hair, with the slightest and first edge of sympathy in his voice. 'Number's in the shop, there's a payphone if you ain't got a mobile.' Michael nodded his thanks, calculating. It would cost at least a hundred in the end just to get towed back to Bath, never mind the cost of getting the van fixed. He could just hitch a lift home and forget all about the van, just leave it to rust here. But he could hardly remove the licence plates in full view of the mechanics, and the registration number would lead them straight to him. Also it was an offence to abandon a vehicle and he was in enough trouble anyway.

'You going to Bath, by any chance?'

121

The pregnant woman was no more than a shivering girl, with large, greenish eyes. She was trying to sound and look casual, standing with one knee bent and her arms crossed. But she had pulled her clothes tightly round herself and over the impertinent bump, which seemed to Michael oddly prominent. It was all out in front, as if the baby had not filled out her sides at all. There was little difference between the colour of her skin and hair, which, in a spectrum between olive and dark gold, might have been striking if she had been warmer and healthier. As it was, she looked yellow in the wrong places, across her forehead and round her mouth, and greenish at the roots of her hair and under the eyes. She was small-boned and long bodied; she brought to mind a snake that has swallowed a watermelon. He tried not to look at her stomach but found himself imaging that she would be very slim after the baby was born. And here she was offering him a lift. He could leave the van here and get them to fix it when they had time, surely in a few days. In the meantime it could be pushed round the back out of sight of the road. He beamed Jeff Stevenson's smile at her.

'Yes! Yes, I am! You can give me a lift? How wonderful, thank you! Anywhere in Bath's fine – drop me anywhere – how kind!'

The girl was taken aback. 'What, isn't that your van? I thought that was your van. I thought you might be going to Bath, that's all. *I'm* looking for a lift.'

Michael stared at her and saw his own dismay in her face. 'It is. It's broken down. I thought you were offering *me* a lift. Is there something wrong with your car as well, then?'

'No. Anyway, it's not mine.' She did not pretend to find the confusion amusing, or try to dislodge the disappointment that now sat on her mouth. She motioned towards the garage shop where the boyfriend, or whoever he was, was just emerging. 'It's his,' she said. 'Him over there.'

'Oh, I see. I see, you're hitching, are you? That was your last lift? I thought you were *with* him.'

'I am, I was, I mean – I'm not hitching,' she said, pushing her hair back behind her ears and shaking her head. 'Mind you, maybe I am, now.' She tried a smile that turned out to be more a wrinkle of her nose, which was red with cold. She sniffed. 'I just thought you was going to Bath, that's all.'

'Well, I am. Or I will be, but I've got to get the van towed back.'

'Oh, well. Never mind.'

'But *isn't* that your car? I saw you getting out.'

The boyfriend had stopped at the door of

his car and was lighting a cigarette. The girl watched him and said dully, 'No. It's his.' With his hands on his hips, he scowled in her direction. She looked away. He shouted something mocking, which Michael did not quite hear. The girl turned, shook her head and the man swore, got in and turned the ignition. Loud and aggressive music pulsed from the car as he drove off with a deliberate scream of the tyres.

The girl watched until the car had disappeared. 'Can't I get a lift with the tow?' she asked.

Michael could not begin to ask what it all meant, for fear that the girl, who was now looking at him with an expectant half-smile, might tell him. Something in the eyes, or perhaps in the droop of the shoulders, or the ripe bulge, or the way she shivered in her inadequate clothing, was crying out to him. Slightly flattered as Michael was by the thought that anyone could turn to *him* for anything, he was also bewildered and appalled. Big eyes or not, she was another thing he did not need, and already she had confused him to the point that he was no longer sure whether he was Jeff Stevenson or Michael. But it was Michael who was stuck with two stolen church effigies in the back of the useless van, the sight of which could get him picked up by the police at any minute. It was Michael who had not been alone in the company of a woman for so long it felt like years, Michael who wanted only to sink into the dark bedroom of his flat. So it was Michael who said, 'Can't help you, sorry. Got to make a phone call,' and strode away. Feeling stupid, he changed his mind, walked back to the van and took the backpack from the back, glaring at Steph as he lifted it over one shoulder and made for the shop.

It crossed Steph's mind that it was not very clever of this man to refuse her a lift and then walk off leaving the van unlocked like that. Not that she made a habit of assessing men's intelligence. She did not assess men at all (except to wonder if and for how long they might be nice to her) so much as react to them. So as she watched Michael's progress across the forecourt, she shivered, wondering if he, with his dark eyes, might turn out to be nice. She was often wrong. Jace had been nice to her for quite a long time before he changed. It had been after about three months that Jace had first muttered in her ear that she was so great, he was dead carried away and he couldn't stop, she didn't want him to stop, did she, not to put on a stupid condom, did she? The truth was that she hadn't. So Steph had spent a lot of time thinking that it was at least partly her fault that when she got pregnant he had stopped thinking she was

125

great, which made it partly her fault that he hit her. And he had only ever taken the back of his hand to her, never his fists. She had spent an equal amount of time hoping that after the baby was born things would change.

A waste of time, she knew. Jace had turned out to be one of those people who did nothing for your loneliness. In fact she had felt lonelier when she was with him than when she was on her own in her Nan's empty house; lonelier even than she was now, stuck at this freezing garage in the middle of nowhere. She stared up the road where Jace had burned out of sight. Had she dumped him or he her? She could have got back in the car. Jace had not stopped her from getting back in the car, but still, he must have dumped her, because she felt so miserable. If she had done the dumping it would be Jace who was in a mess, stuck with no transport and no money. But she had noticed already that Michael's skin was as smooth as bone and there was no threat in his eyes. When she had looked at him, perhaps she had felt a little less lonely. He was out of sight now, in the shop. She opened the van door. There was a solid wall between the van's interior and the seats in front, and no windows in the sides. It would have been nice to find a blanket, but there were dustsheets and a couple of flattened

cardboard boxes. Steph clambered in awkwardly, holding her stomach, and pulled the
door shut behind her.

It was the day after the Dutch couple came
that I noticed the buddleias in the garden. I
must have seen them before, there were four
of them and they were such huge ones, how
could I not have seen them? But it was not
until that afternoon that I really took them
in. Perhaps until then they were simply
waiting for me to pay attention to them.
Perhaps it was the talk of Mother, combined
with the brighter weather that day. Or
perhaps it was just that the buddleias' time
had come. I had already begun to think of
things coming round in their own time.

Anyway, I had allowed myself a little rest
after lunch, feeling rather tired by the strain
of my unexpected visitors the day before. I
had got up about three o'clock and was
looking down at the garden from my
bedroom window, and in the sunshine and a
brisk wind there they were, four enormous
buddleias, waving those disgusting dead
blooms at me.

In an instant I was back in Oakfield
Avenue on that day eighteen years ago, in
Mother's room, the ground floor bedroom
behind the kitchen that she took when she
moved downstairs after Father died. She
was lying in bed on her side waiting to be

wiped, as usual saying nothing and with the butter-wouldn't-melt face on her. I was trying not to look at her backside or think about her face. In fact I was trying not to be there, I suppose, because through her bedroom window I was concentrating on watching the buddleia in our back garden. It was February then, too, and I remember thinking suddenly that that buddleia out there in the garden should not be allowed to get away with it. It should not be allowed to go on waving its branches of dead flowers that looked like Mother's long pointy turds (not a word I like, but there is no other somehow) at me. I cast my mind back to the summer before and it seemed a poor bargain, this plant trading an unreliable memory of a short season, a mere month of butterflies fluttering at its purple flowers, for its intolerable appearance now and for most of the rest of the year. Between a finger and thumb I was holding Mother's big pants that I'd just hoicked off her, and the pad which contained the awful wobbly chocolate-coloured rope that she had squeezed out in the night and whose precise shape and colour I saw replicated on the buddleia bush swaying in the wind. The room was full of our silence, and of the familiar smell like vinegar and lavender mixed with dirt and that particular human clay. Outside, the buddleia waved its thousand old lady's turd-tipped branches and I looked back at Mother's offering in my hand and I thought, oh God, how many more of these, as many as wave at me from the buddleia bush? How many more squalid little starts to how many more squalid little days with me looking through a window on to a view of dead flowers?

Perhaps it would have been enough, then, if I had just gone straight out there and got busy with Father's old saw. Who knows if some savage pruning would have been all that was needed. Then that would have been an end of it, and what happened later that day would not have happened, and life would have gone on in the same fashion for a lot longer. And do you know, weighing it up now, despite everything, I am glad it didn't. I'm glad of the new and surprising turn things took. But eighteen years ago I did not have the knack of clarity that I have acquired here.

So it was here, on this February afternoon eighteen years on, as I looked down at those four buddleias, that it was suddenly obvious what had to be done this time. I found a saw, an axe and a crowbar, as well as Wellingtons, gloves and a waxed jacket in one of the outbuildings in the courtyard, and I got busy. Though pruning is not the word for what I did to those buddleias. It took all my strength. It was dark by the time

I had finished and I got badly scratched and I pulled I don't know how many muscles, and I don't think I have ever been so tired, but I got all four of them out by their filthy brown roots.

No offence intended, nothing personal, but Steve of Corsham Breakdown refused to uncouple Michael's van from the pickup until Michael paid him the hundred quid. Nothing personal, but Steve had formed the opinion after an hour's drive with his silent, motionless passenger – silent but for short replies to Steve's attempts at chat, and motionless but for the gripping and releasing of his fingers over the backpack on his lap – that the guy might be weird and/or broke, despite the clean, regular-looking clothes. It was a little before five o'clock when he pulled over, with difficulty, on the steep road leading up through the Snow Hill estate, and set out his terms. No offence, but I need to see your money, mate. It's not me, it's the boss, all right? Cashpoints still open, aren't they? Time to get down there and get the cash, haven't you?

Mr David closed at five thirty, sometimes earlier on a slack day. Michael set off with the backpack towards the London Road and Mr David's shop in Walcot Street. Steve walked up the hill in the opposite direction to Fairfield Stores and bought a *Sun*, a pasty, a bag of crisps, a Galaxy and a Coke. It was on the way back to the cab to wait for Michael that he heard the banging from inside the van.

When Michael got back with the now flattened backpack over one shoulder, Steph was in the passenger seat of the pickup swigging at the Coke and having a laugh with Steve, for whom Michael's weirdness was now confirmed.

'Oi!' he called as Michael approached the driver's window, 'you never said you got your flaming girlfriend in the back! She could have froze to death. Dangerous and all, illegal that is, I could have got done for that!'

Michael stared into the cab, too depleted by Mr David for anything like surprise. Steph looked back at him with a mixture of defiance and entreaty.

'Needed a rest, didn't I?' she said. 'In the van. Don't mind, do you? He doesn't mind,' she added, nodding at Steve.

Steve patted her knee and said, 'Got a bit warmed up now, have you, sweetheart?' He turned to Michael. 'You want to take better care. Got the cash?' As Michael counted off the notes he went on, 'You should have said. She should've gone up in front between us. There's room for three. Even three and a half!'

Michael, wordless, stared at him. Steve

looked again at Steph, reminding himself that it was none of his business. The girl seemed happy enough to be left with this guy, so maybe she was weird herself.

Steph laughed and handed back the Coke can. 'I'll give you three and a half! I told you, I was asleep. I'll sleep anywhere, just at the moment. Thanks for the drink. And the warm-up.' She slipped down from the cab more easily than would have seemed possible, for her size.

'And the lift!' She sauntered round to Michael. Steve shoved the notes into his jeans pocket and started the engine. 'Van's all yours,' he said, nodding back over his shoulder. 'Uncoupled it when I heard your friend banging to get out.' With a faintly regretful wink at Steph, he drove off.

They watched the pickup truck stop at the bottom of the road, its light winking, then turn into the stream of cars heading out of the city. The sky behind the black twigs of the television aerials across Snow Hill had grown pink. Streetlights were already casting an orange gleam over satellite dishes and roof tiles. Above the noise of traffic from the London Road the shouts of a group of kids on bikes, wobbling home up Snow Hill along the gutter and trading their insults and goodbyes on the street corner, were faint. Twilight crushed the whites and reds and blues out of the clothes of girls with dogs and pushchairs as they passed by on the pavement below; it stole their colours and discarded them in the greying winter air of the afternoon.

Steph said, 'I'm freezing. I'm going to freeze to death if I stay out here.' She placed her hand in Michael's. 'See? I'm freezing.' He nodded but did not tighten his fingers round her hand, nor let it go. People walked home, receding into shadows under walls. Across the estate, strip lights blinked on in kitchens where women dumped bags and made toast and put on kettles; the sick blue pulse of unwatched televisions in rooms with undrawn curtains winked a message to Michael and Steph on the cold pavement – a message about other people, not like the two of them standing there as the sky emptied its darkness into them, but of other people, people who had homes to go to. And when, a moment later, Michael turned without speaking and began to make his way up the hill to his own flat at the end of Maynard Terrace, Steph pulled her T-shirt over her stomach and went too, knowing that the frailty in his eyes and his failure to drop her hand were the nearest she would get to an invitation.

Michael opened the door of the flat and snapped on the bleak overhead light in the sitting room. Dropping the backpack, which sagged at his feet and then fell over, he sank on to a small and unreliable-looking sofa. It seemed to be made entirely of blocks of sponge covered in some brown material which, as he eased into them, shifted behind his defeated back like rectangular rocks in a soft earthquake. Apart from a low table on thin black legs that stood between the sofa and a square fireplace with a cold gas fire, there was not much other furniture: just two chairs, metal folding ones, standing at a small circular table in one corner and two low wicker stools, one with an empty candlestick and a box of matches, the other with a pale blue lamp, at each side of the sofa. Three shelves by the side of the fireplace held toppled-over books, newspapers, a dead plant in a plastic pot, some shoeboxes. On the lowest shelf were a group of small brasses, a stack of plates and jugs, and three or four unsuccessful and empty vases. The arrangement looked as if the things were being stored rather than displayed, as if the person who had placed them there had no faith in them as decorative objects.

Steph, to whom the look of things mattered, gazed for a while, wondering what it was that she recognised in this room. She had thought a great deal about rooms. She had planned rooms in the detailed way that some girls plan their weddings, and just as putative brides mentally arrange in 'the

134

perfect fairytale setting' a full entourage of co-ordinated guests and attendants and bridegroom, but leave the faces blank, so Steph had dreamt up rooms beyond her means in houses that did not exist, where she would imagine living with a family she did not have. The only places where Steph actually had lived, since her mother had moved in with her boyfriend when Steph was fifteen, had been places which, no matter how long she stayed, remained other people's. Even when she had had a bit of money from some job or other to spend on a rug or a picture or some cushions, gestures which she intended to at least legitimise if not celebrate her presence, she found herself still inhabiting places whose surfaces she could not soften and whose depths would not admit her. She only half-recognised that it was a kind of belonging that she ached for, and only half-acknowledging the ache, she fell short of any belief that she deserved relief from it. She grew to believe that the shortcoming was hers, and that something more profound than a different paint colour or new cushions was called for, something beyond aspiration, outlay and some colour sense, beyond even the intensity of her need. Steph watched the man under the pitiless light, collapsed on the sofa, and understood why the room was familiar. His

135

listless attempts at homemaking betrayed the same ache, and perhaps the same lack of conviction.

She stood in the doorway, unsure of what she should say or do. A remark about how cold it was? He was sitting hunched up with his head almost on his knees, and had not moved to turn on the gas fire. How un-welcoming he was being? She was beginning to wonder if he was quite aware of her presence. She should think of something teasing and sarcastic to say, about the cold or the salty smell, or there being no lampshade or proper curtains, something to make him laugh and break the ice. But the window's reflection was showing her to herself, hesitant in the doorway, too heavy for the empty metal chairs and too clumsy for sassy remarks. She pulled the T-shirt down, feeling there was too much of her and that she did not fit; although the walls were neutrally patterned and beige, she clashed with them. Just then from above their heads came the bark of a large-sounding dog, followed by pounding noises, which could have been the upstairs neighbour's feet or missiles missing the dog and landing on the floor. From farther off the sounds of traffic and occasional calling voices from the street reached into the silence of the room through the black glass of the window.

'Got a toilet?' she asked. Michael raised

his head and nodded past her, through the doorway where she was standing. She backed out, closing the door behind her, into the tiny entrance hall. At least now he had sort of given her permission to find the toilet, so she could try the other doors and see what kind of place it was. A tiny, practically empty kitchen. Only the one bedroom as she'd expected, and the smell was coming from there, which surprised her because the man himself was beautifully clean. A freezing bathroom, not exactly fresh but not filthy. Either he kept it fairly nice or he didn't use it. But he must, because he was definitely clean himself and he even shaved. It was a pity about the bedroom, not that she would be sharing it, the way things were going. But just getting warm would be enough. Or almost enough, because now she thought about it, she was also starving.

When she returned, the cold bright air of the room had swollen and grown cruel with misery. Michael was hunched forward, crying. Steph dropped down beside him and pulled his hands away. He turned his twisted face from her and tried to bury his head in the back of the sofa. She looked round, working out that there would be no talking to him for a bit, even if she could think of anything to say. Meanwhile, he had pulled his legs up and was hugging his knees, as if to stop up a great overfilled sump of grief somewhere inside him. The sound of his sobs made Steph want to cry too. She was so cold. At least if they got warm, they might both still want to cry, but how could they feel any worse? She got up and turned the dial on the top of the gas fire. After some cranking and twisting, a blue flame whupped behind the chrome bars and the room filled with the smell of burning dust. Michael pulled himself upright and opened his mouth, gulping.

'Can't do that – costs a bomb, that fire.'

'Got to warm the place up, haven't we? Or we'll freeze to death.'

Michael sucked in a deep breath. He should explain how he didn't ever turn the fire on. He should explain about Ken across the way, how Ken's place was always warm and that Ken was always in. How Ken seemed content to share his heat and hot water in return for a bit of company, even if the occasions when he and Michael were both capable of conversation did not often coincide. He should explain about the money, the fines, getting the stall going again, the electric, the TV licence. He should explain about Mr David and the sudden drop in price, how he only got two hundred and fifty for the figures, half of what he had been promised, and how half of that had already gone on getting the van towed back and it still needed fixing. But talking was too difficult, as would be the effort of making this woman go away. What did she want from him?

'Got any money?' Of course. She had seen him count out the notes for the man in the pickup and must have noticed that he hadn't given him the lot. Michael leaned forward again and covered his face, feeling the backs of his hands soften in the first heat from the fire. Steph picked up the backpack from the floor, watching him carefully, pulled it open and brought out two crumpled magazines. Michael lifted his face but said nothing while she shook them about as if there might be banknotes lurking in them. Then she peered again into the empty backpack, stuffed the magazines into it and dropped it back on the floor.

'Haven't you got *any?* Go on, give us some money and I'll go out and get us something to eat. Go *on.*' She spoke with an odd mixture of authority and impatience, like somebody much older than she appeared. Like somebody much older than he was, Michael thought, looking closely at her face for the first time. Like she was his mother or something, and she must be twenty years younger. He pulled a tenner from his pocket.

'Give us another. Go on, twenty's better. I'll bring you the change.' As she folded the second note she said, 'I could do with a bath. Don't suppose there's any hot water, is there? While I'm out you can put the hot water on, OK? And don't turn the fire off.'

Michael cleared his throat to object, but sank back in the sofa.

'Bloody freezing out there,' Steph said, lingering. Would he not volunteer to go instead?

There was a silence while Michael looked at the slice of pink mottled belly between Steph's T-shirt and skirt. Clumsily he stood up.

'Take this,' he managed to say, pulling off his jacket as if he had just remembered what it was for. Holding it out, he said, 'It's warm.' He retreated back into the sofa.

It was better than nothing. Steph slipped on the jacket, smiling in the manner of all women trying on something new with somebody else waiting to see her in it. It fitted over her bump. She did up the last button, thrust her hands in the pockets and looked up, but Michael's eyes were closed and his face was crumpled again with crying. Upstairs the dog barked and was yelled at once more.

'What's your name?' she asked, fingering the two ten pound notes in the pocket.

Michael's eyes blinked open. 'Michael.'

'Mine's Steph.'

It may have been in the exchange of

names, but when the door closed behind her Michael felt oddly certain that she was not going to disappear with his jacket and twenty pounds, and Steph was confident that when she returned he would not still be weeping.

That evening winter returned. It was dark by the time I came in from the garden, knowing that the sunshine that afternoon had been only the illusion of spring. I ached all over and I was chilled from being out for so long. My exertions had kept me warm for as long as I worked, but as soon as I stopped I could feel that the cold had got right into me. I ran a very hot bath in my lovely white, green and yellow bathroom and lay in it, luxuriating in the knowledge that the drawing-room fire which I had just lit would be blazing for me when I came down. It crossed my mind that it was burning unattended, but I didn't worry. It was such a benign presence, the drawing room fire, I knew no sparks would fly from it and burn the rug. A fire can be a great comfort.

After her bath Jean sat by the fire in her alpaca dressing gown and silk pyjamas. Her face burned from the warm water and the tingle of soft cream after the punishment of the wind in the afternoon. Beneath the pyjamas, that were slipping over her shoulders and breasts and across her stomach as

141

she breathed, her body felt and returned every stroke of the supple silk, yet it was stiffening up after all her work in the garden. The hardness in her arms and legs made her slightly triumphant, aware less of the age of her limbs than of their strength, as if she were a schoolgirl flexing them ready to make a long jump. But although the skin all over her body was soothed, at her core she was still cold and it was difficult to tell if she felt better than usual, or about to become ill. Better, she decided. Better, and more than that: it was as if her mind had just made the discovery that she actually had a body, and her body, just very slightly sorry for itself, was basking in the attention.

The body might, she also thought, be telling her that she was actually very, very hungry, a thing it had not told her, or that she had not heard it say, for years. In fact she ought perhaps to be listening a little more carefully, because she had the feeling that since she had arrived she had grown if anything a little thinner. As Jean had begun to enjoy the loosening of the customary austerity with which she managed her physical needs, she had been considering herself with a new gentleness. Her habitual tone of self-chastisement had quietened down; if she felt like resting in the afternoons, she did so, the word 'lazy' barely crossing her mind. And she did now recall that she had made a little half-promise to herself, on what she now thought of as Wardrobe Day, that she would try to fill out her new clothes a little more convincingly. She was still a little small for them. Now, she recognised, if she were properly to fit her new life, the time had come to attend to the matter of feeding herself as if she still had some growing to do.

First, though, the chill in her joints called for a drink. She had noticed without concern or surprise on her first or second day that the decanters in the dining room were empty. She should have preferred to make her first visit to the cellar in daylight and when she was feeling less tired, but she rose, fetched the key, opened the low panelled door in the corner of the dining room and descended the cellar steps.

In the sudden fluorescent light and thick underground smell, Jean paused. From the bottom of the steps she could see, stretching down both sides of the cellar, a series of whitewashed, arched bays that were filled with metal racks laden with bottles. At Jean's end, close to the steps, stood an old oak table. She looked at it closely. It was like nearly everything else in the house: old, imperfect, beautiful, and although the wood now looked hungry, having been left so long unpolished, Jean could imagine it being used as a dining table in many houses not much humbler than this one. On it sat a small torch, a candle in a metal holder, a leather-bound book and a number of corkscrews, one of which had, inexplicably, a brush on one end. There was also an unnerving sort of circular cutter that looked as if it had been designed for removing fingertips. On the wall behind the table a pair of metal tongs hung from a hook. Jean immediately felt intimidated, as if she had happened upon the instruments of a painful, semi-surgical religious ceremony of quite Masonic abstruseness. She scraped quietly along the flagged floor, peering into the racks and reading labels which told her nothing except how ignorant she was: Léoville-Poyferré, Batailley, Domaine de Chevalier. The shape of the bottles changed; she read Chambolle-Musigny, Vosne-Romanée and sighed, unenlightened. It was easy to recognise the champagne bottles by their corks but it was not champagne she wanted now. Some treacherous-looking bottles on the lowest racks had lost their labels altogether and bore only a number and a daub of white paint, presumably having been caught by a swipe of the brush when the cellar was being whitewashed. Passing by them, knowing better than to open such dangerously old, unlabelled bottles, she walked on, reading names she could not pronounce and feeling, rather aggressively, that the whole thing was unnecessarily complicated. A nice red wine, or a glass of port or sherry, was all she wanted. It was absurd to be frightened by a lot of foreign names, but the trouble was not simply that they were the names of places she had never been to and of wines she had never drunk. They spoke of qualities she did not possess. Permanence and graciousness, let alone pedigree, had scarcely been the hallmarks of her life so far, she thought, lapsing for a moment into old habits and almost forgetting that she was not that Jean any more. She pulled out another bottle, of which there were at least half a dozen identical ones in the rack. Above the words 'Château Palmer 1982' was a picture of the chateau and she sighed again, this time with relief. At last, a name she could read, a nice ordinary English name. She recalled that there had been a Palmer family in Oakfield Avenue. And the château on the label was, really, just a house when it came to it. Or rather not *just* a house like the one in Oakfield Avenue, it was a house like this one, Walden Manor. Her house. The thought gave her confidence. She scanned the drawing, imagining the heavy French furniture behind the tall drawing room windows. There might be a pretty boudoir upstairs with another window looking over the back perhaps, on to a view of a terrace and gardens and vineyards. She turned the bottle in her hand, almost as if she thought that the far side would show the back of the house, and turned it back to the drawing. Who would live in this place? A woman, certainly. Madame, a woman of Jean's age, would be at her dressing table under the window attending to her hair, pinning it into a simple, elegant chignon. I shall grow mine, Jean thought, patting her own which was still damp at the ends from her bath. In fact, now that she thought about it, she would have to grow it, since she was not going to go out any more. The label drew her attention again. What a delightful place it was. On a summer morning, the chestnut trees – that Jean felt sure were there, flanking the courtyard just out of the frame of the drawing – would rustle in the breeze with a soft shivering note that would carry upon it the fluting calls of pigeons and doves. Madame would hear them from the open window at the back as she embedded the final long pin in her coiffure, and then she would look up to see – who? Her son, perhaps. Yes, definitely her son, some way off, moving thoughtfully between the vines, inspecting the grapes. Madame would know by the tilt of his head as he passed down the rows and as he paused to look up at the sky, that he was worrying a little, wondering if the weather would hold. Would the sun

146

shine right up until the last day before the harvest? Jean smiled, then turned and made her way up the cellar steps, picking up a corkscrew as she went. The label had told her all she needed to know about the wine, whatever it might taste like.

It was nice, that first bottle of wine. It certainly loosened my poor old joints, at least. It was strong and I suppose what you'd call dry. I liked it more the more I drank, and it went well with my supper. Because after the first glass by the fire I started to think about food again. I'm no cook, or I wasn't then – I've learned all that since. Up till then I hadn't bothered with the Aga. I only had cereal or sandwiches, or I used the microwave for scrambled eggs or soup if I wanted something hot. I didn't bother much. But that night I needed something more. I got the key to one of the two big freezers in the utility room and found bacon, sausages, butter. I noticed one or two other very tempting-looking things at the same time. For another day, I thought, half-expecting Michael. I'd already got eggs and tomatoes and bread. The Aga behaved itself. There was nothing difficult about it. There was an excellent pan for a big fry-up, and I sipped the wine while I cooked and the kitchen filled with the most wonderful smell. How they would have hated it, the owners!

All of it: the smell of bacon and sausages, the fat-spattered Aga and the way I disobeyed their instructions about where I ate. I took my supper on a tray and ate by the drawing room fire and finished the bottle of wine with some cheese. By then I felt rather sleepy so I made some very good coffee (theirs) and threw out my jar of instant as I waited for the kettle to boil. I wanted to stay awake, because after that wine label and everything that the château had told me, I had been thinking about the importance of pictures. Photographs in particular.

I had taken a look at the photographs round the place, while I was dusting. There were two tables in the drawing room covered with photographs in silver frames, and others elsewhere in the house. I collected them all up and brought them over to the fireside for a proper look. The wedding ones I didn't go for. I was pretty certain it was them, the owners, and the woman – blonde, quite a bit younger than him – looked tall and solid enough to fit my clothes, as far as I could tell by how she looked in the wedding dress which was cream and heavy-looking, not proper white. Not a shred of decent chiffon either, just a flat veil with a little tiara. He was quite heavy-looking in that English male way that often ages well and they were smiling at each other, looking safe and polished and pleased. I suppose I mean rich. They did not so much as glance out of the photograph. I burned it.

There were others of him and her both singly and together, and with older people, parents or relatives I supposed, and some with friends. They seemed to go on holiday a lot. Sometimes they were tanned, or holding skis, or sitting at tables, and her hair changed, both colour and length, but it always looked expensive. Those pictures went in the fire, too. But there were others: proper portraits of the older people, and early snaps taken on beaches when they were white squinting children in baggy bathing costumes, holding up buckets, balancing on rocks. And there they were, older, at their own weddings or with their babies on christening day, and there were black and white pictures of men in uniform who looked hopeful and unironic in a way that you don't get now. It was sad, but I burned all of them too. I will admit I did hesitate, but it would have been wrong to get sentimental about them. They had all begun to jar. The time for their stories had been and gone. They did not belong here, with me and all the other things, the vases and bowls and books and trinkets and little boxes. These people had nothing to do with this house, or with me and my son. It was time for our stories now.

# March

*Hiya Nan! I've picked up my stuff, sorry you werent here you must be at work. Thought you might be wondering where I was, well Jace and me have split, dont worry I wont be in your way, I've got somewhere to stay! Jace and me just wasnt working out, I'm staying with Michael now, he's just a friend, he's really nice, alot older than me, I'll send you the address. Anyway dont worry, but you'r not the worrying kind! I am making a go of it this time, hopefully thing will work out. I took £10 from the draw, I will pay you back, thats a promise Nan. I'm sorry I gave you heartache in the past hopefully thats all behind me now, Luv from Steph xxxxx*
*ps theres also a pan, 2 blankets plus a towel they looked like they were old ones, if you want some money for them I will pay you back.*

On the first few days after Steph's arrival Michael had gone out in the mornings before she was properly awake, apparently embarrassed by her presence. Then one day Steph got up and made him some toast, and as he ate it standing in the kitchen he told her, in what felt like an exchange – information for breakfast – that he would be

151

out trying to do a bit of dealing. That day Steph blitzed the flat and was asleep on the sofa when Michael returned in the afternoon. He made her a cup of tea, sniffing at the air that was vibrant with the smells from plastic bottles lined up on the draining board, with names like citrus cavalcade and mountain mist.

A few days later when he came back his face was tight. When Steph asked him what was wrong, the look had turned to one of slight confusion. He told her about Ken, who was worse and was going into a home. He had just come from there.

'Aw, got no family to go to? Poor old soul,' Steph said, putting teabags into mugs and getting out milk, in the manner of the sort of mildly compassionate, busy wife that she had seen on television.

'He's not old, he's just disabled. He was in the Gulf War. Got divorced after he came back. Doesn't see his kids and his wife's got someone else now. He's got emphysema, other stuff as well, he can hardly walk. He's in a right state.' He paused with the effort of producing so many words at once. 'Got medals. Decorated, he was – he's got medals. That's about all he's got, poor bugger.'

'He's got you. He's got a friend.'

Michael frowned. He had never thought of himself as Ken's friend although it had been a slight surprise to realise, as he was talking, just how sorry he felt about him and how much he knew about him, when he had never noticed being actively sympathetic or curious. He grunted and sipped at the mug of tea that Steph had poured out, struggling in his mind with another surprise: the strangeness of being asked by Steph what the matter was. He had not realised that his face might betray his feelings. Even less had he expected there to be someone else around to notice the look on his face and care. But he had stopped wondering, on his way back to the flat in the afternoons, if she would still be there. He took it for granted that she would be.

'Yeah, well,' he said. 'Thanks for the tea. And for asking.'

'You're welcome,' she said. That was the first time that they exchanged smiles. After that they did so often, enjoying first the novelty, then the habit of it.

Steph had shoplifted a set of fairy lights that she strung along the shelf above the gas fire. But the sofa was too small for both of them. In the evenings, with the remains of that night's takeaway lying in dishes on the floor around them, Steph would stretch out along the sofa and Michael would sit on the floor leaning against it, his long legs bent in front of the fire, which was now always lit. For a while they would not speak of anything and their silence seemed meditative.

Then, full-bellied in the warmth, and in the soft coloured lights and confessional flicker of the candles Steph lit, they talked, unable to see each other's faces.

Michael told Steph the story of his fifteen-year-old mother and the children's home. He hesitated after a few moments, when he had finished the short, true part. From the age of about six he had begun to learn that some facts required decoration; there had been hardly anyone at the children's home whose mother was not a ballerina or a princess, whose father had not commanded a submarine or killed tigers with his bare hands. Michael had so long ago concocted his own story that he felt more its curator than its author; the adult version was by now a carefully embellished artefact that required only occasional polishing. It had never mattered very much that he had made the story up because most of the time he barely remembered that he had. He could, if he chose, reel it off to Steph. It had undergone slight variations over the years and now it went like this: *Most of the papers have been lost. What I do know is that my father was a household name. He was married, and my mother was so young, and of course it was not to be. It broke both their hearts.* At this point Michael was quite used to being asked who the famous father was. *Of course his career would have been destroyed if the story got*

154

*out, I mean this is years ago, it was a different world. So my mother refused to put his name on the birth certificate, though he begged her to. But in high circles, and I mean high, my existence is an open secret. But it's all in the past. Hey, it happens. You've got to move on.*

Instead, he told Steph, 'When I was eight I had to have my tonsils out. They did it to loads of kids then, they cut out people's tonsils all the time.'

Steph said, 'Urgh, do you mind, I've just eaten.' she squirmed.

'There was four of us all sent to the children's hospital, we thought it'd be worse than the children's home but it wasn't. The doctor told me they would put me to sleep and take away the bad bit inside me, and afterwards I would get jelly and ice cream and feel all better with the bad bit taken away. Well I was dead surprised that they even *knew* about my bad bit, because nobody had ever said anything before so I thought it was just me and nobody else had one or knew what it felt like to have a bad bit inside them, so I was really happy it wasn't a secret and they were going to take it away. Only they didn't. It was maybe ten days later I could feel the bad bit was still there, you know? I still felt bad inside but I didn't say anything because they kept looking down my throat and saying it was fine.'

'Didn't you tell anyone?'

'Nah. I just went back to thinking it was just me. I nearly told Sister Beth. She was my favourite nurse, she came to see me a lot and ask me how I was feeling. Sometimes she sat on a chair with me on her lap, one time I just put my head against her and stayed there for ages. The other three boys that had their tonsils out at the same time as me went back, but I stayed. I hadn't picked up, they said. I was there for weeks on the children's ward, in my pyjamas and dressing gown. We did jigsaws. And this boy's parents brought him in this train set – with trailers and goods wagons and stuff that went in them and carriages and everything. Most of the time I just lay on my bed, though.'

'Then what happened?'

'Dunno, really, don't remember. I must've got better.' He hesitated. 'Well, Sister Beth, she didn't have her own kids, she must've felt sorry for me. She set it all up. She arranged to foster me, they asked me if I'd like to go and live with her and I said yes. Well, I thought it'd be great. I was miserable unless Sister Beth was on the ward. I thought it'd be wonderful.'

There was a silence except for the sighing of the gas fire. Steph asked, 'Did you go?'

'Oh yeah. I had to meet her husband and all that first, he was OK, friendly. Barry, he was called, he wanted me to call him Dad. The day they came to get me from the ward

Sister Beth was in tears, hugging me the whole time. I was there till I was fourteen. Then they sent me back.'

'Why did they do that? They sound nice.'

'Oh, yeah, they were. Wasn't their fault, I s'pose I was messing around. It just didn't work out.'

'Why not?'

'Just didn't.' Michael stretched and sighed. 'I just wasn't like them. I wanted to be an actor, for a start. I always wanted to be an actor, they didn't understand that,' he said, trying to close the matter.

'I'm sorry. Honest.'

'S'okay. I didn't become one, anyway, did I? Didn't work out. It doesn't always.' He was sitting in his usual place leaning against the sofa, and now shifted his legs and tipped his head back just a little towards her. It was less than a clear sign but Steph reached with one hand and stroked his hair, once.

Michael sniffed and drew in a deep breath. 'What about you, then?' he asked.

'Me? Oh – I'm a survivor, me,' Steph said, automatically. 'Nothing's going to hold me back. I'm an art student. Only I've got to take a bit of time out, for obvious reasons.' She glanced down at her stomach. 'I'm going back, though. Definitely. When I'm sorted,' she said. But it was no good. She petered out in simple disbelief and stared into the gas fire, remembering that she had once impressed Jace with all the survivor talk. That was when she'd just got into Bath City College, at twenty-two, to do A-level art. Jace had been doing an NVQ in something to do with building and came in one day a week on day release. When she had told Jace she was a survivor, it was not as if she had not meant it. Look where it had got her.

'Oh, that's all bollocks,' she sighed. 'I haven't got a fucking clue.'

'I know,' Michael said, complacently. 'You're as bad as me.'

'Bloody cheek. Who asked you?'

'Well, not your kid's dad, anyway. Where's he?'

'What's it to you?'

'Maybe nothing.'

Or maybe something, Steph thought. She did not dare ask if he wanted her to leave. She had been here for weeks now, and the longer something went on, the more that meant that it was all right, surely? They had worked out a kind of routine; she cleaned and shopped for food, using money that Michael left on the kitchen worktop next to the kettle before he went out in the mornings. To begin with she tended to go through it too fast and once he had complained, but apart from that not one word had been said about the arrangement, nor how long it was to last. Usually she lay down and rested in the afternoons, and Michael would be back by the time she woke up. Quite often now he cooked; he said that takeaways cost too much. At the end of each evening they would say goodnight, Michael would go to his bedroom and she would make up her bed on the sofa with blankets and Michael's coat.

'He's not around, OK? If that's what you mean,' she said.

'OK. So it's not a problem, then.'

A few nights later Steph explained what the matter had been with Jace. She added a little of what had been the matter with one or two others, including the father of her first child.

'He was called Lee. We were far too young, we didn't know what we were doing. I left school and had her. I called her Stacey. I wanted to keep her but I didn't have anywhere, I couldn't get myself together, so they took her off me.'

'Didn't you have no family that could help? What about your mum and that?'

'She told me to get her adopted. They all went on at me. Said I had my life ahead of me and anyway she'd be better off with a mum and dad that could look after her. They said I'd soon get over it.'

'Sometimes the gran looks after it, if you've had a baby too young.'

'Yeah, well. My mum had her own baby then, with my stepfather, my second stepfather. My Nan wouldn't do it neither. She's not that sort of Nan. Got her own life to lead.' After a pause she added, 'Besides I don't particularly get on with any of them. They can be quite awkward. I still think of Stacey, though, most days.'

'So what did you do after that?'

Steph shrugged. 'Usual – bummed around, did stuff, stayed with friends, sometimes with my Nan. She put up with me on and off after my mum moved to Colchester but she don't like it. I had jobs sometimes, retail, shops and that. I was always good at art, though. Got sorted in the end, went to college, met Jace, got pregnant. Bloody hell, I never learn, me. Told you I ain't got a clue, didn't I?'

'Yeah, well. Nobody's perfect.' It really did appear that that would do. Not only was he not going to criticise her and tell her what she should have done instead, Michael did not even seem to expect from her the effort of pretending that she bounced back from failure all the time. The thought made her tearful.

'I'm keeping this baby, though. No way am I giving up this baby, all right?'

Michael said nothing. Later, settling down in the sudden silence that followed the click of the gas fire being turned off, and surrounded by the smell of curry which seemed stronger in the dark and which tainted even the stuffy air under her Nan's blankets, Steph hugged herself and hoped that everything would be all right. Because really, she hardly knew where she stood, or even where she wanted to stand. Michael had never tried anything on with her, and while she supposed she would have been flattered by an attempt, the practicalities might have made it difficult. She was getting so much bigger. She wondered if Michael were one of those men disgusted by pregnancy. She smoothed her hands over her stomach. She quite liked it, getting so round and important-feeling, and she had the idea Michael liked looking at her. Could it be he was old-fashioned, a proper gentleman who would never exact favours in return for bed and board? Or perhaps he was just gay. The filthy soup tins that she had cleared from the bedroom pointed to straight male slobbiness, but the cooking, the nearly becoming an actor, and the suspicious number of books in the flat suggested otherwise. Whichever it might turn out to be, Steph was grateful that Michael had neither asked her, nor shown any sign of wondering privately, when she might be moving on. In the dark she tapped a rhythm on her stomach with her finger-tips, and whispered to her baby that everything would be all right.

I was under instructions to look through the post, bin the obvious junk mail, catalogues and so on, and leave anything else in the desk in the library. The owners had arranged matters, Shelley said. They had given their forwarding address to all the important people, banks and all that, so anything that came to the house could either be chucked out or could wait. I hadn't given it a thought. I've done enough houses not to be curious about other people's arrangements, but I began to think what a cheek to put me to that trouble. Why hadn't they re-directed everything via Royal Mail? Or left a stack of printed labels with a forwarding address, so that I could simply stick them on to things and give them back to the postman, when I remembered? Actually, I thought, why don't they correspond by the internet or e-mail or whatever they call it? It irritated me to have to think about them at all.

In fact the only reason I didn't jam the entire post into the kitchen bin without looking at it was because I had begun to wait for my own letter. The post came early. I watched for the van before I was properly awake, and when I heard the bump and fluttering of envelopes coming through the door I would be down at once, still in my pyjamas, my hair in a dreadful mess. It was quite long now, and it took me a while to learn how to manage it. I frequently forgot to brush it and tie it back at night, and although I found clips for keeping it up in the daytime, they took some time to master. Still, there was nobody to see, not yet. Every day I scanned every envelope but my letter didn't come and didn't come. It was awful to wake each day with such excitement, feeling sure that it must be today, to pick up the post, to read envelope after envelope that was not mine, then to realise that I would have to spend another day waiting, another night hoping. With every day it didn't come I got more convinced that it must come the next. And when it didn't, I would wonder what I was going to do with all the rage and disappointment I felt, where would I put it? For it seemed like some-body's fault, my letter failing to arrive.

But even on those bad days, by the time evening came I would be quite calm, because from the moment I had finished scanning envelopes for my name, the house would begin to quieten and soothe me. It was like breathing in a kind of incense, a faith that since the letter had not come today, the day when it would arrive was drawing closer. After dark, when I had settled in front of the fire with my tray and bottle – wine with supper, I had discovered, made proper cooking worthwhile – my mind and body seemed to be ticking. I ticked with an optimism that had been entering me little by little over the hours of the day, as if with each heartbeat. So the passing of the day turned into hope for the next; not yet, not yet, not yet, it ticked through me, but soon.

The money was running out. After the car battery, the electric, some rent, a bit towards his fines (not enough), gas and food, there was hardly anything left. Michael had bought and sold a couple of things and made a bit, but there wasn't enough for the next deal. He told Steph this, over their toast one morning, with tears of apology in his eyes. But he did not look away from the fixed look in hers. Nor did he pull away when she suddenly got up and put her arms round his neck and drew his head on to her shoulder. Instead he put his arms round her, gently so as not to squash the baby but also because he was not sure if he had permission. He held on but he did not cry. He simply breathed in the scent of shampoo and female skin, the newness and privilege of closeness to her.

Drawing slowly away from him she said, 'OK, then. So we got a problem. We need to do something about it then, don't we?'

She sat down again. She was so tiny, really. Except for her stomach she was tiny, and he marvelled that so much courage seemed to fit in so small a container.

'Okay then. We will, yes,' he said, trying out what confidence sounded like.

It was Steph's idea. It was something she'd thought up ages ago but never done, and she considered it far cleverer than Michael's escapades with church treasures or his little deals among the stallholders in Walcot Market.

'With your church stuff, you've got to sell it on, haven't you? If you ask me,' she said, 'that's where you fall down. My idea needs two of us, so it'd be you and me, in it together.'

Michael smiled.

'What do we do?' he asked, stabbing at the toast crumbs on his plate with one finger.

She smiled back, cleared a space on the table, brought over the backpack that was leaning against the wall under the shelves and sat down again.

'You take the backpack, empty, right?' She handed it to him. 'So, *you've* got the backpack, I've got nothing. We go into a shop, but separately, right? A big shop, a department store or something, as long as there's loads of people and more than one floor? So I go and get something off the rail, right, and I go and try it on, and then I buy it and I pay for it–'

'You *pay* for it? I thought you said–'

'Listen. I pay for it, right? You've given me a bit of cash, right, and I go and pay, and they put it in a bag and I get a receipt and all that, okay?'

'Yea-eh,' Michael said uncertainly.

'*Then* – I meet up with you somewhere in the shop, only miles away from the till and where I tried the thing on, on another floor or something, or in the café or somewhere, and I give you the thing I've bought and you get it in the backpack and then you leave, okay?'

Michael nodded. He would understand it in a minute. Probably.

'Only I've still got the bag and everything, right? Then I go and get another exactly the same as what I've bought, I take it off the rail and I put that in the bag, right? I'll pretend I'm trying something else on or something. So then I go to leave the shop with the second one in the shop's own bag and – right – beep beep beep, off goes the alarm at the door. OK? So, then, I go all surprised, and show them the receipt, the receipt, right, from the one I bought that you've already gone off out the shop with, and they go oh sorry, we didn't we take off the security tag. So they take it off, and off I go, right?'

'But then you've got two things you didn't want, haven't you? Shop stuff's hard to get anything for, there's a couple of pubs but it's dodgy. I haven't got the contacts. I specialise, see, I do old stuff. It's hard. You wouldn't believe.'

'No, no, no – *listen*. First off, we only take

stuff we *do* want. Like I need a tracksuit or something, you need a jumper. Doesn't matter what it is as long as it fits in the backpack and we can get it in a big shop, like M & S, Jolly's, Boots, whatever. And second, yeah we've got two, so next day I take one of them back and say it don't fit, and I get a refund. See? We can get all the stuff we need plus we've got our money back.'

Michael frowned. 'But you still paid. And what about food, and the gas, and the rent?' His throat puckered with the effort of keeping down panicky tears. 'There's the fucking fines and all. And what if we got caught? I'd do time. Straight off, no questions. We need *money*, not stuff. How're we going to get *money*?'

'Look,' Steph said, taking the backpack again and pulling out the two magazines from inside it. If Michael was unimpressed it must be that he had not quite grasped the brilliance of it. 'Suppose I buy *one* of these, pay the cash and I got a receipt, okay? I shove it in here and you leave. Like this. Then I get another one off the shelf,' she waved the second magazine at him, 'and then I try and leave and the alarms go off. I just go, look I've got the receipt. So they let me go with the magazine, and then next day I go in and say oh I don't like this I'm returning it, can I have a refund. So then you've got, one, the thing you wanted, and

167

two, you get your money back so you can go off and get something else you want, like for *free*. *Now* do you see?'

Michael shook his head. 'They don't put those tag things on magazines.' There was a pause while Steph groaned. 'And you can't take a magazine back and say you don't like it, neither.'

Steph sighed, and to stop herself saying something unkind, she opened the magazine in her hand. 'What is this *Lady* crap, anyway?' Oh God, she was thinking, is he gay after all? 'What is this, it's not porn, is it? Oh, it's all ads.' She leafed through. 'Hey, look. We could always get a job,' she said, beginning to read. 'There's stuff here for couples, looking after places. With accommodation *and* a wage. We could do something like that,' she said, idly.

'Need references,' Michael said.

But Steph was not listening. She was stabbing at an advertisement.

'Christ! Christ, this is you, Michael. Listen. This has got to be you.'

56 Maynard Terrace
Bath
9th March

Dear Madam
This letter is in reply to the ad in the Lady, concerning your son. My mother couldn't

168

keep me and so I was given away. I have brown eyes, I am 6 foot 1 and a half inches with dark hair and I would like to meet up with you. If you are my mother, there's a lot of things to talk about obviously, to see if you are her, but it sounds like it, it all fits together. I have always wanted to know about my family especially my father who he really was etc. Due to the circumstances I do not know if he is still alive, maybe you will be able to tell me about him, in addition to yourself.

Yours sincerely

Michael Hunter

ps This is only the name I was given in the home, as I was told you did not give me one (if it was you) or maybe it just didn't get passed on.

Pps I do not have very many papers either, hopefully we will not need them to find out the truth.

Steph wrote out the letter from Michael's rough draft, while his mind lurched between possibilities and impossibilities, starting with the idea that anybody who could be his mother could be living, as the advertisement said, in a 'country house'. He did not try to curb Steph's sudden crazy faith that his mother had been found by pointing out that while he did indeed have brown eyes, he had been born in 1961, not 1955; it seemed unkind to disappoint her. Besides, what if it was just a mistake, a misprint, an oversight? He could miss finding his own mother because of a clerical error! It could do no harm to look into it.

Jean's reply came at once. She invited Michael to come to tea on the following Friday, 15th March, at four o'clock. 'I do not go out, so I hope it will not inconvenience you to come here. The house is not hard to find.' There followed directions.

In the days between the arrival of Jean's letter and the day of his visit Michael worked on the bare fact that his mother had not been heard of since around 1971 until it seemed almost plausible that she should have changed her name, kicked the drugs, married a wealthy man, be living in a country house, and miscalculate her son's birth by six years. By the day of the visit he was ready to forgive her, quite ready to overlook the shortcomings of the drug-raddled teenager, on and off the game, who had given birth to him and then disappeared.

I will admit to misgivings about the whole thing after his letter came. And it was only after I had replied to him that I realised it had been a mistake to invite him for four o'clock, because it would give me nearly the whole day to wait feeling nervous, and worrying. That was why I deliberately gave myself lots to do that day, so that my restlessness could be directed into preparing a proper welcome. It started with food. The immediate problem of what to give him to eat became, almost before I knew it, an obsession with feeding him that I can only describe as maternal. And although to begin with it felt hardly natural (for after all, the last person I had provided food for had been Mother) I gave in to it. I had never until that point bothered much about what I now consider to be proper cooking although since the day I pulled out the buddleias I had found myself looking forward to supper each evening, more than I ever had before. I had been eating more and things were beginning to taste better. I suppose, in the same way that I was now paying new attention to bathing, dressing and sleeping, I had begun to enjoy the little acts of care that I bestowed upon myself when I cooked. These things start, I think, with oneself. Only after I had begun to make myself comfortable (in every sense) did I find myself inclined – qualified, you might say – to care for anybody else. Poor Mother, really. I cared for her in a way, of course, the best way I could at the time, mimicking the manner in which she had cared for me when I was a child. My caring was as perfunctory and spiritless as hers was. Not that that makes it my fault. I wasn't myself.

Anyway, having the whole day to fill before Michael's arrival was the start of it. Thinking first about giving him tea when he arrived, I baked a cake, and standing in the kitchen beating it all up by hand, I tried to remember when I had last made one. It must have been for Father; he liked cake, anything sweet. I had a light hand with a cake, he said. I had forgotten that entirely, and it was nice to remember again. Not that I made many cakes even for him, certainly not as many as I wanted to because although Mother did not bake, it annoyed her if I turned out too many things he liked. She said it was bad for him but the truth was she hated to see him delighted. When she saw him happy, especially if the source of it were anything to do with me, she must have felt she was being done out of something that should have been hers.

While the cake was baking (it was a Madeira cake and I used the electric oven to be certain of the temperature; the Aga has its virtues but I wouldn't trust it for a Madeira) I realised that that would be just the start. Because if things went well over tea he would stay, and I would have to give him supper, and I did not think my usual fry-up would quite do. I looked in the freezer and found fillet steaks. There were broad beans and runner beans, packets of smoked salmon, strawberries and raspberries from the garden, and ice cream. My mind filled with possibilities; in fact I think I permitted myself an anticipation close to greed. Of course they didn't have anything like chips or potato croquettes but I had a few potatoes that I thought I could manage to do something with. That was what led me to the recipe books, because I remembered seeing Delia do something once with a few potatoes and cream and garlic. Well, I had to tear myself away in the end, from those books. The pictures! Not to mention the wonderful-sounding recipes, and all the advice and things to learn. I felt so excited at the thought of reading these books properly, and even put *Larousse Gastronomique* by my bed. But I had so much to do. There was a string of garlic hanging in the kitchen that I had not touched until that day. I even found one or two usable onions in the pantry, while I was getting olive oil and vinegar and mustard and so on, and outside in the garden there was any amount of thyme, rosemary and sage in the borders, and a bay tree. It amazed me, that in the same way that those cookery books were filled with wonders, all these good things were just *here*, waiting until I should notice them and have use for them. Such quiet gifts.

The woman who opened the door was not

his mother. Yet Michael felt, even as he was calculating that she was at least ten years too old, that there was something about her.

'It's me,' was all he said. Her face crumpled, he opened his arms and folded them round her. He liked her lemony warm scent and the smell of her clean hair, that was like a white wire bush tickling the side of his face. As they drew apart Michael scanned her face again for a similarity with his, and he found it in her long, blue eyes. Outwardly they were quite unlike his own, but he saw in them a shade of supplication. Even while her mouth was smiling and producing ordinary, conventional words in a frenzy of flustered politeness – had he found the house easily, he must come right in, would he like to sit down – her eyes were imploring him to belong to her. They held a dignified plea that he not disappoint her, perhaps also a warning that she would be unable to bear it if he were about to deny that she could mean anything to him. Michael recognised it. He returned her gaze and said nothing. It seemed to him suddenly that neither of them could withstand indefinitely, or even for much longer, the dull ache of not mattering to anyone else, and in their wordless acknowledgement of this they were related, conjoined.

I want to write about my first impressions of

him. Since he'll never read this I can, can't I? I was terrified, of course, in case he was going to turn up with all sorts of documents, even photographs perhaps, that would prove I wasn't his mother. And even if he didn't, he would be bound to have bits of information about his natural parents that I might not be able to keep up with. I imagined him saying something like, 'So, tell me about my father's time in Australia. He did go to Australia, didn't he?' Or even worse, *my* time in Australia, I mean suppose his real mother had been brought up there or he knew she'd gone there after having him or something? If the questioning got too dangerous I could always claim a bit of senile memory loss, but only up to a point. All these worries, which I was trying so desperately to hide, almost stopped me from noticing what he looked like when I first opened the door. I was so frightened that he was just going to look at me in disgust, accuse me of fraud or some terrible thing, and leave. But I did notice at once how tall he was. And I could see he was good-looking, although very thin. I realised that when he hugged me. I could almost breathe his hunger, and I immediately felt glad that I had thought so much about food for the visit. It was as if I had instinctively known what he would need, in the way mothers are supposed to. But the most striking thing about Michael was that he looked so tired. Tired in the mind, I mean. His eyes darted round a bit to begin with, taking in me, the house and everything, and then he looked at me and did not move his eyes from mine. There was a mildness in the look he gave me, but also a kind of film over his eyes that made them seem too bright, as if they were concealing, not very success-fully, some terrible fatigue. Would it be fanciful to say that I saw straight in to the weariness of his soul? I don't know. The point was that he let me see it, his eyes did not leave mine.

Of course I needn't have worried. He didn't ask anything awkward at all. Over tea he gazed round a bit more and compli-mented me on the beautiful room and the lovely things I had. Then he asked me, so sweetly and simply, 'Tell me all about yourself. I've never known anything at all about you. Nobody ever told me anything about you, not even your name.'

So I did. The afternoon passed into evening. And he told me all about his life too, until we had learned not everything, but all we needed to know about each other. I couldn't say exactly when I realised it, or when he did (he told me much later that he had felt it too) but within a short time I began to know that I was quite strangely safe, a feeling I had not experienced ever before but which I trusted. I knew that nothing Michael could say would ever disappoint me, none of his questions would challenge me. And he would accept anything I might say; together he and I would find our way to our story, whatever it was to be; it would be a story mutually discovered, shaped and cherished, and in this way we would keep each other safe. He was pleased, for example, to hear (I had thought all this up in advance, of course) that his father and I had been serious about each other but that he had been forced into an engagement, for business reasons, with the daughter of a powerful associate of his father's. I of course had no money, and I had run away to have my baby. He did not even know that I was pregnant, and would certainly have married me if he had, but I felt I could not stand in his way. When he finally accepted that I had gone, he married his heiress and went to live abroad, and the two family corporations merged and became enormously successful. But he never forgot me, and five years ago I received a lawyer's letter telling me that he had died and left me this house with all its contents.

Good stories unite people. Michael had a good one too, and if he had made his up too, so what? We construct our history in order to understand what we are now, that is all, it's a perfectly legitimate way of explaining things.

Historians do it all the time. So by the time I had heard about how Michael broke away from his terrible foster parents and got a job with a small theatre company, then all about his early career on the stage and, tragically, having to give up his first big film part because of his blackouts, we were quite easy with each other.

It was after seven when we got up together, with the sense that these stories had done their work of uniting us and could now be put aside. Now I think of it I don't believe we did refer to them again unless fleetingly, in passing, when it was pleasing now and then to point to, for example, a watercolour of Lake Como and say, oh, your father loved Italy. Or, oh, you hold a potato peeler exactly the same way I do. Silly and fond. But I'm running ahead, all that came later. We went to the kitchen to see about supper, still talking and Michael carrying the tea tray, as if we already had a routine. Without discussing it he started loading the dishwasher while I got things out of the fridge. In all the excitement of preparing for him I had forgotten to think about wine, so I sent him to the cellar to choose some. We had champagne. Lots.

They clinked their glasses like children up to something, with smiling and conspiratorial eyes. Michael had opened and poured the wine inexpertly, saying that it was an excellent vintage, but with his first sip his face contorted with the surprising dry fizz that filled his nose and mouth. Jean laughed, relieved to see that his knowledge of wine stopped at the label. He was as unused to drinking champagne as she was, as unfamiliar with this as with other moneyed, sociable pleasures.

'It's Pol Roger,' he said, trying to reclaim some authority. He swigged again, to drown the pain of being laughed at, not yet able to admit that everything he knew about wine came from a book off the stall called 'Travels with My Corkscrew' by somebody called Anthony Bouvery Hope, whoever he was. He hadn't been able to shift the book even for ten pence, so he had kept it. 'Did you know that Pol Roger,' he said, 'was Winston Churchill's favourite champagne? Do you know, when Churchill died–'

'Roger! Roger Palmer. How funny! Roger Palmer, he lived in Oakfield Avenue, when Mother and I... My mother, you see–' Jean shook her head and sipped from her glass. There was nothing she needed to say on this subject after all. She drank again quickly and said, 'Years ago, it doesn't matter. Roger was a nice man, he did me a favour once, years ago. But we should have some of that nice Palmer too, with the steak. Château Palmer – it's a make of wine. You go down

179

and get it, while I get on. It's down on the right.'

Michael returned from the cellar with two bottles of Château Palmer. 'It's too cold to drink now,' he said, a little importantly. 'It ought to be warmer. You're meant to have red wine at room temperature.'

Jean nodded. It was true. She had noticed that she enjoyed her last glass or two more than the first, after the opened bottle had been sitting for a while on the hearthstone next to the fire.

'The bottles are too high to go in the microwave,' Michael said, dolefully. 'What'll we do? Pour it into a jug?'

'I know,' Jean said with a confidence and efficiency that took her a little by surprise, 'we'll stand them in hot water.'

Michael got down a wide saucepan from the shelf that Jean could reach only by standing on a chair. He placed the two unopened bottles in it, filled the pan with hot water from the tap and placed it on the edge of the Aga. Then he poured them both more champagne and as Jean moved round the kitchen in her apron, he sat in a high-backed chair next to the Aga to watch her and to keep an eye on the softly clunking bottles in the simmering water. Jean worked with peaceful, unhurried concentration, feeling Michael's eyes upon her like a blessing. She looked up from slicing onions

180

and smiled at him sitting there, watching her and drinking his champagne. She raised her glass, and Michael did too. They said nothing. They had exhausted, for the time being, the possibilities of stories told in words, but they could still toast one another silently across the kitchen, and celebrate the combined and unfamiliar joys of vintage champagne and being together.

Steph had made her Bolognese sauce from a recipe on the spaghetti packet. Or sort of; she had had to use vegetable oil instead of olive, had skipped the garlic and herbs and sliced up a bit of leftover, very bouncy frankfurter in place of the mince, but with extra onion and a shake of ketchup in place of tomato puree she thought the result was still pleasing. Unlike Michael, she did not cry easily, and had got through the first hours since his departure feeling his absence but telling herself she was not missing him as such. As she had gone about her routine of cleaning and tidying the flat with a new and unfamiliar energy, even changing Michael's duvet cover, she had wondered at intervals where he would be now and what he would be doing. He had left at two o'clock on a journey that should have taken an hour at most, allowing the extra time in case the van should conk out again, and Steph pictured him in turn desperately poking about under the bonnet, or trying to hitch a lift. Or she would imagine him sitting in the van in a lay-by outside the posh-sounding house, killing time before walking up to the door and seeing his mother for the first time. She imagined his terror. She mouthed the words of reassurance she would give and pictured how she would be keeping him calm with a gesture or a smile, if she were there with him. Then she wished that he had a mobile phone so that he could ring her. She wanted to hear that he had arrived in good time and was quietly waiting for four o'clock, and even more than that, she wanted to hear him say that he just felt like hearing her voice. He would probably find it easier to say something shy and nice like that on the phone, rather than straight to her. He could manage something like that, probably, if he had a phone. And if she had one too, of course, which she did not.

Then she began to imagine that he had had an accident. She saw the van mangled and overturned, blood streaming from Michael's mouth, his lips trying to say her name. He would die trapped in the van, and she would never have heard him say that he liked to hear her voice. He had left her forever and he had never ever said it. Steph began to cry. She wished again that they had mobile phones. She wished she had heard him say it. She wished she had not been left alone. When he got back this evening she would tell him that. He would come back. It was stupid, wishing. She collapsed on the sofa and sobbed. Strange, because she had been alone before, and she did not cry easily.

Darkness came earlier on that overcast and rainy afternoon, and it seemed to Steph that as the day was wearing away outside, here in the flat time was suspended. Michael's absence had stopped the clocks; ambient fear, for him and for herself, would fill all the space until his return. She had meant to buy food, but she began to feel a superstitious reluctance to go out to the shops. She tried to tell herself it was because of the dark and the weather. Then she considered that she simply did not like the thought that Michael might return before she did and come back to find the flat empty, even though he must have done so countless times in the past. And in any case, he could not possibly be expected back in Bath at a quarter to five when he would only just have arrived for tea, an hour's drive away, at four o'clock. Unless there had been some disaster. This renewed the disturbance in her mind enough to halt for a while her fretful tidying and fiddling round the sitting room, and she stood gazing out of the window at the sky, her arms folded over her bump, while in her head she played out new and lurid catastrophes that could befall him. Finally, she turned from the window, accepting that she simply wanted him home.

But she definitely did not cry easily, so perhaps it was the baby that was making her want to again. Whatever it was, it was important that she stop thinking about Michael and the surprising and awful discovery that she missed him. It was then that she had roused herself and gone to the kitchen to tackle the Bolognese sauce with a third of the proper ingredients, so that there would be something nice waiting for him when he finally did come home.

Again, I think it was something instinctive that had caused me to make up a bed in Michael's room long before I had met him, or even quite dreamed of his existence. It's the little practicalities, the things we choose to pay attention to, that so often reveal the desires beneath, desires that are so huge that they really must be concealed if life is to go on in any recognisable form. My life has never been big enough for epic emotions, I now see. I have kept them small, knowing that my life just could not accommodate longing and hope and rage on the kind of scale I could have felt them. I have domesticated my feelings so that I tend them in the little daily observances: making up bedrooms, cooking, gardening. And lighting fires.

On the day back in January when I chose and aired the best white linen with lilac piping for that room and made up the bed, I couldn't have known that Michael would be needing it that very first night. But there was no question of his driving back to Bath so late and after so much wine. I found men's pyjamas, dressing gown and slippers in one of the other wardrobes in my own dressing room, as well as shaving and washing things. Michael did not ask where they had come from but accepted them as his own. I recall that he did not thank me effusively for them, or for anything else, when he left the next morning. Not that he was rude, certainly not. Just that he took it somewhat for granted that his room and everything he needed for the night would be available in his mother's house. He took his leave a little abstractedly after breakfast, in a complete set of different clothes that were all rather better than the things he had arrived in, and I did not mind that, either. Nor did I worry that we did not arrange another visit. Without its being said, we knew that from now on it was his spells of absence from this house that would be temporary, not his presence in it. Besides, what son behaves as a house guest, or thinks his mother needs to know when he might be coming back? He assumes, rightly, that she will be there when he does choose to return, and all a mother needs to know is that he will. But over and above that I felt sure it would be soon.

Michael found Steph huddled and spent on the sofa. She was wrapped in her blankets and half dressed, rigid with cold and with the fatigue of a night spent drifting between fits of crying and shaking and patches of exhausted sleep. Her face was ghastly, smeared with wrecked makeup. Strands of her fair hair stuck darkly to her head where her anxious hands had pasted it down with tears, sweat and mucus.

'Steph? What's the matter? Bloody hell, what's the matter?'

Steph shook her head slowly from side to side. 'You – you didn't come back ... you ... I thought ... I thought you were ... I though you wasn't ever...'

Her eyes were tight shut, so she did not see but only felt Michael's arms coming round her shoulders and pulling her towards him on the sofa. She heard his moan of incomprehension and dismay, and his saying of her name over and over as he enveloped her and held her. As he rocked her against him, she began to quieten.

'You didn't come back, you bastard ... you

bastard, I thought you'd gone. You went for *tea,* you never said you'd be away all fucking *night* ... you might've been *dead*...' She tried to take a breath, but began to gulp. Michael held tighter, taking in the truly puzzling idea that someone else had cared enough about where he was to be frantic with worry. It had not crossed his mind that he should let her know he was staying over for the night. Not that he would have been able to – except, he thought guiltily, he could have phoned Ken who might have been able to wheel himself along and knock on the door. But he had not thought of it. He felt ambushed by two astonishing feelings: grateful joy that she could weep with concern for him, and overwhelming remorse that he had caused her to suffer. He also found that he had an erection. Holding her close and stroking her back, he whispered her name.

'I'm fucking freezing and all,' she said. 'The gas ran out and I didn't have any coins.'

Michael rose, fed the meter and turned on the fire. He returned to her and wrapped her close to him again. After several minutes, she pulled in a deep shuddering breath, and then another. There were several crumpled tissues on the floor. Michael reached for one, lifted it to her face and dried her eyes. She took it from him and wiped her nose, and then buried her face in his chest, but did not cry.

'Are you getting a bit warmer now?'

'Yeah, I suppose.'

'I'm really, really sorry–'

'I thought you'd just gone off, walked out. Just gone.'

'No. No, no I never would ... never. I never would. Honest, I never would.' His arms tightened round her and with one hand he caressed her shoulder. The neck of her sweatshirt was wide, and his hand met her skin and dipped under the edge of the material. The warmth and softness of her seemed to flood him with other sensations; she became not just warm skin beneath his fingers but also taste, a smell. She was almost a sound, both in and of his own head, filling every cell of him with an incredible, compulsive music that his body recognised and wanted to move to. He pulled the sweatshirt from her shoulder and buried his face in her neck, kissing, breathing her in, and with a burst of courage he moved his hand and placed it lightly on one breast. One of Steph's hands was moving up his thigh. Whether he was more terrified than excited, more embarrassed than elated he simply did not know. As her hand roamed closer Michael pressed the round breast beneath his palm. It could have been made of bread for all he could tell, under the thick sweatshirt, but he was unsure if he was allowed to do more, and now something close to panic washed through him in case it was all going to stop. Her hand had left his thigh and was removing his hand. He would explode, surely, if it had to stop. Steph pulled his hand away and drew it under her clothes, and as he touched her bare breast, she gasped.

'Sorry!' Michael blurted, withdrawing his hand.

She replaced it gently and kissed him, pushing her tongue into his mouth. It was only when she stood up and pulled him to his feet that he remembered properly that she was pregnant. He stared at her stomach, trying and failing to conceal his erection, not knowing what to say or do, even less what she wanted. She reached round his neck with both arms and whispered, 'Michael. Michael, it'll be all right. Come on, it's all right,' and there was silence. Michael's hands reached under the sweat-shirt and pulled it off over her head. He gazed at the white-skinned, blue-veined breasts, so lopsided and heavy, while both hands lifted and cupped them and his fingers played over her brown nipples. He searched her face to see if he was getting this right, if his hands being here, doing this to her breasts really could be what she wanted. He took one nipple in his mouth and she moaned and stroked his head. It was incredible; he was almost unable to believe it, but she was unzipping him now. He felt afraid. He had slept with people, of course, perhaps half a dozen, and with one of them, on and off, for several months, but not for ages. And never with anyone pregnant. He did not know how or even if it were possible. What if he hurt her, or the baby?

'Come on,' Steph whispered. 'It's fine. Come on, it'll be fine.'

Michael allowed himself first to be led to his bedroom, then to be undressed, and to undress her. She was beautiful. With the sight of her naked round body came a burst of hope that entering her would be as easy as it was necessary. It was, she made it so. It was easier than he would have believed possible and, beyond that, infinitely happier. She lay on her side and let him travel her with his hands and tongue, moving as and where he wanted. When he began to understand that he had more than her permission and that she was as frantic as he was, he grew bolder, and when he finally parted her legs and found her so wet that he thought he would die from need of her, she reached down and drew him inside her. She showed him how to glide and twist in her. He delighted in the way she instructed and he followed. For ever afterwards he would remember how his delight seemed to please her as much as her own, which she also knew how to take from him. She showed him how, but it was he who delighted her. He touched, pushed and slid and waited, withdrew, touched again as she pulled him back between her legs. For as long as she wanted he sank in and out of her, entering and leaving her, until with her legs gripping him round his waist he felt her tug and tighten over him and she gasped and swore happily. He was long past speech himself.

In a state of amazed exhaustion they lay together through the rest of the morning and into the afternoon. The bedroom was freezing. Under the covers, they could believe themselves just about warm enough if they did not move. Lying face to face, they laughed because their noses, when they touched, were both so cold. Above them the dog barked, and feet pounded. They dozed. Hours passed and they watched darkness come, the time of day an irrelevance. Then Michael wanted her again, and afterwards Steph fell asleep while Michael lay looking at the ceiling, trying to place himself in this new, re-ordered scheme of things. From his bare past, which already he was thinking of in the way that a freed man thinks of prison, it was like stepping through an archway. It almost eclipsed the finding of his mother but was also part of the same thing, marking the beginning of his life as a person who had other people. He turned and looked at

Steph's face. Her eyes, so large, seemed smaller when she was asleep. The eyelids were thin-skinned and bluish and reminded Michael of a baby bird. Her lips had relaxed and seemed fuller. They were still wet. His eyes wandered down to the swell of her stomach over the duvet, the line of her splayed legs. He placed a hand gently on her and let it climb her curve, barely touching. He could hardly bear the distance her sleeping put between them, but he would not dream of waking her. There was no hurry. They had each other. And soon there would be a baby, and all of them, they would all belong to one another. A voice in his head declared it.

When Steph woke she looked even more tired than before, and she had a headache. When she told Michael that she had eaten hardly anything since he had left the house, he went into the kitchen where he found her frankfurter spaghetti in a coagulated mess. He brought her tea and biscuits, feeling slight consternation because he was out of aspirin. Then Steph said she wanted a bath, so he switched on the immersion heater. It only produced enough water for one bath, so he washed in cold water and got dressed. Later he returned to the bathroom and ran a bath for her, fetching a clean towel and placing an old one on the floor. It had occurred to him that the wet floor might be dangerous. What if she were to slip while he was out? He explained all this solemnly, warning her to be very careful and to step on to the towel on the floor, while Steph lay propped up on his pillows and drank her tea, listening and nodding, rather stunned. Michael could have laughed aloud with the pleasure of spoiling her. He still had not told her about Jean, and she had not asked. Things had happened too quickly, and even now he was in a hurry to get her the aspirin. Suddenly he was so busy, life was so full.

'You're nice and cheerful, anyway,' Steph said, looking over her mug of tea.

'Yeah, well, and I reckon you are too,' he said. 'Cat that's got the cream, that's you.' She laughed.

He came back with paracetamol, which the pharmacist had told him was better than aspirin for pregnant women, and two or three carrier bags of food including a chicken and a bottle of wine. He found Steph sitting on the sofa in front of the fire, barefoot, dressed in pyjamas and one of his sweaters, combing out her hair which dangled in wet loops over the towel round her shoulders. She looked up almost shyly because she had planned for him to notice her hair. She wanted him to think it was nice when it was newly washed.

'You warm enough there like that?' Michael asked. Steph smiled and nodded, turned her head and continued combing, while he watched.

They said little else for a while, and their silence lapped generously to the edges of the room and enclosed them.

Then Steph said, 'It's like a little church in here.' It was true. The small room was dark but for the fire, the fairy lights and the candles. Michael stretched himself out on the floor in front of the fire, and said he knew what she meant.

He had seen a chapel like that, once. He had been persuaded to go to Spain for a week, years ago, with three other lads who drank in the pub where he was working. On the first night they had gone round the bars and the other three had brought girls back to the apartment, all of them so drunk they paired off and then, Michael told Steph as she slowly pulled the comb through her hair, 'they just screwed all over the place, right in front of each other, four of them in the bedroom, two in the main room. I didn't know where to look.' He had spent the night on the concrete balcony and woken the next day with mosquito bites on his lips and eyes. The others, when they surfaced in the afternoon, thought it hilarious. Michael had hardly seen them after that. He spent the week alone, disfigured and miserable, keeping different hours. He couldn't face the pool or the beach so instead he took buses inland, alighting in hill villages and walking about in the heat to the silent bafflement of old people and children who watched him from sitting places in the shade. To get out of the sun he would buy soft drinks at cafés that had only two or four white plastic chairs and an umbrella, or he went into churches. He liked the brick floors, dusty here and there with sprinklings of fallen plaster, the green stains in the joins where a little damp seeped between white-washed walls, and the peeling Madonnas in their painted, fairground colours. He knew that these places were in poor taste, mawkish and out-of-the-way, and that the country saints they elevated were obscure, but it had seemed to him that the plastic chrysanthemums, the tinsel and the coloured lights somehow made them precious, contained, intricate.

'If it's like a church in here, that makes us a couple of saints,' he said.

'Sinners more like,' Steph said, with satisfaction.

They grew comfortable. One of the candles burned down. Steph could not lay her hands on the matches to light a new one and Michael found them in her pyjama breast pocket, or pretended to. He set about roasting the chicken, and when Steph suggested they bake potatoes at the same time since the oven was already on, he thought her brilliant. He opened the wine and between them they finished the bottle. Soon afterwards the gas ran out again. Michael had spent the last of his money on the food, so they went to bed. They lay while Michael stroked her bump, and asked her what it felt like to be pregnant. Did she want a boy or a girl? He kissed the bump. Did she talk to the baby?

'You're meant to,' he said. 'I read it somewhere. You're meant to talk to it.'

'That's plants,' Steph said sleepily. 'Anyway, I do sometimes. Hello, baby!' she whispered, to prove it. 'Why don't you talk to it, Michael? Say hello. 'Cause if it's a boy,' she added nervously, 'I was thinking of Michael.'

Michael turned to her and tried to see from her face if she were serious. But the flickering light from the silent television was dancing over her features and he could not tell. 'You mean *calling* it Michael?'

Steph nodded. 'So you'd better get to know it, it ought to know who it's named after. Or it could be Michaela, if it's a girl.' She pronounced it Michael-ah.

'Michael-ah,' he repeated.

'Talk to it, go on. Tell it something nice.'

He kissed the bump again and stroked it, and when his lips brushed the taut skin of her stomach and he felt the ridges of her stretch marks on his mouth he was aghast at the intimacy of it. He whispered something that Steph could not hear, and she realised she was not meant to. She could not fight sleep any longer. Seeing her settle down, Michael switched the television off. As she was letting her eyes close, she remembered with a shock that she had not heard a word from Michael about his mother.

'Your mum! You never said! Was it all right, then? Seeing her? I can't believe you never said. She is your mum, isn't she? What was it like?'

Michael smiled in the dark. He too was almost asleep. 'Oh, oh yeah, it was great. She's my mum all right. It was great. You wait till you meet her. I'll tell you tomorrow. Plenty of time tomorrow.'

Steph woke because the baby had just kicked her much harder than usual. It was not painful, exactly. She lay awake until it happened again. It was somehow *serious*, not in the least playful. This one must be a boy, definitely a footballer. She needed to pee anyway, and she got up, feeling an ache in her back. The baby moved again when she was on her way back to bed and she groaned softly, with surprise rather than pain. In bed she lay and nearly fell asleep again. A little later, she was not sure how long but perhaps half an hour, another kick came, along with a bigger surprise. Was it possible? Steph stared into the dark and tried to remember what giving birth had really been like last time. But she couldn't; it was too long ago and she had been so young, practically somebody else. It was as if it was something dramatic and mildly scandalous that she had been told about, or seen in a film. But even as her mind was trying to keep it from her, her body was digging into old memories asleep in the blood, kicking nerves and muscles awake. These were contractions, not kicks. That last one had been stronger, more like a clamp seizing her round the middle than the baby's foot knocking her from inside. She waited. Twenty minutes later came the next one, the same grabbing and wringing of her body, not painful yet but with the threat of ferocity to come. The struggle to expel was beginning. Still, she had done this before. It would be ages yet, hours and hours. Time enough she hoped, biting her lip, to get Michael used to the idea. It was surely a bit early though, she thought, trying to count back. She had thought she had at least another six weeks or so, judging by her size and what she could recall of the goings-on with Jace. But whether it was coming early or whether she'd just got the dates wrong, she had to get Michael used to the idea not just that she was having it, but that she was having it now, and she was having it here –

at home, or the nearest she had to one. Steph suddenly felt her confidence fail, because after what had happened today, getting Michael to go along with that might be more difficult than if he had stayed as he was at the beginning, tolerant but careless of her. But he was turning out to be so kind. If that thing with the towel on the bathroom floor was a sign of how careful he was going to be with her and the baby, he might panic and drag her off to Casualty.

She had to smile at the picture that made, Michael with his eyes wild and everybody thinking he was the worried father. But it would not happen that way, because she would just refuse. She was not going to hospital. Once she explained to Michael why she had to have it here it would be all right, she reassured herself, feeling for a moment oddly powerful. There was something about having a baby that stopped other things mattering too much. She would get her way. Then the thought of Michael drew her mind back to the memory of him inside her, just a few hours ago, and she found this was easily the nicest thing to think about while she waited for the next contraction. Actually, wasn't it supposed to bring on labour? Steph was suddenly sure now that it did. Once at the clinic, when she was pregnant with Stacey, another woman in the waiting room had said how fed up she

199

was, overdue and still waiting, and somebody else said, you go home and have a nice time with your boyfriend, that'll bring it on, never fails. Another grab of her belly that this time reached right round to her back interrupted her thoughts. Michael stirred, turned over and stretched out an arm for her.

'Michael?' Her moment of calm faith evaporated. Her heart was beginning to beat now with the same fear she had felt when Michael had failed to come home. Perhaps it wouldn't be Michael's care and concern that would land her in hospital. Perhaps she was just wrong again and he would turn out to be the same as others. It would be nothing unusual if he didn't want to stick around; in fact it would be a bloody miracle if he did. Now he had had sex with her, he would probably just dump her at the hospital to go through it alone, and they'd take the baby away before she even saw it properly. Or he might just leave her here again. He'd leave her and go straight back off to his mother. It was almost a certainty that he wouldn't stay. People didn't. Her stomach felt another grip, longer and more aggressive.

'Michael? Oh, Michael!' she yelped, and burst into tears.

But not quite as soon as that. Not at half

past three in the morning of the following day. But even though I was surprised, I felt no fear at the sound of the van coming in to the courtyard. I knew it would be him, somehow, and anything happening at half past three in the morning is enough in itself to suggest a crisis. I remember I pulled on my dressing gown, went down to the door and opened it a matter of seconds after Michael had banged on it, and one look at his face confirmed that it was a crisis. He looked worse than she did, in the time-honoured way of panicking fathers. And she was a funny little thing! She even managed a smile and a handshake, and a 'pleased to meet you', like a child dutifully displaying her party manners, though she was stooped over and holding her stomach, and there was a pinched look about her little face. The eyes were huge. Her legs were buckling under the weight of Michael's jacket and all the blankets he'd put round her. He hadn't had a clue what to do for her, and keeping her warm was all he had managed to come up with, apart from the important thing of bringing her here, of course. Bringing her home.

The minute I saw her in the light of the hall I knew what was happening. The poor thing's manners gave out just then and she made the most extraordinary grunting noise, followed by something like an animal lowing. Then she had a fit of simple crying that was girlish and frightened. I saw then the wet stain on the front of her clothes under her stomach. Even though I had never been in such a situation in my life I was quite calm, at that stage at any rate. I thought quickly. She was well wrapped up but still perished, and Michael was shivering with cold and fear. He could hardly speak at first but I managed to get it out of him that the van heater did not work, and that he'd had trouble finding the house again in the dark and in such a state of nerves. Then she piped up that she'd started about four hours ago. I remember I said something soothing about how he had done exactly the right thing and that everything would be all right now that they were here, and I could see he believed me. In fact they both did. Steph looked so grateful I could see she needed some older and kindhearted person to say that everything would be all right. Well, it seemed I was to be that person, and so I took her in my arms and said it again, and then I believed it too.

She couldn't really stay on her feet. She needed to find a place to lie down, or squat on all fours or however they do it nowadays (I'd read articles and gathered it had all changed). Not their bedroom though, it would be too cold. The heating was off for the night and not due to come on until seven o'clock and it didn't seem like the moment to go fussing with the timer. Besides which I doubted if she could manage the stairs. I took them into the kitchen and she immediately lay down in front of the Aga and started gasping. Michael and I stared at each other.

'I'll put the kettle on,' I said, and he looked relieved.

'Yes! Yes, that's what you do, isn't it? Hot water, you always need hot water, don't you?' Actually I hadn't a clue what people delivering babies were supposed to need hot water for. I'd been thinking of a cup of tea to calm us all down. But obviously Steph couldn't go on lying on that hard flagstone floor, so I sent Michael upstairs for some pillows and bedding. He was pleased to be given something to do and so then I made the tea after all. Steph was glad of it, and so was he, so it was the right thing after all. Then I left them together and went upstairs to put some clothes on. I felt I was dressing to go into a kind of battle. It seemed a shame that I hadn't got old clothes suitable for the occasion, such as people keep for messy jobs around the house. I knew I'd never get the marks out.

In what seemed no time at all Steph stopped being cold and warmed up. She moaned and rocked and pulled herself nearly upright when the pains got hold of her, in fact she got terribly hot. When the contractions came, her mouth stretched in an awful grin of effort; her lips cracked with the dryness and her cheeks grew bright red. It was terribly hard work. She was in a lot of pain and it was awful, just watching the pains gradually get longer and longer and the times between them grow shorter. She sweated until her hair was soaked. Michael dabbed her face with a cold cloth and did not once leave her side. She would tell him to rub her back, or she would take hold of his arm with both hands and squeeze tight, hissing and wearing that grin, and all I could do was stand there. I felt so helpless and ignorant. I had no idea how much worse it was going to get, and so I felt frightened too, but tried to hide it. I brought down more bedding, and some towels, thinking we'd be bound to need them at some point. I made more tea, but Steph sicked hers up a short time later. After about an hour and a half I couldn't bear it any more and got very upset myself. Even though I knew it was out of the question, I said we should get her to a hospital. I was too distressed by the pain she was in to think straight, of course. Because bringing an ambulance or a doctor down here (Michael was in no fit state to drive) and letting strangers in might have risked everything that was important. Who knows where meddling by the authorities might have ended up. There would have been all the business of addresses and names and it would have all got back to the agency and the owners somehow. Not that I had thought all this out at the time. I just wanted the best for her, I wanted something to be done about the shrieking. I wasn't thinking straight, so thank goodness Michael was. It was Michael who said it was too late for that, and then Steph herself got even more upset and yelled and swore she would not move from here. So on it went, for another two and a half hours. By this time she was writhing, and bawling for somebody to help her, and very soon after that she screamed that it was coming.

But it still seemed to take an age. She half sat, half lay, panting, and got Michael to hold her from behind. She pushed and pushed. I don't think I have ever seen such effort. Then she shouted at me, as if she really was angry, to see if it was coming yet, and I had no choice but to look, and there it was, this veiny, foreign-looking dome growing and swelling out from between her legs with a long slick of slime and blood. Also, I'm afraid, foul, gingery, wet rags trailed out from somewhere behind her – I'd had no idea that could happen. I cleaned her up. Steph won't mind my going into such detail; she'll never know. I'm putting it all down because it was so extraordinary. It's such an ordinary-sounding thing, 'having a baby' and I had not realised until that night how very *extra*ordinary it is. It crossed my mind that the only other birth I'd ever had anything to do with must have been my own, and it struck me that birth is simply the most puzzling, immense duet between human beings; nothing ever again in the life of mother or child will demand such struggle and mutuality, and possibly for-giveness. So when one witnesses another birth, one is changed. The ferocity of my feelings for that child and for her parents began then, with the sight of her bald blue head as her mother pushed her out of her own body into my arms, and it has never abated.

Jean stepped out of the kitchen into a freezing pink dawn and closed the door quietly behind her, leaving Steph and Michael holding each other and their daughter, squatting on piles of gore-soaked bedding on the kitchen floor. Outside, the night had been a cold and windless one, and now a frost lay over the walls of the garden and across the bare arms of the trees. Sun-light was slicing through branches and slanting across the grass. Jean took a few steps towards the walled garden, wrapping her arms round herself, breathing in the cold water smell of the almost-spring earth and listening to the rasping of rooks in the tops of trees. Despite the cold she would stay out here a while; she needed a little time to herself. She needed a moment to recover from the terror of it, from the baby's eventual rushed, slippery emergence with limbs jerking and its frowning face squeezed tight, and its appalling silence. God, the silence. And then, as she had been trying to wrap a towel round the wet torso and lolling head, there had come the splutter and the sucking yell, then Steph's answering cry. Between them she and Michael had managed the tying of a length of string round the cord, both taking instruction from Steph who now lay exhausted, but in charge. It was Michael who had claimed, holding up the length of string, that that was what the hot water was for, and had insisted on boiling it first. Steph had lain waiting with the baby resting on her stomach while he tied it, but it was Jean who had finally taken the scissors from his shaking hands and cut the cord. Then she had suggested quietly that the baby might like to suck, and although the idea seemed a novel one to Steph, she had nestled the child at her breast. Jean had been unprepared for the lumps of liver that had slipped out of Steph soon after, but Steph herself had peered over between her legs and watched it without surprise. Presumably it was just the afterbirth, and all quite natural. Jean stopped on the path and looked back towards the house. There would be more to do presently. She had reached the wide crater at the end of the garden from which she had torn the four buddleias out by their roots, and she now recalled something she had heard or read somewhere about burying the afterbirth. Was it Indians, a tribe of Red Indians, she wondered, who buried it in the ground at the base of a tree, or planted a tree in that place? It was, she remembered, supposed to represent the claim of the new child to that very spot on the earth, which was thereafter the place to which it and all its descendents would belong. It seemed to Jean suddenly apt, marvellous, poetic. She hoped Steph and Michael would think it so as well, and turning, hurried to go and tell them.

When she got back to the kitchen Steph and the baby were installed in the large Windsor chair wrapped in a duvet, both almost asleep. Michael, sitting at the table waiting for the kettle to boil, had laid his head on his arms. Steph looked up.

'I thought,' Jean began, pointing to the mess on the floor, 'I thought...' But she found it was impossible even to say the word 'afterbirth', never mind explain about burying it. Steph was staring bashfully where she

208

was pointing. They both had been struck by a sudden, immobilising shyness; hardly surprising, Jean thought, since they had after all met for the first time only a few hours before. The enforced intimacy of Steph's labour and Jean's reluctant midwifery was now receding, leaving each regarding the other with a slight wariness. Jean felt suddenly foolish, anticipating how it would sound in the bright stillness of the kitchen; something about a little ceremony with the afterbirth, a thing Red Indians did, exactly what she was not sure. How mad and, worse, meaningless the words would seem; while those that were not meaningless, that the ceremony would bind them all to one another and to this place, were presumptuous and unsayable.

'Yeah, sorry.' Steph said, trying to ride out her embarrassment. 'Should have got some old newspapers or something down first, shouldn't we? Didn't think. I'm covered in it and all, underneath. I need a bath. So does this one here.' She smiled, dipping her head towards the baby's. 'And I'm dead sore.'

Jean beamed with sympathy and also with relief at finding her role again, as if Steph had just handed her the script. Grandma, mother-in-law, indispensable, here to help. 'Oh, of course! You must be tired out, you poor thing. You're such a clever girl. Now,' she said comfortably, 'would you like a bath straightaway, or a sleep first? Michael will take you both up, won't you, Michael? I'll deal with that,' she added, nodding back towards the floor, 'and then with breakfast. You must be hungry as well. And then we'll just have a nice quiet day. Nothing but rest for you, young lady.'

She rather amazed herself, discovering not just the right tone to take but also what her job would be from now on. Here she was, already talking as if she had never been anything else but the gentle arranger of all domestic comfort; it seemed like a little triumph to add to the day's great one. Jean sighed with the happiness of knowing what she ought to do next.

'She's a great cook,' Michael told Steph, as he helped her to her feet. They were both almost mournful with tiredness. Jean watched the three of them go, and then went to find rubber gloves and a bucket. How easy and clear everything had become. Michael and Steph's bathroom overlooked the other side of the house. So while Michael bathed his daughter and the new mother in soft warm water and found clean and beautiful things to dress them in afterwards, she would have plenty of time to slip the lot into the hole in the garden. It would be a more private and prosaic committal than she had had in mind: just her and the bloody contents of a blue plastic bucket. But there would be enough time, before she had to return to cook breakfast, to linger over the dug earth and whisper a few words (the right ones would come to her) and to watch the bright entrails of her grandchild's birthing soak into the soil of the place that would be ever afterwards charmed.

'Steph was thinking of Michael-ah,' Michael said shyly, from the chair by the window. He and Jean had brought breakfast up on trays to the bedroom which was now his and Steph's. From where she sat in a chair on the other side of the bed Jean considered this, drinking her coffee. Steph's head rested on several pillows and her eyes were closed. She was lying in the largest and most comfortable bed she had ever been in in her life, and Michael-ah, dressed in new baby clothes that Jean had directed Michael to find in the nursery, lay sleepily in her arms, feeding without urgency. Her hand was covered by a too-long sleeve, which had been folded back. They had picked out the smallest baby suit with a label that said 'newborn', but it was much too large. Michael reached over and pulled the material back so that he could see the tiny fist stirring the air, as if its waving were a necessary part of her sucking. Three teddy bears and a white baby shawl lay on the bed next to the tray with Steph's empty plate.

'Michael-ah. Or Michæla, perhaps?' Jean murmured. Michael looked embarrassed, so Jean went on quickly. 'It's a lovely name. It reminds me of Miranda, it's got the same number of syllables. I think it means miracle.'

Into the warm silence came Steph's slow voice. 'Miranda. I like that better. A miracle. Michael, would you mind if we called her Miranda?'

Michael smiled. 'She is a bloody miracle,' he said. 'Miranda, then. Miranda,' he yawned.

Jean tiptoed out and went to her own room, knowing that she was going to have to cry at the honour of choosing the baby's name. They all slept until the day was over, except that Miranda, stirring from time to time, would feel the skin of her mother against her face and with her soundless mouth she would seek and find a nipple, clasp it between her gums, and tug.

Of course it wasn't all plain sailing. You'd think, wouldn't you, that once we'd all found one another, and the baby having come safely into the world, that all we'd have to do then would be to settle down to life in our new house. And there could be no easier house to settle in, I knew that already; and they were so pleased to be here. I don't believe we ever did discuss it in the formal sense, it was just understood by us all that we would all be living here from now on. Everything we needed (or very nearly) was here, in a way that seemed quite magical to them. I think I had stopped being astonished at how the house somehow went on providing what we needed, starting with the time and the privacy just to be our best selves. Or perhaps I had begun to take a little credit for it myself, as if the house and I worked together, or at least had begun to reflect each other. It was close to the feeling I had first had when the two Dutch students turned up. It had become personal. The house and my life now were like things I could shape in my hands, like arranging flowers, or painting, something I was creating and of which I was also a part. Steph and Michael ended up feeling the same. But the important thing to start with was that they stayed. Any other arrangement would have been unnatural. I never did quite get to hear much about the place where they'd been living, but they were certainly not in any sort of hurry to get back to it. It was at least a week before Michael went off in the van and came back with the rest of their things, none of which quite suited the new way of life. I don't think we kept any of them except for some of Michael's books.

No, it was the baby who worried me from the start, in a niggling way that I told myself was due to my own inexperience. And thinking it was inexperience, of course I said nothing, not wanting to start up any doubts about my not actually having had any children. I mean I don't know what they thought of my story at that stage, but it seemed a courtesy not to challenge whatever they had decided to believe. I know new babies seem impossibly small, but Miranda was so tiny. I didn't like to say so and her size didn't seem to worry her parents, but I wondered all the same. On the day after she was born Steph was still in a bad way and I volunteered to change Miranda's nappy – there were plenty, thank goodness, in the nursery – and I slipped downstairs and popped her on the kitchen scales. It was difficult! I weighed the biggest mixing bowl first and then put her in it, which she did *not* like. She wriggled so much I told myself that it couldn't be a completely accurate reading. But four pounds five ounces! Still, I said nothing. Steph was only slightly built herself, so maybe the baby would just take after her. And it seemed that Miranda had arrived on the early side, so you wouldn't expect her to be big. As long as we kept her well fed and cared for there didn't seem anything to worry about. Babies grow, don't they? In fact it's all they do, really.

It was Steph who was doing the feeding.

She wasn't a natural at it though. She got very tired and cross over it and I remember she was often in tears. With Miranda bawling over her shoulder she would nag at Michael or me about getting Cow and Gate or something. *There must be bottles and that in the nursery! There's **everything** in there! Can't we give her a bottle?* We had to tell her there weren't any. Miranda would get used to the feeding, I was sure of it. I mean, it was natural to take mother's milk, and must surely be better for her. It wasn't as if she'd ever had a bottle, was it, so why should that be any easier for her than the natural way? It seemed a reasonable argument and I really did believe it, and I could see Michael did too. We couldn't suggest going out to buy baby milk and bottles. We both honestly thought it would be better to spend what we had building Steph up so that she could feed the baby herself.

Money. Of course, it was mainly to do with money, though at the time we convinced ourselves we were doing it for better reasons than that.

Miranda blurred Steph's nights and days by waking her almost every hour, chewing her till she bled and vomiting up curds. She writhed and groaned in her arms when she was not actually fretting at the nipple. Steph's right breast swelled up and became so red and sore that she could hardly bear it to be touched even by bathwater, then it grew so hard that she had to squeeze the spurting milk from it, yelping and crying with the pain and the waste of it; it was mixed with blood and serum from the cracked nipple so that she could not slip it into Miranda's mouth from a spoon. Her temperature rose. She grew feverish and woke from wild and anxious dreams. Her heat entered the baby, who did not seem to know if she screamed for want of Steph's milk or out of disgust for it. Steph lay beached on the soft bed, or sat for hours in cool baths to ease her breasts and the stinging from what she called her exit wound. She could only lie and hope that the burning, if it were not to stop, would just consume her altogether. At appallingly frequent intervals she would take the baby from Michael or from Jean, clamp her to the breast, and suffer. Later it seemed to her that in those weeks she cried not just in the bath or when Miranda was mauling her, but at every waking moment, even when eating, or drinking the glasses of water which were also brought to her too solicitously, and too often. Miranda's periods of sleep were snatches of exhausted respite from what seemed her personal awareness-raising campaign at the injustice of having been born; she would wake from them freshly

216

enraged and renewed for the fight. Steph herself felt cowed by her ferocity and at the same time enslaved to the task of appeasing it. Sometimes she cried for shame at her own inadequacy. Nobody understood. All Jean's brightness and Michael's doggedness were irrelevant, merely atmospheres that she sensed dimly against the background of the days and nights, as they moved about bearing trays and glasses or bringing the baby to her again. They took care of the practicalities as best they could, but there was no relief. Miranda screamed and would not feed, or she screamed and then attacked with her pitiless mouth, later sicking up most of the milk she had pulled from her weeping mother. Not once did anyone suggest calling a doctor.

When Steph's temperature eventually fell and her infected nipple shrank and dried, she ate. She had been torn during the birth and walking was still painful, but she began to come downstairs for meals, dressed in clothes that Jean had put in the wardrobe in her bedroom. Michael had brought her few old things from the flat but she discovered she could not bear to look at them. It was Jean who sized her up and chose from her own collection the 'youngest' trousers and shirts that would be comfortable, though fashionless. None of it much suited her. Steph did not care.

Michael and Jean exchanged a smile when she came into the kitchen early and slightly sheepishly for breakfast one day, taking her presence as a compliment to themselves. Perhaps kindness was becoming a habit with them all, for Steph did not spoil their pleasure by saying that it was not their company she was in need of but simply more to eat. It was the smell of bacon that had brought her down, and she thought it might be easier to get a second helping or extra toast and butter if she were nearer the food.

Jean's beautiful trays, with flowers and napkins and silver, had been getting a little short on quantity.

## *April*

Life acquired fluency. On good days, which came more frequently, there were long stretches of peace, even glimpses of grace. The weather improved and bulbs came up all over the grass and around the garden. Jean brought in tulips and daffodils by the armload and for the first time in her life was amazed by them. How had she missed them all these years, she wondered; their colours, the clinging, yearning scent, the slippery sap and the stamens, so unbearably naked and tuned to the air that it was impossible to believe they were not receiving some strain of music too fine for human ears. She discussed with the others what vases she should use and where they would like them put, and she was pleased when one day Michael said he didn't much mind, just whatever she thought, anywhere was fine as far as he was concerned. His mildly distracted indifference struck her as affectionate; she felt promoted. His taking her somewhat for granted confirmed not just their familiarity but also his security in their relationship, and perhaps there really was something endearing about her, something elusive that only a son could see. She hummed as she trimmed stems and filled vases, to show that her prettifying efforts were for fun and she was not being fussy and anxious. Most of the flowers went in the drawing room for Steph, who said that she might get around to doing a painting of them some time. On days when Miranda consented to sleep (which she did more and more, and even took on a slight listlessness when awake which they all agreed was a sign that she was nice and relaxed) Steph would settle on the drawing room sofa in the afternoon while Jean and Michael flitted about on little tasks which seemed to please them, Jean most often around the kitchen, Michael ranging more widely about the garden and outbuildings as he searched out things that needed doing.

One morning early in the month the telephone rang while they were having breakfast. A man, who introduced himself as Stan, told Jean wearily that he could send one of the boys round later in the week to mow the lawns. As long as that was convenient to herself, he added, as per the arrangement.

'Oh! Oh my goodness, arrangement? What arrangement? *This* week?...' Jean turned to see Michael and Steph sitting upright and alarmed, and realised that her voice had sounded frightened.

'Ma'am? The arrangement for the grass. I was told you'd know all about it. Shan't inconvenience *you* at all, ma'am,' Stan said, implying that the inconvenience would be his.

'The grass? Well, I ... I couldn't say. How – I mean I'm not sure...'

'The arrangement, ma'am, didn't they tell you? They said there'd be somebody here that knew the score.' When Jean said nothing he went on, even more wearily, 'Ma'am, I farm the next land. Mr Standish-Cave lets me have his hay from the fields either side of his driveway, and for that I get one of my boys to cut his grass when he's away. Suits us both, except I'm short of hands. So I'm not saying we'll be round every week but I can spare Darren Thursday, most probably.'

There was a silence. There had been something on the owners' list about the grass but Jean could not remember what. Until this moment she had not given the grass a thought beyond thinking it was getting rather long; it was silly of her, for of course it would need mowing. But not by an outsider. She said, 'Well, actually, if you're short of hands, there's no need. I'm sure we can manage. It's only a bit of grass cutting.'

'There's a lot of lawns, ma'am. You're not planning driving the mower yourself, are you?'

'Well, no, I don't suppose so. But we, I...'
She looked at Michael. 'I have someone
here. I'm sure he's perfectly willing. Then
there would no need to bother you, would
there?'

Stan brightened. 'That's made my day,
that has. I don't mind doing it, mind, but it's
hard to fit in, come summer. If your visitor's
up to it, good on him, and you thank him
from me. Only,' he said, 'I wonder, ma'am,
if you'd mind not saying ... you know, to Mr
Standish-Cave. Thing is you see, I'd still owe
him then, wouldn't I? You with me, ma'am?
I mean I *would* do it, only if you're telling me
there's no need ... and it's only a bit of hay
at the end of the day, isn't it?' He laughed.

'Quite right,' Jean said. 'You're quite right,
I shan't bother to mention it. Goodbye.'

After she had put down the telephone they
remained tense for a few moments. Then
Steph said, trustingly, 'No problem, is
there?'

'No. Oh no, it's just–' It was just *what*, Jean
wondered. That matters such as grass-
cutting, and a hundred others, were not for
her to decide because the house was not
hers and she had somehow not been able to
bring herself to spell that out? That Michael
and Steph had no right to be here because
she herself was only temporary, transient,
and belonged, in the end, nowhere? It was
all too unsavoury. Jean looked slowly from

one to the other and decided that they understood it all anyway, and more than that, they understood the need not to go into any of it.

'It's just – oh, *arrangements*,' she said. 'You know. If it's not the grass it's another thing. But I don't think we want to be disturbed, do we? I should think we can manage by ourselves.'

'Definitely,' Michael said.

Steph shifted Miranda to the other breast and nodded. 'We don't need nobody else.'

Jean reached for the coffee pot and refilled Steph's cup. 'You keep your fluids up now. Michael, I think the mower keys are in the jar on the window sill.'

Michael cut the grass that day, chugging pleasurably on the tractor mower, learning how to corner just at the right moment for the blade to snatch the edges of the grass without munching into the plants in the borders. The smell of the cut grass brought Jean and Steph outside, and Michael made a note that later he would scrub down the wooden table and chairs by the kitchen door so that they could sit there when it was warm enough.

Over the next couple of weeks he made it his business to discover the extent and nature of the grounds, the condition of window fastenings, door latches, furniture. He even inspected the roof, tutted over blocked guttering, and spent two days clearing out wet and wormy leaves, wearing huge industrial gloves. He cleaned and oiled garden tools. It was a house with more behind-the-scenes arrangements for comfort than he had ever seen; it felt like a theatre. He found out what appliances, machinery and systems made it all work and came to understand the boiler, the septic tank, the water softener, the plumbing, the Aga. Mentally he stored up projects for himself for the next day, the week after, next month. He bled the radiators, sawed up some felled logs on the edge of the woods. Thinking of Steph and Miranda, he planned that soon he would master the swimming pool.

Yet in all these things he was a little less than proprietorial, behaving more like a respectful and discreet householder-elect. It was with a sense of his filial duty, a grown-up obligation to help his capable but ageing mother with such a large house, that he took some of the weight on his younger shoulders. Jean observed him with increasing pride that she should inspire such quiet and solid devotion, and that he should express it in ways that she thought so apt and so manly.

But perversely, as the good days became more frequent, the bad days when they came grew worse. There were days on which

Jean woke with her heart pounding so hard that she felt she had been thrown out of a dream about an impending collision, just a second before the moment of impact. Saying nothing, she began to dread her trips to the freezers, whose pickings were growing thin. She felt guilty about her early lavishness with the beef, salmon and game of which the supply had once seemed endless. Her generosity and the sense of celebration she attached to feeding everybody, had been, she now saw, simple profligacy and poor husbandry. One morning she came back from the freezers with a packet of sausages to find Steph in the kitchen.

'Oh hiya,' Steph said, backing out of the fridge with a packet of bacon in one hand and a butter dish in the other. 'I'm starving. *Got* to have a bacon sarnie.' She set the things on the table and pulled a baking tray (the wrong one, Jean observed, not the one to use for bacon) from the pan drawer. Jean watched her as she peeled five slices from the bacon packet and laid them out on the tray.

'But you've already had bacon for breakfast. About two hours ago,' Jean said, in a rather ringing voice. 'That's all that's left now.'

'I *know*,' Steph said, turning flat eyes to Jean's. 'Isn't it awful. I'm that hungry. I'll get huge. Must be the feeding, I'm just really hungry the whole time.' She smiled lazily. Jean watched in silence as Steph slid the tray of bacon that was meant to be tomorrow's breakfast into the top of the Aga. She tried to expel, in a long sigh, the resentment she felt at the commandeering of her oven. Her oven, her kitchen, *her* baking tray (the wrong one for bacon).

Steph was nosing in the bread bin now. 'Bread's finished as well, once I've had this,' she said, taking out the end of a loaf. She sniffed it. 'Needs using anyway.'

'Steph–' There were no more than two or three loaves of bread left in the freezer now. Jean hesitated. She was in danger of saying something tight and mother-in-lawish. There was flour in the kitchen cupboards, after all, and dried yeast. They would be all right for a while.

'Know what I was thinking?' Steph was saying, as she went about sawing the bread into slabs. 'I was thinking Miranda's room could do with–' She glanced at Jean apologetically. 'I mean it's lovely and everything – but it's like, kind of serious? A bit old-fashioned? What with the panelling, it's kind of dark, you know?' When Jean did not answer she went on, 'I mean it's *lovely*, as panelling. But I've always wanted to do a baby's mural, you know, paint things on the wall. A cartoon character, maybe. Life size, and like in a kind of setting that you paint them in, maybe a castle or a forest or on a mountain or whatever.' She waved her hands in the air. She did not seem to notice that Jean was not filling the silence with an enthusiastic response. 'Saw an Aladdin one in a magazine once. I'd only need a bit of paint in maybe eight, ten colours, and the brushes. I could do a really nice job. I mean I'm not professional but I'm not rubbish, I could do it really nice. *Is* there any paint, sort of, around anywhere?'

She wandered along the row of wall cupboards, opening them until she found tomato ketchup, which Jean considered a ruination of good bacon. The plastic bottle wheezed two long red worms of the stuff on to the slices of bread. Then Steph set the bottle down so hard that a bead of ketchup still hanging from the top flew off and spattered on the worktop, which Jean had lately wiped clean.

'Though it doesn't matter if there isn't because it doesn't cost much, paint. I mean if I could get it myself I would, only I'm not exactly earning anything at the moment, am I? I mean soon as I was I'd pay you back and everything.'

Dear God. Paint in eight colours, brushes, nursery murals featuring cartoon characters? Jean opened her mouth but could not trust herself to speak. Was Steph blind? Could she not see that she, Jean, was standing in front of her holding six frozen sausages that were making her fingers numb, wondering if she could spin them out with rice or something and call it supper? Jean put the sausages in the fridge and sat down at the kitchen table. What could she say to Steph, round-eyed and trusting, no more aware than a child, who was calmly eating anything that wasn't nailed down and asking her to find the money for *paint?* She would have to face up to a few things.

But what Jean actually heard herself saying was, 'Oh yes, how lovely. I can just picture it. I wonder what Miranda would think – she'd be thrilled, wouldn't she?' She knew no way to point out that buying paint was out of the question, to tell her that there was hardly any money even to buy more food; to suggest that actually, they might all have to learn to manage with less to eat. Nor could she mention that even if they had the money, it would have to be Steph or Michael who would have to get up the courage to go shopping, because Jean herself could not.

But she could not point any of this out because to do so would amount to saying that life could not be lived in this way. And how could she suggest that when life together here was now, for them all, a simple necessity? Jean was protecting them all by saying nothing. Things would sort themselves out. In the meantime it was still true (in a way) that whether or not they could buy the paint Steph's mural sounded lovely. And since it would never happen, Jean would not have to say anything heavy-handed about not touching the seventeenth century oak panelling. It could not matter, then, that she said again, 'She'd be thrilled, wouldn't she?'

Steph was now laying out flabby bacon slices over the bread, murmuring that she thought they'd be a bit crisper than that after this long in the top oven but she was too hungry to wait. Jean rested her elbows on the table and tried to think seriously about what else she might give them with the sausages that evening, knowing that by luxuriating in this immediate but com-paratively small problem she was displacing temporarily the huge, intractable one. They could not live forever on the contents of the freezers, but in the meantime, until she absolutely had to decide what to do about it, there were a couple of onions and a tin of tomatoes. Jean brightened. And she would see if Michael could find anything more in the garden. He had already found some potatoes in the large walled garden that Jean had never explored properly. She would ask him to dig it over again, there were always a few more. Everything would be all right.

Steph was finishing her sandwich and Jean

was sifting through a collection of jars of dried herbs when Michael came in, bringing a blast of outdoor air with him. He strode over to the Aga, crouched over the temperature gauge and groaned. 'Thought as much,' he said, straightening up and turning to them. 'I've just been out and checked the tank and it's practically empty. We're out of oil.'

Just then there was a wail from over their heads. 'That sounds like a hungry cry,' Steph said informatively. Her desperation over her daughter's feeding had vanished, and in its place was a kind of contented weariness which was easier on them all. But she was wrong, Jean was thinking, about the cry. Miranda cried very little and was never hungry. It was not a hungry cry, but a cry of bewilderment and despair, and it grew louder. It was then that Jean burst into tears, sank her head into her hands and sobbed almost hard enough to drown Miranda's yells.

I had almost put my desire for a tree to one side, knowing that there simply was no money for such things, but when Steph announced that she was after paint for a mural, I found myself thinking that I did want my tree, and why shouldn't I have it? I wanted a magnolia to plant in the spot where I'd buried the afterbirth, but I had contented myself with just the wanting of it and had not hankered much after the getting. Old habit. But why shouldn't I get, too? I really wanted that tree. Still I didn't say so, because on that very same day we had the business of the oil to deal with. It put other things out of my mind. Things rather came to a head, and I had to face the fact that even here, life can only go on with a certain amount of involvement from the outside. The oil was a shock to me, I admit.

Michael was wonderful. He sent Steph up to feed Miranda and then sat quietly with me until I was able to speak. He got it out of me at last that I wasn't quite the owner of the house, a thing I had never really spelled out. I don't think he was altogether surprised. But we both felt such distaste for this fact that, without having to say so, I think we both resolved to get the practical difficulties of the oil and the money situation dealt with without delay, and ever afterwards to refer to such things only when absolutely necessary. I told him what the owners notes had said, which was that the tank was full and wouldn't need refilling. But Michael pointed out at once, being good at these things, that there would have been enough if I had been here alone because then I wouldn't have been heating the whole house day in day out since January. It was obvious, of course, and not the sort of thing that I would ordinarily miss.

Of course I didn't know how to get hold of more oil. Then he asked if there might be any papers kept anywhere, to do with the house, that would tell us. For example, what happened about the post? I explained that I had been picking the post up first thing before he or Steph could see it, and that I put it in the library desk, as instructed. But then I remembered the study upstairs, and I told Michael that there were lots of papers there, and filing cabinets. He took it out of my hands, told me not to worry about another thing, he would deal with all of it. He and Steph together, he added, and I could tell that he felt he needed her help. So I gave him the key to the study, and knew I could trust him to do as he said. And he did, of course. Steph too – she's a clever girl, easy to underestimate a girl like that. They took care of all the money matters. In fact, until I started coming up here to use the typewriter to write all this down, I had no call to come in here at all. They have saved me from having to worry about that kind of detail.

I suppose I never have been very skilled with money; I mean look at me and Father's clock for a start. I found myself wishing that somebody like Michael had been around all those years ago to help me with the business of Father's clock. Not Michael, of course, how could it have been? I was only sixteen myself. I mean somebody older than me at the time, who would have known what to do. Mother was useless, not that I would have consulted her in any case; we had by then set out our positions about me and university and I knew she would have done nothing whatsoever to help me get there. She did not single out that one thing to be useless over, she was useless in everything from that point on, because when Father died Mother simply declined to be of any further use. She declined even to get up much any more. I think at first it was mainly to make sure that I didn't go off to college or indeed anywhere else. Whether or not she was actually ill at that point I cannot say, but she kept to her bed. Not *their* bed, note. She couldn't abide to be in the bed she had shared with him (I did think to myself, well, she probably couldn't abide it while he was alive) so she took the room at the back of the house, beyond the kitchen, that the previous owners had built on for a lodger. There was some money from somewhere that Father left to her, and that went on putting in a bathroom alongside. No, I was on my own over the clock.

I went to Hapgood's in the High Street. It sold jewellery and clocks and also mended them, so I thought they would know about my clock, even though mine was an antique and they sold mostly new things. Mr Hapgood was about thirty, I suppose. He had a wide face, not like a grown-up's at all, but even so I thought of him as old. He had sandy hair and sharp little teeth, and very careful hands, and he was kind. He asked me how a young lady like me came to have an antique longcase clock in the first place. It was only two weeks since the funeral and the question made me cry, and Mr Hapgood took me behind the counter and into the back of the shop. It was quite dark except for the space over the two long benches that were lit by angled lamps, and very warm, with the smell of an oil stove. He sat me down on a torn leather sofa, surrounded by boxes of bits of metal and cogs and sharp-looking tools, and made me a cup of tea. And he said he would come and see the clock if I gave him my address. I was grateful.

Steph and Michael shut themselves in the study, leaving Miranda, newly fed, with Jean in the kitchen. Now alone, they assumed the authority of the young taking responsibility for the supposedly incapable old. Michael could hardly admit to enjoying the slight sense of crisis that Jean's collapse had brought, but there was something uniting in the idea that he and Steph were now being relied upon.

In the filing cabinet under *Suppliers* Michael found receipts and details of the oil supplier's quarterly debit scheme.

*'It couldn't be easier! Simply ring to order your oil whenever you need it. As a valued direct debit account customer your payments will not fluctuate, whatever the current oil price. Then once a year we will work out the credit or debit on your account and arrange with you for part or full settlement!'*

It did sound easy, but would they take an order by telephone from Michael? Could just anyone ring up and order oil for any address?

'Say you're the handyman,' Steph suggested, but frowned. It might work, and it might not. What if the oil supplier would deal only with the customer direct? There were receipts going back five years, so presumably the suppliers knew Mr Standish-Cave, even if only as a voice on the telephone. 'No, better not. No, you'll have to say you're him, Mr What's-his-name.'

'Well, that's not a problem, is it?' Michael said. 'I can do voices, remember.'

'Yes, I know that,' Steph said witheringly, 'but you've got to know what he sounds like first, haven't you?'

'He'll be posh, that's all. Won't he?'

Steph looked even more withering and said, 'That's not the only problem anyway.

What about a signature? They might want a signature, when they deliver.'

They fretted along these lines until she said firmly, 'No, it's too risky. We need to get hold of cash and just pay for the oil. What would it cost? We could sell some of the stuff here, couldn't we?'

'Jean wouldn't like that. She likes to have all her things round her. Anyway, we need the oil now, today.'

'Okay, but all this office stuff, she doesn't need that. We could flog some of the stuff in here, for a start. The smaller bits, like them.' She nodded towards the disconnected fax and answering machines and moved across to inspect them. Michael watched her dumbly, with nothing better to suggest.

'Michael,' she said, peering into the answering machine, 'there's a tape in here. Reckon it's got what's-his-name's voice on it?'

Within half an hour Michael had produced a very passable impersonation of Oliver Standish-Cave, whose voice on the tape had sounded unsurprisingly public school, yet surprisingly pleasant. It was true that there was only his *Hello. This is the office line at Walden Manor, 01249588671. Please leave a message at the tone and we will return your call as soon as we can* to go on, but with Steph's encouragement Michael quickly found both the vowels and the correct pitch

236

of assumed authority. Steph tried it too, until they both collapsed with laughter. Steph was finding that laughing hard could make her pee in her knickers, just a little, and when she told Michael this, he said, 'Oh how absolutely frightful, for Heaven's sake, woman, *contain* yourself' in Oliver Standish-Cave's voice, and they collapsed all over again.

'But even if you phone up for the oil,' Steph said, 'we'll need to sign something when it comes, won't we? There'll be stuff to sign some time.' The thought sobered them again. Further rummaging in the filing cabinet produced any number of examples of the swirling, enormous signature on receipts and photocopies of letters.

'Give it over here,' Steph said, with determination. 'I'm good at art, remember.'

And forgery, it emerged. The trick, she discovered, was not only to copy the shape of the signature but to work quickly. Oliver Standish-Cave had long ago given up signing his name in discernible letters; Steph had little trouble with the double hillocks of his first two initials and the huge, pretentious letter C that embraced them. Then all she needed to do was place, at just the right point, the long waving line of the rest of his name. It looked like a small rolling field, and one flick of the pen to dot the 'I' of Standish became a bird tossed in the sky above it. She sat and practised at the desk, covering sheet after sheet of paper, while Michael carried on through the filing cabinet. Absorbed, they looked up at each other from time to time. Quiet elation at what they were doing hung in the air.

'I think I've got it now,' Steph said eventually, holding up a page for Michael to see. He shook his head in impressed disbelief and she turned pink with pleasure. 'Go on, Michael, ring them. Say you won't be in when they deliver and they should drop the receipt through the door. Then you can just send it back signed.'

Michael's mouth had gone dry and his heart began to pound in his throat. For a moment he felt so dislocated that he was back in his old life, about to become some not-Michael or another from *Crockford's Directory of the Clergy*, his entire body flooded with fear. He wondered about asking Steph to leave the room while he spoke, just in case he couldn't do it. What if his Oliver voice gave way, or if he bottled out and slammed down the receiver? What if he burst into tears, or laughed? But he wanted her to stay and watch him, because he was doing it for her. It was for her, for all of them really, because now they were all – Steph, Jean, even Miranda, and he sensed it also in himself – growing blurred around the edges, more like one another. It was the resemblances he noticed, not the differences. They were becoming so alike in warmth, in little affectionate attentions to one other, that they were at times almost indistinguishable, fused into a trusting conglomerate of needs, all equally expressed and met. Even Miranda as she lay awake and motionless in her Moses basket reminded him of Jean's smiled thanks when he brought in a load of logs, or tightened a washer on a tap, and he felt it, too, in Steph's languid arms round his neck and it was there, too, when his mouth touched her skin. Perhaps that was what a family was, a sort of large healthy organism made up of smaller ones who did not have to survive everything on their own, or merely for their own selves' sake. Nothing important that he now did or thought or felt could occur in the absence of these other people. Steph probably knew this already, as she somehow knew other things that he did not tell her, and so while he lifted the receiver and dialled, she stayed. She seemed also to understand that the joking part was over. She walked over to the window and looked out at the garden so that he could not see her face. She turned to him just once, to whisper, 'Tell them we've run out and it's urgent.'

As he stood waiting for the telephone to be answered he watched the halo of light that blazed round her head. Her hair was smoothed and pinned up today, and she had dipped her head forwards and was resting her forehead against the glass. How was it possible that such a little thing, daylight slipping through a window and falling on the simple curve of a neck, could inspire him to vow to himself that he would never, ever leave her? Michael stared at her head. He could see the back of her earring. He had no idea what the earring itself looked like from the front (he supposed he ought to) but now he set himself to memorising every tiny detail of the back of the metal clip, the private pinch and squeeze of gold on her earlobe. It was delicious to him in a half-forbidden, unofficial way, that he should know the *back* of her ear. It was like being admitted backstage, surreptitiously and discreetly, to discover that the guile and artifice behind some spectacle was even more thrilling than what the audience saw. He understood both the earring and the ear; he could almost feel the nip as if it were his flesh the little claw was clinging to, or his own teeth tugging at the lobe. He pictured the skin beneath her hair from which her hundreds and hundreds of thousands of fair strands sprouted and grew. How many? And why? Why did they grow like that, unless to hang like long threads that she could collect up and brush and fix in this almost-falling-down way, exposing her neck, whose beauty almost stopped his heart? It was only hair and skin and skull, after all, she was made of the same things as everyone else on the planet. He imagined the fine white shell beneath the scalp, round and hard, and under the helmet of bone, the warm coiled brain that made her think and talk and move and laugh. The ordinariness, the miracle of her. The telephone was suddenly answered.

'Ah, hello?'

Steph did not turn from the window.

'Hello. Yes. We need some oil. Urgently, I'm afraid, we're out. Yes, bit of a cold snap, took us unawares! Yes, it's Standish-Cave, Walden Manor. That's right.'

Michael sailed through the negotiations; fill up the tank, about 3,000 litres please, put the receipt through the door, and then he confirmed breezily that they could manage to wait until six o'clock. He thanked the person at the other end for helping them out of a spot. Just before he rang off the woman said, 'And how's your wife doing?'

'Oh, oh. My wife? Oh, she's, er...' Michael looked up desperately at Steph, who turned just then and smiled at him, lifting and twisting a loose lock of her hair. Michael said, 'Oh, she's absolutely fine, thank you. Very well indeed.'

'Oh, glad to hear it. Do tell her I was asking.'

Men were deceivers, ever. Shakespeare, but I can't remember where from. Father would know. And only half right, because women aren't above a bit of deception either. I have come to believe that just about anyone will deceive to get what they need, if they have no other way open to them. In that strict sense there is no difference between me, Michael and Steph, and Mr Hapgood (in other, crucial respects there is all the difference in the world). And people who think oh no, they could *never* do the kind of thing we did, well, perhaps they are just people who have never had to, and who lack the imagination to see that if one day they found themselves in the same circumstances, they probably would. People who have landed in another category, who have somehow got what they needed by easier means, are no different from us. No, that's wrong, they are different. They are luckier, that is all. Not better.

What Mr Hapgood did was this. He came to see the clock the next afternoon after I'd got back from school. I thought it only polite to offer him a cup of tea in return for his the day before, and while I was making it he had a good look at the clock. He came into the kitchen while the tea was brewing

242

and leaned against the draining board. He would have to go and consult somebody, an 'associate in the trade' he said, but it was without doubt a fine clock. I poured out a third cup of tea and took it to Mother who was in bed, and when I came back he asked all about her, and I found myself crying again. He said he understood perfectly because his mother was much the same, not at all well. He said we should make ourselves comfy in the sitting room because life could be very difficult and what we both needed was a little cuddle. I think he might actually have been right about that.

The next day Michael and Steph returned to the study, bringing with them the pile of unopened post that had been accruing in the library desk. They opened the bank statements, which showed that whatever the Standish-Caves were living on while they were away, it was not being drawn from the Household No 1 account. Twelve hundred pounds a month were going in, and the account was in credit for a little over six thousand. Outgoings amounted to rather less. There were direct debits for electricity, water, telephone and oil, and to the local authority for council tax. Jean Wade's monthly salary was the only other regular payment. They guessed that the statements for other accounts, that the owners must be using, were being sent by the bank directly to them.

They began to feel clever. Steph found reams of specially printed Walden Manor stationery. In the filing cabinet they found previous letters from Oliver Standish-Cave to his bank so that they could copy the style exactly. Michael fed a sheet into the type-writer and together they began to compose their letter. Steph lost all sense of propor-tion and wanted to clean out the account.

'But it's a *fortune,* six thousand quid,' she said. 'Once we transfer all that lot into Jean's account we'll be laughing, won't we?'

'And then what? Suppose the bank thinks it's a bit funny and investigates? We got to do something quiet, something that'll just slide past them without them noticing. Just a little rise that nobody'll notice, so it can go on and on, see? Look, Jean gets four hundred a month. We just make it six, it'll make a big difference.'

The clatter of the typewriter keys sounded cheeky and illegal, and it was hard not to laugh. The extra would make a difference, but not all the difference. And Jean's next payment was not due for three weeks in any case, Michael thought, as he watched Steph sign the letter. She was laughing a little too triumphantly, not really taking in that the problem had been eased, not solved. They would have to do something more.

Michael sifted again through the post. Among the other unopened letters were credit card statements which proved the existence of a credit card that had not been used since shortly before Christmas. But the statements did not give the card's expiry date, and that was essential, Steph declared, before they could order things by telephone. She had stopped laughing.

'If only we had the card,' Michael said.

'Or a chequebook,' Steph said, looking round as if one might be lying to hand somewhere. Then they heard Jean's soft footsteps downstairs, crossing the hall from the drawing room to the kitchen. She would be putting the kettle on, and soon would come upstairs to fetch the sleeping Miranda. Then she would call them both down to tea, for which she might have made scones or a cake, although there had been less of those lately. It might be just toast, then. Since her outburst the day before she seemed again to move in her own unhurried way, perhaps even a little more slowly, Steph had remarked last night. Getting on, she and Michael had agreed.

He would not, could not fail Jean over the money. Because Michael thought that her slowing down was not entirely to do with ageing; the tread of her feet seemed to have something to do with a simple absence of strain. Perhaps Jean had ceased to strive. It was strange, he thought, remembering his desperation over paying his fines, that while there was now more point to everything, life for all three of them had grown less effortful. It was not that the struggle to find enough to live on had lessened, but rather that there was no longer any need to outrun a lurking sense of futility about everything. The question *is it worth it?* did not arise any more. There was peace in Jean's footsteps, the work of her hands, her look of concentration as she peered at recipe books. She was sedate, but still busy most of the time. Her self-appointed duties in the house undoubtedly made demands upon her energy; towards seven o'clock she would sink into the big chair in the kitchen, tired, and Michael would give her the glass of sherry which she always said was just what she needed. But it seemed to Michael that her energy was freely and willingly expended. She had no need to hoard any, to hold a little in reserve against the day when it would be required in the struggle just to stay cheerful. He recognised in her a picture of himself in his freezing flat and remembered the tight battles fought between himself and the persistent nag in his head, telling him that nothing was ever going to get any better. It was an almost forgotten picture, now abandoned in the old attic of his life before Steph had come, but looking over at Steph now he could tell, now he thought about it, that the same voices had nagged in her head too. They must none of them ever again have to squander energy trying to hold off the conviction that nothing they did made any difference.

Steph and Michael resumed their search through the desk drawers and filing cabinets. Jean's footsteps were crossing the hall again, and then they stopped. They listened to the silence. Jean must have paused in the hall, perhaps to consider the tall vase of daffodils on the carved chest opposite the stairs. She might have been drawing out the stems that were yellowing now and proffered flowers too crumpled and papery to deserve their places any longer, adjusting the fresher ones to fill the gaps they left. She would be humming to herself. Now came the faint creak and the sound of her climbing the stairs, another pause while she rested for a moment at the top. She might turn left to go to her room to change her shoes (sometimes she put on her slippers before tea) or, as they could hear her doing now, she might turn right along the broad landing. She did not, nor did they expect it, come into the study, but walked past the closed door towards the nursery. Michael and Steph smiled at each other. In a moment they would hear her talking softly to Miranda as she changed her, and then she would call them on her way past and they would all go down to tea. But the sound they next heard and which froze them where they stood was a rising, disbelieving scream.

It might have helped to be drunk. In a way I felt as if I was, in the sense that I still have no clear memory of the days following that one when I came upon Miranda dead. Glimpses, that's all I have, and although I can't be sure how many days it took, I know that Steph kept Miranda by her for too long, and that by the time Michael could persuade her to give her up so that we could bury her, some terrible things were happening.

I want it understood that the child was not neglected, whatever she might have died of. I hope that's clear. Don't think it hasn't worried me, not getting a doctor. There must have been something wrong with her, perhaps her heart. I think now of the slight frown she sometimes wore when she was lying awake quietly; it seems to me now that she might have been listening to her little heart. I think it must have been her heart. It is hard to accept, but if that was the case then perhaps it was better to let her slip peacefully away, undisturbed by strangers. In the end, what do doctors know?

I prepared her with my own hands. There

is no pain like it, the washing and dressing of the dead, because it is unbearable that one should be doing such things to a body that is so dear yet so changed, and equally unbearable that these necessities should be left undone or trusted to other hands. I used a strongly scented soap which I thought might do the trick at least for a while, but her skin began to wrinkle and slough, gentle though I was, and I feared that I was hurting her. I whispered that I was sorry, isn't that silly? People sometimes say that dead people don't look dead, they look as if they are sleeping. Miranda did not look asleep. Miranda was dead in my arms, gone. How else could I have contemplated placing her in the ground? I dusted her with talcum powder until I realised that it made me think of quicklime. I wrapped her in two white silk handkerchiefs. They covered her, tiny thing she was. She had hardly grown at all. I fancied that she looked even smaller than she had on the day she was born, though sometimes that happens when people die, they look emptied of something. I remember thinking that the silk would be soft against her skin, another silly thought, but it's the kind of thing that comes to you in those circumstances.

Next I wrapped her white shawl round her tightly so that her mother would not feel the stick limbs. I had meant to dress her properly, in bonnet and bootees and everything, but I could not do it, not for the want of caring. Her hands and feet were too far gone. Then I slipped her into a pillowcase. Then I had a good idea; there were lots of lavender-filled pillows in the bedrooms, so I gathered them all up, ripped them open and poured all the dried lavender flowers in the pillowcase with her so that she would be buried with sweet flowers surrounding her. So that we might be distracted a little by the lavender scent and not have to notice the state she had got into. Then I bound her round and round with white ribbon, covering her completely.

Because by now Michael had managed to get through to Steph and almost bring her out of a kind of blindness that the death had plunged her into, and I did not want her to see (I do not think she really had seen it yet) the colour that her baby's face had turned to.

So it wasn't a tree, after all, that the space in the garden had been waiting for. We put Miranda there, in the same spot where her afterbirth lay buried. I hardly remember what was said. Michael had found volumes of poetry in the library, and he seemed to know what to say. I'm sure it was all beautiful, I remember parts of it, but of course it was not enough. A funeral is supposed to explain the whole thing, is it not? But not even my sweet Michael could find an acceptable way to say that this little one was dead and that she should be left in the dirty cold ground while we went back into the warm house without her. Steph could not be persuaded to come with us. So Michael buttoned her into her coat, and let her be. She stayed out until well after dark.

There followed several days when we could neither be together, nor bear not to know one another's precise whereabouts. We could not rest in one spot, or seek out places of refuge. I roamed somewhat, trying to go about the jobs that needed doing, as did Michael, and even Steph. But we tired so easily, and would go to lie down and not manage to settle, and then we would come across one another wandering through the house again, or going about the garden. We could neither talk about Miranda, nor silence the clamour of her in our heads. I am speaking for myself, of course, and in truth there were times when I scarcely noticed what the other two were doing – but from what I did manage to take in, it was much the same for us all.

If there were any comfort to be had, it was in the knowledge that at least our child had not been taken away. She was dead, but nobody had been allowed to interfere. So we were all still together, all of us, including Miranda. Although she was dead and buried and gone from us, at least she lay not far away, and at home.

Steph's days wasted one into the other, a cruel mirror of the time just after Miranda's birth. Daylight lapped somewhere at the sides of the things she noticed, while Michael pushed and pulled her through the everyday and surely pointless practicalities of getting dressed, eating, bathing. In between times her brain swam, her empty arms stiffened and ached, her legs felt heavy and too weak to carry her far. She could not say whether it was through her body or her mind that she hurt more. It was as if loss jellified her. She felt boneless, a floating, absorbent thing that existed only to soak up pain. Then when her breasts began to ache with Miranda's milk, she knew she had become some kind of efficiently functioning system for suffering. Night and day she processed raw material in the form of waves of perfect grief, which lapped and receded in her body, pricking, breaking, stabbing. Her breasts lifted, hardened and filled through countless incoming and ebbing tides of milk.

In the daytime she took long baths, as if she hoped to soak away her pain. She changed her clothes three and four times a day, swapping one anonymous, spotless shirt for another, yet her unhappiness clung;

it lay beneath her pink skin and gleaming hair and beyond the reach of soap and water, or got itself caught up and buttoned in tight under her immaculate clothes. She walked about, ignoring the weight of her legs until she failed to notice the heaviness. Michael gave her little jobs to do, putting away a garden rake or carrying kindling, taking clothes to and from their bedroom to the laundry room; sometimes she would accomplish these tasks and sometimes stop them halfway through, forgetting. One day on the windowsill halfway down the stairs she came across two shirts, some socks and an empty tumbler that she had simply wandered away from, having paused at the window earlier on her way down. She spent a lot of time outside neither far from Michael nor yet with him, while he did what he could in the vegetable garden, but she was insensible to the sunshine which at times punched its way out through clouds and raised the smell of warm, dug soil into the air. She paced the paths and yards, the pool pavilion and outbuildings. She would stop and look at things for no apparent reason, and it was hard to know if she saw anything.

One day as she stood by the covered swimming pool, Jean, trudging back from the walled garden with a few sticks of rhubarb, stopped and watched her contemplating the turquoise rectangle. Had the pool been uncovered, would she try to drown herself, or was she imagining a summer day when Miranda might have been making her first splashes in the water? Steph roused herself, walked on towards the gate in the fence at the edge of the lawn, and stepped through it into the paddock. Jean turned towards the house, frowning at the bundle in her hand. Supper was going to have to be the last of the potatoes and an onion, and more rhubarb. It hardly seemed to matter; the walk to the garden and back had exhausted her so completely that she thought she might go back to bed anyway. Whilst thinking this Jean did not notice that Steph had already crossed the paddock and was now walking quite fast, making her way down the drive towards the road.

As she went further from the house, Steph wished she could stop thinking. It would have been a relief to be free of thought, free of the thousands of quarrelling and contradictory memories of the past few months: Jean's house and how she had arrived that night, the birth of Miranda and before that, Michael and the flat, then Miranda, the awful first weeks. The miracle of waking up slowly, over several days, to the idea that her daughter would not be taken away, that she now lived in this amazing place with her, and with Michael and

Michael's mother. Even as she had been lulled by her new and gentle circumstances, there had still been space in her mind for Jace and at an unreal and distant point there had been Stacey, college, her pictures, her Nan. But as these thoughts tramped softly through her memory, now she wondered if, even as she had been learning to feel safe from that old life, she had been aware of a shade of disbelief. For how could she appear first in one life and then leave it for another, like the same small detail in two pictures – a jug, a scrap of lace, a tulip – that an artist might have arranged and painted twice on different canvases, for some sentimental reason or just through laziness or accident? In that sense she was, in a manner of speaking, simply the jug or flower or trinket that had come to someone's hand. Perhaps it was her fault. Perhaps this happened to her because she continually consented to be picked up and placed in surroundings which might turn out to please or displease her, but over which she had no power in either case. She could even, as she had this time, grow convinced of her happiness, but her inability to change anything did not alter. She had been determined that Miranda should not be taken away, and had been shown her powerlessness over that.

As she walked, this idea too got left behind, along with other thoughts of the past. They took their leave lightly, like tentative visitors who had come just to remind her that once they might have been important but would not be staying. She walked on in some expectation that now something else would have to happen to her. New things would have to come along; the things, whatever they were, that were to be important next, the things she was to be placed among, in whose canvas she was to occupy a space. She opened her mind, inviting new thoughts to come and fill it. She walked, but none came.

She was wearing trousers and boots and began to notice that both were too big, while the white shirt (whose, for God's sake?) was a little tight over her chest. Her clothes had an indoor, bready smell, or was that the smell of her milk? And the clothes felt no more hers than any of the sensations they created, the trouser stitching chafing a little on her hipbones, the pressing of the shirt over her breasts, but suddenly nor did they, or she, seem to belong to anything she could remember of the past three months. She liked the feeling of neutrality. She carried on walking.

It may have been just the sound of passing traffic as she got nearer, but at some point it seemed to Steph that the long drive had, invisibly, begun to belong more to the road that ran past it than to Walden Manor, with its stone arms outstretched more than half a mile behind. Nothing as simple as curiosity turned her in the direction of the village, but when she took the turning that led to it after another twenty minutes' walk along the edge of the noisy road, she found herself slowing down to look at it properly.

Most of the houses were old and the stone built ones along the curving main street were joined together. Many of them were double-fronted and had steps leading up to their doors. Some had window boxes, others had Bed & Breakfast signs in their windows. Trees were planted at intervals along the pavement. Most of the traffic ripped past along the top road that Steph had turned off, leaving the village quiet. In the middle, the street opened out round a small triangle of grass surrounded by railings and beds of flowering plants, where a stone monument stood, its steps and inscription worn away. On one side of the triangle was an empty bus shelter, across the road on another side was a peeling semi-detached house with a sign saying 'Vicarage'. The church sat behind, down a road that led off at the side. Next to the vicarage, well set back, stood a grander, older house, the only one with a drive and a front garden full of trees. The slate sign on the wall read 'The Old Rectory'. Next to that stood two empty cottages, a shut-up garage, a modern, bright-green painted shop with orange star-shaped notices on its wide flat windows, a litter bin and a sign announcing that lottery tickets were On Sale Here. It was all very pretty, of course, Steph could see that, but empty and pointless unless you lived there. Perhaps even if you did, she thought, as a familiar feeling stirred in her. She wanted chocolate, suddenly, or crisps. Anything, and she had no money.

At the ting of the bell, Steph stepped into the shop and was surrounded by the smells of cheese, wrapped cake, newspapers and ageing vegetables. There was silence but for the dismal buzzing of strip lighting and refrigerators, and the almost audible expectation that she should buy something. From behind the counter a man with big yellow hands was stabbing at buttons on a calculator that sat on an open ledger. He nodded at her over his glasses without smiling. Steph raised one corner of her mouth and turned her back, browsing a rack of biscuits, fly sprays and birthday cards. The man looked down again, and Steph sidled along past shampoo and tins of soup. She couldn't take crisps without making a noise, the biscuit packets were too big, and the sweets were on display right under the man's nose. There was a tall, freestanding row of shelves that divided the shop in two, but there was also a round mirror high on one wall that gave the man a view of whoever was behind it. The stuff on the shelves round the back was only light bulbs, soap powder and tin foil, anyway. Unless somebody else came and distracted him, she had no chance. She turned and looked through the door on to the triangle of green grass, willing someone to come in with a long shopping list.

'You looking for a tent or a lawnmower, you're in luck,' the man said, distantly. 'Four new ones in yesterday.' Steph turned and smiled cautiously, wondering what he meant.

'Small ads, four new ones. Good price, the tent. Only got used once, bloke said. Selling it after one go, the wife didn't like camping, apparently. He's giving it away at that price, just wants rid of it.' The man was motioning now towards the door, and Steph saw that he was pointing at a cluster of handwritten postcards pasted over the top half of it. She turned back and looked at them, pretending to be interested. She couldn't have cared less about a tent or a lawnmower, but if she spent a minute or two reading the ads, something might happen. His phone might ring. He might even go through to the back or something.

'Tent's a fantastic price. He was going to put the card in for a fortnight, I said don't. It'll go within the week at that price, I said, take just the one to start with. At that price it'll go in one. Tempted myself, if I'm honest.'

Steph smiled again and turned back. Clipped to the postcard was a blurry photograph of the quite resistible tent. Below it on another card Steph read:

WANTED: Childminder, hrs tbc, for Charlie, four months. Lively baby. Non-smoker. Kind personality req'd. Start IMMEDIATELY. Apply Bell Cottage Green Lane. Or tel (after 6 pm: 583622).

The man looked up again at the ting of the bell and noted that the pale young woman had left without buying anything. He sighed and returned to his ledger. She hadn't looked the type to buy his tent, and he was beginning to lose hope that he'd ever shift it.

Bell Cottage was a small, double-fronted house down a narrower street that ran parallel to the main one where the shop stood. Steph found it by wandering. The signs on most of the lanes leading off the main street gave also the names of the streets they led to, and there seemed to be no more than a dozen or so at most in the old part of the village. The door was opened by a dark-haired woman in bare feet, who stared at her without speaking. Steph thought she looked too old to be the mother of a baby.

'Hello ... I was wondering if–'

'I'm just about to go out.'

'Oh. Oh, but I was just wondering,' Steph said, sure now that she had got the wrong house, 'if this is where the job is. The childminding?'

The woman hesitated for a moment without smiling. 'Oh. Well, I have to go out when he wakes up. But you might as well come in,' she said, turning back into the house and evidently expecting Steph to follow.

The narrow hallway had been painted some dull, pale colour that had been streaked and scraped black on both sides. The smell reminded Steph of something earthy, cold and none too clean, like mud or certain kinds of cheese. A long, dark bulge of hung-up coats and jackets padded most of one wall. Underneath lay a heap of boots and shoes, umbrellas, a crash helmet, walking sticks, a riding crop and one ice-skate. On the floor next to a low stool that was covered with newspapers sat a telephone directory, on which several milk bottles and a camera had been placed. Next to that stood a folded child's pushchair whose detached plastic rain canopy leaned against the wall. On the floor nearby was the telephone, a bowl with a spoon and the brownish dregs of breakfast cereal in it, two or three listing carrier bags and an open briefcase with papers fanning out of it.

Steph followed the woman down the

passage, past the staircase and into the kitchen at the back. She said, not asking, 'Coffee', pulled a kettle clear from a clutter of things on a worktop, filled it and switched it on. Steph wondered where she was supposed to put herself, and decided to stand still. There was nowhere not filled with other things. The worktops and table were laden with jars, utensils, little bottles, a tub of baby wipes and a pacifier, two radios, a toaster, a blender, the kettle, a feeding bottle steriliser, as well as assorted bowls which contained something or nothing: Steph took in papery-looking garlic, pens, bananas, cassette tapes, some pursed-up lemons, rubber bands, an assortment of hair ties, keys, scraps of paper, cut-out coupons, dried up garden bulbs. Only a fraction of space was clear for anything that might be expected to happen in a kitchen, such as cooking or eating. A notice board held curling fragments of cards, lists, takeaway menus, envelopes and postcards of beaches. On a blackboard alongside it were chalked the words *Bags Coff Spread Milt tabs. O. Chips bleach.* The cooker top was spattered with burnt spills which all seemed to be dark orange, the grill above was covered with a rag of tin foil that smelled acrid and rubbery. Two of the wall cupboards had no doors. Any patches of floor that were not covered by cat bowls, litter tray, sheets of spread newspaper and squashed crumbs were more homogenously dirty. The windowsill behind the sink held a few jars of brown water with slimy forgotten herbs or attempts at cuttings of something or other, more milk bottles and a heap of pacifiers on a saucer.

'I'm Sally,' the woman said. 'Charlie's next door asleep, I'll show you him in a minute but I'll go mad if he wakes up again. He's hell to put down.' She hesitated. 'I don't suppose I should say that, I might put you off. I mean, he's coming on. The thing is, he's not such a good feeder. I've got to go back to work and he's still getting used to the bottle.'

'Oh,' Steph said.

Sally turned, and as she poured water from the kettle, which had not yet boiled, into the mugs, she said breezily, 'Still, at least I've got my tits back. Not that they're much use to me now.'

Steph made a small noise that was half surprise, half laugh. That was the trouble with educated people. At some point in their lives they simply managed, somehow, to go beyond embarrassment. Or perhaps they were born incapable of it. Whichever it was they made you take on double the amount because you had your own and theirs on top. They told you things that you could never reply to. What was she meant to say?

'So.' Sally was putting milk into two mugs of instant coffee, another thing she hadn't asked Steph about, and shifting stuff – a baby's jacket, a purse, some keys and half a croissant – off a chair so that Steph could sit down. She didn't offer sugar, either, but she was watching Steph carefully. Steph, knowing she was being sized up, put on a bright face. 'Charlie's a lovely name,' she said. 'They're coming back, aren't they, the traditional names.'

Sally ignored her, but went on watching. 'I did have somebody all lined up weeks ago but she rang to say she's not coming now, less than a week before she's meant to start. Got a better offer, I suppose. So I'm stuck. I've got to go back fulltime next week.' She leaned against the worktop and sipped her coffee. 'If I don't get somebody local I'll have to take this girl an agency's offering me and they charge a fortune. What's your name anyway? You're local, are you?' She smiled in such a way that Steph could tell she had had to remind herself that smiling was a thing she was meant to do.

'Yes, I'm staying here. I mean, yes. I do live here now. I'm Stephanie. Well, Steph, really. I'm twenty-three and I've had ... a lot of experience with children.'

'Yes, but what about babies. He's only four months. Have you done babies?'

'Oh, yes,' Steph said, 'I had sole charge of

a newborn.' She took a mouthful of coffee while she tried to assemble the words for the story she had worked out. 'I took care of my sister's baby. She couldn't. She was depressed after it, the birth. You know, post-natal, she got it really bad? So I did everything, more or less, the lot, all the looking after. She couldn't do a thing, hardly.' Then, in case the woman might think she was complaining, 'I really enjoyed it, I had a knack, everybody said. My sister's husband, he was away at the time as well, so I had sole charge, I held the fort. Then they moved away.' She paused. 'To America. Her husband was American.'

That should put the question of references on ice for a bit. She began to feel slightly inspired.

'And so now I'm staying here with ... with my aunt, I live with my aunt.'

She had rehearsed on the walk to Sally's house the phrase 'my boyfriend and my boyfriend's mother', and decided that it sounded too flaky and impermanent and might make her sound like a hanger-on. And she wasn't wearing a ring; suppose this woman advertising for the childminder was a religious nut or something, who disapproved of people living together? A niece helping her aunt sounded solid and respectable.

'I'm staying with her and helping her with

the house, she hasn't been too well. At Walden Manor.' Risky to give the name, perhaps, but she had guessed, correctly, precisely the effect it would have.

Sally raised her eyebrows and made an 'oooh' shape with her mouth. 'Walden Manor? *Oh.* I know, yes, I think I know where it is. Off the Bath road, that no through road marked private? I've never seen the house.'

'You can't see it from the road. It's more than half a mile up the drive.'

Sally sighed. 'There are lots of beautiful places round here, actually. But I didn't know Walden was owned by a... Actually,' she looked mournfully round the kitchen, 'I don't really know many people. I haven't been here that long, we only moved here after I got pregnant. I thought it'd be all playgroups and community stuff and all that. But everybody under seventy's at work all day, in Bath or Chippenham.'

Steph made a sympathetic noise. 'You've got a nice house, though,' she lied bravely.

'Oh yeah, thanks, well, it is nice, or it could be. Haven't done much to it, been too tired.' She waved with the hand holding the mug. 'As you can see.'

Steph said, bracingly, 'Anyway she's much better now, you know, my aunt, but she likes having me there so I'm staying on, but now there's less for me to do I thought it'd be

266

nice to find something.' She smiled competently.

'Your, er ... aunt, I mean, it's not, is she... You don't seem ... has she lived there long, I mean? Has it always been in the family, the house?'

Steph beamed with sudden understanding and said, with a slight lowering of her voice, 'In the family? Oh no. Not at all. Look, if I tell you, will you promise not to say, not to anybody? Not to anybody at all, *ever?*'

Sally's eyebrows shot up with interest. 'Sure. Of course.'

'Because she doesn't want all sorts knocking on the door, you know?' Steph paused. 'Lottery win,' she said. 'Five week roll-over. Only she wants it kept quiet, because she's not that sort of person, she's just ordinary. She's not, you know, *flashy.* I mean she's always had this thing about a house in the country, so straight off she went and bought this big place and well, I think it's a bit too much for her, but I can't say. I mean she can do what she likes at the end of the day.'

Sally nodded respectfully. 'I promise I won't say a word. I didn't even know the house was up for sale.'

'Oh. Oh no, well, it wasn't *advertised.*'

'No, they aren't always, the big places, it's all word of mouth.' She drank some of her coffee. 'We don't get much of the big stuff.

Though we get farms from time to time, and then of course I don't get a look in. Farmers have to deal with a *man*, apparently, can't cope with a woman handling things. The firm goes along with it, doesn't matter what I say. The senior partner says,' she twisted the words sarcastically, '"in this outfit political correctness comes second to complete client confidence."'

Steph cleared her throat. She was not sure she had understood a single word. 'Only with my aunt – you won't spread it around, will you, because she doesn't want the publicity, she's a very private person. Not unfriendly or anything, but she likes to get to know people at her own pace, what with everything. You can understand. So you won't tell anyone, will you? I mean I'm only telling you so you know the score. About me, for the job I mean.'

'No, no, of course I won't say anything,' Sally said, in a way that made Steph wonder if she were interested enough even to remember the story, let alone divulge it. But she roused herself from her thoughts about the senior partner to ask, 'But that is a point. You – I mean, what do you want a child-minding job for? I mean you can't need the money, can you?'

Steph looked her in the eye. 'My aunt, she's dead generous, she's doing a lot for me, but I've told her no way am I living off her for everything. So Okay, no, in a way I don't really need it, but I like earning a bit of my own money, you know what I mean?'

Sally had begun to peel off a splitting fingernail with her teeth, but Steph thought she might still be listening. 'Like if I earn a bit I can surprise her, you know? Make a little contribution. Get her a bunch of flowers now and then, something like that. It's the independence.'

'Independence,' Sally said distantly, dropping her fingernail on the floor. She snorted. She looked directly at Steph. '*I'm* independent. Not all it's cracked up to be, let me tell you.'

She was doing it again. What was Steph supposed to say to a remark like that? She gave what she hoped was an interested murmur and hoped Sally was not taking them completely off the point.

'I'm a solicitor,' Sally said, wanly.

'Oh, right. So, what I mean is, I don't want you thinking I'd be unreliable, just 'cause I'm not like, living on the money.'

'Unreliable?' Sally gave another uneasy smile. 'Oh, no, I wasn't thinking that. No, I can spot unreliable. I know all about unreliable. I might not even be going back full-time if Charlie's father wasn't *world class* unreliable.' She turned to tip the last of her coffee down the sink. 'He was training to qualify too. Was. As a solicitor, I mean.'

Steph knew that Sally was waiting for her to ask more.

'So ... do you mean ... he isn't any more?'

Sally sighed so dramatically that Steph felt in some way responsible for whatever might be coming next. 'Oh, no, *no*,' she said with slow sarcasm, 'Oh no, he decided being a solicitor wasn't enough for *him*.' She sighed again. 'He's tried lots of things. He was going to be a priest then he decided no, that would just be trying to live up to his dad. So he gave that up, tried other things, travelled a lot. Oh, he wants to save the world, basically. Law was just the latest thing, the thing he thought he should be doing while he went through his husband and father phase. But he's given up on that, too, by the look of it.'

'You mean he's not here?'

'Nope. No, he's gone to Nepal. I don't mean he walked out, oh no, my dear husband never does anything he could be *blamed* for. He only does things he feels he *ought* to do, never admits it's what he *wants*. So then he can't be criticised, can he, because he's only doing what his conscience tells him is *right*.'

'Oh.'

'Don't get talked into having kids, Stephanie, that's what I did.'

'Oh. Oh well. No, I won't.'

'He was the desperate one. Gets me to

270

agree, gets me pregnant, and just when I thought this time he means it, he's growing up *finally*, he gets another fit of conscience about privilege, east and west, all that. So practically the minute Charlie's born he gives up law and wants us all to go off and live in Nepal and work for some leprosy charity. I said no.'

'But he went?'

'Yep. Now he's out there working for this bloody charity, principles all intact and all for bloody nothing of course, so I've got no option. And oh, not only is he not providing a penny but *I'm* the one holding us back. He's still waiting for us to join him, you see, thinks I'll give in and go. And know what? I won't. The main thing about it is, and you should listen to this Stephanie because it's amazing how often this happens, the things is he thinks because I've got the baby I shouldn't mind where I go or what I do. Because I'm a mother now, aren't I. He thinks I'm selfish, staying in a rich country and being a lawyer when I could be making a *contribution*. I'm perpetuating global inequality, apparently, going back to conveyancing and wills in Chippenham. Me. *Me*, selfish.'

Sally's voice as she spoke had been getting louder to drown out badtempered wailing from another room. Practically shouting now, she said, 'Well, global *bollocks*. But it's amazing the number of other people that think I should have gone. His dad, for instance, he comes out with all the 'for better for worse' stuff. Oh shit, he's awake. Well, you might as well meet him.'

Charlie squirmed in a nest of covers on the padded floor of a playpen in the dining room. A carrycot stood on the table in the middle of the room. Sally pulled him out kicking. 'He settles better in the playpen,' she said wearily. 'Dunno why. Doesn't like the cot.'

Steph looked round. A smell of salt and pepper and old meat still rose from the dark green carpet, but in all other respects Charlie had taken over. Both the mantelpiece and a high, polished sideboard that was too large for the room were littered with baby paraphernalia. A baby changing mat, nappies and a heap of unironed baby clothes filled one end of the table. Dozens of baby books and plastic toys covered the sideboard and the four upright chairs, and a bank of soft toy animals formed a colony against the wall on one side of the cold, green-tiled fireplace. Steph caught sight of a teddy identical to one that had been in Miranda's nursery, and felt something kick suddenly in her throat. She opened her mouth, but did not speak and managed not to gasp, and then the moment had gone, supplanted by a sense of safety. Because absolutely nothing else in this chaotic house – not Charlie's bewildering mother with her aloof but embarrassing way of telling her too much, certainly not the streaked and bawling face of Charlie himself – sounded even the thinnest chord of memory, painful or otherwise. Steph simply did not recognise it, this bulging, crammed and messy place that so many things had been spilled into, as if the house were a repository for the thoughts, ideas, plans, all the *stuff* in Sally's head. It was a place where myriad fragments and layers that made up her life had substantiated somehow into wave after wave of bits of beached rubbish, which Sally then used, abandoned, dropped, broke, lost or cherished, without explanation, apology or, it seemed, particular concern. Charlie was perhaps just another item in her collection. The very idea that one person's life could so casually produce such rich and overwhelming disorder was unknown to Steph.

Sally had Charlie on the changing mat and had wrestled him out of his wet nappy. The sight of him insulated Steph further from any link with Miranda. Charlie had a standard pouting, apelike baby face, quite unlike Miranda's ladylike and slightly worried one. And he never stopped moving. His flailing limbs creased into their own peculiar folds and bends like a badly stuffed

273

toy, while Miranda had now and then waved her spindly arms and legs without conviction, and they had been what Jean called finely made. Steph darted forward and handed Sally a baby wipe from the carton, and deftly took the sodden clump from Sally. 'Bin under the sink,' Sally said flatly. When Steph came back Sally was walking round the room jiggling the angry bundle on one shoulder. For the first time since she had arrived Steph saw on Sally's face not only impatience and distaste, but complete exhaustion.

'I'm supposed to be going in for a meeting this afternoon. They keep doing it, I'm not due back till next week but oh, will I pop in to discuss this or that. I said okay but I'd have to bring him with me and they said oh really, well with a bit of luck he'll be asleep.' She shifted him on to the other shoulder and blew gently in his ear, to no effect. 'He probably would go back to sleep if I gave him his bottle now but he fights it and takes ages over it, so if I do that I'll be incredibly late and *that* won't go down very well.'

'Tell you what, you go,' Steph said, 'why don't you go to your meeting, and leave him with me? I'll see to the bottle and everything. Just to help you out.'

'What? Oh, no, I don't think, I mean I'd like you to take the job, I mean for a trial period, but you've only just... I mean you, we – we don't really know each other, do we?'

Steph smiled and nodded understandingly. 'Oh, you're quite right. I *know*, you haven't got my references or anything – but look, I'd love to do the job, and you could do with a hand now, couldn't you? Look, he's got a wet patch on his bum, he needs a dry suit. Shall I take him a minute while you get a clean one, only I don't know where you keep them.' She held up her arms and Sally, a little taken aback, allowed Charlie to be taken from her. She rummaged in the pile of clothes while Steph rocked Charlie from side to side. In a lower voice, she said, 'Tell you what, Sally, suppose I come with you, then I could look after him in the car or take him for a walk or something while you're at the meeting. If you're not sure about leaving him here with me. I quite understand.' Charlie's yells seemed to subside as she spoke. 'Don't I, Charlie?' she said softly in his ear. 'You don't want to be left all alone with a stranger, do you? Do you, little Charlie?' Charlie grew quiet. Steph smiled beatifically. 'Hello, poppet. I'm Steph, all right? *Aren't* you a lovely little man, *aren't* you a good baby?' she told him softly, rocking him with gentle confidence.

Sally straightened up and looked hard at Steph for several moments. 'I suppose you have *got* references, haven't you? Good ones?'

'Oh yes, only not with me. I was just in the shop, you see. I was just out for a walk. I wasn't expecting to see the perfect job there on a card in the window. But I just came straight along 'cause I didn't want to miss the chance. I was scared I'd be too late and somebody else would get it.'

Sally said, 'And how many years' experience did you say you'd got?'

'Oh, it was ten months with my sister's,' Steph said, 'and loads of other little jobs child-minding, babysitting and that. Babies and up to age five. But you need to see it all in writing, that's okay. I understand. If you don't feel comfortable.'

Sally looked at her watch and studied Steph's face again. 'No,' she said, 'no, I've decided. I can always tell, I'm good at reading people. And if you're going to do the job I'll have to leave him anyway, won't I? I can tell I can trust you, Steph. I can feel it. And it's very, very good of you to offer.'

Steph smiled up at Sally. 'He's a lovely baby,' she breathed. 'Now are you sure? Because I mean I could come with you, in the car.'

But the whole idea was suddenly cumbersome and silly. Sally shook her head. 'No – decision's made. As long as you're sure...'

'Go on, you go. We'll be fine. I'll give him his bottle.'

For the first time Sally gave a genuine

smile. 'Really? Oh God, you wouldn't, would you? It's all made up, just needs microwaving. I'll be back in about an hour and a half,' she said, with sudden energy, 'if that's not too late for you? I mean, you are taking the job? I didn't expect ... oh, *brilliant!*'

'You go,' Steph said serenely, 'And you and I, young man, we're going to get on just fine, aren't we, while Mummy's at her meeting?'

'He'll fight it. He hates the bottle, I'm warning you, you have to insist. It's in the fridge. Twelve seconds on six,' Sally said, on her way through the door. 'And you mustn't ... do you know how a...'

'And leave it for about another minute and give it a good shake, and test it on the back of my hand. I know,' Steph said, more to Charlie than to Sally. 'Don't I, Charlie? I know.'

When the front door had closed behind Sally, Steph waited for a moment with the feeding bottle in her hand, then unscrewed the top and tipped the plastic-smelling formula milk down the sink. In the sitting room she removed a cat basket with a pair of sunglasses in it and a tilting stack of magazines from the sofa. Then she settled back with her feet up and placed Charlie on her stomach. Opening up her shirt, she lay back and gazed up at the cracked ceiling.

Tears ran down her face as he gorged. She could feel the fingertips of his greedy little hand closing and unclosing over the skin of her breast, while his gums pulled milk from her bursting nipple almost faster than he could swallow it.

Michael listened to make sure that the house was quiet. Then he pulled a tartan rug from one of the library sofas, brought it into the utility room and spread it out on the floor. He thought that he would be safe from interruption here, even if Jean should wake up.

They had not had lunch until after half-past three. Neither of them had commented on Steph's absence. They had chosen to assume that she must be resting and therefore did not remark on it – in this way they disallowed the possibility that there might be any significance in her failure to appear. Because as long as a thing remained unsaid, it could be deemed to be not happening. It would remain untrue, for as long as they did not draw attention to it, that dozens of little hairline cracks in their arrangements were about to open into fissures. They were afraid to refer even to how late it was to be eating lunch, lest it make them take a mere irregularity in mealtimes seriously. Since Miranda's death everyone had been rising late and, in between daytime naps and lie-downs, scratching effortfully at things, in search of some sort of purpose in anything. To mention a lapse in the punctuality of lunch might be to suggest that they were failing to find it, or even that they might be falling apart. What did it matter, anyway, what time they had lunch? It was only *time* after all, told by a clock somewhere, and these days, except to notice that there seemed to be too much of it, they were hardly aware of it. Time did not seem to have any need of them nor they for it. Lunch itself, a sparse soup that had been getting weirder as well as sparser by the day, had not been worth waiting for anyway. This was its fourth manifestation, and since flavour had quite deserted the original stock, which had been made with the last cube, today Jean had added a shake of angostura bitters and a small tin of macaroni. Defeated by the effort of pretending it was edible, she had left hers unfinished and agreed to lie down for the rest of the afternoon.

Michael moved silently in bare feet through the house while he pictured her sleeping above, trusting but unaware. He was conscious of the first pleasurable sensation he had felt since before Miranda died, an agreeable certainty that what he was working quietly at now, without her knowledge, would please his mother. From the library he brought first a set of leather bound volumes with the title *The History of Scotland, during the Reigns of Queen Mary and of King James VI* dated 1752, and placed them on the tartan rug. Then from the library desk he carried a brass inkstand, a pair of Sèvres inkpots, and two lace and ivory fans from a glass case that contained seven or eight others, and put them next to the books. That would do for the library. Jean would not notice. In the dining room he opened the corner cupboard that held some of the silver. He took a ladle, a sugar shaker and four salt cellars and spoons, and altered the spacing between the things that were left, dozens of them still, so that the losses were concealed. From inside the sideboard he took a porcelain tureen with a ladle and two or three lace cloths, but left the decorated blue and white pieces that stood on the top.

Back in the utility room he notched it all up. Even at Mr David's prices there should be at least three hundred quid's worth here. In fact, he might take the books to a proper dealer and do better. The thought of actually declining to sell to Mr David anything that Mr David was prepared to take was un-familiar and delightful. He might make a point of doing it. He could afford to, he really only needed to make a couple of hundred to keep them all going. Michael felt a hot, excited bubble of pride rising inside him. He would take care of them; even if he had not been able to save Miranda he would take care of them now. He thought of coming back tomorrow with fresh milk, bread, meat, eggs, vegetables, fruit. Then he pictured Jean taking one of her cakes out the oven, with happiness written all over her hot face, and told himself not to forget butter, sugar, flour, syrup, dried fruit. Chocolate for Steph. Her huge appetite had vanished since Miranda's death, but she might be tempted by chocolate.

Using dusters and newspapers from a pile in one of the sheds he wrapped his haul carefully, arranged the pieces in the back of the van and covered them with the tartan rug. First thing tomorrow he would go over to Bath. If he got off first thing then he might even be back before Jean and Steph were up, and he would make breakfast for them and they would wake to the smell of bacon and toast and coffee. The little smile that had been on Michael's face all afternoon widened. He closed the van doors and turned to look properly around him.

The afternoon was wearing to its end now but evening had not come; the earthy, growing smell of the spring day would not leave the air. He strolled out of the courtyard, drawn by the red gleam of the sun going down behind the hills miles away, far beyond the limits of the house. He followed the wide bend where the drive curved round to the front of the house before it straightened out to the half mile that ran down to the invisible road. Steph was walking towards him, though she did not appear to have seen him. Her arms were rigid against her sides, her hands apparently pushing the pockets of her jacket to the ground, and her head was down. Then she looked up and it seemed to Michael, from the angle of the lift of her head and the infinitesimal shake of her hair, that she had experienced pleasure at seeing him, perhaps for her, too, the first sensation of pleasure since before her baby had died. All at once the thought of tomorrow's grand surprise breakfast seemed inadequate. He wanted Steph to be in on the secret too. How much better it would be if they did it together! He began to run towards her. She would be so delighted when he told her the plan; he would take her with him in the van tomorrow, and they would do the whole thing together. He would include her in everything, even show her off to Mr David.

'Steph! Steph, listen! I've had this idea, it's all set up, I've done it all, it's ready to roll.' He stopped, gasping. He felt sick and light-headed; it was such a long time since he had eaten properly.

Steph looked faintly interested. 'Oh?'

'I've took some stuff from the house, not much, nothing we'll even miss, but worth a bit.' He took her arm and steered her towards the house as he spoke, as if she had not been heading that way in any case. 'Listen. It's in the van, all ready, tomorrow we go and see my contact, you know, I've got this contact.'

'Mr David. The one that rips you off.'

'Yeah, well, this is better stuff, more saleable. It's not the best in the house, so it's not like it'll get noticed, right, but it's nice stuff, small stuff. He'll take it. It'll give us enough, anyway, and it's cash, right? Enough to see us right till the next pay cheque's due, and there'll be an extra two hundred quid there, don't forget. Six hundred instead of four. And if we need to, I can always do it again, there's loads of stuff. I've only touched two rooms. Come with me – we'll go early before Jean's up, get the cash, go shopping, surprise her. You are coming, aren't you?'

'Oh, Michael. You and your small stuff. I can't come with you.'

'Why not? We won't be out that long. If you're worried about leaving Jean on her own ... I mean we can always–' He stopped, panting, his hands on his hips.

'Aren't you even going to ask me where I've been?'

Michael looked at her, stricken. Why had

it not even occurred to him? She was leaving.

And she was smiling, actually smiling in a way Michael had not seen for weeks. She placed her hands on his shoulders and stood on tiptoe with excitement. 'I can't come. I can't come with you tomorrow 'cause I'll be at work. 'Cause I've got a job, haven't I?'

## *May*

It was all very difficult for a time. As I said, there was a patch when I could not be sure how many days passed. And it hardly mattered except that our supplies, which were low, dwindled to nothing without anyone noticing. Or it's possible we noticed but just could not consider it important. So by the time Michael took matters in hand it was serious. The only thing we had plenty of was wine (although even the cellar was looking rather emptier than at the beginning). That, and unhappiness. Unhappiness was everywhere in layers, layers all the same colour folded and unfolded over and around us; we carried wads of it everywhere, we left it in every room and then it came flapping after us. I neglected the housework, I will admit, and so after a while I thought I could actually see it, this unhappiness everywhere – it had come to look the same as the coating of dust that flattened all the surfaces.

But things did get better, starting with some very practical developments. I date it from the day after the one when Steph had not been home for lunch and Michael and I, saying nothing, had sat over bowls of some awful stuff we were trying to call soup. Michael's silence was kind, as is everything about Michael, and afterwards he shooed me off upstairs for a lie-down. The next morning I decided I would stay in bed. Michael brought me up a cup of tea and said he'd be back later and not to worry. What I did not find out until later that day was that he and Steph had both gone out. If I had known, I wonder if I would have worried (even worrying was beginning to require more energy than I could find). How that day passed I still do not know. I had gone beyond being hungry so it wasn't that, though at the back of my mind I was aware that this was the fifth or possibly the sixth day when there literally was not enough to go round. We had got to the stage of eating rhubarb from the garden, without sugar because there wasn't any, and there's a limit to how much of that a stomach will stand. We had all but finished the potatoes, and there was scarcely another thing except for a tin of anchovies and some dried chestnuts, nor any money to buy anything until my next salary was paid. Steph and Michael for a time had been as unable to care about this as I was, but they kept turning the study upside down looking for a way out of our problem. Michael in particular got to know all about the investments and so on but there was no way of getting ready cash. So nothing more came of that, except that Michael and Steph fell out. That *was* to do with hunger, I'm sure.

Anyway, it crossed my mind that day that perhaps if I kept upstairs in bed and out of the way, Michael and Steph would not feel bad about dividing what there was between the two of them. I felt that perhaps I was the problem. I was dragging them down with me. I was an old woman and the time had come to relinquish my hold. A bleak idea on the face of it, but I swear that just the thought of their survival filled me with joy, even then. I was hopeful, even as I lay there (as I thought dying) that with me out of the way they would find some way to manage. After all, they had done well over getting the oil; that had gone without a hitch and Michael had even managed to relight the Aga without any trouble. My mind wandered in and out of all the things we'd done and said we would do, until I was a little confused between what had really happened here and what had not.

So by the time it came to afternoon on this day, I'd dropped off to sleep again and was dreaming about food. Surprisingly, not so much the taste of it in my mouth as the sight of it being prepared, and the smells, the savoury air of a good kitchen. The relish of those sensations is not just the prospect of eating but also the homeliness of a prosperous, well-ordered house and somebody generous-spirited at the stove. It makes me happy again to think of it. So in this dream I could see and smell food, and it's not true that a starving man dreams of a feast. What I could smell was toast. Plain, simple, lovely toast. And then I realised I was awake and Michael was at the foot of my bed. My first thought was oh, my goodness has the day gone by already, and here's me still in bed and I haven't managed to do a thing.

So there he was, Michael, and he was holding a tray with a pot of tea, some toast and scrambled eggs, which he knew I was very fond of, and some black grapes, and chocolates. Actually, very expensive chocolates. And from his face I could tell there was nothing to worry about. He'd got hold of money from somewhere, he said, plenty to keep us going. He sat on the chair over by the window while I ate (I'm afraid I did bolt it all down, rather). He said nothing, just looked out across the courtyard and down the drive, and refused to taste the grapes.

I'm not stupid. I was still eating when I said, what did you sell to buy all this? Must be quite a bit, I said, and just to show him I wasn't cross with him, or even in the least upset, I smiled. So then he told me about the books and fans and bits of china and all of it, and he was surprised at how little I cared. I was surprised myself. All I said was that they were only things, not even in perfect condition. I was thinking to myself that I could always doctor the inventory if the need arose (which I didn't anticipate) until I remembered that I'd burned the inventory months ago. So there wasn't even that to worry about. Then he looked out of the window again and said he could see Steph coming, and he would walk down the drive to meet her. Now that did surprise me, because I didn't know she had gone out, and I said so. Michael just gave me a look and said no, he would explain, and everything would work out. I wasn't sure he meant it. But already I felt much better so I got up and went downstairs.

That day, looking out of Jean's bedroom window while she ate, Michael watched Steph in the distance bending in to the wind on her way up the drive, just as she had done the day before. Once again he felt that she was escaping danger by a hair's breadth; by the merest chance she was being delivered back to him rather than borne away and destroyed. She was oblivious, of course, like a sleepwalker gliding across a motorway. He watched her with growing anger, feeling that he had been dangerously inattentive. How could he have allowed her to go off like that in the first place? If she had no sense of danger then clearly it was up to him to have it for her, and he should have been more insistent. He had almost forgotten that when he had told her that morning about the risks she was taking she had seemed not so much to disagree with what he was saying as simply not to be hearing him at all.

They had sat at the kitchen table over mugs of tea and all the time that he was talking, she had appeared to be waiting. And then, without the least hostility, she had patiently drained her mug and declared that she must be off, just as if he had never opened his mouth. Michael had set about adding water to the teapot to get another cup out of it for Jean, feeling so angry and miserable that his hands shook. He had calmed himself down so that he could take Jean her tea without her seeing the state he was in, but he need not have worried. She had been so dopey – just sleepy, Michael tried to tell himself – that she would not have noticed anyway. Back downstairs again he realised that he would have to get a grip on himself if he were to accomplish the tasks he had set himself for the day. He had no choice but to concentrate on those. It was not possible to deal with so many dangers all together; selling the stuff that he had already put in the van, getting cash and buying food were as much as he could cope with. In fact, an agenda of such complexity and risk was beginning to fill him with the kind of depression that in the old days would have immobilised him for a week. Because it *was* risky: driving the untaxed, uninsured, un-MOT'd van into Bath, selling to Mr David, shopping openly with a large sum of cash. Any one or all of them could go wrong. If something did, if the van were spotted, if Mr David (always of uncertain temper and sometimes malicious) screwed him over, then Michael's entire new life would fold in upon itself and disappear.

Michael had never developed the habit of anticipating too closely the consequences of his actions, beyond taking the usual steps to avoid immediate chaos. He had never been convinced that anything he might do could be important enough to have consequences that would matter that much. That had changed. With the knowledge that he now had something worth keeping came a huge fear that he might lose it. He saw that what he was about to do might destroy everything, but he was also looking straight into the blank fact that he had no other options. His existence, and Steph's and Jean's, were at risk anyway, endangered by a simple lack of money. He could not make them safe from that without first exposing them all to other risks, and he would have to concentrate. It would not be his fault if, while he was fending off one danger, Steph was out God knows where creating others. He would deal with her next.

So when he saw Steph trudging along, head down (her mood never was reflected in the way she walked, it was always the same slow tread, hands in pockets) he thought, here it comes, the next thing. She was still making her way up between the fields. The sight of her alone, not yet within the boundary of the garden, appalled him. He watched from the window, timing it carefully until Jean had finished eating. Then, anxious not to hurry or show his fear, he took the tray and reassured Jean that everything was fine. He clattered downstairs and ran outside, his panic rising.

Steph might be making her way back, but he was not fooled. She was shaking herself loose, moving beyond and away from them. What was wrong with her, that she needed to go outside, to mix with other people? What was wrong with *him*, that he was tolerating it? Was she blind? As long as they lived quietly, keeping themselves to themselves, there would be no need for actual secrecy, certainly nothing as blatant as outright lying. But if other people came poking in, if other people were actually being *encouraged*, how long before certain things came out? God knows what she might already have told them, these people she was 'working' for. And who, anyway, were they? He suspected that not only did she not really know, she was so blind and trusting that she did not even recognise the importance of knowing.

She had no right to spoil everything like this. He marched down the drive to meet her. As he drew closer he broke into a run, shouting, and the noise shook a few birds out of the trees at the far side of the paddock. Steph stopped, looked up and watched them rise and fly off, in that moment realising that Michael would reach the point where she was standing within the next ten seconds, and that he was probably going to hit her. She lowered her head and waited for it to happen so that it would be over. She had no firm opinion on the matter, but it had come as a slight surprise that he was turning out to be the same as the others, after all.

Out of breath and half-sobbing, Michael grabbed her by the arms. His voice was a thin wail. 'Jesus Christ! Isn't it enough for you! Isn't it enough? Don't you see you'll ruin it? Look at me! What's the matter with you?'

But Steph barely raised her head.

'What's the matter with you! Isn't it enough, all of us here together?'

Steph tried to pull away for a moment and then, throwing him a look of puzzlement, she cried, 'Together? All of us? Oh sure, all of us, minus Miranda!'

Surely he would hit her now, after a remark like that.

'Miranda's *dead*,' she said, 'in case you'd forgotten.'

He was bound to hit her now. But Michael let go of her and wiped a hand over his face. 'Oh, look, I only meant – Steph...'

He raised his arms as if to hug her, saw her face, and dropped them again.

'Oh, Christ. Look – Steph, it's ... look, I know, I know. I do, honest.'

Without saying more, Steph walked on. Michael followed a few steps behind. 'Look,' he said, 'it's not all bad. I mean I've sorted the money. I've done it. We're OK. Come *on*.' He pulled at her arm and drew level. She shook herself free, but walked along beside him, at least.

'Steph, listen, you don't have to. You don't have to, there's enough money now,' he said. 'Please. Please don't go back.'

'But it's not just the money.' She stopped again, turned to him and shook her head. 'It's Charlie.' Other words of explanation were stranded in her mouth. Her face crumpled, because she could tell from his eyes that Michael was not, after all, going to hit her, and never had been. He was frightened, that was all. But she could not help that, not now that there was Charlie. She turned away, sobbing.

'You wait! Just wait, Michael, you'll see!'

Then she spun past him and ran the rest of the way back to the house, where Jean was already in the kitchen wondering which of three massive joints of meat to put in the oven for supper. Steph flung herself at her and wrapped her arms round her neck.

Michael hovered in the doorway. Jean looked carefully at him over Steph's shoulder as she patted her heaving back. She was feeling rather unsteady on her legs and Steph had nearly knocked her over, but she would have to find the strength from somewhere. Taking a deep breath, she said, 'Oh, Michael dear. I think a drink's called for. Would you, dear? Then we'll all settle down and talk things over.'

And then there was Charlie. Suddenly, there he was. From that day onwards, he was ours. It was all Steph's doing, the clever girl, and she was proud of herself for doing it, and quite right too. I was with her over Charlie right from the start, without even having to think about it. It was in her face, for one thing. The necessity of it, I mean. Charlie was, purely and simply, a necessity. He still is. When she burst into the kitchen that day, there was, I don't know, a very *important* look on her face, I can't describe it any other way. She was in need of something – exactly what, of course, I didn't know just that minute – but she was in very serious need. I still cannot see that there is anything extreme in the idea that people should have what they need, particularly if they have had to go without it for most of their lives.

That same evening we managed to settle Michael down about it all. You know, it is amazing how much more amenable people are when they have been properly fed. I wonder less, now, at Mother's permanent irascibility when I was growing up, remembering what we ate in that house! Mother's meals were not just unappetising, they seemed take more out of you than they put in. We would rise from the table debilitated, thwarted and restless; afterwards I would wash up and clear away but I could never wipe the surfaces clean of my disappointment.

So over dinner, together Steph and I persuaded Michael about Charlie. Because of course the minute she told me about her job, I saw it as clearly as she did. She began to explain it to me when we were doing the potatoes and beans together in the kitchen, while Michael was in the cellar deciding on something to go with the beef. I still feel some pride in the way I took control that evening, weak though I was myself. Because they needed me; my two young people were quite ragged with tiredness and hunger and with this matter of Charlie, so I kept them both busy and away from each other until we were at table. The little jobs I set them to were those pleasant tasks that fill the hungry waiting time and slowly transform a dining room while the cooking proceeds: replacing candles, setting out the beautiful claret glasses and the silver (we always used the dining room in the evenings, but did so that night with special ceremony), decanting the wine. I sent Steph out to pick flowers for the table and she, bless her, came back with hedgerow flowers: some late primroses, buttercups and campion. She wasn't sure if she was meant to pick the garden flowers, she said. I point this out because that's the sort of girl she is. Not greedy. Not inclined to assume that things are hers for the taking. But if it's a question of necessity, well, that puts a different complexion on it. Anyway, by the time we sat down to dinner the tension had almost gone; by then we could think of little else but the food. And afterwards, such a happy atmosphere, it's funny how you remember the details.

I have thought about this since I began to cook, and I believe that it is very much underestimated, the effect of food on one's outlook. I do not mean just being hungry or not. I mean the very things we eat. That night we ate red meat, a great deal of it. I roasted a sirloin of beef. To begin with, the smell of rich meat like that belongs in a house like this. It made us feel optimistic and at home, although we were too hungry to feel quite happy until after we had eaten. We were so hungry that we could not wait, not with the smell of it tormenting us, so we ate our meat very, very rare. And that sort of food makes one courageous, even slightly bolshy. Perhaps it's the blood or the chewing, something metallic that sharpens the air, an edge of steel, but that beef did something for us that another dish (poached salmon, say, just as nutritious, and delicious too) would not have done. Not an obvious summer dish, a sirloin of beef, but it was exactly what we all needed; it resisted just a little against our teeth before melting down our throats, it was so sustaining and rich, and the potatoes and vegetables were so sweet.

So, I agreed with Steph that Michael was worrying unnecessarily, because of course there would be no question of her spending her days apart from us, going off to that house in the village and staying there all day with the baby. I knew that without having to be told. She would bring Charlie here. His mother already thought she was some sort of genius with children after just one day. I gathered that Sally was getting her head round (Steph's phrase!) the idea of going back to that job of hers, and Charlie had already slept right through the night, for the first time, the night after Steph's very first visit. So in Sally's eyes Steph could do no wrong, right from the off. We didn't see a problem with her agreeing that Steph could bring him to the manor. We'd win her over with the thought of all that space, the gardens, and the pool (where of course Steph would not let go of him for so much as a second). She'd probably go along with it. And if she didn't, how would she even know? Steph could get him back to Sally's in good time, if need be, at the end of each day. A detail.

Bit by bit our confidence soaked into Michael, so that by the end of dinner he was as full of it as if he had mopped it up himself along with the juices on his plate. Afterwards we sat outside with glasses of brandy to watch the sunset from the terrace that faces west. It must have been the first time we had all sat there together, for we had not had many fine evenings. This was a perfect one, full of contentment, the sun such an improbable, huge, burning orange, the pinks and blues in the sky so painted-looking. Such a hazy evening sky seems to hold neither air nor colour but is like pure, liquid light just melting over empty land. Steph said it was like a Turner. She and Michael were sitting quite cuddled up by then, all happy. It did us all good to be sitting together looking outwards, beyond the boundary of our own place.

I began to wonder what we had been so frightened of. I was beginning to think we'd been a bit over the top, with all this keeping ourselves so apart, even being frightened about Michael going shopping. I said so, and it turned out they had been thinking much the same. After all, as Michael said, his trip to Bath had gone off perfectly. Steph pointed out that she had taken herself off to the village and come back not just un-harmed but actually bringing us a baby boy. I said I did not want to be furtive about everything, it made me feel as if I were doing something wrong. Perhaps we did not have to be quite so cautious. Private, yes, and discreet – we were not about to fling the doors open to all and sundry – but if we were sensible and clever about it, there was no reason why we shouldn't be a little more relaxed. Life would continue just as before. It was Steph who said oh, but it'll be even better than before. And we agreed.

Michael had brought back a vanload of food and over the next week or so we all grew strong again. But in no time at all the need for money reared its ugly head again. We weren't hungry any more, but we found there were other things we needed. Steph admitted that she couldn't bear her clothes (the things she had from my wardrobe were, in truth, much too old for her, and she was tired of borrowing Michael's shirts). She wanted to make herself something to wear, she said, and it wouldn't be expensive. That's fair enough, she's young, and these things matter especially if you're pretty, as Steph is. Her shape had changed, so she needed things that were looser. She had noticed that we had lots and lots of white sheets made of real linen, scores more than we ever used, and white linen would be just right for summer clothes and she knew how to make what she wanted. She didn't even need a pattern, she said, just thread and a few buttons and a sewing machine.

Well, we hunted high and low for a sewing machine, even in the attics, but there wasn't one. I thought it odd, but there you are. Although our money situation was much better, with what Steph was earning and with my rise in salary, we still did not have the wherewithal for big purchases like that. Never mind then, Steph said, but we could tell she was disappointed, and it was such a modest request. So Michael and I surprised her. One day when she thought he had just gone shopping for food, he came back with her sewing machine. I had told him, you see, to take a pretty little brocade-covered button back chair from one of the other bedrooms, and a pair of watercolours of Venice, and get what he could for them. It's marvellous, our sewing machine. You can even do embroidery on it. Steph was delighted and said she would learn how to sew CHARLIE in big letters, and customise all his T-shirts, but in fact she's never got round to it. But she set to work on the linen sheets while I minded Charlie. (Charlie, even if I say so myself, took to me from the start, and even though I couldn't feed him myself, he was very happy in my care.) Steph worked quickly, so that after only a day or two she had made some pairs of pyjama-like trousers and simple tops, a wrap-round skirt and some dresses. Everything was loose and summery, draping and elegant, in simple shapes and layers that allowed her to move easily and gracefully. Michael could hardly take his eyes off her. But she only wore her linen clothes here, never to fetch and return Charlie. She wore a sort of uniform of navy trousers and floral blouses for going outside.

Steph got used to arriving at Sally's to find both her and Charlie in a state of fractious semi-undress. During the first week she had walked into the house each day eating a bar of chocolate that she bought from the village shop on her way past. (She very soon got, with her chocolate and her change, a 'you all right, then?' from the man in the shop, whose name was Bill. And as a regular customer she was no longer invited to buy the bargain tent, which was still for sale.) But very soon Steph sensed that her chocolate-stopped mouth diminished her authority in Sally's eyes and, more importantly, she realised that authority over Sally was going to be the key to success. So she left the chocolate in her pocket for later and walked in smiling, pulling Charlie from Sally's hip or lifting him from whichever location he had been dumped in while Sally tried to organise herself. Without speaking, she would fill and switch on the kettle, and then she would track down whatever it was that Sally was at that moment most frantic about not having immediately to hand: often her keys, the briefcase, her diary, a pair of tights, her other shoe. On bad days, it could be her first cup of coffee, the vital papers she had been working on last night, a tampon, and once, a new bottle of shampoo (it being, apparently, a surprise to the dripping, naked Sally that the bottle she had finished the day before and left in the shower was still empty the next). Then Steph would shoo Sally upstairs (or better, out of the door, on days when she was halfway ready to leave on time) and settle in a kitchen chair to feed Charlie, always ready to whisk him away from the breast and plug his astonished mouth with the bottle if she heard Sally begin her clattering and swearing descent down the uncarpeted stairs.

When the door had finally closed behind her, Steph would keep the smile on her face until she heard Sally's car start up and drive away.

At the end of the day Steph would be waiting, still smiling, when Sally banged in shouting that she was *bloody knackered*, dumping her briefcase, bag, keys and usually also carrier bags of shopping in the hall, and walking out of her shoes on the way into the kitchen. Charlie would be bathed, in a clean sleep suit, and fed; Steph always placed an empty, apparently drained bottle of formula on the table next to her elbow. Steph would rise, sit Sally down, deliver Charlie into her lap, make her a cup of coffee and, because Sally usually asked her to, pour her a glass of wine as well. If not actually asleep, Charlie would be sleepy enough not to mind how his mother's arrival shattered the peace, and would drop off gratifyingly in her arms.

Steph was pleased that she did not have to say very much at the end of the day, beyond confirming that Charlie had been 'absolutely fine'. In between slurps of coffee and wine, Sally would talk as if she had been forcibly gagged for hours, throwing out what sounded to Steph quite manic and incomprehensible details of the day's confrontations: with colleagues, clients, pedestrians, idiots in shops, but also with machinery – chiefly computers and telephones – as well as the traffic and the weather. Although neither of them realised it, it was Steph's very stillness that stimulated Sally into such torrents of speech. Because just in case there were something judgmental in Steph's silence, Sally filled it with authoritative babble about how impossible life was and how she was managing to overcome its many obstacles. It sounded simply like an impassioned and colourful account of Sally's heroic daily struggle with a world hostile to intelligent, well-qualified lone mothers, but the implication was that this was a struggle that a humble childminder knew little of and would be unequal to, and so had no cause to be smug about. Into her patronising commentary Sally continued to drop expletives and throwaway revelations so personal that Steph was further robbed of any power to reply. But Steph, though she did not become more talkative, grew not to mind. Sally seemed to speak this way to other people too, she learned, when Sally, answering the telephone and blaring down it (obviously in reply to a polite enquiry about how she was) more information about her cystitis than Steph could imagine anyone would need to know, then returned to the kitchen and reported that that had been her father-in-law, miserable uptight bugger.

It was while we were turning the place upside down looking for a sewing machine that Michael came across the silver picture frames that I'd torn the photographs out of in January. After I'd burned the pictures I'd put the frames away and hardly thought of them. He said we ought to have some of our own family pictures, and of course he was right. So he sold more of the old books and bought a digital camera. I had no idea what was meant by 'digital' (I still don't) but Michael laughed and said it was all done by computers and that he didn't even need film! Sure enough he spent a couple of sunny afternoons taking pictures and he actually developed them in the study. I'd always thought you needed a dark room. Michael did explain – he said he was new to it himself but if you spend a bit of time on a computer it's amazing how fast you pick it up and in any case the computer tells you what buttons to press half the time – but the details escape me. I'll never understand it. There were some lovely shots of Charlie and Steph, the garden, and even some not bad ones of me. You don't notice how you change until you see a photo of yourself, do you? All that hair I have now! It has grown bushy as well as white and thick, but I fancy it suits me. When I noticed my hair in those photos I thought back to that night in the cellar and the label on the wine bottle, and saw how far I had come in a few months. Steph had taken some pictures of Michael, too, so we are all there, somewhere or other; the pictures are all still here, in their frames, all over the house. Steph and I had great fun trimming them for the frames and sticking them up all round the place. The very best one of Charlie was too big for any of the frames, though. That's the one that's still on the door of the fridge, under a toy magnet shaped like a carrot that Michael picked up at the garden centre.

Oh, yes – the garden centre. Well, I had begun to think seriously again about a tree for Miranda's grave. In fact that was another thing. It became easier to talk of Miranda. We all learned how, even Steph, we helped each other, persevering even when it was difficult. Not that we can ever speak of her casually or without longing, even to this day. Still when her name is mentioned, more often than not one or other of us weeps. But there is a certain sweetness in that. We learned to speak of her often, always fondly and sadly, and one day I told them about my idea of a tree. They both said very firmly that I should have it. There was a rather florid Edwardian dinner service that we none of us cared for and agreed we could spare. We never used it, preferring the very thin, plain white porcelain. So I got my tree.

I sent Michael off to the garden centre with careful instructions and he brought back a very large magnolia that we planted all together.

Michael had been amazed by the garden centre. It turned out he had never been to one before (well why would he, with no garden?) and it was a revelation, all those tender shoots, just waiting to be put in the ground and allowed to thrive. He thought he would like to plant a proper vegetable garden. Everything he needed was there, he would only have to buy the seedlings and put them in. I can see it now, how his face was shining. He was already taking a pride in this garden, which existed at that point only in his mind. It was yet to be planted, but just the idea of keeping us supplied with fruit and vegetables for the summer made him proud. I at once encouraged it, so he picked out some more things we could do without (I left it to him this time to choose what – I knew he would be sensible). I believe it was more furniture from the bedrooms. He filled the walled garden with row upon row of fresh, bright little plants, and he tended them every day. There was no end to the care he took with them, and he kept the lawns cut and the flowerbeds tidy, too. We were all in a kind of heaven – not sitting about on clouds, you understand, but busy doing things that made us happy.

I do not think we were ever afraid that it might not last, but perhaps we were half-expecting that somebody would come and try to spoil it. I do know that we acted extremely quickly to stop Shelley.

The weather grew warmer. One morning Sally told Steph, unnecessarily, to be sure to put on Charlie's sun block, which Steph took as approval in principle that she might take Charlie out and about in the pushchair. That evening Steph told Sally that she had taken Charlie up to the manor to 'meet my aunt', omitting to mention that Charlie had, in fact, spent every single day there so far. The following day, Steph made a point of saying that she had taken Charlie there again and that he had enjoyed the walk up the drive, and she brought back a lemon cake for Sally 'with best wishes from my aunt. She's great at cakes'. After that Steph filled a vase with buttercups that, she explained, Charlie had been charmed to see growing in one of the manor paddocks. The next day she reported how 'my aunt' had been reading his baby books with him. Then Steph had a brainwave.

The following day, instead of taking Charlie up to the manor, she got Michael to come down to the house after Sally had left. Together they blitzed the place, resisting the temptation to throw most of Sally's junk away, instead cleaning round it and tidying it into more rational arrangements. That evening Sally arrived home not just to the silent, smiling Steph and a bathed, fed and sweet-tempered Charlie, but also to a pine-scented and gleaming house. It was still cluttered, but there were at least enough clean surfaces to allow her to walk in and put her things down without having to move other things first, and then find places (by shifting other things) for those things she had picked up in order to make room for the things she had come home with. She seemed slightly confused by the tidiness, but grateful. She even offered Steph a glass of wine but Steph, anxious to get home and feeling fairly sure that she was unlikely to enjoy the Côtes du Rhône that Sally was uncorking, declined, and slipped off.

'Sally,' Steph said the next morning, 'you don't mind me taking Charlie up to the manor, do you? I thought it'd be nice to have him up there and save messing up the house. Now it's all nice, shame to get it all, you know.'

'No, I don't mind, you take him, it's fine,' Sally said, slightly absently, looking round the kitchen. The wine bottle she had emptied the night before stood on the draining board. 'But he does *live* here. I mean I'm really grateful, but we don't want things so perfect we can't touch them, do we? I'm not bringing him up in a bloody *sterile environment*, after all. Am I?' She began picking through a basket of onions to find her car keys. 'Maybe I should pop up there one day, you know, just to see he's settled. I'd like to meet your aunt, anyway.'

Steph had been expecting this. *I'm going to check up on where he is all day and who he's with*, is what you really mean, she thought. Jean had suggested that any half-normal mother would want to do that.

'Oh, yeah, right,' she said. 'My aunt was saying she'd like to meet you, meet Charlie's mum. She said suppose you take us up there in the car one morning and drop us off, on your way to work?'

'Well, we could do. It's in the other direction. We'd have to be out of here half an hour earlier,' Sally said, her interest waning.

'OK. I'll tell her you'll be up tomorrow then, OK?'

'What? Oh fine, yes, tell her that's fine.'

'Glad you like the spring-clean, anyway. Nice to have it a bit clearer, isn't it?'

'Oh yes, but I mean in a way, now it *is* a bit better, it seems a shame not to be here a bit *more.*'

'Oh no, of course, I didn't mean–' Was it all going to backfire? Steph thought fast, and delivered her masterstroke. 'It's just – well, I think Charlie likes to see new faces. You know. He likes my auntie. He gets tons of attention up there, you see.'

'Oh, yes, yes. Oh, *where* are my keys? Steph, have you seen my fucking keys?'

'Here they are. Anyway, I think the stimulation's really good for him. You know, especially when he doesn't see very much of you. You know, when he doesn't see you *all day*. And with him being an only.'

The next day Sally drove them up to the manor, cursing at the early start. Jean came out to meet them in the drive, shook hands with Sally and invited her in. Sally refused coffee, spent all of five minutes in the kitchen where one end had already been transformed into Charlie's play area, smiled and said she must be off. Jean saw her back to her car, chatting amiably. When she returned, she and Steph exchanged a look. Jean put plates to warm and made a pot of coffee while Steph, with Charlie on her hip, laid the table. After another minute or two, just to be cautious in case Sally came roaring back up the drive for any reason, they called to Michael who had been waiting upstairs, and then they sat down to the breakfast that Jean had ready in the oven. That was all it took.

I've gone woefully off the point, because looking back a few pages I see I didn't get to the end of the Mr Hapgood story. He took Father's clock away and stored it at the back of the shop. He reported that he had found out that it was a Vulliamy clock of 1788. Unfortunately, however, it had only a number (169) rather than the maker's signature, indicating that it wasn't among his best work. He showed me all this, how the number 169 wasn't engraved on the backplate along with a signature like the finest examples, but punch struck on the reverse of the brass bob at the base of the pendulum, somewhere inconspicuous. It would have been signed if it had been a superior clock, he said, but it was still an attractive piece and could be worth as much as £150. It seemed an awful lot for a clock, I said. But inside I was thinking it didn't sound like enough to go to university for three years. I hoped I was wrong. I hadn't looked into it. Although Mother had rallied, a little – she had been up and about quite a bit in fact, supervising the people putting in her downstairs bathroom – it still hadn't seemed the right time to raise it with her, the question of me leaving home. Did I say, it was always difficult to talk in that house? It was no easier with Father gone. With him gone there were no more kind little blinks or never-mind looks between us when Mother's back was turned. So I didn't broach the subject.

Mr Hapgood went on to say that it was very important to find the right buyer. Why didn't I ask what he meant? I don't know why, except that he made it sound as if I should already know, or as if there was a sort of buyer who was 'right' in some way over and above wanting the clock and having the money for it. He said that even though he himself wasn't in the 'mainstream antiques business' I had done the right thing in coming to him, because he would see me right. For a start I wouldn't be having to pay an 'extortionate dealer's premium'. I didn't ask what that meant, either. But it might take a little while to find 'the right buyer', however, and he suggested that I pop in once or twice a week to see if there was any progress to report.

So I did. I must have been living in some fug that stopped me barely noticing, let alone minding, that there at the back of the shop in the drowsy oil-stove heat, he always had more tea for me than progress to report, and soon a lot more cuddles than tea, and before long he said we were very good at comforting each other and cheering each other up, and could get even better. Soon enough his hands had been everywhere and I was confused by the way he seemed both a little impatient if I showed any reluctance, but at the same time pleased with me. He was gradual, and clever with his hands. So by the time he took my hand and put it down his trousers and made me keep it there, I was at the very least curious. And on the day he unbuttoned himself and showed me everything, I was almost as ready as he was to go (as he said, brandishing it) the whole hog. The whole hog did not take long and was carried out in silence except for the creaking of the rickety old sofa. I remember thinking it was the sofa that was taking the brunt, because I felt in a curious way rather out of it and at a distance. Then Mr Hapgood was saying I should be on my way and I remember the slipperiness and the smell like raw potato that I thought was me, so that I was embarrassed and only too ready to go.

These days it would be called abuse, of course. But it was what he did later that still seems to me infinitely worse.

In the third week of May Michael unlocked the door at the back of the low stone pavilion by the pool. Old, trapped summer air poured out, peppery and slightly damp. White cotton curtains had been drawn against the French windows on the far side, so he crossed the room through the milky light and pulled them apart, finding the material just slightly tacky under his fingers. A few dead flies stuck in old webs in the curtain folds spun with the sudden movement; one or two fell and clicked faintly on the floor. He opened the French windows, strolled out on to the stone terrace from which shallow blue steps led down into the water, and made his way to the end of the pool. Slowly he turned the handle at one end of the horizontal spindle that stretched the width of the poolside, and wound in the winter cover. After its last edge had been pulled free and was hanging dripping from the spindle, Michael crouched down and dipped his hand in the water. It was extremely cold, and the level of the water was lower than he expected, but he was surprised at how clean it looked.

Turning back on his bare feet, he could feel as soon as he re-entered the pavilion that the sun was already striking the terracotta tiles of the floor and stirring up the faint reek of warming earth. Michael's body tingled as he breathed it in. He liked the way the smell seemed to come to him almost through the soles of his feet. It was both fresh and fertile, so *new*, and made him think of earthy things that were workaday and practical, the slap of water over clay, human sweat, and the later, sweet baking of the sun on bricks and tiles. Yet the smell carried in it also a dank note, a threat from the sour underground it came from. Heavily and inexpressibly ancient, it was also lifeless, and although dead, it was at the same time so darkly erotic that Michael felt simultaneously animated and destabilised.

It was not an unpleasant feeling. He smiled, thinking of Steph, picturing her unpeeled from her solid nursing bra and engrossed in the steady nursing of Charlie. She had become capable and authoritative on every practical detail of childcare and breast-feeding but if, when Charlie was nuzzled up and sucking from her, her attention would wander, a look of such distant, private sensuality would come over her face that Michael would find himself staring like a voyeur. Watching her made him feel quite helplessly joyful, as well as aroused. She did not seem to mind.

But the matter in hand was to get the pool working, and first he had to locate the machinery. He was hopeful that there would be some sort of instruction book that would tell him what to do, but if there wasn't he had another idea. It would be well within his capabilities to ring up a pool maintenance outfit, posing as Oliver Standish-Cave of course, and get somebody round to do it for him. The idea rather appealed to him, in fact he had already rehearsed the mock-exasperation he would express at being 'just hopeless I'm afraid' at this kind of thing himself, and 'a bit too snowed under to see to it personally'. But both Jean and Steph had looked worried when he had suggested it, and it would be, he had to admit, intensely satisfying to manage such an unfamiliar job by himself. He could see the admiration in their eyes already. He had discovered since coming here not just that he had a definite practical streak but that there was pleasure in having something to accomplish; he liked having a few projects on the go. So although his mind was quite ready to take him off further into his reverie, perhaps to the mental picture of Steph and Charlie naked in the water together, he turned his attention back to the place where he was standing.

Most of the room had been made into a space for lounging around in and was furnished in a kind of green and faded English garden style that he imagined Jean would like. Steph would like it less; perhaps once she had finished the nursery mural (she had said this morning that it would be ready by the end of the day, and was up there now painting, while Jean looked after Charlie) she might fancy doing something here. Something to do with water would be better than these white walls with prints of ferns, he thought, looking round at the bamboo sofas with their white and green cushions.

Against one wall, set into a long, white-painted kitchen unit, stood a sink with worktops on each side. A row of glass-fronted cupboards, containing nothing but ice buckets and tumblers, was fixed along the wall above. On either side of the cup-boards were two identical doors. Through one he found a large, neglected bathroom with corroded taps and chilly white tiles covering the floor and walls. The other door led into a bare, stone room like a scullery where the pool machinery was installed. Here, on a shelf next to several tubs and bags of chemical-looking cleaners, Michael found what he was looking for: a damp notebook with the words *Pool Maintenance Checklist* on it, and a colour brochure entitled '*Enjoy Your Pool*'. He picked them up, returned to the green and white room, stretched himself out along one of the sofas and began to read.

It turned out to be quite complicated, but with the book in his hand Michael eventually identified the pump, filters, motors and heater. He cleared out the valves and pump head, charged the filters with water, primed the filter pump and checked for leaks. Back outside he re-installed the water surface skimmer baskets and, following the measurements prescribed, gave the water a dose of chlorine. Then he tested and adjusted the alkalinity and calcium levels. He felt like Einstein.

It was while he was hosing down the paving round the pool that he heard a shout from Jean. Looking up, he saw that she was approaching across the grass, moving as fast as she could, and if she had not been holding Charlie she would have been waving her arms. Her hair had shaken free of its clasp and the few clumps of it that Charlie had not managed to grasp in his fists flew out behind her. Her usual serenity had vanished, not a vestige of poise remained; she was jabbering and distraught – only a few jerking steps away, it seemed to Michael, from complete breakdown. Just then Charlie, jiggled almost insensible by the dash across from the house, got enough breath back to start up with a high-pitched, bewildered bleating. Michael dropped the hose, turned off the tap on the wall and strode towards them across the grass. He took Charlie from her a little roughly, which upset him even more. He pulled round from Michael's arms and stretched back to Jean, wailing louder. His confused eyes scanned the space around and behind, looking for Steph, and then he arched his back and screamed. His brown arms pumped up and down in rage. Jean was shouting incoherently above him, but Michael was too busy struggling to get a better hold of the writhing Charlie and keep his face clear of his waving fists to hear what she was saying.

But how, he was managing to wonder, *how* had this happened? Two minutes ago he had been calmly working on the pool. He had left Jean a little over two hours ago, baking bread in the kitchen while Charlie gurgled and watched her from his reclining seat, happily flinging his rabbit to the floor from time to time. Steph had been painting upstairs and presumably still was; she would be up a ladder, humming to herself and too far away to hear that once again their peace had been obliterated. How? What had gone wrong this time? Why could they not be left alone?

'Come on, sit down. Sit here on the grass and tell me what's the matter,' he said, in his most coping voice, pulling her down. He set Charlie gently on the grass and Charlie, perhaps bamboozled by being plonked in yet another unexpected location, stopped crying and stared up at the sky instead.

'What's up, then?' Michael was managing to sound calm, but oddly, he realised that he was not just putting on the right voice, it actually was his voice, and he really did feel the way he sounded. Jean needed him to be this way. Whatever the matter was, he would put it right for her.

Jean was rocking to and fro on the grass. 'I've just had a call. From Town and Country, the agency, the house sitting people.' She raised frantic eyes to Michael. 'I don't know what to do! Shelley's coming. Shelley, she runs the agency, she says she's on her way. Here! I couldn't stop her.' She buried her face in her hands and moaned.

Charlie, kicking on the grass, gurgled and gave a short wail.

'Oh, Christ. Christ, *when?*'

'Now! In about an hour. She phoned from the car – she said she wrote and gave me the date and to tell her if there was any problem with it. She said, "Well Jean, since you didn't object I assumed it was fine, and now I've scheduled it in"!'

'But did she? Write and give you the date?'

Jean burst into loud sobs. 'I don't know! You know what we're like! We don't bother with the post any more, it's never for us. I ignore it, I just shove it in the library desk, I hardly look at it!'

'Oh Christ.' Michael got to his feet and stood looking round wildly.

'Michael, I tried to stop her, I really did. I said I'd be out, but she just said that's why she was ringing, to make sure I'd be here. Oh, *Michael!*'

'But why? Did you ask her *why* she's coming?'

'I couldn't! She's so definite and so, I don't know, so *official*. I couldn't exactly *demand* to know. I did say, oh you've never done that before, visited when I'm doing an assignment, and she said it was a new company policy, it was all in the letter. Oh Michael, I don't believe her! She knows! She knows, and she's coming to spoil everything! She'll ruin everything!'

'Oh no, she won't,' Michael said quietly. He took a few steps away, leaving Jean sitting on the grass. He had to think. Crying softly, Jean collected her hair and twisted it anxiously into a tight bundle at the back of her head. Then she picked Charlie up from the grass and rocked him gently as his little voice creaked in unconvincing half-complaint.

Michael turned away, trying to think, but found himself considering the house, wondering for one wild second if it might be looking back at him. It never changed in itself, but he liked the way it wore the changing colours of the light so trans-parently, remaining always the same behind them however varying the cloaks of certain times of the day or year. Though the hours and seasons changed, the light this summer must be the same as in summers past, and come the next one after this, it would be no different. In the early afternoon in summer-time, the same warming light would glow on these walls, always like this.

Now the sun was slanting across the stone tiles of the roof and glancing off the glass of the upper windows. Light fell and dappled the wall behind the wisteria whose boughs hung in their motionless, frozen writhing as they had done for hundreds of years. Perhaps in the droop of the leaves there was a touch of complacency that flowers would come again next year and every year after that, and that time would bleach the colour from them by such tiny degrees that the blossom would not so much lose its purple as grow graciously towards whiteness, as if acquiring dust. And while the wisteria would flower with or without Michael's attention, he felt that his admiration was somehow necessary; it was as if he were being shown some important small treasure that lay in the scooped palm of the house, something fragile and elusive in this play of light and shadow on flowers and leaves, of summer sunlight on stone. He must not neglect the privilege.

It seemed that with the same slow, quiet skill of insinuation that bound the wisteria to its walls, this house had woven itself in and among them – Jean, Steph, himself, even Charlie – had gathered them all in towards itself and to one another, and it seemed also that whole centuries of summers and winters were caught in along with them, trapped, stilled, and kept tight in its web. The house seemed to be saying, do not struggle, and do not move from here. Every important thing that ever was, or could be, is here. Like you, it is held in the very stone, it lies under the brushstrokes of the pictures on the walls, it sits on the pages of books and is woven in with every thread. It grows in the garden, is warmed in the sunlight, rests in the darkness. Stay.

Of course. How could he ever have doubted it? He returned across the grass and crouched down next to Jean. She looked up. Her eyes were still frantic.

'Michael?'

Michael said, 'Shelley – she can't *know*. How could she? Tell me exactly what she said.'

'She said they were introducing Management Visits. A friendly drop-in, she said, just to see there are no problems.'

She began to cry again. Michael got up, swung Charlie up into his arms and helped Jean to her feet.

'Oh Michael, what are we going to *do?*'

'You're not to worry. We'll do whatever we have to.' He looked back at the house. 'We're staying.'

Jean came out from the back of the house at the sound of Shelley's car on the gravel, patting her tidied hair and intending to give the impression that she knew her place and never used the front door. She had an idea that Shelley would notice and appreciate that sort of observance. But all of Shelley's attention was concentrated on heaving herself out of the hot car. She moved with a sense of grievance, as if she were being made to carry a weight that she considered privately was heavier than anything she should reasonably be expected to shift. As she straightened up, puffing herself into composure, she took in the courtyard, stables, outbuildings and the front of the house. She gave a breathy whistle.

'Oo-ooh. Well Jean, you've landed on your feet here, haven't you?' she said. She made a face. 'Look at all this. Just your thing, I should say. *Very* cut above.'

Jean winced as her words rang round and bounced off the walls of the courtyard. She had forgotten how loud Shelley's voice was.

'I didn't get a chance to tell you,' she said, 'on the phone. There are other people here. I tried to tell you on the phone but I didn't get a chance and then all of a sudden you'd gone. The owner's cousin's here.'

'Oh? Nothing was said about *that*.' Shelley drew herself up. 'In fact, Jean, nothing's been said, *period*. You're meant to ring in once a month.'

'No, well,' Jean said.

'Slipping down on the details, we don't like it.'

'Yes, but–'

'No way do I like slipping down on the details, Jean. Not in this company. You're getting paid to take sole responsibility, and now you're saying – oh sugar.' A rising burble of *Yankee Doodle Dandy* was sounding from inside her bag. She fumbled and found the mobile phone and began to prod at it with fingers too large for the tiny keys.

'It's the office.' Shelley cast her eyes heavenwards. Jean took her chance to wander off a distance while Shelley shouted at the caller. The ringing of the mobile phone was silently noted by each of them as proof of a slight superiority over the other.

Shelley rang off, turned to Jean and made another face. 'Sorry about that! Sometimes they do need to access me. Technology!'

Jean had stooped to pull at a few weeds among the catmint and pansies that grew in one of the stone troughs on the edge of the gravel. She jammed the small green clump into her dress pocket. How stupid of her. Had it looked proprietorial, lifting weeds like that?

'Oh, never mind. It doesn't matter to me, I assure you.'

'It was just the office. They needed my input on a decision.'

'I see. Do you want to come in?' Jean set off to lead the way round to the back.

'So who did you say was here?'

'The owner's cousin, that's all. It doesn't make any difference. I'm still doing the job. I'm still house sitting, they're just relations, they're just staying for a while. It doesn't bother me, them being here. In fact, I quite like the company.' She wondered if she were saying too much. Where on earth was Michael?

Just then he called out from behind them and they turned to see him appear from the front door. He sauntered out of the house towards them, his arms folded. He was wearing old khaki shorts and a soft, floppy shirt and sandals. He had tipped his tattered straw hat back on his head but it was still obvious that he needed a haircut. His dark hair gleamed blue-black in the sun and his fringe flopped in his eyes. Pushing his hair away with one hand he beamed a friendly, nonchalant smile and advanced, extending one hand.

'Well, gosh, how do you do? Umm – Michael Standish-Cave,' he said slowly, with what Jean thought was unnecessary languor. 'You're the famous Shelley from the agency, I gather? Down for a visit? Good for you!'

'I, er ... the agency, we weren't aware that there would be any other occupants in residence during the agreed period. Our client–'

'Oh, um, yes, *occupants in residence*,' Michael said, carelessly amused. 'Good old Oliver. He came up trumps, and thank God, quite frankly. I'm his cousin, by the way. On our fathers' side, obviously.'

'Mr Standish-Cave hadn't made us aware–'

'No, of course, well, we weren't aware ourselves. We did just rather descend, I'm afraid, Oliver said not to hesitate. We're between flats, actually. I knew Oliver's place was empty so I just rang him up. I admit I was rather relying on him to come to the rescue, don't know what else we'd have done quite frankly. He said oh, go straight on down and make yourselves at home, only for God's sake ring the house sitter first and tell her you're coming or she'll have a fit!'

He turned and laughed at Jean, who laughed decorously in reply. 'I must say it's grand to be out of town in the summer! And she took it jolly well, didn't you, an invasion of Standish-Caves!' He turned to Shelley. 'She's doing an *awfully* good job, you know.'

'An invasion?'

But Michael had started to lead the way down the path between the rose beds and Jean rather delicately dropped back and allowed him to. He was striding along rather fast now. Behind Jean, Shelley struggled along last with a lumpy shoulder bag on one arm and a ladylike black briefcase in the other. There was another volley of *Yankee Doodle Dandy*, which Shelley this time silenced with a couple of exasperated stabs. Jean turned and watched her. She was wearing low-fronted black shoes with heels like short pencils, which gave the impression that her thick legs ended in hooves. With each step her foot sank deep into the gravel, so she was taking dainty little steps, as if doing so would somehow make her lighter.

The effect was of a cow trying to tiptoe.

'An invasion? I mean, Jean, she– How many are there, here, I mean?'

Michael turned and walked backwards without slowing down, as he called back to her, now several yards behind, 'Oh, just the three! My missus, and Charlie, that's the son and heir, five months. But we'll be gone in another week. I say, you're not wearing the right shoes for the country, are you? Poor you!'

He stopped and waited with his hands on his hips, grinning. 'Course, we wouldn't have been stuck in the first place without a roof over our heads but God, decorators! They're on another planet, aren't they? Three weeks behind already. Here we are!' He was steering Shelley through the back door into the kitchen. 'Gosh, you do look hot!' he beamed.

Jean silently filled the kettle, watching Shelley out of the corner of her eye. Michael was right. Shelley's suit was made of something that sparkled very slightly in the sun and was of a light sage green colour. Two thick slices of dark green, like watermelon skins, grinned beneath her armpits. With a tinkle of her bracelet she lifted one hand to move her frizzy hair, which today was sticking to her scalp like clumps of damp wire. Her round face had started to ooze like a carelessly kept cheese. Jean disliked Shelley enough to feel a sharp and unworthy pleasure that she looked such a mess. In fact, it was more than that, Jean realised, with a slight shock, as she set about making tea. Her pleasure stemmed not just from Shelley's wrecked appearance but from watching her in the role of underdog. Michael had taken up his customary place with his back to the Aga, where he stood with his hands on the rail.

'Do sit down, Kell – er... – Shelley,' he said graciously, gesturing to a chair.

Shelley sat down, confused. She had stepped out of her car very clear about who was in charge. Of course the owner could invite whomsoever he pleased to use his house in his absence, but the balance was upset. He was under no obligation to do so, but Mr Standish-Cave had not had the courtesy to inform Town and Country that his cousin and family would be appearing out of the blue, and Shelley felt undermined. *'She's doing an awfully good job, you know.'* That was plain cheeky. It was her place, not his (cousin or not), to comment on how well Jean was fulfilling her duties. This cousin was behaving almost as if he owned the place, and while everyone seemed quite clear that he did not, he had been invited to treat it as if he did, and by the owner. Did that amount to much the same thing? It was confusing.

Shelley looked up at him, his lanky, relaxed body towering above her, and an affable, head-of-household grin on his face. He was being friendly, of course, but she knew that sort of friendliness. He was as status-conscious as she was, friendly only for as long as it cost him no effort. They both knew that at any moment he could decide that it no longer amused him to be charming to her, and could switch the tone of their exchanges to one as if between employer and employee. And Management Visit or not, employees cannot insist on making tours of their employers' premises. Shelley tightened her mouth and breathed noisily through her nose. Jean was no help. True to character, she was flitting about in the background setting out cups and saucers with that sly smile of hers. Jean was either slow and superior in an unassuming way, or unassuming in a slow and superior way; Shelley had never quite decided which. But now that she looked at her properly, she could see that Jean had changed. Shelley reached into her bag for her inhaler and took several puffs.

Jean said, 'So, these spot checks you're doing. They're a new thing, are they?'

'Management Visits,' Shelley corrected her. 'You've grown your hair, haven't you? I knew there was something different about you.'

As she expected it to, this caused Jean a little embarrassment. She was the sort of tight old spinster who would always prefer not have any attention drawn to herself, least of all if it concerned her appearance, and Shelley was the sort of person who made a point of ignoring such outdated and inexplicable preferences. Nonetheless there *was* something different about Jean. 'Or is it your dress? Nice to have a change from separates. It's not Marks, is it? Very unusual colour. I've never had you down as a yellow person.'

'It's not yellow,' Jean said, weak with offence, 'it's old gold.' She lifted a hand to her throat. 'I don't wear it very often, only in this weather...'

Just then Michael lunged forward from his station in front of the Aga. With a terrifying cry of *'Haaaaaa!'* he dived towards them and banged his hand down hard on the table, just inches from Shelley's elbow. The table shuddered. Shelley's hands flew up to her face and for a moment both women stared at him, wide-eyed and speechless.

'Gosh, close thing. That,' he said cheerfully, 'was an earwig. Making a beeline for your sleeve, Shelley. Lucky I saw it!' He dusted his hands together and returned to the Aga rail.

'I gather they can give quite a nasty nip,' said Jean, smooth and smiling now. Clever

Michael. She poured out three cups of tea and pushed one across the table to Shelley. 'It must have been hiding in the roses.'

'I hate the fuckers, don't you?' Michael asked, conversationally.

'Ugh. *Yuck*,' Shelley said, in Jean's direction. She realised that she could not openly complain about being 'subjected' to 'language', and was pretending instead not to have heard him. She took a sip of her tea, noting with dismay that it was Earl Grey, and looked with suspicion at the jug of roses on the table. They were already overblown and Michael's sudden mad attack had caused several of the heavy-headed flowers to moult even more petals on to the table. The drooping, denuded remains in the jug were now surrounded by a moat of curling, pink and yellow velvet discs.

'That's the trouble with garden flowers. You end up bringing in all sorts,' she asserted.

'Jean does all the flowers,' Michael said. 'Don't you, Jean? Jean, is there any of your cinnamon and honey cake left? She makes the most marvellous cinnamon and honey cake, you know.'

'Oh, really? Not for me,' Shelley said, 'thank you very much.' She gave a professional cough, signalling that she was ready to start ignoring Michael. Quite where she stood in relation to him she could not work

334

out, but she was a busy woman with a job to do and she would not be deflected from it any longer. She cleared her throat again, and reached down for her briefcase.

'Jean, there's a short questionnaire I'm required to go through with you, it won't take long. This is your opportunity to voice any issues or concerns.'

'Issues and concerns? Wouldn't I just have told you if I'd had any?' Jean asked mildly. 'Issues and concerns?' She repeated the words with suspicion. 'I haven't got any, anyway. Everything's going fine.'

'I'll say!' Michael chimed in. He had found the tin with Jean's cake in it and cut off a large lump. 'Sure I can't tempt you?' he offered Shelley, lifting up his fistful of cake and pointing to it with the other hand.

Shelley smiled and shook her head. Because she had scoffed a KitKat in the car this morning, she had skipped lunch and was now starving, but she always felt it looked better to refuse anything offered between meals. Looking back at Jean, she said, 'But it can be useful, can't it, to *identify* issues and concerns in the first place? That's good management practice, pure and simple.'

She had arranged a stapled sheaf of papers in front of her. Next to that she placed her mobile telephone and personal organiser. She now popped the top off a pen.

'Now there was that breakage for a start, wasn't there? You never did supply the details, Jean, though I do remember we asked. So if you'd just get the inventory, we can action that one, for a start.' She smiled efficiently.

Jean's mind swam. 'I kept the bits,' she said, hopelessly, 'it was a teapot.'

'That's no good,' Shelley said, busy filling in boxes on her form. 'I need to work off the inventory, so if you can just get your copy.' She looked up. 'You do have the paperwork, don't you?'

'Oh well, of course. Somewhere, though I can't quite think...'

There had been no time, in the alarming hour between Shelley's telephone call and her arrival, to work out quite what they would do or say if the question of the inventory came up. They had torn around tidying up, removing their group photographs in the silver frames, the funny pictures and messages on the front of the fridge, trying to make the house look less relaxed and lived-in. They had decided that whatever else happened Shelley must not be allowed upstairs. The smell of fresh paint from the nursery that was obvious even on the landing would be difficult to explain; temporary house guests do not usually embark on redecorating, particularly when their hosts are absent. But Michael had been quite bumptious by then.

'Oh well, if we have to, we'll just wing it!' he had told Jean. 'Just stay in character. Remember, you're the house sitter, me and Steph and Charlie are Oliver's relations. Just hang on to that and stay *in character*. And wing it!'

That was all very well. But how was she to stay in character and wing it when she actually *was* the house sitter, one who had filled the house with her own family? And burned the inventory, emptied the freezer, altered whole tracts of the garden, moved into the best rooms, purloined clothes, destroyed photographs, sold furniture and artefacts? It sounded quite unreal, put like that, not at all an accurate way of describing what she *had* done, but that was how somebody like Shelley would look at it.

'Jean? The inventory? You're not saying you've lost it, are you?'

Jean felt as if her brain were melting. She shot a look at Michael, who grinned at her. 'Oh, mea culpa, I expect! Blame us!' he told Shelley, suddenly. 'I'm afraid we've rather turned the place upside down, descending out of the blue. I have made it clear that Jean's not here to clear up after us, haven't I Jean, so things are not as pristine as they were. It was hunky-dory when we arrived. Sorry!'

He moved over to the teapot and refilled

Shelley's half-empty cup. 'Tell you what though, I did shift a load of papers upstairs. Didn't I, Jean? Let me see if it's there. Shan't be a tick.' He loped happily from the room.

His absence hung awkwardly between the two women. Jean got up and wandered over to the window. There seemed to be not a single safe thing to say. She grasped for a remark that would be *in character*. 'They're pretty, aren't they, these windows, with the lavender growing in the border there, just outside, underneath?' she offered. 'It's a lovely kitchen, don't you think?'

'You sound well at home,' Shelley said, flatly. 'I'll say that.'

'Oh, no, you just notice things after a while,' Jean said, backtracking. She felt like screaming at the woman. 'I just mean, the flowers. That's honeysuckle growing through that tree, for instance.'

Shelley did not reply. Just then Michael reappeared, followed by a shyly smiling Steph, dressed from top to toe in white. Her hair hung like long, gleaming cornstalks and Charlie's fingers turned and twisted in its thickness as he stared round. His skin was the same colour as Steph's, a mixture of gold and milk, and their faces wore the same sleep-soothed shine. Jean, for a moment until she remembered herself, looked at them with unguarded adoration.

'Hello! Charlie's come to say *hello!*' Steph trilled. She stepped forward and shook Charlie's forearm in the air. 'Charlie says hello!'

Shelley had no option but to lift her hand and give a tinkling wave back, with a sort of *Watch With Mother* smile. 'Hello, Charlie!' she said. Jean did the same.

'No sign, I'm afraid,' Michael was saying, scratching the back of his head. 'Bloody paperwork, never where you think it is. Know it's there somewhere, but need to have a bloody good look. Sorry!'

But Shelley was not listening. Steph had advanced towards her with Charlie, who had given a sudden beam and stretched his arms out towards her. He was now being settled in Shelley's lap and Shelley was taking off in an unselfconscious flight of rapture. It was not clear to whom she was speaking, Charlie, his parents, or herself, but she was making kissing faces and letting loose with a burble of words and noises of admiration. Charlie gazed up at her, impassive and open-mouthed. A bead of saliva that had been gathering on his bottom lip fell on to the back of her hand. She did not even notice.

It was Charlie who saved us. I never would have taken Shelley for the type to go helpless over babies, but once she'd got Charlie

339

on her lap I knew we would be all right. I apologised nicely about the inventory again and Michael kept butting in saying the fault was his; between us we bored Shelley into the ground over the inventory until she said it wouldn't matter. She was hardly listening. By then Charlie was smiling and laughing up at her and she was completely taken up with talking to him and shaking his bunny rabbit at him. We just bombarded her – Charlie with his giggles, I with cup after cup of tea, Michael with all sorts of banter to show what a scatty but charming sort he was. Steph just sat nearby looking luminous and drinking up the compliments about Charlie. Michael offered to check over the house himself with the inventory, when he found it, and report anything amiss direct to her in Stockport. Shelley said that would be fine.

I suppose Michael simply wore her out with protestations about what a good job I was doing and how he had said so to Oliver on the telephone. Now that was an awkward moment, because Shelley was a bit surprised at that. For a minute I thought we'd gone too far. But it was just that the agency had been instructed not to contact 'Oliver' (as Shelley was now calling him, even though she had never met him) unless there was some dire emergency. He did not wish to be disturbed, apparently. Oh, but of course the family keeps in touch, Michael said, so barefaced I could have blushed for him. So when he finally pulled her off to see the swimming pool nobody even remembered she was supposed to be here on this stupid 'management visit' and she'd long since lost any hope of seeing over the house. But by then she didn't really care. After all, she had satisfied herself that the place was still standing.

I point this out because even though I've never been a fan of Shelley's I don't think the agency can be blamed for anything, except for trying to get rid of me before I was ready.

Charlie grew fractious just in time. First he got a little cranky, and then he twisted in Shelley's arms until Steph took him firmly, settled herself back in her chair and flipped out one enormous blue-veined breast. Shelley at once turned her startled eyes away, embarrassed at being embarrassed. Nobody else was.

'More tea?' Jean asked, cupping her hand round the pot and frowning. She glanced at the clock. 'You've got a bit of a journey, haven't you?' she said pleasantly.

'Yes, poor you,' Steph murmured, smiling down at Charlie who was slapping and guzzling happily.

'I usually go round and close the windows

about now,' Jean went on. 'So if you'll excuse me–'

Shelley said quickly, 'Oh, perhaps I ought to come with you, normally I would, you see, on a normal Management Visit, if there was just the house sitter in residence. If you don't mind, I could just go round–'

'Oh, *don't!* We'd die of embarrassment, wouldn't we?' Michael almost shouted. 'If we'd known you were coming, of course it would be different. We wouldn't have dreamt of letting you see what utter piggies we are, we'd have had a proper tidy round. I'm sure you understand. But with babies, well, they do rather take over, it's a bit messy. But I'd *hate* you to see.'

'Oh, well, of course I wouldn't like to intrude, but–'

'And anyway you *know* Jean's marvellous, don't you. She keeps us in order, doesn't let us get away with too much. Eh, Jean?' He almost leered at her before turning back to Shelley. 'Come with me and see the pool,' he commanded, in a new onslaught of friendliness. 'For a bit of fresh air, before you're all cooped up in the car. Haven't got a cozzie with you by any chance – no, too bad! Still, you could always have a paddle!'

Shelley was torn; reluctant to follow the striding Michael outside and God knew where, in the wrong shoes, but pleased to have a reason to get away from the spectacle of Charlie feeding. 'Oh, well, I suppose. Just for a minute, then,' she said, with a careful smile. Michael was already at the door.

Fifteen minutes later they all trooped out to see her off, Charlie now latched to Steph's other breast, Michael once again wearing his straw hat at a silly angle. Jean was careful to stand a way off from them, and lifted a hand once at the departing car with a courteous but disinterested wave. They watched until after the car had gone from sight, and stayed listening until long after the noise of the engine had died in the evening air. The returning silence seemed newly their own after Shelley's cooing baby voices, her noisy breathing and her *Yankee Doodle Dandy* telephone.

'Party time,' Michael said, under his breath.

Well, we did go a bit daft after that, I will admit. It was late for Steph to be taking Charlie home, so Michael drove them down to the edge of the village and Steph walked him in the pushchair from there. She wanted to arrive on foot, thinking that Sally might already be home (she wasn't). She knew she would go berserk if she saw them and found out that Charlie had been travelling in her arms in the front of the van, not in a proper car seat, and of course on top of that Sally knew nothing of Michael's existence. Do you begin to see the trouble we took to keep everybody happy?

It happened to be Steph's payday, and when she met up with Michael again they went off to Corsham and bought a Chinese takeaway. They had decided between them, the sweethearts, that I had had too demanding a day to cook that night! In fact they bought so much food that the man taking the order threw in free Cokes and prawn crackers, a calendar and a bottle of soy sauce. It felt like a sort of approval. They came back giggling. Then Michael said the occasion called for something special and got four bottles of champagne up from the cellar. I don't have a good memory for the names of wines, because we tried so many. But Steph stuck a candle in one of the empties from that night and it's been on the table ever since, so I know that it was a 1988 Krug, which Michael would insist is marvellous. It wasn't the ideal thing with sweet and sour though, and I think it was the combination of the two, plus the release of all the tension, that caused me to be ill so suddenly that evening. I would like it to be understood that afterwards I made every effort with the carpet. By the way, the rings on the dining table date from that evening too. There was such an air of celebration we didn't even notice how much soy sauce was escaping down the side of the bottle.

Actually, when we did, it didn't seem to matter. After all, it's only a table, Michael said, and I recall that that led on to us talking about possessions in general, and how it is that the objects that bear the marks of events in our lives are always the ones most precious to us. There was general agreement on this point.

# *June*

Oh, it was a like a life from the pages of a magazine for a while. There was the weather. I don't believe I have ever noticed the weather so much before. Here, the seasons get themselves noticed in the way that does not happen in towns, and by the time the summer really arrived I had developed something of a countrywoman's eye for it. The garden burst into bloom, of course, a thing that I would have observed without much interest before I became the kind of person who would stick her nose into flowers and bring masses of them into the house. My choice of reading expanded out from the cookery books. In the library there were dozens of books on gardening. There was one in particular that had pictures and descriptions of just about every flower that grows in England, and I took it into the garden with me and learned the names of all the ones we had. I found that the Latin names went into my head and straight back out again, but even now in August I can still recite the common names of the flowers that came up in the garden in June. There were some I already knew, of course: fat daisies that were almost spherical like pom-poms, candytuft, forget-me-nots and wallflowers, catmint, and the peonies: both white and red ones, so many! I watched the peony buds swell like wet green fists in the rain and when they split open and the flowers came I could hardly get over them, they lolled on their stems like upended tutus, all those petals with their edges ripped into tiny points. And the colour! I wondered how that shade of crimson could be brought into existence without some juice deep underground in the root being crushed and distilled and sucked up to the very tips of the flowers. There were also Canterbury bells, columbines, leopard's bane, bishop's hat, foxtail lilies, Chinese trumpet flowers – every one a delight to me.

On and on it went. Birdsong woke me at five, and I wore the same three or four dresses over and over until they grew soft and familiar. I could feel something dancing inside me, all day long. It was my first barelegged summer since I was a girl, and I almost gave up on shoes. Mine had never fitted me, quite. Then Michael brought back for me and for Steph some espadrilles that he had seen on sale at the supermarket, which turned out to be just the thing. They were such a success he bought us several more pairs, all in different colours. Our feet were as happy as the rest of us.

One day when they were finishing breakfast Michael said, 'Am I the only one who's noticed? We're all bigger.'

He looked round the table. 'Haven't you noticed it? We're *bigger*.'

They always had breakfast late. They preferred to wait until Steph had been to Sally's and returned with Charlie, by which time they were all hungry. Jean's breakfasts had resumed their original lavishness. It did not matter that they seldom got round to doing anything else before about half past eleven; the days were theirs to spend as they chose. Steph smiled her sleepy smile, and nodded without speaking. She was sitting with Charlie, who had fallen asleep with his mouth open against her skin.

'Speak for yourself,' Jean said. 'I may have filled out, a *little*. Cheek.'

'No, I mean bigger. Not fatter, just bigger. In every way. As people.'

Steph sighed, shifted Charlie and buttoned herself back into her clothes. She didn't really understand or care. She had some news for them, but she was enjoying, for the moment, having it all to herself. The pleasure of giving it could wait a little while, and anyway, she liked listening to them talk. They were always talking, these days. They just were words people, Jean and Michael, and really, she was not, never had been. What was different was that she no longer felt inadequate about it.

'All right, I have put on a little weight,' Jean said, complacently, 'I suppose.' She fitted well inside her clothes, now. 'Is that what you mean? Isn't that all it is?'

'No, we're bigger in every way.'

'Not *taller*.' That was impossible. Yet Jean began to wonder if he could be right. She liked the earnestness with which Michael would explain new things to her. She did not always succeed in seeing things differently, but she made a point of being receptive to all his ideas.

'I mean,' Michael said, 'we take up the space more. Not that we take up *more space*.' Jean and Steph raised their eyebrows at each other. 'Don't you see? We displace the space more, we breathe more air, we take more of everything, we're more solid, we're as solid ... as,' he waved one hand around vaguely, 'as everything else here.'

Steph laughed. She laughed a lot, now. Charlie stirred and groaned, decided that the noise was familiar, and settled.

Michael looked at her. 'See? That's part of it. All that sound you make. It's because we're not just *here*, it's because we're *in* it.' He gestured round the kitchen with both arms. 'It's like we've entered the walls. We're so big we're in the walls. Don't you know

350

what I mean?'

He hardly did himself, and perhaps it was asking too much for them to grasp it. Perhaps, he thought, it was impossible to understand unless you had first of all lived in Beth's house in Swindon. Not that there had been anything wrong with it, certainly nothing that Michael had been able to explain at the time, and barely could now. Beth and Barry were proud of it; they had bought the house brand new, they told him, on the drive there from the children's hospital. Michael had sat in the back of the car not really paying attention, because he was busy trying to get used to Beth in ordinary clothes. He had only ever seen her in her uniform and had somehow imagined that was the only thing she wore. In the slacks and jumper she had on now she did not seem quite the same person, although she chatted as before; even her hair did not seem properly her own. Michael sat watching the back of her capless head, feeling jaded and dismayed. Their house, they said, was on such a friendly estate. People's doors were always open. You could see green fields from it, in fact the estate itself was built on a hillside, and you could even see it from the motorway. When Barry pointed it out ('See up there? That's home from now on, son,' he had said, and Beth turned in her seat with brimming eyes and squeezed Michael's knee) Michael looked and saw half a dozen broken rows of semi-detached houses stretching horizontally across the landscape. In the distance they looked tiny, like dislocated, uncoupled container wagons from a derailed train, just like the toy ones from the fancy set that the boy in hospital had been given by his parents.

After that Michael had never quite rid himself of the feeling that he lived in a form of transport, only temporarily halted, or in a container, just a square vessel with thin walls and different compartments for putting things in. It turned out to be true that everyone's doors were open. Beth's were, usually the front and the back. She might be in the back garden hanging out washing or something, and some neighbour would arrive at the front, walk in and call out for her, and stride straight through and out the other side of the house as if the hallway were just a continuation of the pavement and the front path. Or Beth, looking from the sitting room window, would catch sight of somebody walking along and wave and yell, and rush to the door to tell them to come on in for a minute. Even the neighbourhood dogs ran in and out; one Saturday afternoon Michael, sprawled on the carpet watching football on television, suddenly heard behind him a noise like something frying in a very hot pan. He turned round to see a brown dog with an enthusiastic face peeing up against the doorframe, rattling the woodwork and carpet with yellow urine as if the sitting room were just a bus shelter or something. Michael had burst into tears. That particular incident seemed to generate even more droppings-in, callings-out and visits, full of explanations, apologies and finally gales of adult laughter. Never let it be said that Beth and Barry were the kind of people who couldn't see the funny side.

Barry drove a long distance lorry, and he worked a shift pattern that Michael never got the hang of and that added to his sense of transit. Just when he felt sure that Barry was off working for four days he would walk in, or when Michael expected to find him at home, he would have vanished. Beth would try to explain, using words like 'earlies', 'split' and 'doubles', until Michael stopped asking. Beth's hours were easier to understand, but all day long at school on the days when she was at work Michael would feel wistful and anxious, picturing her in her uniform on the children's ward. He could see all too clearly a boy just like him but *not* him, lying motionless on her lap with his head against her body, and it gave him a pain in his chest. He told the teacher about the pain and Beth was summoned to take him home, but after the third or fourth time and a visit to the doctor, Beth said, kindly as always, that it was not to happen again. He was getting to be a big boy, she told him, too big to be jealous. So Michael tried to shrink the feeling in his chest by shrinking into the house-container that he thought of as merely parked on the friendly estate where people's doors were, alarmingly, always open. From the sitting room, whose huge flat window reached almost to floor level, he watched the traffic of neighbours, children and dogs, and looked out for Beth coming home. He still felt conspicuous, even though he had shrunk himself so much by now that he was almost managing to live in his allocated space without touching the sides.

'The thing is,' he said now, 'we've expanded to fit our space. Even our voices are louder. Don't you know what I mean?'

Jean thought about it. She knew the sounds of the house now. There was the faint rush of water as the washing machine filled or emptied that she could hear upstairs in the nursery, directly above the laundry room. There was the faint gurgle of the water softener, the creak of espadrille soles on the waxed upper floors, the friendly burble of music when someone, usually Steph, left the radio on in the kitchen. (She said that music helped her milk flow, it was well known, the same thing happened to cows.) Also, these days, Jean could spend hours in the house going about her tasks, and though alone, hardly for a moment would she be in any doubt about where the others were or what they were doing. She might hear a distant, mechanical cough and then the whine of the saw, and she would know that Michael was cutting logs at the woodpile behind the far wall of the vegetable garden. She would know that he was breathing in the smell of resin and the faint warm stew of the compost heap a few yards away. Sawdust would be flying in the air around him, and he would look up from time to time and see the world streaked and skewed by the plastic safety goggles, which would be making his face sweat. She might hear the chug of the mower, or the clack of the ladders against a wall and the rustle and snap as he pruned the climbers. From the other side of the house she might hear Steph at the pool chanting a counting game with Charlie, dunking and lifting him in and out of the water, or pulling him about with a lulling sing-song, as he perched, with her hands supporting him, on a massive, duck-shaped float.

Or there might be a very particular silence from the white plastic loungers (another purchase from the garden centre) on the grass in front of the kitchen windows. At such times Steph might be drawing something.

She would only draw things she could see, a detail of the roof, a lavender bush, sometimes even an impromptu still life of whatever was to hand: an apple core, sun cream tube, sandal, or empty glass. But most often, she would draw Charlie. She filled page after page with silvery pencilled lines out of which emerged his little buds of toes, the coiled ends of hair slipping behind one ear, his closed eyes, the warm cheeks bulged in sleep, the fanning fingers and pink scoops of fingernails. Sometimes Jean would peep out of the window and see that Steph was dozing along with him, her drawing pad collapsed and pressed against her chest. Then, not wanting to disturb them, Jean would think to herself that it would make no difference if she vacuumed the kitchen tomorrow instead of this minute, or if she blended the herbs and nuts for pesto later on (she had gone from Larousse to the River Café by this time).

Sometimes she would hear Michael and Steph going about something together, talking in a continual, contented banter about the score of a croquet game, the amount of fruit to be picked, how slowly Steph read, how fast Michael did. Even, once, she heard them arguing gently about which one of them Charlie resembled more, stopping just short of actually using the words 'takes after'. And then there were the shrieks, the calling out, the yelling from one end of the place to the other when one of them wanted the others for something, doors opening and closing, footsteps.

'We make more noise,' she said, 'if that's what you mean. Because we go about things just as we like. As if nobody is ever going to mind,' she said, smiling at Charlie.

'And nobody is,' Michael said, as if his point had been proved.

'Oh, by the way,' Steph said, 'Charlie's staying the night.'

She had been waiting to tell them this, and now looked round with shining eyes. It was great fun, being able to tell people something that was going to make them pleased with her. She had never realised. 'Aren't you, little Charlie-arlie, little Charlie's going to sleepy-byes in his cot, going to stay all night and be a good baby, aren't you, Charlie?' she crooned at him, drawing out both her pleasure and their surprise. 'Sally's got a boyfriend,' she said. 'She met him at work, he's a lawyer as well, in her firm, he joined when she was on maternity leave. She goes on about it all the time. Philip. He's younger than her. And she doesn't know if she should tell her husband about him or not, she sort of wants to. *I* said she should wait a bit.'

She looked up at them importantly. 'Anyway, the thing is she asked me to baby-sit. Ages ago. She's asked me loads of times

357

and I kept saying I couldn't, so she got somebody else from the village, only tonight they've cancelled. So this morning she's all desperate and I said I'd do it but it'd be better if we just kept him here instead of me taking him back for six o'clock and baby-sitting him there, better for her so she's got lots of time to get ready, and he can sleep over here so she won't have to worry about getting back afterwards or anything. And,' she smiled again, "cause it's a Friday, I said we might as well have him tomorrow so she can have a Saturday to herself for a change, we'll keep him till six. So we've got him nearly a whole weekend.'

'Are you *sure* she doesn't mind?' Jean asked. 'She doesn't see much of him in the week, are you sure she doesn't mind us having him on a Saturday?'

'If you ask me,' Steph said with a knowing snort, 'she's dead pleased. She keeps asking if I think she's lost the baby weight. And the other day she asked if it was true a man can tell when a woman's given birth. If he could ... you know ... feel anything.'

'Really!' Jean exclaimed. She wanted to sound as if she were only pretending to be shocked but in fact she was, a little.

'I said, as if I should know!'

'What's that got to do with you baby-sitting?' Michael asked, wondering about the answer to Sally's question and promising himself he would think about it properly another time.

Steph looked witheringly at him. 'S'obvious. She's obviously planning on bringing the boyfriend back tonight, isn't she? If Charlie's away she can shag him all night, can't she? And probably all day tomorrow as well.'

'Really!' Michael cried, mimicking Jean. 'Really, Stephanie! How can you use that word in front of Charles!'

'Shagging? But that's exactly what *she'd* say!' Steph told them, laughing again, this time louder.

It was not exactly what Sally said. But she did say that it had been a treat having Charlie out of the house overnight. 'Because if anything, Steph, since I've been back at work he's been even worse at night. He's still waking for a feed and he's gone bloody *backwards* with the bottle, I'm up for hours with him. Don't you think he's gone backwards? Don't tell me he takes the bottle for *you*.'

'Well ... you know, he might just be playing you up a bit. You know, just for the attention?'

'Oh don't *you* start making me feel guilty! Bloody hell, I've got to earn a living, haven't I? Aren't I entitled to some fun and a bit of time to myself?'

'Of course you are! I didn't mean that. We're happy to have him. I mean, we haven't got your sort of pressure, have we? It's easier for us. In fact my aunt says he's ever so welcome to come again next weekend. Then you could have another peaceful night, couldn't you?'

Sally accepted the offer. And on the weekend following that, Charlie was allowed to stay away for two nights, and after that it became the norm that on a Thursday morning Sally would kiss him goodbye and not see him again until Saturday evening. She made a point of saying that she was not enjoying herself, not entirely.

'They're chucking work at me like it's going out of fashion,' she told Steph. 'If you ask me they're trying it on – can she or can't she cope with it now she's got a baby, oh, they want to think it can't be done. They're waiting to see if I'll go under, well, I'm buggered if I will. I can work all Thursday night if you've got Charlie, can't I? I mean, if I wasn't a single parent I'd have somebody to help me handle Charlie in the evenings, wouldn't I? All I'm getting is what millions of people get. And if you've got him Friday as well, that gives me a bit of time with Philip, and I don't see what's so bloody unreasonable about having a bit of fun, do you?'

'Of course it's not unreasonable,' Steph

said, smoothly. 'Charlie's perfectly happy and that's the main thing, isn't it?'

'Of course! There's no reason to feel guilty about it and you know what? I don't. People don't understand that. I mean you should hear Charlie's grandad – he was on the phone again, when am I going out to Nepal, when is Charlie getting christened, et bloody cetera. Christ!'

As Sally grew happier her house became even more untidy and the range of things left lying around widened. It now included many more pieces of makeup, sometimes squashed into lardy pink lumps on the floors or tabletop, wine bottles and theatre programmes, matchbooks from restaurants, a couple of books on hot air ballooning (Philip's hobby) and, once, an unworn pair of black stockings that had been, as Sally explained to Steph, 'ripped to buggery' on their way out of the packet. Steph would clear up these things into prim little heaps that made Sally laugh.

At the end of June there was to be a hot air balloon festival near Deauville. Sally informed Steph, in what sounded like a prepared statement, that Philip had been very generous about Sundays, quite prepared to share them with a six-month old baby who was not even his. He complained about it really very little, especially when, it should be remembered, Philip was five years younger than Sally and had no ambitions yet to be a father himself. So it seemed to Sally quite reasonable that he should now make it clear, of course in a gentle way, that he wanted to go to France without Charlie, just the two of them, leaving on the Wednesday and returning on Sunday the 29th of June. In fact it was not just reasonable, it was rather sweet and romantic, although it did mean that Sally now had to ask a favour. Not that she did so lightly. She had thought about it and discussed it with Philip. They both felt that it was terribly lucky that Charlie was not the clingy and difficult baby he had been a couple of months ago, and that Sally could contemplate leaving him with Steph for four nights with a completely easy mind.

I suppose I'm of that generation that is meant to believe that everything is worse than it used to be, including mothers. But they could be bad in my day, too. I've been painfully aware from an early age of how bad mothers can be. So it's just in general that I think I don't understand mothers (with the exception of Steph, of course) and not, as you might expect me to say, 'modern' mothers. Nor am I saying that Sally is necessarily a bad mother. She committed no sin; inattention is not in itself a sin, though I am of the no doubt old-fashioned opinion that there is considerable vanity in the belief that one can attend satisfactorily to so many things at once. But no, the puzzle is mothers generally. There's no explaining them or, to be more accurate, there's no explaining why the people who make the best ones are not necessarily the ones who have the babies.

Although I'm not referring to Mother, is that clear? I daresay Mother and I each blamed the other for our situation, and I am prepared to admit that I cannot have been without fault. No, I mean my own, actual mother, the one who (I like to think still) was killed in an air raid on Cardiff just before my fifth birthday, in 1940. The one who I am sure must have made the dress I was wearing on the day when Mother collected me from the children's home and brought me on the train all the way back to Oakfield Avenue. The one of whom I do not have a photograph and cannot recall a thing, not the colour of her hair, the sound of her voice, nor the smell of her skin, nor the feel of my arms round her neck. It may even be a presumption that I ever did put my arms round her neck, but I cannot imagine I did not. Not knowing how that felt is what I most miss – and this is important, the point being that it is perfectly possible to miss something one has never had. It is not the contrast between having and not-having that is at the root of the pain. You simply go without and feel the lack.

In fact I don't know why I think about necks and arms when what I recall most about that time is knees. Not even hers, my real mother's, but Mother's. That day we had walked from the children's home to the station without saying anything. Mother carried my case in one hand and held on to the strap of her shoulder bag in the other. Was that why she did not take my hand? While we were in the waiting room I needed to go to the lavatory, so I raised my hand and asked to be excused. Mother pushed my arm down and said very quickly, 'You should have gone before we left. What a waste of a good penny. And you're to call me Mother.'

Then in the train there were Mother's purple and white knees (like two not very meaty ham hocks, as I now picture them). It was freezing, and so crowded that there was nowhere for me to sit, so I stood next to her the entire way. My ankles were stinging with tiredness, and I kept lurching over on to the sides of my shoes until she told me I would ruin them. Sometimes I tried to lean against her knees just to take the weight off my legs, but they were too hard and wide, as clenched as fists, and she would move me off and tell me not to fidget. She did not take me on to her lap because she was knitting most of the way, something that had no colour. There was a bit of conversation in the carriage, I think about me, there was an atmosphere of slight congratulation; Mother behaved as if she had acquired something quite covetable that was nevertheless proving awkward to cart home, like a new ironing board or a stepladder or something. A lady told me she was sure I had a nice smile, would I not show her how nice my smile was? I think Mother was pleased at that, but she never stopped knitting. I remember watching the needles going up and down and from side to side, and I could tell she was doing it to fend me off.

Anyway, all that is beside the point. I don't know why I digressed, unless it's to show that I have never, at least not since the age of five, been starry-eyed about mothers. Yet I was taken aback that Sally handed Charlie over so casually. Glad, too, of course, because Charlie made us complete, but at the same time almost annoyed. It was no doubt perverse of me but I kept thinking, how could she? I would never, ever have let Michael be taken off by virtual strangers at that age. I told him so and I think he liked knowing that if he had been in my care he would not have been dumped with just anybody for any reason at all, let alone for a hot air balloon festival. What is that, anyway? Sally had her priorities all wrong. In fact it's hard to believe she even thought of herself as a mother in the true sense. There's some excuse, you see, for Mother (I see that now) who never actually gave birth to me, but none for my actual mother or, in my opinion, for Sally. Though I am not without sympathy for her. I do realise that she will be terribly upset.

Steph wheeled Charlie back to Sally's house on Sunday evening trying not to mind that Sally's holiday with Philip was over. Four days and nights with Charlie had been just long enough to get used to having him with her all the time, and he fitted so perfectly into whatever else they did, observing what they were up to with such amused interest, that sometimes it even seemed that they went about jobs just so that he could watch. The planting of her marigolds, for instance. They had been almost as much for Charlie as for Miranda.

The stock of Bill's shop in the village had been expanding as the summer progressed; he had set out slanting tables outside from which he sold local fruit, vegetables and plants, spending long hours, when it was warm enough, sitting out there himself on a picnic chair with his newspaper. On Wednesday morning, walking Charlie back to the manor for his four day stay, Steph's eye had been caught by trays of bright yellow marigolds. On an impulse she had bought three of them, earning Bill's undying respect, and had taken nearly twice as long as usual to walk back to the manor with two of them wedged into the carrying shelf at the base of the pushchair and the third balanced on the front bar. While Charlie watched, she planted them out later that day in the shape of a wide letter 'M', over Miranda's grave under Jean's magnolia tree. Of course she got a little tearful, and Charlie watched her solemnly and almost seemed to understand.

But it was Sunday now; the marigolds had been watered in and were doing well, and it seemed a long time since Wednesday. Still, she would have Charlie back again in the morning, she told herself. But all the way down the drive and along the main road to the village she was thinking how crazy it was, all this ferrying back and forward to Sally's just to leave Charlie there for a few hours overnight. Sally would be going back to work the next day, and Steph knew that on Monday night the old pattern would resume; Sally would barge in loudly, and she would have to be waiting to hand Charlie over to her again. It was becoming harder and harder to do. Even as she would be calling out 'Hi! In here!' in response to

367

Sally's crash of the front door, she would be silently begging Charlie to understand that she was not betraying him. She would nuzzle one more time into his neck and breathe in his ear that she would be back in the morning, but she could not bear to look at him closely for fear that she might see abandonment on his face. Giving him back at the end of each day felt pointless and inappropriate, especially as Sally more often than not did not stop yapping long enough to take much notice of him. When she did quieten down long enough to acknowledge that he was actually sitting on her lap, she seemed reluctant to break some train of thought of her own in order to pay him any proper attention. Steph sometimes wondered if she ought to remind her that she had spent the past nine hours away from her baby son and should be more delighted to have him back.

Steph reached the house and saw that Sally's car was parked outside. 'She's back, Charlie,' she told him as she unstrapped him from the pushchair and carried him to the door. 'Never mind,' she whispered, bracing herself to part with him.

She had to leave the pushchair in the front garden because the hall was too full of a freshly dumped consignment of new stuff. With Charlie in her arms she picked her way across the threshold, past Sally's luggage, a plastic picnic box, supermarket bags, cases of wine and Sally herself, who was leaning against the wall with the phone at one ear, listening grimly to what must be a long speech at the other end. She squeezed up to let Steph by, ruffling Charlie's hair and pouting at him. In the kitchen Steph came upon a huge, glass-eyed, orange teddy bear, perched up on a chair. It was wearing a leather balaclava, a fringed white silk scarf and a sash that read 'Fête de Deauville'. Charlie took one look at it and began to wail. Steph backed out and carried him into the dining room where she set about changing him and getting him into his pyjamas. She felt she could hardly turn round without bumping into things; even though none of the fall-out from Sally's trip seemed to have made it this far, there still seemed to be less space than before for her and for Charlie. The room itself seemed smaller, as if during the past four days the walls had been quietly and malevolently shuffling forwards and closing in. She realised that Michael had been right about getting bigger. In this house she felt the opposite of how the manor made her feel. Here, she wondered if she ought to try to shrink. She said little enough in Sally's presence, but even the voice inside her wanted to make more noise and use up more air than this house was prepared to allow her. She felt as if even the taking of a deep breath would cause her to expand into some place she should not go.

Steph could hear through the open door that Sally was now talking back aggressively to whoever was on the telephone. She sounded slightly drunk. Steph could not quite catch the meaning, but as the hissing voice reached their ears, it seemed that Charlie was picking up the atmosphere, staring up at her with a kind of mourning in his eyes. 'I know, I know,' she told him softly, 'but don't you worry.' She was praying to herself that it was not Philip at the other end of the telephone. What if the holiday had been a disaster and Sally was right now giving him his marching orders? It was just the way Sally would do it, she thought; full of indignation and certainty, as if Philip had all along simply been wasting her precious time. Heaven forbid that Sally might find herself without the diversion of a boyfriend and with more time and energy for her son. Just then the telephone was banged down.

'Bloody bastard!' Sally shouted down the hall on her way to the kitchen. 'Want a coffee, Steph?'

Steph had grown accustomed to proper coffee, not Sally's brackish instant, but if she were being asked to stay and have coffee it meant that Sally was about to go off on one of her rants and wanted Steph there to listen. She called back that that would be lovely, and made a 'yuck' face at Charlie, who grinned. When she took him into the kitchen a few moments later she found her mug of coffee and Charlie's bottle of formula waiting. But he was barely awake now, full to the gunnels with the last feed he had had from Steph before leaving to come back. He sucked his thumb in her arms, while his eyelids floated reluctantly down over his eyes and slowly up again.

The orange teddy had been dumped on the floor and Sally occupied the chair where it had been sitting. She had a glass of wine in front of her and was eating pistachio nuts out of a box on the table. Steph slipped into another chair, glad that the bear was out of Charlie's sightline even though he was probably too bog-eyed to notice it.

'Oh, look at him,' Sally said, with her head on one side. 'Tired out.'

'Oh, just glad to be back with his Mum, I should think,' Steph said. She made a point of coming out with this sort of rubbish. She took a sip of her coffee.

'Oh, Steph – *France*,' Sally announced, raising her glass and waving it in the direction of the nuts, 'France is fantastic. They're a third of the price over there, pistachios. Have some, go on. And the wine's amazing. This was two quid a bottle. D'you like wine?

Oh, I should have offered. You can take a bottle home with you if you like, we brought back loads.'

'Oh! Oh, thanks!' Steph smiled. She was getting quite choosy about wine, although not as choosy as Jean and Michael who could hold quite long conversations about it. In fact at this time of day, she never drank coffee. Michael would usually be handing her a drink, probably champagne, about now. It was funny to think of Jean taking Sally's bottle of plonk and considering whether or not it was good enough to cook with. She could picture her wrinkling her nose at the label, raising an eyebrow and murmuring about some recipe or other. She smiled. 'Well, we've had a very nice time, too, haven't we, Charlie?' she said in a rather bouncing voice.

'Oh God. *God*, so did we!' Sally drawled, stretching her arms up behind her head and lifting her hair. 'Oh, God, the joy, not being woken up at six. And Philip, really – he's fantastic.' She looked away, yawning and rapt in some luxurious memory. 'I'm bloody *shattered*, actually.'

'Yes, a lovely time we've had,' Steph said. 'He was absolutely fine, 'cause he's a good little baby, aren't you, Charlie?'

Sally gave a small snort and drew her arms back down on to the table where they landed heavily. 'That's exactly what I said.

On the phone just now. He'll be perfectly happy, I said, he's as happy as Larry with her. At this age they're very adaptable, I said, but he doesn't get it, though. His generation can't.' She slurped some wine.

'His generation?' Steph looked at her. 'I did sort of wonder, I mean I wondered if that was ... so it wasn't...'

Sally looked at her scornfully, as if Steph had not being paying proper attention. 'That was Charlie's grandad, miserable old sod. My father-in-law. He's still on his campaign, ringing up and fretting. Been trying to get me all weekend, apparently. Like it's a crime to go away! I mean it's not like he's ever on hand, he hardly ever bothers to come and see him – Charlie wouldn't know his grandfather from the bloody Archbishop of Canterbury! But he's all het up because I dare to have a few days' break and leave Charlie with other people.' She snorted again and filled up her glass. 'He's never once *really* asked about *me*. Doesn't want to know how *I'm* managing. Because God forbid, what if I asked him to help? Oh, he's not up for that. So just now I told him straight,' she said, in a tone that left Steph in no doubt that she had, 'straight out, I told him, your precious grandson is fine, as I keep telling you, but no, I haven't a clue how your precious son is, because he doesn't ring up here any more. He hasn't phoned for three weeks, that's the sort of father and husband *he* is. And you might as well know, I said, I've been away. On holiday. In France, and with someone else.'

When Steph said nothing Sally went on, 'I did. I just told him. I said you might as well know I'm seeing someone, and he's a bit more clued up than your precious son. Clued up in every way. I did! I'm past caring.' She giggled at Steph's shocked face.

'And of course that didn't go down too well but I *knew*, you see, I knew he'd get all embarrassed and change the subject, and sure enough all of a sudden he's back on his favourite topic: when are we getting Charlie christened. Been on about it since he was born.' She sighed and drank some more. 'Wants it sorted out before he goes off on holiday. I said I wasn't taking that sort of pressure.' She leaned back in her chair until it creaked. 'Frankly, I preferred him when he was depressed. At least it kept him quiet.'

'Charlie's asleep now,' Steph whispered. 'Want to take him?'

'Oh,' Sally said, starting up and fixing a look of enthusiasm on her face. 'Oh, sure. But what about his feed? Shouldn't he be hungry? He hasn't had his bottle.'

Steph had got up and was now easing Charlie gently on to Sally's lap. 'He's getting on for six months now. Perhaps he's ready to drop a feed,' she whispered. 'He might not need so many. I'll put this in the fridge, shall I?' She tried not to show her distaste as she picked up the baby's bottle. 'He might want some later on, around ten or eleven. And then I bet he'll sleep through.' She smiled reassuringly.

'What would I do without you, Steph?' Sally said, looking down at Charlie.

It was only as Steph was letting herself out quietly, trying not to pay attention to the now familiar, awful moment when she left him behind, that it struck her as odd that Sally should think it was Steph she could not be without, rather than Charlie. But Steph would be the last to complain. She would be back in the morning, and in the meantime there was a new and important matter to consider. Because she had decided, following the conversation about Charlie's feeds, that it was time to think about weaning.

Mr Hapgood – I never could call him Gerald – found a buyer. I went into the shop one day to find him smiling secretly and saying he had a surprise for me, which turned out to be an envelope with a hundred and seventy pounds in it. He had got an even better price for the clock than he had hoped, and how about coming through to the back for a cup of tea and a bit of a cuddle 'to celebrate'. The 'to celebrate' bit seemed unnecessary because that was what happened almost every time I went anyway. Only the arrival of a customer would put him off, and there weren't many of those at the end of weekday afternoons. Anyway, it wasn't disappointment with the amount that upset me that day, or even with what Mr Hapgood immediately started doing (he was tending to skip the preliminaries by this time), it was the empty space where the clock had been standing all those months. Suddenly it wasn't there. Of course it was silly of me to be upset and surprised. I knew it was being sold and now I had the money in my satchel, so how could I expect the clock itself to be there? But I burst into tears. Because it suddenly seemed as if it was Father himself who had gone, rather than his clock. It felt as if I were just understanding it for the first time, that Father really had gone, as if one minute I had been helping him to sit up, supporting his head while he swallowed his tablets, and the next he had suddenly been wrenched away, leaving me with his water glass in my hand staring at a dent in the pillow, the empty blankets and a bedside table cleared of his spectacles and book of crosswords. At this point, you realise, he had been dead for over six months. Why was I so slow on the uptake? I don't know. But the empty space on the floor at the back of Mr Hapgood's shop was suddenly the most desolate place on earth. I stood and howled. Every single part of me ached because I wanted to see Father's face again, and talk to him and hear his voice, and that empty space was telling me that I never, ever would.

Mr Hapgood got rather flustered and said I was sixteen after all and he hadn't forced me. When I could speak I said no, it's not that. He was clearly very relieved. Then he said he knew what the matter was, and I was to dry my eyes. What a silly girl I was being, to think that just because the clock was sold he wouldn't want to see me any more. I wasn't to think that. In fact, the last thing he wanted was for my visits to stop. I promised to keep popping in. And I did. The space where the clock had been soon filled up with other stuff but in any case, for ever afterwards I always ignored that spot.

Not long after that, Mr Hapgood sprang another surprise. This time there was no secret smiling and 'celebrating'. Instead he sat me down and told me very solemnly that sometimes people have to do one thing when they might want to do another, that some things are just not meant to be, and that people have to accept disappointment and make the best of things. Well this wasn't exactly news, but he talked as if I hadn't thought of it, and as if he was being terribly brave. I had an idea he was thinking I was being terribly brave too, but in fact I was thinking how young he sounded. That's odd, I suppose, that I thought him young, but by then I think I was abnormally old. Anyway, all his 'making the best of things' didn't seem to have much to do with me. The thing was, he said, he was getting married. He had been engaged for so long that he sometimes even forgot that he was, and I should forgive him if he hadn't mentioned his fiancée. They had been engaged for eight years, but what with his mother, and the flat above the shop being too small for all of them, he had stopped thinking they would ever actually tie the knot. Now finally, they'd managed to make a down payment on one of the new houses that were going up at Rectory Fields. They were getting a semi-detached with lounge and dining alcove, kitchen, three bedrooms, bathroom, he said, counting them off on his fingers. Lovely indoor toilet. But meanwhile, there was no reason for me to stop coming to see him. We could go on being very special friends. It was just that he respected me too much not to tell me the truth. I was The One, but the age difference, and a promise is a promise, and Veronica wanted kiddies. But he wanted me to keep coming to see him. I said all right, then. Congratulations, I said.

Michael and Jean had been picking strawberries for days, since the middle of June.
First they had eaten them just as they came,
warm off the plants, or with cream and
sugar. Black pepper had been tried. Then
they had had strawberry ice cream. Then
strawberry shortcake, and a strawberry
mousse. By the time bottles of strawberry
vinegar were maturing in the larder Michael
and Steph were begging for mercy. With the
fruit that was left, Jean announced at
breakfast on the last day of June, she would
make jam.

They waited until the afternoon, after the
sun had been on the strawberry patch all
day, and together they picked the last of the
crop. Under a canopy, Charlie in a white
brimmed hat and white cotton clothes lay
drowsy in a nest of white blankets at the end
of the strawberry beds, presiding over the
pickers like a large and rather viceregal fruit
fairy, kicking arms and legs as smooth and
golden as butter. His serious eyes, when
they were not inspecting his hands to see if
they had pulled anything more surprising
than a trapeze of saliva from his mouth,
would follow birds and insects, and from
time to time he would chatter in reply to the
others' voices or to the sound of far-off
buzzing – Michael had set wasp traps a good
distance away from him. Every few minutes
he or one of the others would rise from the

picking and sink down on to the rug nearby to chatter back to him and put on more of his sun cream, or tickle him under the chin or touch his cheek with a stained hand, to make sure he was not getting too hot.

After a time Steph stood up, groaning, and licked her fingers clean of strawberry gore. Clutching her lower back, she sauntered back to the house and returned with a tray with bottles of water and glasses, and a bowl and spoon. They plonked themselves down while Steph, sitting next to Charlie, mashed up two strawberries in the bowl with the back of the spoon and then, to Jean's slight horror, added a few drops of breast milk.

'Steph, are you *sure*, I mean is one supposed to...?' She looked round at Michael for support, but he was simply gazing at Steph with that look on his face, the one of soft but total absorption that so often came over it when he watched her with Charlie.

Steph smiled as the resulting pink paste disappeared into Charlie's mouth. After a second's astonished smacking of his lips and widening of his eyes, he opened his mouth for more. Within four mouthfuls he was laughing and turning the stuff over in his mouth. Everyone applauded. It was his first taste of anything besides milk, and because they had watched it together the event was, it went without saying, theirs alone, a private joy; nothing whatsoever to do with Sally.

They went back to the picking. The strawberries mounted up in a large plastic bowl that Jean had brought from the laundry room. It was the end of the season. Most of the whole strawberries had lost their gloss and grown dull and deviant-looking; this was the riff-raff, the small, the reticent, late-forming and grudging fruit, and it was already almost too late. Some of the berries were so ripe that as they were picked they burst in the fingers and landed in the bowl as wet, scented rags. The warm heap of exposed flesh in the bowl would, within a very few hours, begin to mist over with a blue-green bloom of mould.

Even though they discarded the rotten fruit and all the stunted berries that were almost white on one side, the quantity was almost threatening. Jean began to re-calculate the amount of sugar she would need. But there would have been even more strawberries, Michael said, if he had known more about them back in April.

'In April,' he told them when they had nearly finished, 'you've got to nip off the first blossom, it encourages more fruit. I read it in one of the gardening books, only,' he said, heaving the bowl of strawberries from the ground up on to his hip, 'not until May.'

Steph had already picked up Charlie and was following Michael back to the house, trailing his blankets on the grass behind her. So they were too far away to hear, that was all. They were simply too far away to hear, so of course did not reply when Jean said, dreamily, 'Oh well, never mind that now, we've got plenty. And there's always next year.'

They could not have heard. They had reached the end of the walled garden, crossed the sunlit lawn and were moving between the borders of rose bushes into the jagged shadow of the corner of the house. Jean stared after them until they disappeared round the side. She thought, watching them go, 'They didn't hear me. So I could pretend that I never said that, that it was never even thought of, let alone said. I could pretend that, even to myself.' She stooped down, ruffled through the clumped leaves of a couple of strawberry plants, with a hand that was shaking. She could hear her own heart beating. Finding nothing worth picking, she stood up again. She should go back to the house. There were things to do. There was no reason for her to stand out here, with the sun beating down, as if she were waiting for something. But then it came, as she knew it would, as she stood unwilling or unable to move, an old ache gathering weight somewhere inside her.

Of course I never did go to university.

Mother wouldn't put up the money and in any case, she said, she needed me at home. (By the way, I'm sorry to keep going back to Mother, and I'm not confessing anything in the sense of owning up to something I should not have done. She drove me too far.) The clock money paid for a secretarial course, and the rest went on my board, Mother's point being that I had left school and until I was earning why should she stump up for everything if, after the course was paid for, I was still 'sitting on a goldmine'. Hardly a goldmine. I began to get angry with Father for saying the clock would get me through college. I even began to wonder if by 'college' he actually had meant Technical College, a year learning to type and file and do shorthand and organise the boss's diary? If so, it was just cruelty on his part to have let me run on with thoughts of proper university. I could scarcely believe it of him, and he had always told me I could be a teacher, like him. But then his dying and leaving me felt like an act of cruelty also. All those years I spent thinking ill of him, of course I regret them now, but I was misled.

After college I was never out of work, Mother would have to concede that. I kept the money coming in, not that secretaries earn much, and I was there at the end of every day. I fed her the usual things at the usual times, making sure that nothing on the plate had a noticeable taste. Anything that might be described as having what I now consider flavour she would have refused, because she did not like anything unexpected in her mouth. She said anything with a taste came back on her. Steamed fish, mashed potato. Semolina. Yes, I looked after her and I was never out of work, and before I knew it, those two facts were all I had to put in place of achievements, not that they added up to enough to be proud of. Nothing in the actual work I did, in any one of the places where I was employed over the years, interested me in the slightest. Most of the time I scarcely noticed what I typed or took down in my shorthand pad or filed away or said politely on the telephone. I was a pleasant enough colleague, I think, not difficult or hostile, but I did not care one way or the other about the work that went on, and over time that becomes indistinguishable from mental dullness. I could be relied upon to do as I was asked, nothing more. It seemed enough to me. Ditto at home with Mother, although I did develop what she called a 'nasty sarcastic streak'. I know what she meant. I could sometimes come out with remarks that were rather bitter-sounding. And sarcasm without wit (which I have never possessed) comes across rather sourly. Without quite realising it, I became sour.

I had long, long since stopped going to Mr Hapgood's, of course. Once or twice towards the end I saw through the glass bit of the shop door that there was a woman with dyed blonde hair behind the counter, and on those days I walked on home. Gradually I stopped even looking to see if she was there and didn't go near the place. Mr Hapgood had grown a little distant, anyway, by then.

Incredible, you will be thinking, that she could even think of carrying on with that awful man, even after she knew he was getting married? How could anyone be so naïve? But it wasn't naïveté, quite, although I was as ignorant and unwise as the next provincial schoolgirl in 1951, and out of my depth. If you think depravity's involved, I'm not even sure I was much less depraved than he was. But there was more to it than that. I had been lonely since Father died and at the end of every school day my heart sank at the thought of going home. At least going to Mr Hapgood's put that off for an hour. At least, in the smoky back of the shop, I got a welcome of sorts.

And I think I was overwhelmed by something else, a sort of knowledge that had been growing over the years, more in my bones than in my brain, a thing I just knew without noticing I'd been learning it. So when I told Mr Hapgood that yes, I would keep coming, it felt not like a decision that I was making but like a reflex reaction to a blow that I had been expecting. It was quite clear and unsurprising. The fact was that with Father gone, I had nobody. Nobody. The feeling this gave me was unbearable, as if I was made of something weighty but without colour or life, like damp ashes, so worthless I could be swept into a sack and tipped out somewhere and never be missed. So I would have clung to anyone who stopped me feeling like that. I would have stuck to anyone who wanted me, and I was in no position to much mind who they were, or even what it was they wanted me for.

So for a time Mr Hapgood was a kind of intermittent relief from that feeling. But when that episode finally closed the feeling came back, of course, and I managed to live for years and years either feeling it or in danger of feeling it, so it turned out not to be unbearable after all, in the strict sense. I bore it, I even learned to pretend it wasn't there. But I've done enough of that now. I cannot bear to feel like that ever again, not now that I been truly free of it, living here.

It was my own fault, that day of the strawberry picking, letting a mention of next year slip out of my mouth, but it helped me. Because when that unbearable feeling stole over me again, as I stood there, after I had watched them walk away from me, that was the moment when I knew I would do anything, I mean absolutely anything, to keep us all together.

# July

Steph was pressing the little studs on Charlie's pale green shorts and tucking in his T-shirt, wondering which of his several hats he might wear today. It was going to be hot again, too hot for jam making, really, but the fruit had been picked yesterday and would not last out the day.

'We're going to make jam, Charlie,' she told him. 'Aren't we? Are you going to help me make the jam? Are you going to have a taste of the jam?' She popped an acorn shaped hat of green gingham on his head. Charlie looked back at her coolly. It was a morning on which Sally had, surprisingly, left calmly and in good time, so Charlie had already had a peaceful breakfast with Steph and apparently was scrutinising the day ahead with equanimity. They were both startled by the sudden loud pang-pang-pang of Sally's doorbell.

A very tall, elderly man wearing smeared glasses and dressed in a light linen jacket and an open-necked shirt stood on the doorstep. He raised his panama hat and smiled experimentally. 'How do you do. I hope Sally told you to expect me?'

He asked this in a way that suggested he assumed she would have, so Steph felt somehow in the wrong when she told him that Sally had not. The man wriggled his full lips. 'Oh, dear. I did tell Sally. I told her expressly that I would visit today. I was supposed to pop in yesterday evening which frankly would have been more convenient, but she rang and said Charlie was too tired. So I said I would come today instead, and she said I would have to be here early. Do I take it I've missed her?' He looked at Charlie for the first time and chucked him under the chin. 'Hello, young man! Helloooh!'

Steph wondered how she could ask him who he was without sounding rude or suspicious. Before she could say anything he turned from Charlie, who now had hold of one of his forefingers, and said, 'And you must be Nanny, am I correct?' The words were followed by a parting of the lips, offering Steph a view of greyish teeth that appeared to be huddling in his mouth for shelter.

'I'm the childminder. Steph.'

'Well, how do you do, Steph. I'm Charlie's grandfather. Mr Brookes, or Reverend Brookes if you like, but in mufti today, not in fancy dress! Actually I'm on holiday.' He grinned at her. The sun was falling directly on his face and Steph, seeing nothing

390

beyond the obscuring rainbow glint of grease across the lenses of his glasses, could not be certain if his eyes were friendly.

'Oh. Oh, that's nice. Nice weather for you.'

'Yes, only wouldn't you just know it – I gather it's wet where I'm going! I'm off later, you see, for a week's walking. Up north, probably in the rain! Anyway, I thought I'd pop over before I head off, and see my grandson. I did tell Sally I would, but evidently she's forgotten to tell you. Eh, Charlie?'

'Oh.'

So this was the, what was it Sally had called him? The uptight bugger, the miserable old sod, the one Sally preferred when he was depressed. Steph's heart went out to him. He was just old and awkward, a big embarrassment of a man, too tall for his clothes and too helpless to clean his glasses, yet here he was on the doorstep making an effort. But what could she do?

'Well, I'm sorry Sally's not here, but we were just going. Charlie and me, we were–'

'Going? Going where?'

'Oh, we don't stay *here*. We don't spend the day here. Didn't Sally tell you? We always–' She stopped. It was clear from the falling of the man's already long face that Sally had told him nothing at all. Steph could almost hear it, Sally barking down the phone at him that he'd better be early and she wouldn't be hanging around, *she* would have to get to work, and he would have to sort it out with Steph. It was suddenly much less surprising that Sally had gone off so promptly today; she had deliberately left the two of them to deal with each other. Steph immediately felt rather sorry for herself, as well as for him. In fact Charlie's grandfather was not at all as she had imagined him. He was quite kind-looking, really, just a bit unfamiliar with babies.

'I take him up to my house. There's lots of room and the garden and everything, and a pool.' She added, 'Sally knows. We keep lots of his stuff up there, there's nothing here for him. And er, well – well, I need to get off, they're expecting us. Takes a little while, what with the pushchair.'

'Oh. Oh, I see, yes, I'm sure, but you see, I've come nearly eighteen miles. Though of course you've got your routine, I wouldn't want to…'

'Well, come on in for a minute, anyway,' Steph said, comfortably. He was nice, she was deciding. And he had come specially, and must be wearing that hat just as a sort a joke. It was typical of Sally to take against him. Sally did seem always to be furious with the wrong people. 'Come on in and have a cup of coffee. What a shame, you coming all this way and Sally never saying.'

Charlie's grandad seemed as mystified by the cluttered house as Steph was. He stood frowning, looking round the kitchen as if he were wondering if he could bear to stay in such a muddle even long enough to drink a cup of coffee.

'Tell you what,' he said. 'Don't bother with the coffee. I'll give you a lift. And then perhaps I could spend–'

'Oh, no! No, don't, there's no need, honest. Kettle's on, won't take a minute. And we like the walk. Don't we, Charlie? It's only a mile, it's just along the road, really. We count the cars, don't we, Charlie?'

'Along the road? The top road? That settles it. They tear along there, there's no proper pavement, is there, and they just tear along ... it's not safe. No, never mind the coffee, I'm giving you a lift. What can Sally be thinking of? I'll have to speak to her. So dangerous!' He had already found his car keys.

Steph tried to protest. 'But we always walk! I'm careful! I wouldn't let anything happen to him!'

'I'm sure you wouldn't, but I won't have it. I'm taking you in the car.'

'Oh, but you can't! I've just remembered. You won't have a car seat. And Charlie's is in Sally's car, and she's gone to work, and she wouldn't like it. He's got to be in a proper car seat. He's only safe if he's in a proper car seat, she says. So we can't come with you.'

The man gave a dismissive tut. 'Oh really, as if that was the point. Anyway, there's a car seat in the hall. I'm sure I saw one in the hall, on the way in.'

Steph had not noticed. There it was, partly hidden under a thrown-down jumper of Philip's. She remembered now. Philip's car was a BMW two-seater, so they had gone to France in Sally's Volvo, folding the back seat down flat to make room for the cases of wine. The car seat had been taken out and, true to form, Sally had not yet put it back.

Mr Brookes's car was almost as crammed with things as Sally's usually was. While Steph tugged the rear seat belt round the car seat, Mr Brookes cleared stuff out from the front so that Steph could sit there. He first chucked over some books, folders and a number of cardboard tubes, and then he brought out several boxes with no lids, that contained bundles of brightly coloured paper strips held by elastic bands. They all carried the same words: SAVE YOUR LYCHGATE. Several identical strips were stuck all over the windows and rear windscreen of his car. He opened the boot and began rearranging things to make room for the boxes.

'What are they?' Steph asked.

'Oh, a parish project of mine. Car stickers,

good for awareness-raising. I've still got plenty, printer was most obliging, twenty thousand cost hardly any more than five. Want some?'

'But what is it, a – whatever, a lychgate?'

'Oh, the lychgate's where you park a coffin if it's raining. You must have seen them, quite a lot of churches have them. We've done a bit of a blitz on ours, coat of paint, got a few plants in containers round it, that kind of thing. Petunias and busy lizzies, mainly. Trying to get a volunteer warden scheme going for the watering, discourage the graffiti merchants.'

'Sounds nice,' was all Steph could find to say.

Perhaps because all she could do was sit there passively, Steph felt, as soon as she was in the car, that Charlie's grandad was trying to take over. He said, 'Stephanie, please don't think I'm being at all critical of *you*. But the thought of a pushchair on this road, *well*. But it's not you, it's Sally I blame.'

'But I'm careful, I stay on the grass, we've never once had any trouble. I – oh, turn off here, the next left, this is the drive. Where it says Private Drive.' The car swung in suddenly. 'You could just drop us here,' Steph said, optimistically.

'Oh no. No, I'll take you right up. In any case, I should like, if there's no objection, to stay for a few minutes. I don't see much of my grandson, after all. Do I, Charlie?'

He turned to Charlie in the back and beamed luridly, and Steph wondered, gazing at his nostrils which opened much too wide when he smiled, if perhaps she didn't like him so much after all. Still, she thought, turning back and staring through the windscreen, it won't do any harm. She would prefer not to be giving Jean and Michael the fright of an unexpected visitor, but he wouldn't stay long. They had coped with Sally coming here, and that woman Shelley, so they could easily manage this.

Michael had moved the croquet hoops off the side lawn, which he would mow later on, and had set them out ready for a game on the stretch of grass between the back of the house and the pool pavilion. He was fetching the mallets and balls and carrying them round when he heard the sound of the car. Jean appeared at the kitchen door. Together, exchanging a look, they made their way quickly round the side of the house to the front. Steph had stepped out of the car and was hurrying towards them with an appeasing but doubtful smile. Jean stopped and was wiping her hands on her apron and Michael stood some distance behind her, tossing two croquet balls up and down in one hand. They tried to smile back.

'It's okay!' she said breathlessly, as she

reached them, 'honest, it's okay. I couldn't help it. It's only Charlie's grandad.' Jean and Michael looked past her to the back of the figure bending into the rear of the car, fiddling with the straps of the car seat. Michael stopped his half-hearted juggling with the croquet balls. 'Only I couldn't help it. He just turned up at Sally's, and then he wouldn't let me bring Charlie along the road in the pushchair. He's okay, though. He never sees Charlie and he wants to stay a minute. Just act ordinary.'

'Oh, Jesus Christ,' Michael said slowly. He was staring at the man, who was now smiling broadly and walking towards them with Charlie in his arms. 'Jesus fucking Christ.' He stepped back a few paces, but it was too late to disappear. He had been seen. 'Jean, go on and say hello.'

Mr Brookes pulled off his hat and called out, 'How do you do! Forgive my descending on you out of the blue, did Stephanie explain? Bit of communication breakdown, I'm afraid! Here we go, young man!' He shifted one arm under Charlie's bottom and handed him over to Steph. Then he extended a hand towards Jean. 'I'm Charlie's grandfather. Gordon Brookes. And you're?'

'Er, Jean,' she said, in a voice that sounded out of practice. 'I'm Jean. Hello.' Steph bit her lip. Jean looked rather wild, standing there in a strawberry smeared apron, her hair wandering. She sounded rather out of it, too.

'What a *marvellous* house!' the man was saying, taking Jean's hand and pumping it while he looked past her at the façade. 'Have you lived here long?'

'Quite long,' she managed to say, suspiciously.

'What's the period? The usual hotchpotch? Tudor origins, later additions? Glorious stone!' The man was turning his full charm and attention equally on Jean and the house, and Jean seemed about to collapse under it.

Steph shot Michael a darting look. Michael must see what was happening. Why was he simply staring, and not doing something to rescue her?

And why was Charlie's grandfather now staring so hard at Michael? The smile had gone, and his mouth was opening and closing. 'You? My God. *You.* I – I'm going to– My God, it *is* you, you're the – the–' Gordon Brookes's face was reddening.

'Steph,' Michael said quietly, 'Steph, take Jean and Charlie indoors. Please, go now. Now. Right now.' He took a step backwards.

Gordon Brookes was advancing, and growing agitated. He gasped, 'It's not, is it? It is! It's *you!* You little, you...! My figures, my St John and St Catharine. Oh good God ... you–'

Being a man capable of fury yet unused to

398

physical contact of any kind, least of all fighting, Gordon Brookes did not move smoothly, but his hands flew up and one fist caught Michael on the shoulder, half pushing, half punching. The blow seemed to take him almost as much by surprise as it did Michael, but he followed it with another before Michael could raise his arms to protect his head. Gordon Brookes had long ago been civilised into churchy mental habits, so it was a shock to him to realise that hitting somebody could feel, while unfamiliar, the only natural and appropriate thing to be doing. His outrage was overtaking all his beliefs about the pointlessness of violence; he was instead almost dancing, animated by an angry energy that he would never, ever have imagined he could expend on any response as 'mindless' as punching someone about the face. He landed a hard kick on Michael's leg. Michael's whimpering stopped him for a moment. He raised a shaking hand. 'That curate ... that poor man. You ... have you *any* idea what you did? We know you did it, you know! I'm getting the police down here, right now! Good God, you're – you won't get away with this–!'

'Steph, take Jean and Charlie away, *now*. Do it.' Michael's voice was wavering, and when he lowered his arms from his head, his eyes and lips fluttered with fear. Yet he did not move from the spot where he stood, nor take his eyes away from Gordon Brookes. Brookes moved in again, this time kicking wildly.

'Steph, go! Go, for Christ's sake!'

Steph, still holding Charlie, managed to pull at Jean's arm and she, now dumbly bewildered, allowed herself to be led. They hurried in the direction of the house. And Steph even managed to prevent them both from looking back when, a moment later, they heard the hard crack of a croquet ball against the side of Gordon Brookes's head and the first of his long, despairing cries.

Michael got him helpless on the ground, though not completely unconscious, after seven or eight blows. But he would not be quiet. Michael dropped the croquet balls, raced down into the walled garden and returned with the wheelbarrow to find Gordon Brookes attempting to crawl in the direction of his car, shrieking in disbelief and pain. Sweating and weeping with the massive effort, Michael dragged him up by the shoulders. He began to resist, and succeeded in scratching Michael's face. He would not go in the wheelbarrow, but after another blow on the side of the head with a croquet ball he gave a squealing kind of scream and Michael hauled him over and left him draped across it. He heaved the barrow up and pushed it slowly and windingly round to the back. Setting down the barrow on the grass at one side, out of sight of the kitchen windows, he stood up and took several deep breaths. Gordon Brookes lay quiet at last, and limp, facing downwards, his clothes more off than on. Michael wiped his eyes and looked round.

There were roses still blooming against the wall. Was it only yesterday he had wondered about the best time to prune them? He looked down at the wheelbarrow. That would be just the kind of thing Gordon Brookes would know, and now here he was, bleeding from the side of his head that was beginning to look like a cut aubergine. Michael looked away, shaking with pity for the man and with fear for himself. For it was terrifying, how quickly it was possible to go from one to the other, from considering the pruning of roses and setting out croquet hoops, to this moment, looking at a bleeding man heaped in a wheelbarrow and facing the inevitability of the next step. More terrifying still was how much further Michael now had to go. From not far off, birds were singing above the snuffling sounds coming from the man's slack mouth. But when Michael breathed in he could smell roses and warm grass. He grew still, and then quiet, and then he wiped his hands over his eyes again, crossed the lawn and entered the kitchen. Steph and

Jean were standing in silence, waiting. Charlie waved and jiggled in Steph's arms when Michael appeared in the doorway.

'Right,' he said, still breathless, 'don't worry. Stay here for a bit. I want you to stay here, okay? Make some tea.'

But neither of them could reply. Steph opened her mouth first. 'I don't know what I did, I don't understand. Why–'

'Never mind, I'll explain. It'll be all right,' Michael said, tightly. 'It'll be all right. I'll make it all right. I've got to–' And then he began to feel that strange thing at work again, that way he actually could begin to believe himself when he had other people to convince. 'It's okay. It's just that, well, I know him. I mean he knows me, he knows about this thing I did. He'd bring the police here and we'd all, well – think about it. See? I'd end up in jail. We all might.' He smiled grimly. 'You see? What with everything. The stuff I did, the fines, us, the things here. It'd finish everything. I mean, we've got to – you see? Look, just stay in here for a while. I'll deal with it. We've got to be normal.'

'All right,' Jean said, finding her strength. 'All right.' She took a deep breath and smiled round bravely. 'We'll just be normal. Won't we? We'll just get on and make our jam, won't we, Steph? The fruit's all hulled already.' In the moment's silence after she spoke it became understood that neither she nor Steph would ask Michael exactly what he was going to do when he went back outside, and he would not volunteer to tell. They all knew.

Michael wheeled the barrow slowly round, limping from the kicks he had taken on his legs, and stopped at the side of the pool. He had begun to shake again just at the thought of touching Gordon Brookes, who was sliding so far over to one side that his head almost scraped along the grass. He did not dare think about what else he now had to do to him, and could not look at the face as he heaved him over and pulled him off the wheelbarrow. Laboriously, closing his eyes when he could, he dragged him to the edge of the water; it felt as if Gordon Brookes were filled with loose stones. Then he seemed to become aware of what was happening; he mouthed and moaned, and succeeded in raising one hand, flexing his fingers for a second over Michael's bare arm and scratching hard. Michael hissed in pain. Gordon Brookes gurgled and coughed, and his moans rose to pitiful yelping when Michael hauled him over and tipped him into the pool. He landed with a crack on the water. Michael followed, feeling through the cold shock on his groin the warm flow of his own urine. Gordon Brookes, revived by the slap of the water, flailed desperately, as if trying to grab armfuls of it. But he did not have the strength to protest much when Michael grabbed the back of his head and pushed it under. Michael turned away from the sight of the mouth taking great choking bites of water but could do nothing to avoid hearing the panicked snatches of screams as, time after time, Gordon Brookes managed to force his head up hard enough under Michael's hands to snatch at the air. Michael's legs were shaking so much that but for the water he would have collapsed. For it came as a dreadful, slow-dawning shock, how long it took. It was unbelievably long; incredible how much fight and life and air and struggle there was in one man, how often his arms tried to reach and grab at Michael's hands, and how hopelessly; Michael was filled with a kind of respectful horror until, almost exasperated and suddenly fearing that he might not be able to finish this, he gave a great roar, thrust the head down deep into the water with both hands and held it there. Brookes's mouth, still gaping and searching, surfaced only twice more. In its final, slackening, waterlogged gasp Michael thought he heard a note of sorrow. For at least ten minutes more he stood holding his head under, until long after the last throes had stopped. Michael turned his face up to the sky and saw merely a flat, blurred blue through his stinging eyes. Nor, as the minutes passed, could he hear very much, save his own bitter sobbing and the slap of water as the waves made by Gordon Brookes's thrashing arms smacked and subsided against the pool walls.

Michael waded down the length of the pool and hauled himself up. He sank on to the grass at the side and lay stretched out, shaking and weeping, until he had to turn his head and vomit. He shifted some feet away and lay down again. He closed his eyes. The sun's heat pulsed down on him, water dripped from his clothes and soaked around him into the grass, flies buzzed over and landed on his still twitching body. Then he began to sense that the air carried another scent, freighted with sweetness. He could hear that in the kitchen someone had turned on the radio. Voices from a studio somewhere had started up in polite and amused discussion. The sound rose and mingled and was borne along, bubbling in a commixture with boiling strawberries and sugar that perfumed and corrupted the air. Michael opened his eyes and watched butterflies pass above him. Turning his head, he saw two or three ants among the droplets of water, scaling blades of grass inches from his face. It seemed, then, that life was continuing. He refused to focus on the gently lapping water of the pool some yards away but could not help seeing that its surface sparkled under the sun, as before. Was it outrageous or miraculous, he wondered, that it could look so much the same when everything had changed? How *could* it be the same if, the next time this bright, turquoise water flew upwards in glittering drops into the sun-laden air, it were to be Steph's hand flicking little playful splashes on to Charlie's golden shoulders, rather than Gordon Brookes's desperate, dying limbs jerking and grabbing for a few more seconds of life? Was it possible, that you could just lift a corner of this pretty world that Gordon Brookes was suddenly no longer a part of, push him out and drop the corner back in place, and go on as before? For it really did seem as if that was what was happening. Michael closed his eyes again, breathing in sun and the smell of fruit. The voices on the radio stopped, there was a second's pause, a burst of laughter, then the tap of polite applause. Another voice, and then came the pips. He had just killed a man while people somewhere chatted and an audience clapped. Life was just going on. And it was incredible to him, as well as a little unnerving, that it was not just other things that were going on as before, but that he himself was, too. Here he was, lying wet on the grass but feeling the same sun, hearing the same birds and voices, smelling the same flowers and fruits.

The thought comforted him. He knew he should be changed. He should be inconsolable, but instead was soothed. He knew himself to be filthy, but felt cleansed.

There would be more to do, of course. Michael lay out on the grass for a long time, dozing and thinking, the sun washing him with calm. He glanced at the pool once or twice, fascinated by the tinting of the water around Gordon Brookes's submerged head, until he vomited again. He got up and stretched, made his way into the bathroom of the pool pavilion and washed himself all over. He thought further. There was so much to think about, so many crucial details that he must get right that his head was now filling entirely with them; there seemed to be no space left now for simple terror about the next stage. Nor could he afford to be appalled. He was beginning to realise that if he carried on being sick he would not be able to see the thing through. So he would have to behave as if a part of himself were simply absent. It would be like acting. Neither outrageously callous, nor miraculously calm, just acting. Only in that way would he be able to do what had to be done, but it would not be *him*. Something at his core would be uninvolved.

He presented himself almost nonchalantly at the kitchen door. Inside, the heat was as thick as paint. Steph and Charlie were dozing in the Windsor chair, apparently stupefied by strawberry fumes and just waiting to melt down completely. Jean looked up, with a hot frown, from stirring the glooping, crimson, boiling bath on the stove. She scraped a tide of scum off the surface of the jam with a wooden spoon and blatted it into the sink, then moved over to the fridge and took out a saucer.

'There are some things we have to do,' Michael said, uncertainly. Steph opened her eyes and murmured. She had not been asleep, after all.

'Oh! Oh, at last it's done! It's setting!' Jean stood with one forefinger held up. 'Steph, it's done it, it's set. We've got a set!'

'Well, thank God for that,' Steph said.

It takes forever to get a set on strawberry jam, I know that now. That day, as I got tireder and tireder, and hotter and hotter, watching the fruit boiling and waiting for a set, I began to regret embarking on the whole thing. I was tempted to tip the whole sticky mess in the bin and forget about jam altogether. Steph thought I should. It's not worth it, she said. She went completely floppy that day, as if she was suddenly too exhausted to take anything in. Bin it, she said. But you can't, can you? You think: if this next little test on a saucer popped in the fridge for a minute doesn't set, it's never going to. If this one doesn't set I'm binning the lot and I'm giving up on jam, full stop. And of course the next test *doesn't* set, but you don't carry out your little threat to yourself. You realise the threat came from the part of yourself that wants to see you fail, and the better side of you thinks: oh no, I've gone this far – I've picked fruit and hulled it, measured sugar, washed and warmed jars, I've stood here stirring and testing till I'm at boiling point myself – I've made too much mess to give up on it all now. But even as you stand there knowing you've got to see it through, you're starting to wish you'd set about it differently. Added pectin from a jar, used some apples or redcurrants, something. You begin to think you'll never, ever get a set and somehow it's your fault. And then suddenly it sets. So it's all come right in the end, and the struggle has been worth it. Then you understand that this combination of self-chastisement and wisdom after the event was not helpful in any way whatsoever.

We very much regret the vicar, all of us. I'm going to put down as exactly as I can what happened, and then you'll see that although Michael did it, it's impossible to say who was responsible. Was it Steph's fault for bringing the vicar here? She had no idea that he and Michael had, as it were, met before. Mine, perhaps? I'm practically an old woman, but could I have done anything to prevent it? The shock of this stranger turning up with Steph and Charlie was considerable, the shock when he suddenly lashed out at Michael more considerable still, but I am not saying I was too shocked to know what was happening. It simply did not occur to me to do anything other than what Michael asked of me. I wanted to do as he asked. But suppose I had resisted, or said something to Mr Brookes right at the beginning such as, Oh, now, let's all calm down, we can sort this out, surely? But no, I just went back into the house as Michael told me to. And look, even if Michael had instead forced me into the house and threatened me with violence if I tried to interfere, I still wouldn't have been able to prevent what happened, so where's the difference? So I, and Steph too – we did what he told us to. We went into the house and got on with the jam.

So, was it Michael's responsibility, entirely? Not in my opinion. He responded to a crisis, that is all, and in the only way open to him. Because that man would have got the police down here, and that would have been the end. By then there were too many things to answer for: the church figures, Miranda, the house, the money. Not to mention Michael's previous misdemeanours, of which I had heard the gist. What would have happened to us then, Charlie included? Michael was only seeking to protect his own, and why should that be considered an admirable impulse in some circumstances and not in others?

But it was a puzzling, upsetting day, and the difficulty in getting the jam to set was just a small part of it. And it may sound trivial, but when I got the jam to set it changed my outlook. I suddenly believed that we could achieve anything, and come out of this mess all right, and more than that, I saw that we absolutely had to. *Had* to. It all became clear.

What happened was this. We had to give immediate consideration to the unpleasant fact that it was a very hot day. Now please do not think I write of this with anything like relish. We were all horrified by what had taken place, all but immobilised by the magnitude of it, as well as filled with disgust at its implications. But it had to be thought of. The degrading of flesh is horribly quick. Well, you know what would happen to meat left out on a hot day. In a matter of a few hours the man's presence would be obvious. So after we had talked the whole thing over and made decisions about how to proceed, Michael went back outside, pushed the wheelbarrow into the shallow end of the pool, then he dragged the body to the edge of the steps and hauled it up into the barrow

411

and managed to pull it back up on to the grass. Then I helped him drag Mr Brookes's clothes off him. That was when I first cried, at the sight of his dripping fawn socks and sorry green underpants. It was so sad. I thought of him getting dressed that morning, not knowing what would happen, and it seemed so unfair. The world is deceptive, it looks so solid, yet people can leave it so abruptly. Perhaps that is the purpose of vicars, actually, to explain that to the rest of us. Steph picked up his broken glasses and the panama hat from the front drive and I took the hat with the clothes, got the worst of the stains out and hung everything over the Aga to dry off. Together she and I raked over the gravel where they had kicked it about fighting, while Michael took the wheelbarrow with the body in it and pulled it off the grass and up the steps into the pool pavilion, out of the sun. The bathroom had no window and was quite cool, and he managed to tip the man into the bath where at least he would be out of sight, for the time being.

Then I had a brainwave. At least the other two said it was a brainwave, but to me it seemed suddenly obvious. I remembered that there were sacks and sacks of salt tablets for the water softener lying stacked in the utility room. I had been reading up about preserving methods; the jam, you see, using sugar, is one way of preserving fruit, and of course salting is what you do to meat or fish. The sacks weighed a lot, over 20 kilogrammes each. Steph could barely lift one, and Michael did not let me even try. But she and Michael between them, using the barrow again, fetched nine or ten sacks of the salt and emptied them over the sorry sight in the bath, packing it in all around him. He was completely covered, which made us all feel much better. Even more important, we could be confident that he would not smell.

Then the three of us together tried to make sense of the pool instruction book that Michael brought from the room with all the pool machinery. (A mistake: trying to understand complex machinery isn't an ideal team activity, and we were all very upset and agitated. Things got quite snappy.) But eventually we worked out how to drain the pool. The odd thing was it already looked quite all right again, but none of us fancied going back in that water. We had to fix up a pump that sucked all the water out, and attach the pump to a hose that drew it all the way across the grass and let it run out down on to the long paddock. Of course it took hours, which turned out to be a blessing. It forced us to take the time to think.

Because we had to work out what to do

next. Steph remembered that almost the first thing Mr Brookes had told her was that he was on his way up north on holiday, and sure enough when we looked in the boot of his car, there were his backpack, anorak, walking boots and so on. Going by the maps he had with him it looked as if he was going to the Pennine Way. There didn't seem to be any bookings with hotels or anything, but perhaps he was planning to take pot luck, stopping when he felt like it or booking a day or so ahead once he was up there. Or he might have been planning to camp; he might have been meeting up with friends who were bringing the tent. We just didn't know. If he was going on holiday with other people he might be reported missing almost at once; otherwise we would have several days' grace. But in any case his car was still here and that was, of course, a problem.

Steph is a clever girl. While we were grappling with the question of the car she went rather quiet, and then she suddenly came out with something her art teacher had told her. She had once done a water-colour of some trees and painted the trunks brown. Her teacher said, if I sent you out and said come back when you've found a brown tree trunk, I would never see you again. Why have you given me brown tree trunks? Well, Steph said, wood *is* brown, see? The whole room was full of tables and chairs, she said, all wooden, and brown, as you'd expect. But why look at tables and chairs if you're trying to paint a tree, he asked her. Go and look at trees. And don't think, he said, that I am teaching you to draw and paint, I am teaching you to *look*. People don't see what is actually there unless they look. Artists must learn to look, most people never do. They see only what they expect to see.

Up until then I hadn't really been getting her point, but she explained it. The point was, the vicar's car might have been seen this morning, in the village, outside Sally's, perhaps even turning off up our drive, and so while we had to get rid of it, we had better not try and say he had never been here. We had to get ready to say that he had been here, but had left after spending a bit of time with Charlie. Then she said that Mr Brookes had better drive back through the village again, this afternoon, so that somebody might see him again, and confirm what we would say about him leaving here. Well, this sounded mad to Michael and me.

'You're as tall as him,' Steph told Michael, 'and there's that hat he was wearing so the hair won't matter. You just have to drive through the village in his car, wearing his clothes. *Somebody's* bound to notice the car, aren't they, with all those stickers on the windows. You couldn't miss it.'

They were sitting with mugs of tea at the kitchen table. The sandwiches that Jean had made just in case anyone felt like lunch sat untouched. Only Charlie's appetite was unchecked; today Steph was trying him on banana. Michael pushed his empty mug away.

'But I'm *not* him! I can act like somebody else, I can't *be* somebody else.'

'But I've e*xplained*. The thing about most people,' Steph told him with weary patience, 'is they see what they *expect* to see. Like me and the tree trunks. Nobody's going to say oh yes, I saw somebody wearing Mr Brookes's clothes and hat, driving Mr Brookes's car, in the village on Wednesday afternoon. They're going to say they saw *him*. He's not the vicar of the church here, is he, so it's not like anybody actually knows him, it's just the impression they'll remember.'

'But what's the point? Why take the risk? Why don't I just drive the car off and dump it?'

Jean said quietly, 'Because if you do that, and if somebody in the village saw Steph and Charlie in the car this morning, the police will know he was here. If we deny he was here, they'll be suspicious. And if we admit he was here but just say he left, the police will have this place down as the last place he was seen. They'll be very interested in us, they might be suspicious enough to turn the whole place over. Dig up the garden.'

'So? We'll have got rid of the car by then, and we can dump him too. He won't even be here.'

'No. But Miranda is. What if they find her? And anyway,' she said, 'how long before they find out more about us? Find out everything?'

Steph said, 'And haven't you ever watched those detective things on telly? They can find traces of people, you know, even a hair or a bit of spit or something. If they really look hard, they'll find something. We've got to do something that shows he left here. Even though he didn't. If somebody thinks they saw him later on, it makes it really look like he left here, doesn't it? And then we'll be left alone.'

So Michael put on Gordon Brookes's dried and pressed clothes and his hat, removed the broken lenses from his glasses and put those on too. Jean managed to stop him, just in time, from touching the car without gloves. She found some thin plastic ones in the box with the silver polish. A backpack with Michael's own clothes went into the car, and Gordon Brookes's backpack, boots, anorak and Charlie's car seat came out. Four hours after Gordon Brookes had driven his grandson up to the house, Michael drove his car back down the drive and along the road into the village. He was alarmed but pleased to see a knot of people, mainly elderly ladies and youths in baggy clothes, at a bus stop, and a man sitting outside the village shop next to a banked table of fruit and vegetables. He pressed the hat further down and drove by without turning his head.

The tank was more than half full. With the map open on the passenger seat he drove, according to what had been decided with Jean and Steph, first to the M4. He joined the M5 northeast of Bristol and left it at junction 19. By half past two that day he had parked Gordon Brookes's car at the far end of the Avon Gorge Nature Reserve, in an almost empty car park displaying a warning about theft from vehicles. Here and there little heaps of ice-blue fragments of windscreen glass glittered on the ground.

A picnic was in progress nearby on a patch of grass dotted with tables, rubbish bins and notices about litter, dog walking and wild flowers. Keeping as far away as possible but remaining within sight of the picnickers, Michael took his backpack from the boot and set off down the path, marked with fat yellow arrows, towards Nightingale Valley at the heart of the wood. The path rose and fell along the steep, thickly planted banks of

Leigh Woods. From the map Michael had hoped for a more remote, less public sort of place; there were arrows and maps everywhere, even little metal badges on some of the trees. But it was simple enough to keep his head down and ignore the grunted 'g'afternoons' of the few people he met, most of whom sped past him on mountain bikes. He doubted if any one of them saw anything more of him than his feet, or would remember seeing even those. Where the path branched Michael took always the smaller and less-frequented one, and after an hour or so of walking, and checking that the path was deserted in front and behind him, he scrambled up a bank thick with brambles and bracken. He found a place where a stand of rhododendrons under some conifers made almost a secret room, several feet wide but only about five feet high, and he crouched inside, panting, waiting until he was sure that the only sounds he could hear were his own breathing, and birdsong. He looked round to make sure that he was quite out of sight. Very carefully and quietly, he pulled his own clothes from the backpack, slipped out of Gordon Brookes's things and put on his own, as quickly as he could under the low concealing arches of the rhododendron. He placed Gordon Brookes's clothes – jacket, shirt, trousers, shoes, hat and glasses – in the backpack, and fastened it up. He settled back on to the ground and waited. Strange, how birds calling in woods sounded somehow hollow and far away. He lay listening to the stillness, broken by the wind sighing through the trees above him and from time to time by murmuring voices, a crying child, from the path below. Once, a dog came crashing by quite close to him before being whistled away back to its owners. The afternoon passed. It seemed to Michael, overwhelmed now by fatigue, that he was waiting here only until he could be granted some sort of permission to admit how tired he was. His eyes drooped and he leaned back on his backpack.

Steph set off at the usual time to take Charlie back to Sally's, tucking a cotton blanket around him in case he might feel a slight chill from the evening air. She called out to Jean that she was off now, and crunched away across the gravel. She had adjusted the pushchair seat so that Charlie was now facing outwards, to see the direction in which he was going, rather than facing her. He was old enough now to want to take an interest in the things around him and no longer needed to keep Steph constantly in his sight. But that was not the reason, or not the only one, why she had done it. Although she did not understand how it was possible, she knew that outwardly she was behaving quite normally. She knew too that Charlie had seen nothing 'unpleasant' and that, as Sally had remarked, he did not know his grandfather from the Archbishop of Canterbury; yet there was something in his long, considering stare that she did not feel quite equal to tonight.

Still, she was finding on her familiar walk this evening that she noticed the same things: the length of her own shadow slanting in front of her, the summer smells of grass under her feet and the sweet cow parsley at the roadside that sprang back bruised from the pushchair wheels. And when others carried on behaving normally it was even easier; Bill was stationed, as usual on a sunny evening, in his chair outside the shop, reading the Bath Chronicle. He lowered the paper and sent a grunt of recognition her way.

Sally arrived back in her usual manner. As usual Steph was waiting with a peaceful, immaculate Charlie in her arms.

'Oh, hi, Steph. God, I'm shattered. Look, did Gordon turn up here today? Sorry! Forgot to say. Everything all right?'

Steph smiled. 'Charlie's grandad?' She looked down at Charlie, widened her eyes and shook her head at him and he, laughing, reached for her hair. She was suddenly afraid that Sally might choose right now to pay attention to what she was saying, to look her hard in the eye and probe. She could manage this better, she felt, if she told it to Charlie. So she planted a raspberry on one of Charlie's hands and prattled at him.

'Oh, yes! Charlie saw his grandad today, didn't he? Didn't you! Didn't you, Charlie-arlie, you saw your grandad, *didn't* you?'

When she looked up Sally was at the sink sponging at a mark on the front of her blouse. 'Bloody nuisance, clean this morning. Bloody mayonnaise, plopped out of a sandwich straight on to my boob. So – did he stay more than five minutes? Did he behave himself? What did you think of him?'

'Oh, yes, he gave us a lift. Yes, I put Charlie in the car seat, don't worry. I've brought it back. He gave us a lift up all the way there and then he stayed for a while. He was pleased to see Charlie, I think. I thought he was nice.' Well that's true, she was thinking. All that's true.

Sally snorted. 'Oh, yes, he can *put on* nice. He hasn't been near Charlie for months, so don't be fooled.'

'Well you wouldn't, would you? You might not feel up to it. Not if your wife had just died.'

'That was months ago!'

'But he got depressed just after, you said. Didn't you say he was depressed?'

'Yeah, he says he's on Prozac. Who isn't? I suppose you got the whole lychgate story?'

She had thrown the cloth back in the sink now and was pouring a glass of wine. 'I reckon he just claims to be depressed, to make me feel sorry for him.' She swallowed some of her drink. 'Maybe the Pennine Way'll perk him up. Did he tell you about that? He's off up there on holiday. They used to do it every year, the Pennine Way, only last year they missed it because Wendy – that's Simon's mother – she was too ill. So Gordon's off this year on his own.'

'Aw, that's sad. He must miss her.'

'I suppose. If you ask me he feels guilty. They were never that close, according to Simon. Anyway, you're off now are you? Here, I'll take him. God he's getting heavy, isn't he? See you tomorrow.'

'Yeah. 'Bye then. Night-night, Charlie.'

When Michael woke, it seemed as though the sheltering woods had turned against him. The wind had risen and now filled the trees with a sound like breaking waves; his bed under the rhododendrons was sunless and damp. It was only seven o'clock and the sun had not quite set, yet he was cold and lost, feeling a kind of loneliness in his bones that told him that it was too late to be out. He listened until he was sure everything was quiet. Cyclists, walkers and dogs had left the paths and birds had deserted the air. Picking up the backpack, he scrambled down the bank to the path and continued along it until he reached the point where the edge of the woods met the banks of the River Avon. From here a broad path, he knew from the map, followed the riverbank all the way into Bristol. He met nobody until he had almost reached the suspension bridge. From here onwards other people passed him on the path, not the manic mountain bikers of the afternoon, but young, evening people from the city flitting about in small groups or strolling in couples, absorbed in one other, thinking about having a drink soon and finding a place for dinner, wondering if they should have booked. Michael tried to slow his pace to match theirs. The country merged into town; the path became the pavement of a 'waterside development' passing by buildings that, unless they were brand new, had been prettified and adapted for purposes other than the ones for which they were built. Warehouses were galleries, boathouses were wine bars. He crossed the river by a footbridge into Hotwells and from there, passing the moored barges and houseboats, restaurants, shops and pubs along the river, he trudged into the centre of the city. At Temple Meads station he caught a train.

When he got out at Chippenham it was quite dark. He was so hungry and exhausted, as well as parched with thirst, that he was tempted for a moment to take a taxi the rest of the way. Instead he bought a can of Coke from a vending machine outside the station, heaved the backpack up on his shoulder again and set off on foot through the town. When he reached the roundabout on the outskirts, where there were no pedestrians, he halted. Cars were still streaming round, shooting off at tortuous exits to McDonalds, Sainsbury's or the DIY store. He felt too visible. The next and final part of his journey was in some ways the most difficult; if he kept to the roads, which would soon be emptier of homing traffic, he might be noticed. There were no proper pavements, and a lone man walking along the roadside in the dark might be more memorable to a passing driver than the same man making his way along the streets of Bristol or Chippenham. God forbid, he might be stopped by a police patrol car; they had a habit of cropping up, and he still had Gordon Brookes's clothes and car keys in his bag. He climbed a stile and set off on the last eleven miles to the manor, following the line of the road through the fields, keeping on the far side of the hedges.

Michael returned late that night, after midnight. We had waited up. His appearance was a shock. Steph and I had collected our wits hours ago and had been going about things as normal and that being so, of course we looked more or less the same, except that our worry showed. Michael had aged in a few hours.

All that day I had taken my cue from Steph and although my head was full of Michael, I had carried on as normal. While she was occupied with Charlie I potted the jam and labelled the jars. We had both been surprised by how easy it was to get on with the usual things, even though every single minute we were thinking of Michael. We mentioned him to each other on and off throughout the day, wondering how he was managing things, hoping he would find the strength for it all and not forget any important detail. But we did not fool each other, Steph and I. We both knew that the other one was thinking of nothing else. I kept the frown from my face for her sake, and she smiled and sang to Charlie for mine. Not being hungry myself, I nevertheless made a cake that afternoon, and for me she ate some of it. But we longed to have Michael home. I have never before in my life so much wanted for a day to be over, and that is saying something, for I have had other difficult days in my life.

Steph was calm that day. Some stillness seemed to come over her, and in fact after that day it never left her. From that day on, her mind went into a permanent and steady gliding state. She opted for it, I think. She decided to keep her mind in a neutral, unfearing territory somewhere between helplessness and trust.

There was a breeze that afternoon after the still heat of the morning, not ideal swimming weather. But once the pool had refilled Steph spent some time in it with Charlie while I sat out nearby and watched. I am sure that it helped us both, to see and hear Charlie just as happy and excited in the water as he had ever been. Something compelled us, I believe, to fill the garden and the pool with playful noise. It was necessary to exorcise any lingering spirit of ugliness. And it is certain that nothing sees off the looming atmosphere of strife that adults create around themselves faster than a delighted, shrieking child.

But Michael's appearance when he returned brought back to us the awfulness of what was happening. He was starving, but he couldn't eat until he had had a bath, he said. Steph went up to run it for him. We were all hungry by then, as Steph and I had not been able to eat until he was home safe. I had roasted a chicken, and we sat in the kitchen until quite late, eating with our fingers. It began as a performance that we all consented to appear in for the sake of the others, and slowly it mellowed into something else that was less of a charade, because our relief and happiness to be together again were real. Afterwards Michael needed another bath, he said.

That night we were all exhausted, but we hardly slept. I lay awake wondering if I should feel guilty. Or rather, wondering if I actually *did* feel guilty – wondering, really, if this sleepless going-over of my life *was* a sense of guilt. Michael, not me, had done the deed, of course. But was it his proximity to me that had turned him into the kind of person who *could* do it, I mean kill another person? I dwelled on this for a time. Does the mere presence of one person whose hands are not exactly clean make it inevitable that another person will sooner or later dirty theirs? I lay in bed getting quite depressed, because despite all my efforts, it seemed that all this might go back to me and Mother.

Mother's own baby 'wasn't born right' and died when she was three, eight years before I came along. I suppose they'd tried to have more babies of their own in that time. So I was meant to fill the space that was left, I suppose, which I now know to have been a doomed hope, because nobody can ever replace another. Charlie consoles us all but he does not, nor do we want him to, replace Miranda. Miranda's tiny spot on this earth will always be precious and it lies in a place of its own, somewhere beyond a margin that

Charlie cannot cross. All that Miranda meant to us remains with us and in us.

It didn't work, me and Mother. Not that direct or cruel comparisons were made, for the first little girl was never mentioned, but I didn't shape up. Perhaps Mother tried, at the beginning. I know I did, probably right up until the time that Father died. It was around then that she first told me the truth about my real mother. She wouldn't have dared to while Father was alive. She told me only to hurt me or, as she put it, to get me off my high horse about going to university. Because my real mother hadn't died, after all. She hadn't been the frail, tragic heroine in an air raid I'd made her into. I was the natural daughter of a 'common prostitute', who'd had me and handed me over to a children's home the minute she'd been able to. And hadn't she (Mother) and Father done enough, bringing me up as their own, even handing over valuable property (the clock)? Did I not think, in the circumstances, that I should be a little more grateful, content with what I had (a secretarial course)? It was the theme whose many variations have played over and over in my life until I came here, that good things: opportunity, security, affection, happiness, should come to me, if at all, only second-hand, and in second rate scraps.

But I remember that I was not really

listening to all that, for my mind had just stopped and could not go any further. It stopped, just like that, at the idea that my real mother had not died when I was five. *Which meant that she was still alive.* Inside I was rejoicing, and I decided there and then that I would hold on to this feeling. I did not recognise it for what it was. It was hope. That's what hope is, isn't it, something between a decision and a feeling; it is the giving of permission to oneself to be optimistic about things yet to be. I had not developed the knack, nor ever did. It has always taken effort. But then I was thinking, as soon as I can I'll find her. I'll track her down. Exactly how I had no idea, but it certainly would not be with Mother's help. In fact I should probably have to be very patient and wait at least until I was twenty-one when, it seemed to me, I would suddenly, magically know how to go about it. I could imagine the uproar it would cause. But I rejoiced also that Mother had just created a purpose for me and would never know it, because I was going to keep very quiet about it. I was intrigued by the prostitute part, and frankly unbelieving – I knew, because I could just sense it, that even if it were true there would be a reason for it. Something must have happened to her, something she couldn't help. I would find her and make everything all right.

I'm getting to the guilt part of it. So, with my beautiful secret, the years went by. Twenty-one came and went, of course. Mother got worse and really did need looking after. I got sour, as I think I mentioned. So by the time I was forty-six, on that day eighteen years ago when the buddleia outside Mother's window offended me so deeply, I am afraid there was a bit of a row. I am afraid my patience deserted me and I raged at Mother about the incontinence. At the heart of it was her notion that I was only worthy to clear up her mess, and yes, I admit that I shouted at her, and not for the first time. She of course screamed back, along the usual lines. But this time she added something. She said it wasn't *her* fault I was still here. What's that supposed to mean, I yelled at her. And then she said, in the way you would, the only way you *could* say it if you'd been saving it up for about thirty years, that if I hadn't been so stupid and gullible over the clock, I could have left years ago.

I got it out of her, finally. She had spoken to Christie's. They had told her that that series of numbered, unsigned Vulliamy clocks are the earliest and best. The records, the first surviving *'Vulliamy Clock Book'*, begin with Number 297, delivered in 1797. Mine was 169, predating the known records by at least ten years. It would have fetched about £1,700, possibly £2,000, in the early nineteen-fifties. The longcase clock had been worth at least ten times what I'd got for it. More than enough to go to university.

Mother herself had always had a shrewd idea that it was worth something, though Father would never spell out to her how much. That was why she had checked up and, of course why she was furious that the clock was mentioned specifically in Father's will as going to me. But why didn't you *tell* me, I asked her, why? Of course I knew the answer: if I wanted to flounce off on my high horse and sell it to some two-bit shop, that was my own lookout. She loved it, telling me all this.

It explained Mr Hapgood's three bedroom house in Rectory Fields. I think I'd realised something of the sort.

Anyway, since I've told this much, I might as well tell it all.

It wasn't even Mother's bombshell over the clock that day that did it, in the end, nor the way she kept quiet so that the money for university never came my way. No, it was what she went on to tell me about my real mother that really did it.

You see, I hadn't quite realised until that day that I had been living all those years, all of my life to date, not *with* the hope that I would find her, but living *on* that hope. It had been feeding me. And with what

432

Mother told me, the hope died. That day, I saw that I would never know how it felt to come first with somebody. I had been holding on to the chance that I might still come first with my real mother, once I found her. But what Mother told me, the information she tossed at me as if it didn't matter, was that although my mother had not died when I was five, she had died since. She *had* been alive, all those years ago, when Mother first told me I was a prostitute's bastard. But now she was dead.

It will keep for later, what happened next. It still makes me cry to think about it and really I think I've said enough on that subject for now. I have searched my conscience and concluded that what I did was not my fault.

So let me get back to that night after Michael came home. I did sleep a little, burdened still with something that, on balance, was not a feeling of guilt. This may surprise you if you are the sort of person who puts people like Michael, Steph and me in a different category from other people. But for some reason I find myself incapable of believing that I am significantly worse than everyone else.

Michael slept dreamlessly and woke early. But Steph was lying on her back staring at the ceiling, and he could tell that she had been like that for hours. Even in the half-light, he thought her features had sharpened overnight; around her mouth it seemed that an old tightness had returned. Turning on his side, he reached out and, starting at her hairline, with one finger traced the line of her profile. When he touched her forehead she did not move, but when he reached the soft little lift of flesh between the base of her nose and her upper lip she tipped back her head and caught his finger in her mouth. They had done this before so many times that it was by now their customary foreplay. But Steph did not this time keep hold of his finger, running her teeth gently along its length. She did not then turn to him without letting go for a moment, and take her mouth to his, and only then gently remove his hand and place it between her legs. Instead she took his finger from her mouth and pressed hard, dry kisses all over his hand, pulled the fingers open and smoothed his palm over her face. Her cheeks were wet. Michael drew her close and they held each other tight in the silence of the room. Outside, the first creamy light of the day was melting to yellow sunshine. They heard Jean get up and go downstairs. Then they lay listening to the yammering of the birds as light tried to burn through the curtains, until Steph's body relaxed against his and slowly she drew him into her. They did not hurry; all too soon this sweet time would be over, anyway.

By six o'clock the next morning we were all downstairs. I had made a pot of tea and got out all the maps I could find, for I had already begun to grapple with the practicalities and had an inkling of how we would have to proceed. We had been set upon a path that we simply had to follow to the end. We had no choice. We hated the necessity for it, and wished desperately that we could undo the events of the day before. I could tell by their faces when they joined me at the table that Michael and Steph felt this, too.

There was so much more to do, and in some ways it would be even worse than what had been done yesterday. And there was the extra worry of not knowing how much time we had. So if I say that we became brutally practical, don't misunderstand. I mean it only in the sense that one might say it of people attending to the consequences of accident or misfortune: firemen or paramedics or surgeons. (That was, in fact, exactly what we were doing.) There is a need to get the job done, and what it looks like, or feels like to attend to it must not be allowed to interfere with physical skill, courage or resolve to see it through. What good ever comes of people ceasing to think clearly? So we became brutally practical, but we never acted with brutality. We merely mustered the strength, for one another's sakes, to do what we had to. In fact I would go as far as to say that in our case, the killing of that man was attended by nothing but regret. Even what we did next was carried out only because we had to, and it was done with respect, even with something like tenderness.

He couldn't stay here, at Walden. That was certain. Not just for the obvious reason that he might be found but because he would somehow dirty our surroundings. We were already thinking of the poor soul as a kind of pollutant. Wherever we might have put him, and there were dozens of places where he could have been buried, we just could not bear to keep him anywhere on the premises. The earth here was Miranda's, and her presence sanctified it. I imagined myself lying in bed in a week's time at four in the morning, knowing that he was lying not far off, and I knew that unless he was got rid of I should never feel that this place was ours or was quite clean, ever again. We had to get him away. We had to put far from us the ugly, terrible thing that Michael had been forced to do, we had to take ourselves beyond the whole episode. If we could, we would rid ourselves even of the memory of what had happened. We had to be allowed to go on as before and that would not be possible if he were anywhere close by. Besides, what if the police came digging?

No, he would have to go, and this brought a number of considerations. For one thing, I could not leave the house. Quite apart from my own inclinations (I had not felt like leaving the house since my day in Bath) I was the house sitter and what if Shelley telephoned about anything? Steph also would have to carry on as before, appearing each day at Sally's and looking after Charlie. So it would be up to Michael alone. He would have to do it by himself, and here came the first of several quite appalling practical difficulties. Michael could barely lift him. In one piece, I mean.

Jean seemed to know that the police would not do anything about the disappearance of an adult until at least forty-eight hours had elapsed. Even then they would point out that people have a perfect right to absent themselves without being considered as having gone missing. But eventually the police would have to take it seriously, and when they did, she told them, they would be sure to come asking questions. Neither Michael nor what remained of Gordon Brookes must be anywhere near Walden when that happened. Michael's presence was in itself a problem, because trivial though it now seemed, the matter of his unpaid fines meant that he could not risk giving the police either his real name or a false one. By this time tomorrow Michael would have to be well clear, and the business of disposing of Gordon Brookes underway. Jean waved an arm over the maps that covered the table.

'I'm trying to work out where you could go. But it's hard to tell,' she said, apologetically. 'A map only tells you so much.'

'As long as it's quiet places,' Michael said. 'And a long way from here. Just write me down a route and I'll improvise.'

Steph squinted at the maps, then at Michael. 'It's hard on your own,' she said, suddenly eager, 'trying to read a map and drive. You need somebody with you. Jean, he needs somebody with him, doesn't he? Jean, suppose I go as well?'

But of course she knew even as she asked that it was out of the question. Steph and Jean must stay, and carry on precisely as they would if Gordon Brookes had actually visited and left, as Steph had already told Sally he had. Nothing must change on the surface; life must go on in its usual way. Meanwhile in their heads, they must create a yesterday in which everything had happened as it should have done, and as they would claim it had. They must construct a yesterday like a film that would play over

and over in the imagination, with conversations and events whose details they
must rehearse until they were as real as
memories. This must be the yesterday they
would reel back to and remember and talk
of, when they were asked about it.

'Steph, of course you can't go with him.'

Michael said, 'You've got things to do
here. You have to stay here and wait. If they
come, you've got to be here to tell them. You
tell them Mr Brookes stayed all morning
but he left before lunch. He spent the
morning with Charlie, right?'

Steph stared at them both for a few
moments. Then she said, 'With Charlie *and*
me. He wasn't used to babies. He just
watched. We were outside on the playmat;
me and Charlie played with his cars and the
blue rabbit.'

'Mainly he watched. But he did put on the
Cookie Monster glove puppet and did some
funny voices for him,' Jean suggested.

'Charlie *hates* that puppet,' Steph said. 'Mr
Brookes just watched. He didn't seem very
happy.'

'Yes! You're right, he did seem withdrawn.
Perhaps he was depressed, but we hadn't
met him before so we thought it was just
shyness,' Jean said. 'He said very little. He
didn't say anything about his holiday. But he
read to Charlie out of one of his books.'

'Yes, he read him *The Very Hungry*

*Caterpillar*. Then he carried Charlie round the garden and showed him the flowers. Oh, yes, and he gave him his bottle,' Steph said, with finality. 'Don't you remember?'

'Now you've mentioned it,' Jean said, 'yes, I think I do.'

'We said to ourselves when he'd gone, what a nice man.'

'Very serious, and quiet, but nice. And we noticed how he said goodbye to Charlie, didn't we?'

'Yes, oh yes. We noticed – *what?*'

'How he whispered in his ear and held him tight, and for such a long time. How his eyes were watering when he handed him back, as if he was leaving for the other side of the world! After he'd gone, we said, well, he clearly adores that grandson of his.'

'We said, lucky little Charlie.'

'So we did.'

'And we thought no more about it.'

Michael put on gumboots, found goggles, heavy gardening gloves, a long gardening apron. Jean found two rolls of plastic bin liners and a bag of carefully folded supermarket carrier bags that she had saved from Michael's shopping trips. He fetched the chain saw and took it, with bin liners and bags, to the pool pavilion. Carefully he closed the French windows behind him, entered the bathroom and closed that door

440

too. A little later, when Steph and Jean heard, faintly, the cough of the motor, they did not remark upon it to each other. They were busy. There were the clothes from yesterday to burn, including shoes and a panama hat. There were the clothes Gordon Brookes had packed for his holiday, the backpack itself, his walking boots and anorak, too. Together they carried armloads down between the vegetable rows to the patch of ground behind the walled garden. Michael had forbidden them to use petrol, so Jean scattered a whole box of firelighters under a heap of kindling, sloshed a bottle of methylated spirit over it and flung in a match. She and Steph stood back and watched as flames whirled upwards, sucking breath out of the air that began to tremble against the sky. It was still early, but presently it would be time to fetch Charlie. Steadily they began to feed the fire. It would smoulder for at least a day and a night, giving off the choking smells of charring and melting cotton, canvas and plastic, but without discussing it, Jean and Steph both knew that they wanted the first and fiercest blazing of Gordon Brookes's belongings to be over before Charlie came. They wanted to give him a nice, ordinary day. They all needed it, and they would try to make it so, despite the edgy smell of burning that would hang in the air, and the constant background noise of raw grating, as a chainsaw blade some distance away met and sliced into something solid, yet wet-sounding.

The surface of the day passed. In the house the hours and minutes presented themselves and were filled conventionally. Outside it clouded over and rained for a short time, reducing the fire to sullen smoking and keeping them indoors. Charlie was now eating variously coloured forms of creamy slop that Steph prepared for him, and he slept off his lunch of mashed banana and avocado while she began on a drawing of a jar of honeysuckle that she had picked and placed on the kitchen table. But even after the rain the day remained close and muggy. Steph's head began to ache and she fell asleep.

Jean fussed around over unnecessary jobs in the house, with a set look on her face. Late in the afternoon, after Steph had left to take Charlie back, she began to assemble and wrap sandwiches, cake and fruit. She filled flasks with tea. She brought down rugs, and folded clean clothes for Michael and put them in his backpack. It soothed her to have such sensible, innocuous things to do. An aspiration to wholesomeness felt important and necessary now, so as she worked on the preparations she kept well to the back of her mind the actual purpose of the journey. And she curbed a wish to whirl round tackling six things at once, and forced herself to move slowly, concentrating on doing everything that a good mother should to ensure that Michael would be as comfortable as possible in the circumstances.

But she was fretting about Michael's being disqualified to drive, and the van's being uninsured, details that he had overlooked so often in the past that it seemed to Jean that perhaps it was pernickety to worry about them now. She had not worried, had she, the countless times he had gone off in the van with her careful shopping list in his hand, smiling and pretending not to hear the last minute things she would be reminding him about at the door. 'Only get asparagus if it's English, don't forget. Oh, shampoo! Shampoo, I forgot! Oh just anything, as long as it's for dry hair. No, get Wella. Or Pantene, but make sure it's for dry hair. Oh, anything will do.' But those trips had been short and local. Then there was the van itself. It was perfect in one way, being solid-sided. But it was old, a liability on a long journey.

Among the keys in the teapot had been sets of car keys. Jean had never even looked properly inside the double doors of the old stable buildings farthest from the house, but now, with the keys in her hand, she made her way across the gravel, past the log store and outbuildings flanking the courtyard, round to the line of disused stables. She unlocked the doors and hauled them open. There were three cars. She dismissed the sports car at once. There was a large jeep-like thing that looked new and tough, just right for a long journey, but it was full of seats and had windows all the way round it. There seemed to be no boot to speak of. The other car was a more ordinary-looking thing – a Mercedes, Jean thought, knowing little about cars –that seemed solid and safe. Most important, it had what looked like an ordinary boot. Satisfied, Jean returned to the house.

Michael emerged from the pool pavilion that evening at around eight o'clock. He pulled off the boots and stripped, and wearing only underpants, walked straight into the pool. He did not swim, but simply stood twisting his hands in the water, scooping it up over his shoulders and torso, rubbing cupped handfuls of it over and over his face. He plunged his head under for a few moments and when he brought it up again, he was shivering. Still he stood with his arms clasped round himself, his eyes clamped tight shut and teeth clattering. It was early July, but when the sun had set it had taken all the heat from the air, leaving a coolness in the sky that claimed the evening for itself. He tramped out of the water and back to the house, looking pinched; a stooped, walking ache, Jean thought, watching him through the kitchen window. She handed him a towel at the door, because he would not come inside.

And still he was not finished. He went back to the poolside through the greying light, and got dressed. He once again put on the gumboots and then unhooked from the wall the hose that was used for cleaning the pool, and took it into the pavilion. Inside, he snapped on the lights. A brash yellow glare spilled through the windows on to the grass outside, and as he moved around, daggers of light and shadow lurched and split on the surface of the pool. In the bathroom he ran sharp jets of water up and down the walls and ceiling, and over and around the sealed bags on the floor. He lifted the circular drain cover, and then he shot blades of water into every corner of the bathroom, every surface and angle, until he had sliced and whipped every crumb of salt, every hair, every shard and unnameable remnant of Gordon Brookes down into the drain, and watched them disappear. Then he returned to the poolside and replaced the hose, pulled off the boots and clothes and waded in again, where he lay, floating, shivering and weeping with cold and shock. This time when he came back to the house Jean demanded that he go upstairs and get in a hot bath. Afterwards he tried to rest, but could not sleep. Later Steph tiptoed in with a tray, but he could not eat. Jean picked up his soaked, stained clothes from the poolside and put them in a bag to burn later.

It was about one o'clock in the morning when Michael backed the Mercedes out of the stable garage and across the drive to the edge of the side lawn that led down towards the pool. Through the dark the sound of the wheels on gravel was confiding but dismissive, like the gentle rustling of paper being scrunched carelessly in large hands. Next he drove his own van into the stable garage and locked the doors. Silently he made his way across to the pool pavilion, and under the private light of a slice of moon he began the solitary ferrying of bags from the bathroom to the open boot of the car. He could not help counting them. There were thirty-one of them, a fact that he found strangely helpful. Michael's memory of the man was beginning to seem implausible now; any idea that Gordon Brookes had until very recently been a living, talking person now seemed un-reliable. In fact it was difficult even to sustain the thought of him as a dead, silent *person* any more. It seemed like some trick of perception, too dislocated from the ponderous, overwhelmingly physical and

446

troublesome fact of these thirty-one filled bags to be true. Gordon Brookes had, in the course of events since yesterday, been receding in the way that Michael now imagined must happen when an animal goes for slaughter. For how else could it be done? Since he had been living here he had seen them on the road now and then, those lorries with slatted sides whose interiors clattered with caged life, and he had overtaken one once on a slope, glimpsing as his van strained past a tender nose pushed up against the slats, trailing strings of slime, and one silk-lashed, fearful eye. How could anyone go about the task of transforming that into a number of pink rolled joints on polystyrene trays, unless some human mental law came into force, some benign slackening of the logic that bound the two states together by the act of killing?

So it must be with Gordon Brookes. Gordon Brookes must now be thought of now as a packaging, transport and disposal operation. The separation of the man – alive, talking, gesturing – from the stuff he was made of – lumps of gristle, bones, offal, cords of muscle and fat – was essential if Michael were not to go mad. He was still aghast from the discovery of just how much *stuff* there was and how in all its appalling quantity it had split and spurted, and how parts of it stank, too.

Jean and Steph prowled round between the car and the lighted kitchen doorway, trying to help Michael without looking at or touching the bags. They loaded his food, backpack, blankets and torch into the car, went back for a spade, a pickaxe and the maps. Jean hovered, thinking, and added another sweater, two long raincoats and boots, a box of Charlie's baby wipes, a bottle of brandy. Just as Michael was ready to go Steph tore back to the house and returned with a photograph of herself, Charlie and Jean. Michael looked at it and tucked it in the top pocket of his shirt.

It seemed somehow too cheery, even profane, to wave at the departing car. Jean and Steph walked alongside as Michael edged it round to the front, and then they stood, each raising a hand, as they heard from the sudden silence that the car's wheels had left the gravel of the courtyard and reached the start of the drive that threw its black ribbon down into the night.

What I remember thinking most about the day before Michael set off with the bags was how ordinary it must have looked on the surface. Steph and I kept well clear of the pool, and that was all, really, apart from the smoking bonfire that we went out to see to in turns, every now and then.

Once again it was the house that rescued

us, with its demands and its rewards. I found things to do: dusting as usual, flowers to arrange, the hearth to sweep, bathrooms and the kitchen to clean. One of the tiebacks of the drawing room curtains had lost one of its tassels, so I sewed it back on. Oh, it's never-ending, the upkeep of a house like this. A house like this claims a number of one's daily hours no matter what, and it's a pleasure to surrender them to it. Because when the flowers are freshened up, the silver cleaned, and the whiff of beeswax and the faint, delicious oil smell from the Aga mix and spread themselves through the rooms, it feels like a reward, or rather, a contract honoured. What a rich repayment for one's willing attentions to a house, to be given a home in return. With Michael so conspicuously absent and the noise of the saw going on in the background, I thought this on and off during the day, until it seemed to me that we owed it to the house itself, and not only to one another, to keep strong. It may sound silly but it was as if the house would be hurt, too, if we were to neglect it now, or fail to see things through. I worried too, of course. Towards evening I got busy with things that I thought Michael might need, and that kept me occupied until it was time for him to go.

We were grateful for an uneventful day that day. Steph managed to sleep in the afternoon but I could not, for thinking of Michael. She took Charlie back to Sally's as usual, and when she returned she reported that Sally had been absolutely the same as ever. This was as we had hoped. Steph still seemed to be existing in this half-sleep, taking in things, responding and reporting back as if her brain were some patient machine. There was no question of panic. All in all, things were going well. But that night, after Michael had left, I was reluctant to go to bed. Tired out though I was, I stayed up and walked round the house, going from room to room, slowly and quietly, so as not to wake Steph. I believe I was seeking comfort. Eventually I went to bed and lay awake, praying that Michael would be all right.

For two weeks nothing happened. With Michael away, the grass grew. Jean felt she walked through the lawn, rather than across it. She would go slowly, with eyes down on her way back from cutting flowers, and ache for Michael's return. Life had become more modest; an air of quiet waiting descended, befitting a household that is observing a period of formal mourning.

One evening in the middle of July Steph entered Sally's house with Charlie to find Sally sitting red-eyed in the kitchen. She took Charlie from Steph's arms unceremoniously, with none of the singsong endearments that Steph considered phoney in any case. The silence was uncomfortable so for once Steph, who expected Sally to initiate the talking, started first.

'All right, Sally?'

Sally answered by sinking her head into Charlie's neck. When her face reappeared she said, 'There's a problem with Gordon. Or there might be, they don't really know.'

'Gordon?'

'You know, Mr Brookes, Charlie's grandad. They don't know where he is. The police, I mean.'

'But he's on holiday, isn't he? Didn't he go off walking or something?'

'He was meant to be back a week ago. His church lot just thought he must be taking a few extra days, but now the police have found his car. It was abandoned.'

Steph swallowed. 'Oh, no!' She could not for a moment remember what she was supposed to know and what she was not, so she sat down hard in a chair. What did the police know? Had they found Michael? Sally's face disappeared back into Charlie's clothes again and she began to rock gently. Steph looked round and forced herself to think. 'Want me to put the kettle on?' she said.

Sally nodded, her head still buried. Steph rose, filled it and switched it on. As she was washing mugs – every mug in the house seemed to be in the sink – she said in a worried voice, 'So the police – what is it they're saying, exactly?'

Sally presented her exhausted face again. 'They've found his car, or what's left of it. It was miles and miles from here – in a lay-by some place near Chepstow, all vandalised and burnt out. They don't know how it got there. It's miles and miles from where he's supposed to be. He's supposed to be up north.'

'You mean, he isn't, then? Then where is he?'

'Oh, for God's sake, Steph, that's what I'm telling you! They don't know. They say *he* won't have left the car there. They say it was probably stolen and dumped there and set alight.'

Steph drew in a shocked breath. 'Oh, Sally! They're not saying he – he wasn't, you know, *in* it, was he?'

Sally seemed slightly surprised. 'No, of course not. They don't know where he is. That's what I'm saying. They don't know if the theft of the car's got something to do with where he is, or if it's a separate thing altogether. But the police want to find the people who took the car. Obviously.'

'But are they... I mean they must be ... are they looking for him? Up north, I mean?' Steph asked, picking up the kettle. It was easier, she was finding, to ask questions casually when she was doing something else at the same time. She filled their coffee mugs and brought them to the table.

Sally shook her head. 'They won't even say he's definitely missing, they say he could have left the car somewhere to go off walking, assuming it'd be safe for days and days. I think they're making enquiries up there, along the Pennine Way, but they're not even sure he went. Nobody would steal a car up there and bring it all the way down here, according to them. So they think it was nicked from round here, and he never went up north. They said he could've changed his plans and decided to do his walking down south instead of going all the way up there.' She sighed. 'I don't know exactly *what* they're doing. *They* don't know what they're doing, if you ask me.'

'Maybe he did change his mind. You said he used to go up north and walk there with his wife, didn't you? Maybe at the last minute he couldn't face it on his own and went somewhere else instead. Here, I'll take Charlie while you have your coffee.'

Sally looked at Steph with respect and interest as she handed him over. 'That is possible,' she said, nodding. She drank some of her coffee but as she put down her mug her face crumpled. 'But those awful people ... the people that took the car, you don't think … I mean maybe they … you know, they might have … you know, hurt him … and just left him somewhere. Oh *God!*'

'But what for?'

'Oh God, Steph, *I* don't know! That's what the police are for, isn't it? And there *is* such a thing as motiveless crime, you know.' She blew her nose on a paper tissue from her sleeve and looked up. 'That's not the only thing, anyway. The point is I had to ring Simon in Nepal to tell him. I've rung the place he's in anyway, it's just this tiny hospital. I couldn't actually speak to him. I was going to tell him he should come home, only he can't. He's ill.' Her eyes filled with tears again. 'All this time, for over a month, he's been really ill. That's why he hasn't phoned. And he can't travel yet, so I'll have to go and be with him and bring him home. I've got to go to Nepal.'

'What about Charlie? You're not taking Charlie, are you? Shall I … I mean, it'd be better, wouldn't it? It'd help, wouldn't it, if we had him at the manor?'

Sally looked gratefully at her, as more tears ran down her cheeks. Charlie, interested, began mimicking her sniffles with little grunts of his own. 'Would you, Steph? Could you, I mean if it's no trouble? I haven't got anyone else he's so happy with. He's so good with you.'

'Of course! Of course I'll look after him.

And of course it's no trouble. Is it, Charlie?'

'And look, as long as you don't need to... I mean, I've been a bit outspoken about Simon and his dad. Not that it's not all true but it's been a difficult time, you know? I mean, I've told the firm I've got to go to Nepal, and I've told Philip. They're OK about it and so's he, but I suppose everybody wants to know where they stand. I can understand it.'

'How long are you going for?'

'That's what I'm *saying*, I don't know. I've got to get some jabs first anyway, and I can't get a flight for another ten days. And I'll be away three weeks. Minimum, it might be longer. Simon's got this recurrent thing, he might be all right to travel soon or he might not. Why, is that a problem?' Having got the favour sealed, Sally was now ready to defend her right to ask it.

'No, of course it isn't,' Steph told her smoothly. 'We'll be fine. You can stay away as long as you like.'

If we needed encouragement to feel that what we were doing was appropriate and somehow meant, was perhaps even being surveyed and assisted from beyond by some approving deity, we got it, with this news of the car being burned out and abandoned. Over the next few days, as Sally got her trip to Nepal organised, Steph heard new

455

snippets from her. The vicar's depression and recent erratic habits did us no harm to start with. More and more of his parishioners were adding to the picture of a man with a skewed sense of proportion, a man making a terrible fuss over one lych-gate, a man brooding about trouble with his bishop over a recent church theft, as well as his wife's death and the break-up of his son's marriage. Sally stopped short of mentioning suicide, at least to Steph, but the thought hung in the air between them whenever Gordon was spoken of.

But for the car not simply to be discovered (as we assumed it would eventually be) where Michael had left it, but to have been stolen, in all probability by joyriders, then vandalised and set alight somewhere just over the border into Wales, was a minor miracle. Because it muddied the picture. Should the police be combing the Pennine Way for an accident victim? Tracking down the brats who had stolen the car and establishing what they might have done with the car's owner in the course of their thuggery? Dragging rivers? Alerting the ports? The Somerset police now had to work with the Welsh police and two different police authorities up in the Pennines, which was requiring additional layers of effort.

The day after Sally left for Nepal, the police came. A uniformed officer, with the words 'liaison' and 'community' in his title, I recall. We were ready, of course. He seemed particularly anxious that he wasn't disturbing us and said he wouldn't take very long. There was concern about the whereabouts of Mr Brookes, and he merely wanted to corroborate, if he could, what was already known about the day Mr Brookes came to see his grandson. He opened up his notebook. Mr Brookes, according to his information, had told his daughter-in-law on the telephone the previous evening, and remarked to the parish secretary that morning, that he was going to visit his grandson before heading up north on holiday. Could he start with our names? Yes, I confirmed, I was the house sitter, and did he want Town and Country's number? No, he didn't think that would be necessary. Steph was my niece, staying with me for the time being. (We decided that we should be quite open about the house sitting, in case the police knew of the Standish-Caves. It was wiser also to stick to the aunt and niece story that Steph had told Sally right at the beginning, just in case there should be any cross-referencing.) When I said this I watched him look at Steph, playing on the drawing room floor with Charlie, that lovely hair swinging over her face. She looked up, pushing back her hair and smiling at him with her strange, green-gold eyes.

He had more questions, which we answered. Yes, Mr Brookes had kindly brought them down here from Sally's house that morning. His mood? Difficult to say, as we had not met him before, but he had seemed a quiet sort of man, pleased to see Charlie but in a muted sort of way. Perhaps a little preoccupied. You might think, Steph said hesitatingly, and she hoped it didn't sound cheeky, you might think that vicars would be happier than other people, believing in Jesus and all that. The policeman said he supposed vicars had their fair share of problems like everybody else, and in fact several members of Mr Brookes's parish reported that he had been a changed man in the months since his wife passed away. We paused at this point for long sympathetic murmurs, which for myself were quite sincere. Yes, the police officer said, quite chatty now, Mr Brookes was always known to have been a workaholic, but had lately been driving himself even harder, throwing himself into things. We told him that Mr Brookes had left here at some time between twelve and half-past, after refusing an invitation to lunch. Yes, the policeman said, the man who ran the shop in the village believed he might have seen his car. That must have been quite soon after. The policeman pulled the rubber band back over his notebook and thanked us.

Seeing him to the door, I said, meaning it in a way that I truly don't understand, that I hoped poor Mr Brookes was all right. The policeman said (and this was unofficial) that if you asked him the poor man had done away with himself, possibly from the Clifton Suspension Bridge. Left the car somewhere in the vicinity, from where it was later nicked, and driven by joyriders, most probably, straight up the M5 and into Wales. A lot of that went on, joyriding over the Severn Bridge, but could you get the Bridge Authorities to co-operate in a clamp down? You could not. And Mr Brookes wouldn't be the first, it drew suicides like a magnet, that place, and if you asked him they should shut off pedestrian access to the Clifton Bridge, full stop. People were always tipping themselves off it, often at night; he wouldn't be the first, poor devil – on average it was about ten a year. And it was notorious, the Bristol Channel. The tides could wash a body up and down the estuary for weeks and months before they had finished with it. I do hope you're wrong, I said. So do I, he said, so do I. They were keeping an open mind. But if that was what had happened, and he wasn't saying it had, mind, then it would all 'tie in'.

## *August*

When the telephone rang it was just after one o'clock in the morning. Jean woke at the sound of it, her heart pounding.

'Hello?' She could hear a rushing noise, and piped music. 'Hello?'

'It's me.' It was Michael, fractured and afraid.

'Oh, my goodness! Michael! Michael, are you all right? Where are you?'

'I'm in one of those service stations. I want to come home. Is it all right? Is it all right to come home? Is everything all right?'

'Yes! Yes, come at once! Come home, come straightaway. Where are you?'

'In a service area, I'm not sure, on the M6, no, the M5, I'm near Birmingham.'

Jean said, *'Oh!* Oh, that's *miles*, I thought you meant you'd be– Oh, you'll be hours still. Are you sure you're all right?'

'I'll be back as soon as I can. Don't stay up, I just wanted to check it was okay – it *is* okay, is it? There hasn't been any trouble with – you know, anything?'

'No! No, everything's fine. We just want you home. Oh, hurry, won't you – I mean, no – don't, *don't* hurry, drive safely. Be very

461

careful. Oh, Michael!'

He arrived at three o'clock. Jean had got dressed again and was lying awake listening for the car, and as soon as she heard it she got up. Steph was downstairs before her and was already leading Michael into the kitchen. He was crying with tiredness, and was visibly thinner. They put him in a chair by the Aga. He seemed to have forgotten how to breathe; he sucked in air and held it in the top of his chest and swallowed, as if fearful of letting it go. When he did breathe out, he sank physically as the air left his body and waited, it seemed for long minutes, before gulping in another chestful. It was painful to watch. Jean made tea and fussed, to conceal the fear she felt for him. Had he been eating? He was so thin, he must be starving! Michael shook his head.

'No appetite,' he said. His voice was rusty from lack of use. 'I had no appetite. I was too scared. But now I'm here I am quite hungry. In fact, I really am hungry. I'm starving.'

Jean smiled. 'Oh *well*, I can fix that. What would you like? A bacon sandwich? Scrambled eggs?'

Michael looked at her as if he were struggling to understand what she was saying. But the tea was already beginning to calm him. 'No,' he said, 'not bacon. I really couldn't eat anything salty.'

'Something sweet, then? What about something sweet?'

'Maybe. I – I think first I want a bath, if that's all right.'

Steph went ahead to run the water. When he came down again he looked even more tired. Jean had made a mound of toast and another pot of tea, at which Michael managed a smile, a little like one of his old ones. He sat down. But when he lifted the lid of the pot next to the butter, peered in and smelled the strawberry jam, he had to get up quickly, unbolt the back door and dash outside to be sick.

You read about such things in the papers, don't you? Head in suitcase, torso in canal, that kind of thing, you think, how on earth has that come about? And you picture some monster getting up to all sorts, enjoying himself, and phrases like 'pure evil' pop into your head. I know better, now. I know that the blackest deeds are not necessarily done by those with the blackest hearts. I know that in the first place we did not want to kill Mr Brookes; we had to. Second, we most certainly did not want to deny him a proper burial. Even less did we want to plant bits of him all over the country. But it was the only way to deal with the situation we found ourselves in, and he was dead anyway after all, it's not as if we were doing any worse to

463

him than had already happened.

But I fretted and cried after him. I tried to think, if there is a God, He knows all about it already. If He is there and serving any purpose, doesn't He know everything anyway? So He'll take care of poor, blameless Mr Brookes's soul without the need for the coffin and prayers, surely. It would be a little trite of God, I thought, to insist on the coffin and the prayers in the circumstances. I prayed, yes, literally I prayed as if God might still be listening to me, that He would be above all that and see His way to dispensing with the niceties in Mr Brookes's case. It worried me. Actually, it began to lose meaning, this connection we cling to, between the person lost and the stuff in the coffin. They're not the same. Let's be grateful they're not the same. Let's not burden ourselves with talk of souls, but let's just separate the man from the meat; regret the passing of the man, even if only to shield ourselves from the fact that the meat has been jointed, carved, and distributed all over the place. We wish it could have been otherwise.

And if there is no God, well, what then? Then we're all in it together, we're all the same, there's no escaping it. If there's no God, then no one of us can be closer to him than the next person, so that dispenses with the religious haves and havenots, and what a relief that is. When it comes to our deeds, I am not without conscience, but I think we all do what we have to, according to who we are and where we find ourselves. We cannot preserve the delusion that we are not mere creatures of clay, or that some of us are at heart any better or any worse than anyone else. Unless you believe in monsters, which on the whole, I do not. The point is, the whole Mr Brookes episode is as horrifying to us as if we had read it in the paper ourselves and shaken our heads in pity and disbelief. We are not monsters.

The night Michael returned he would not go to bed. Steph kissed him so tenderly when she went up, saying that Charlie would be awake and needing her in three hours' time. I saw the tears start in his eyes when she said that, but he let her go, telling her he could not sleep just yet and would be up soon. We sat until the silence that followed Steph's leaving us was absolute. I was waiting for him to talk, and he knew it. We sat downstairs until dawn. Still he would not go to bed because he did not think he could sleep just yet. And then, as I almost feared he would, he told me all about it.

I shall not, could not give you all of it here. But Michael had gone east and then north, disposing of those thirty-one bags, in thirty-one different places, between here and Scotland. He brought the road atlas and showed me, as much as he could remember. He had tried to work by night when he could, and in the daytime he would park up somewhere to sleep. The car parks of those large supermarkets on the edges of towns were often suitable, if he used one of the spaces furthest from the store entrances. But he never dared stay for more than two or three hours. He was afraid it might attract attention to be in one place too long, so several times a day he would move and find somewhere else, keeping his eyes open all the time for places to bury the bags that he could return to after dark. He used the washrooms in motorway service areas when he could. He wanted, he said, to keep looking slept and clean and shaved, like somebody who might own a Mercedes, not some ragbag. When a person is described as 'suspicious-looking', apparently, it usually means they look tired and poor and not very clean. But he couldn't eat, and he knew he was beginning to look half-starved and haunted.

By night he would park in as concealed a place as he could find, and then take the spade, a few of the bags, the torch, and go off. After the first night or two he decided the spade was not such a good idea. He bought a trowel and handfork, and another backpack that he lined with plastic sheeting. Each night, with two or three bags from the boot in the backpack, and the tools in his pockets, he would set off looking for burial places. It looked less suspicious, he said, as if he was just setting out on a night hike.

It is amazing when you start to look, he said, how many places there are that never get walked over or noticed, even though nearby people are coming and going all day. He dug holes on those patchy and desolate stretches of ground where people do not go, not even to walk dogs, the soft ditches at field corners where no footpaths cross and where no ploughs go. He even buried two bags deep in the middle of a huge roundabout, planted with thick shrubs and trees.

As he went further north he began to seek out remoter places, though it was hard to judge how suitable the ground would be. He walked long distances in the dark, managing whenever he could by moonlight. On some nights he would hit rock not far below the ground's surface, and then he would have to give up, the night wasted, and take the bags back to the boot. And the boot was beginning to smell. But he never gave in to the temptation just to drop bags in a litter bin and get away, or to scratch shallow holes for the bags and cover them over quickly. He always dug deep, emptied the contents of the bag in with the remains of the salt, filled the hole and trod over and around it carefully, replacing any turf. The thought of an excited dog with a wagging tail dropping some freshly dug-up part of Gordon Brookes at its owner's feet filled him with horror. Not one of those bags must ever be found.

But just in case any should be, he avoided leaving them in any discernible trail. He branched off the Ml and wound through the High Peak District of Derbyshire, then continued due west into Cheshire and turned north again on the other side of the country, on the M6. From there he made detours into the Forest of Bowland and Swaledale. He crossed the country again south of the border, and drove east to Newcastle and then set off northwest through the Cheviots, entering Scotland at Hawick. But he could only get rid of three or four bags a night, at the very most. The boot seemed almost as full as when he had begun. So he pressed on, beyond Glasgow, across the Forth Road Bridge into Fife, burying bags where he could. The last two went into the North Sea at a place called Garron Point, north of Stonehaven. The next day he bought a large container of disinfectant, emptied it over the boot of the car, and headed south.

As he told me all this I asked questions: but how did you manage it, were you not frightened, how could you drive so far, on next to no sleep and little food? To my ears it was heroic. It hadn't occurred to Michael to see it that way, but I was overwhelmed with admiration. Bit by bit as he talked and the day grew bright, some of the flint that was in him began to melt out. It came gradually, his understanding that it was all over. I sent him up to bed just as Steph was coming down. He went willingly. Now he could rest. The massive effort was over and we were back together again, and safe.

Jean was kept busy with the plums. There were six or seven trees, some bearing red fruit and some purple, and a golden one that she told the others were greengages. She decided against jam. But she read up about stewing, puréeing and freezing plums; she made them plum tart and plum charlotte, working in the kitchen with the radio on. She paid special attention to the news, dreading to hear anything about the discovery of human remains. No news came. She was now even more grateful for every day that passed. Each morning she would wake with the thought that another twenty-four hours had gone by which, even as she slept, had been doing their degrading, natural work. With every moment that passed Gordon Brookes was being returned to earth, dissolving hourly into the elements in which he lay.

She watched Michael, willing him to mend. After several days during which he did not get out of bed, he re-emerged with a white face and unsteady eyes. He blinked too often and glanced away to the side every two or three seconds, as if he had suddenly heard a soft but unwelcome noise over his shoulder. He had also developed a habit of giving tight little sniffs which would momentarily convulse the muscles in his throat. But the days of August stretched on, the time between the present and the past grew longer, and the events which had threatened his near-collapse seemed to fade in his mind. He did not get any worse. Jean trusted to the passing of more time and to the house itself to heal him, as she knew they would.

The summer continued hot. Some of the trees all but dried up and began to drop their leaves ahead of time, before their colours changed. They lay like torn paper strips painted dark green on one side and pale grey on the other and set out on the ground to curl under the sun. Jean pointed out to Michael the jobs in the garden that she considered mellow, soothing, and in keeping with the season, sending him out to be among the fallen leaves, not because she wanted them tidied up (she very much liked the dry swirl of them under the trees) but because she thought it would please him to feel their papery weightlessness in his arms.

It was not a particularly theatrical August. These days a mist lay on the garden until late morning. Amber blisters broke out over the remaining plums. They oozed and then rotted on the trees and on the ground; wasps feasted. In the flower beds it was the turn of the geraniums and carnations to eclipse the waning early flowers, the roses and monkshood, but everywhere the colours looked a little exhausted.

Charlie was less content to be carried round the garden on Steph's hip having the names of colours told him; he wriggled now to be put down on the grass where he would sit for a moment, pointing, and then lunge forward trying to reach the flowers, desperate to get among them. He could bounce along quite fast, and needed constant watching. Steph fretted pleasurably about his increased independence and mobility. She was worn out, she said. What with Charlie being here all the time, she was being run ragged. And he would put anything in his mouth. One day Jean came out to the garden to find her entire wooden spoon collection in a circle around him on his mat and Charlie sitting with his arms stretched up towards her, two bright red circles on his cheeks. He was teething.

There followed some disturbed nights and days of frantic gnawing, bad temper and a burning temperature. It was Steph and Michael together who saw him through it. They took it in turns to rise as soon as they heard him cry and dose him with Baby Calpol. For four nights in a row they walked the hot little bundle up and down with a cold flannel against his face. Then there were two twin white stumps in the centre of his lower jaw. It seemed to bring Michael round. His smile, which had been tight, filled out again. He laughed. Sally, who rang Steph once a week or so, sounded sorry in a remote kind of way to have missed her baby's first tooth. Steph promised to take a photograph. In the meantime Simon, Sally said, was no worse, but neither was he much better. She could not come home yet. Steph told her not to worry.

Not only the colours in the garden faded, but the skies changed too, and in the afternoons the light shining on the walls of the house was gold. Inside the house Jean noticed the scent of roses and from the windows, looking up from what she was doing, she liked to watch Michael and Steph in the garden with Charlie, whose good humour was quite restored. Now once again there would be singing, and shrieking and laughing, and Michael and Steph swinging Charlie up high between them, then quiet spells. That was when Jean liked to walk slowly outside to join them. Charlie would be either asleep, or amusing himself on a rug in the shade, Steph would be lying or strolling about nearby. Michael most often would be reading. A pretty picture they made, or perhaps they created something more like a line in a poem than a picture, because the faint reluctance Jean sometimes felt to walk in and become part of it was not a fear of sullying the thing visually. It was an appreciation of the scene's completeness, and her utter contentment in standing there beholding it, that sometimes made her wonder if adding herself to it would be clumsy. For she was beginning to feel the slight separation that comes with being the first to realise something important, ahead of other people. The date was beginning to weigh on her mind, and, with her face as calm as ever, she now, as she went about her work, would be wondering about it, thinking what to do. She would not discuss it with the others, not yet; she liked to be thinking it over for herself as she watched them out in the garden, oblivious. She did not want to burden them with it yet. Then they would look round and see her, and call out, and she would go towards them, smiling. So they would lie about talking and playing until it was time to go in. They were impossibly happy.

I did say earlier that it is amazing to me the

way this house seems to provide what we need. It amazes me further that it provides it just *when* it is needed. For it is only now, in August, that I have remembered about monkshood although I have been tending the flowers, picking them, learning about them from the gardening books, arranging them, all this time. And I have known for years that monkshood is a poisonous plant, but it was only when Steph was talking about Charlie who is now crawling and putting all sorts in his mouth, that I wondered how safe he would be in the garden, and then, as if I had only just seen it for the first time, I became aware of the monkshood. Aconitum, to give it its proper name.

And I also see, but only now, that the things I have been remembering and writing down here about Mother – things which I have not thought about for years – are part of all this. Not just rambling digressions on my part, but stopping places on the way to where I am now. All this time I have been becoming the person I am. I have always been heading this way.

This is the point. On the day of that row with Mother, eighteen years ago, with the buddleia swinging in the wind outside, it wasn't the news about the clock that did it. Mother and I had stopped screaming at each other. The row was over, really, and we had reverted to our usual calm hostility. But in the silence, when I was going about all the things I had to do to her: the washing, the wiping, the hair, the tablets, the breakfast, the cleaning up, the rubbing of her elbows and heels with meths to stop her getting bedsores, tidying the bed, we were both thinking up things to hurt the other with.

Who can say what might have happened if she had not got in first? But worse than the actual information she gave me was the offhand pleasure she took in it.

'Oh, yes, moan moan. You can moan,' she said. 'Go on, I'm used to it. But if you didn't have me you wouldn't have anybody, would you? I'm all you've got. It's not as if you've got any friends, is it?'

'May I remind you,' I said, 'may I just remind you that in actual fact I *do* have a mother?' I was plumping up her pillows, bashing them with my fist. 'Not *you*. I don't mean *you*. I'm talking about a *mother*, a real one. *I* at least have a blood relation.'

'Oh,' she said, looking past me, 'you still think that, do you? Well, allow me to inform you that you are sadly mistaken.'

I was confused to begin with. But hadn't she said, just after Father died, that my real mother had *not* died when I was four, she had given me up? Wasn't that what Mother had said? (Wasn't that what I had been holding on to, the hope that I would find her some day?) Mother said, still breezy, oh, yes, but she died later. She had not bothered to remember quite when.

I wanted to die myself then, for shame perhaps. For shame that some ordinary day, any dull old day when I got on and off buses, filed carbon copies, ate biscuits, bought stockings, God knows what banal things, was the day on which my real mother died. On that day I had been oblivious. I spoke no word, took no farewell, did not grieve. I did not know the day or even the year she died. Oh, well, Mother said, relishing it, it was maybe fifteen or twenty years ago. Then I thought, she's lying, the whole thing is a lie. But no, she knew this because my real mother had kept in touch with the adoption bureau, keeping them up to date with her address, in case one day I ever wanted to contact her. Mother had never told me that, either. The bureau had been informed when she died and had passed the news on to Mother but, as she pointed out, what was the use in telling me? It wasn't as if I knew her.

Until that precise moment I had considered the Mr Hapgood episode as the worst thing that had ever been done to me. In a way it was – as a deed actively done, I mean, or a set of deeds performed but then over and finished with – but now I suddenly saw that

Mother's treatment of me so outclassed Mr Hapgood's in malice that it amazed me that I had not seen it before. For Mother, without actually *doing* very much, had been busy. Over the years, forty-one of them by that time, she had been so constantly and perniciously denying me her care and approval that my state of permanent want had become a strand, no, the very substance of my character. I suppose I had grown to think of it as an inability on her part, something she couldn't help, but suddenly I saw that she had withheld things from me so conscientiously, in so meticulous and thorough a manner, that it must have been deliberate, worked at. It had not occurred to me before then that I had a right to be angry. But now I thought, what sort of person would do that?

Mother's bedroom was on the ground floor, behind the kitchen. I opened the top pane of her window, because the room really did need freshening up, though she complained that it was too windy. I left her door open a crack. Perhaps I was in shock and perhaps I wasn't, but I must have omitted to turn off the burner of the cooker when I had made her usual breakfast of porridge. Then I fetched my coat, bag, purse, keys and shopping bag. And before I left, I must have dropped a teatowel carelessly, because one edge was touching the burner and the other fell over the worktop where there were three or four cotton wool pads soaked with methylated spirit (left from when I had been rubbing her elbows and heels to keep the skin strong). The bottle stood alongside the roll of cotton wool, and evidently I had omitted to replace the cap. The wind must have blown it over. I left the door from the kitchen into the front hall open, too. I didn't go to the office that day or, in fact, ever again. I did some unnecessary shopping, slowly. Then I sat for half an hour over a cup of coffee. Then, as it was a fine, blustery day, I took a long walk along the towpath, and I thought about my mother, my real one. I must have been out for over four hours, but what with the through draught and our old-fashioned kitchen cupboards of painted wood (I had been on at Mother for years to change them) the ground floor had gone up in less than two hours.

Everyone was so kind. Mother had been found in the kitchen, they said, obviously trying to make herself a cup of tea or something. I kept quiet about the fact that Mother would rather lie for a week with a mouth like a desert than get up to make her own tea. They said she could not have noticed what she was doing with the tea towel, and she must have panicked when the meths caught alight. Anyway, although she might also have suffered a mild heart attack, it was smoke inhalation that killed her.

The fire almost destroyed the house, which turned out to be under-insured. The sale of the house was just enough to pay off the builders for the rebuilding work. I have been a house sitter since, joining Town and Country with a reference from nice Roger Palmer of Oakfield Avenue, who agreed with me that there was no need to mention the house fire business. All this time I have been becoming the person I am today.

So, as you see, I am capable of such an act. I admit it, but because I am still not sure what I intended, I cannot say exactly just what the act was. I do know that it was the opposite of cold-blooded. My blood that day was close to boiling, but I certainly was not out of control. I am not sure whether or not that makes what I did deliberate.

Nor am I cold-blooded now, in considering the monkshood. If I can contemplate the next step calmly, it is only is because I know that that is the state of mind necessary. Besides, I am doing it for all of us. And I feel responsible, and that always has a calming effect, I think.

I looked it up in the garden book, just to be sure. It says, 'Monkshood is a useful plant, bearing graceful, small bell-like blooms of an intense blue up and down its stem. Its leaves are attractively pinked in appearance, and it makes an effective filler for the back of the mixed border. No attention is necessary. All parts of the plant are very poisonous, especially the roots.'

Because there is nothing I can do to stop the Standish-Caves coming here. They are expected soon. I have the date. In fact I have always had the date, though I have been unable until now to connect it with something that might actually happen. But Shelley rang to check up on me again and to confirm the date. She has informed me that they will be taking a taxi from Heathrow and will be here by half past four on that day. They want me to be here to hand over the keys, and expect me to be ready to go by six o'clock.

That being so, I thought, I shall have tea ready for them. They shall be received with such ceremony and circumstance, by this humble, fawning, slightly embarrassing house sitter, that they will not refuse. I shall make such an obsequious fuss and show of this cake I have made for them that they will indulge me. I shall bake them a cake to welcome them back, made with apples, honey, fruit and spice, which will mask any foreign taste, assuming that monkshood has any. I think it more likely that it imparts a bitterness, that is all. And with the spices to distract the tastebuds, any slight bitterness on the tongue will not be noticed until after enough has been swallowed.

Jean began to glow with her idea. As she worked in the house, she planned it in detail. On the day when she believed that she had it perfect in her mind, she went to the walled garden. Michael stretched up from picking beans and together they strolled down towards the paddock. It was after five o'clock, and Steph had taken Charlie indoors for his bath.

It was, of course, unthinkable. But it was less unthinkable than all of them having to leave Walden and have all the other things catch up with them. Only that would be truly unallowable. Michael saw that at once.

'A cake? Are you sure it'll work?'

'I'm going to use the roots. They're the most poisonous part. I'll grate it up small, it'll look like ginger. All the books say it's deadly.'

'But even if it works ... even if it does, somebody will know, won't they? People will know they're coming back. They'll be missed.'

'Listen. I'll tell Town and Country that the Standish-Caves came back as planned but then they decided not to stay here after all, and went off back to the States. But even though the contract with Town and Country has expired they're keeping me on themselves, privately, because I know the house so well by now. And it's for an indefinite period, because Mr Standish-Cave's been developing some business interests over there. All right?'

'But what about money? There won't be any more coming in. How will we manage?'

'We can write to their bank again, can't we? We can instruct them to carry on paying me, double my salary even. And they'll have credit cards on them. Chequebooks for their other accounts, passports. We'll be able to get at all their accounts.'

'I've already got stuff on all their investments. It's all in the study. I could set up an email address. I'll say I'm him, I'll email the whole lot of them, the bank, the advisor, everybody, tell them to use email now, because I'm living abroad. Oh God, it'd work.'

'And you could say that all statements and all the correspondence are to be sent to Walden Manor from now on, because you might be moving about and there would be arrangements there for forwarding things.'

They had walked round the paddock and returned to the garden. Now they were sitting side by side on a bench green with mould, looking down the path towards the gate in the far wall. Beyond, across the back lawn, stood the dark wall of the house. Jean waited for Michael, who looked excited but still fearful, to speak again.

'We could just go on as before,' he said

softly. 'We won't be greedy, will we? When we get the statements for the other accounts we'll see what comes in from the investments and what they spend. We'll just make sure we don't get through any more than that. There'll be enough for everything. Repairs when we need them, everything.'

'Yes, and I was thinking ... Charlie's going to need a swing soon. You could fix one up in one of the trees. And we could get him a slide.'

'And Steph quite fancies getting a cat. Somebody's selling kittens, she says, there's an ad in the village shop. We could get a cat.'

'Well, yes, we could. We should get two, though, I believe they're happier in pairs. Oh, we could do all sorts of things.'

'It'd work. Nobody would ever know.'

'We just need to get through the ... the necessary part, the awful bit. Without making mistakes, or getting frightened and giving up.'

'It'll be easier this time. We weren't expecting it last time, it was crazy, horrible, it just came at us out of the blue. This time we can plan it. We've got time to get everything right.'

'And when we – you know – when we have to get rid of them, you won't have to do all that again. You needn't go off with them, in a hurry, like last time. We'll think of something else. There must be easier ways, more gradual. Burning, maybe.'

'We've got to manage it somehow,' Michael said, looking straight ahead. 'Otherwise we won't ever be safe.'

'We will. Because we've got to,' Jean said. 'And when we do, we'll be safe forever.'

It was twilight when they walked back down the path to the house. Steph had come back downstairs with Charlie and had switched on lights as she went. Their yellow glow shone from every window into the surrounding dark.

Michael got down to some serious planning the next day. What, he said, if they decided to do a tour of the house and garden the moment they arrived? Jean shook her head.

'I suppose they might. But I'll be at the door when they arrive, I'll tell them tea's already poured in the kitchen. Even if they do look round quickly, it won't look so different, will it? Even if they notice one or two things, suppose they see there are no photographs on the tables for instance, I'll say I put them away for safe keeping.'

'What if they go upstairs?'

'They won't. And just in case they do, I'll move my things back into the tiny little room they gave me. Move your things up to the attic. And I'll lock the nursery and not be able to find the key.'

Over the next few days, together they

made lists of what had to be done. Michael bought Jean a cotton skirt and top from the supermarket to wear on the day, since Mrs Standish-Cave might well recognise even the blandest of her own clothes on Jean. They planned that on the day they were due back, Michael's van, and Michael and Steph and Charlie, would be nowhere in sight. But Michael, having left Steph and Charlie somewhere with the van, would walk back and stay out of the way but close at hand, ready to come the moment Jean called out for him.

Jean found the pieces of broken porcelain at the back of the cupboard where she had put them in January, and made a passable attempt at reassembling the teapot. Back in one piece, though crazed now with a frenzy of fine golden glue lines, it sat once again in its place on the sideboard in the dining room. Nearer the time Jean would replace the keys in it, in case the Standish-Caves wanted to get their hands on them even before tea. Jean also decided that if she set a large bowl of flowers on the dining table, it would prevent their noticing the black rings that had appeared on it since they had seen it last. Michael said that the day before they came back he would clean the pool, replace the winter cover and close up the pavilion. But all these were precautions. Jean could not imagine that the Standish-Caves would do anything other than come to the kitchen and sink their grateful teeth into her cake. She would have slices of it cut and ready for them on plates, waiting.

Shocking, isn't it? It shocks me. And I do truly hate violence. I do not say this with any pride, but if I am a killer, I am a gentle one. After all, I saw to Mother with a tea towel, and this time I'm doing it with cake. Hardly offensive weapons. But I hope the necessity for it is understood, and I shall make it a very strong dose that works quickly. I intend to do all I can to avoid unnecessary suffering.

There has been, however, a change of plan.

It was Mr Standish-Cave's telephone call. He sounded nice. I don't know what I had been expecting, but not such a concerned and pleasant person. He said he was ringing just to ask me to be very, very sure that there was nothing in the house that would remind his wife of babies. He was certain, really, that he had put all the baby things into the nursery and locked it, but just in case, would I go round and check before they arrived. I must have sounded surprised because he went on to explain. They had not been able to bring their baby home. He had died in hospital when he was five months old, after a number of operations. His wife had had a breakdown over it; that was why they had been abroad for so long. She was much better now, but frail, and he wanted her to be eased gradually back into things, not be reminded too suddenly of the previous terrible year. And, he was delighted to say, she was pregnant again. So I said oh, how lovely, now you have everything to look forward to. And he said yes, we feel so lucky. His voice grew slightly hoarse when he said that.

You see? It changes everything. It's one perfect chance. One perfect chance to get the important things right. A curled, waiting, perfect chance, and it's theirs. When I think of all the messes and inadequacies we have been caught up in and have, no doubt, contributed to – there's me and Mother and my real mother, Steph and her hopeless parents and her first baby, and Miranda, and then there's Michael's poor child-mother and kind, puzzled Beth and Barry and then there's Sally treating Charlie like an encumbrance, and that husband who's waltzed off to put other people's lives right – I think, we got it spectacularly wrong, didn't we? Somehow we got it all spectacularly wrong, and for the most part it wasn't even our fault. And here in this house, we've been able to put so much right. It fills me with happiness that we have been able to do that. It redresses a balance.

And that, surely, should be enough. I'm still tempted to think that we really could arrange matters so that everything goes on just as it is, and forever, but in the end, we are not greedy. We are not monsters. We made our own and our only perfect chance here in this house, and we took it, with whole hearts and together, and we lived it out, every moment. And with our hearts still full, and still together, we should leave others now to their perfect chance. The Standish-Caves might make wonderful parents, and they might not, but I think they should be allowed their perfect chance, too. The truth of it is that even before we came here, time was pretty much up for us all. There can be nothing good waiting for any of us beyond this. We seized our perfect chance at the last possible moment.

Besides, how long would we have? How long before our lovely lives unravelled again? It would not take much; do the Standish-Caves not have parents, or other family, or friends? For how long would they be content to communicate by email, even supposing we made no disastrous mistakes? How long before someone discovered that the Standish-Caves were not 'abroad', and came knocking on our door to find out where they really were? I've come to the conclusion that the world just will not go away. That's all we want it to do, just go away and leave us in peace. But it won't. It never does. It keeps at you, prodding and pricking till you're demented, slicing at all your defences till you'd do anything just for a place to lie and gasp, and even if you're lucky enough to find one, it's just when you're beginning to breathe normally that it comes after you again. The whole idea that we could keep the world away indefinitely was, of course, desperate. You can go ahead and call it mad if you like, I wouldn't.

So the change of plan came into my mind, and my mind, I assure you, is as clear as could be. And when I changed the plan, I began to come up here to the study to write my report in the afternoons, feeling that I should like everything to be understood, even though I am not sure who I am writing to, exactly. I have been coming up for a few hours each day for about twelve days now. The Standish-Caves are due back on the 3rd of September. It is the 31st of August. Tomorrow morning I shall put all these pages I have written into an envelope and send Michael to post it, first class, to Shelley. That's the obvious destination, I can rely on Shelley to get things moving. But I do not know who will be here first (the post is so unreliable these days), whether it will be Shelley herself, or the police, whom Shelley is sure to contact at once, or the Standish-Caves. I do apologise to whoever it is for what is sure to be an unpleasant discovery. I should like to leave things somewhat tidier, but I don't believe that's possible.

You see, I have told Steph and Michael that it is my birthday tomorrow. I think that right this minute down there in the garden they are discussing what they might give me as a birthday present, but of course they have given me everything already. Thanks to them I am not just an agoraphobic old woman with wild hair, I am Michael's mother, a devoted mother-in-law and grandmother, a homemaker. They gave me that. Steph is not just a sleepy, tongue-tied girl in strange baggy clothes, nor is Michael to be dismissed as a depressive with nervous eyes and an occasional facial tic. We are a family. And for that reason, I'm afraid it is necessary to include Charlie in this. He would be lost without us. You may say he would still have Sally, but that would be to overlook an important point. I have met Sally, of course, and spoken to her on the telephone and heard enough about her from Steph, to know that as Charlie grows up Sally might take on the world for him. She'll be shrill on his behalf, abuse his teachers, insist on his rights. He'll get the best in car seats, bicycle crash helmets, orthodontics and for all I know hot air ballooning lessons, but will he know a moment's peace? What will she do when he is frightened, lonely and unsure? Do you think she will wrap him round quietly, with wisdom and warmth, make him feel strong, and secure, and wanted? No, it has to be this way, to save him knowing what it is to grow up with a mother who does not really want him, not enough. He must be spared that.

The sun is leaving the garden now. From about now until sunset the edge of the house will cast a shadow like a sundial across the grass, between the willow tree whose leaves Michael swept up the other day and Miranda's grave, where Steph's marigolds are finishing now. There is a coolness in the air already; I shall ask Michael to light a fire this evening. I wish every remaining hour of today and tomorrow to be gracious and pleasant.

I have made a cake for my birthday, of course. It is in the oven now, a honey cake with the necessary amount of spice added. I shall give it a layer of icing for extra sweetness. I expect they will find some candles for it. And at teatime tomorrow I shall blow out my candles and cut the cake into slices. I shall mash up a little bit with ice cream and feed it to Charlie myself, and when I have seen Steph and Michael bite into theirs, I shall eat my own. I shall spare them from knowing, beyond a little bitterness on the tongue, that the end has come.

Now I realise that it is the house that has brought us to this. For this house is itself a kind of deep and slow-ticking clock, in which our days have spent themselves as imperceptibly as a perfect mechanism winds down or a living heart beats towards its own end; the days have ticked out so quietly that it seems that our hearts have beaten with more mellow calibrations than before. Our passing lives have slipped by us here in the way that a song cheats time. When I hear Steph singing her song to Charlie,

*Row, row, row the boat*
*Gently down the stream,*
*Merrily, merrily, merrily, merrily,*
*Life is but a dream*

I want every note to float to the next, not caring that in the very singing of the song, time is being depleted. The house has shaken out time itself upon us like a garment that we have gathered around ourselves, Steph, Michael and me. So we shall spend a last day here. Steph will sing her songs to Charlie and I shall listen, smiling. Michael will watch over us all with his careful eyes as the last of our finite, peaceful days passes, wrapping us at the end in time's warmth and in our great and reciprocal gift of love.

# ACKNOWLEDGEMENTS

I would like to thank Vanda Joss, Patrick Toynbee and Ben Wright for sharing expertise and giving advice, and I am grateful also to Jonathan Ray for help with wine cellars.

Thanks for their faith and hard work are due, as ever, to my friend and agent Judith Murray at Greene & Heaton Limited, and to my editor Wayne Brookes, to Lucy Dixon and the sales and marketing teams at Hodder & Stoughton.

Most of all, my thanks to Tim and Hannah, for everything.

Morag Joss

The publishers hope that this book has given you enjoyable reading. Large Print Books are especially designed to be as easy to see and hold as possible. If you wish a complete list of our books please ask at your local library or write directly to:

**Magna Large Print Books**
Magna House, Long Preston,
Skipton, North Yorkshire.
BD23 4ND

This Large Print Book, for people
who cannot read normal print,
is published under the auspices of

**THE ULVERSCROFT FOUNDATION**